*Doctor*
*Copernicus*

# Doctor Copernicus

## A NOVEL
by John Banville

DAVID R. GODINE · PUBLISHER · BOSTON

*This edition first published in 1984 by*
DAVID R. GODINE, PUBLISHER, INC.
*306 Dartmouth Street, Boston, Massachusetts 02116*

Copyright © 1976 by John Banville
Title calligraphy by Julian Waters

First published in the United States by
W. W. Norton & Company, Inc., in 1976.

First published in Great Britain by
Martin Secker & Warburg, Limited, in 1976.

*Library of Congress Cataloging in Publication Data*

Banville, John.
Doctor Copernicus.

Reprint. Originally published: London:
Secker and Warburg, 1976.
1. Copernicus, Nicolas, 1473–1543—Fiction.
I. Title.
PR6052.A57D6   1984    823'.914    84-4163
ISBN 0-87923-513-6

*First softcover printing*

*Printed in the United States of America*

*in memoriam*
*Douglas Synnott*

# *Acknowledgments*

A fully comprehensive bibliography would be wholly inappropriate, and probably impossible to compile, in a work of this nature; nevertheless, there is a small number of books which, during the years of composition of *Doctor Copernicus*, have won my deep respect, and whose scholarship and vision have been of invaluable help to me, and these I must mention. I name them also as suggested further reading for anyone seeking a fuller and perhaps more scrupulously factual account of the astronomer's life and work.

The standard biography is Ludwig Prowe's *Nicolaus Copernicus* (2 vols., Berlin, 1883-4); it has not, however, been translated into English, so far as I can ascertain. Two brief and delightful accounts of the life and work are Angus Armitage's *Copernicus, Founder of Modern Astronomy* (London, 1938), and *Sun, Stand Thou Still* (London, 1947). A more technical, but very elegant and readable explication of the heliocentric theory is contained in Professor Fred Hoyle's *Nicolaus Copernicus* (London, 1973). However, the two works on which I have mainly drawn are Thomas S. Kuhn's *The Copernican Revolution* (Harvard, 1957), and Arthur Koestler's *The Sleepwalkers: A History of Man's Changing Vision of the Universe* (London, 1959). To these two beautiful, lucid and engaging books I owe more than a mere acknowledgment can repay.

For the light which they shed upon the history and thought of the period I am grateful to F. L. Carsten, whose *The Origins of Prussia* (Oxford, 1954) was extremely helpful; Frances A. Yates, who, in *Giordano Bruno and the Hermetic Tradition* (London, 1964), revealed the influences of Hermetic mysticism and Neoplatonism upon Copernicus and his contemporaries; W. P. D. Wightman's *Science in a Renaissance Society* (London, 1972), and M. E. Mallett's *The Borgias* (London, 1969).

I must emphasise, however, that any factual errors, willed or otherwise, and all questionable interpretations in this book are my own, and are in no way to be imputed to the sources listed above.

*

As well as the numerous extracts from Copernicus's own writings which I have incorporated in my text, and which I do not feel I need to identify, I have quoted from six different sources, which are identified in the Note on p. 225.

*

For their help and encouragement, I wish to thank the following: David Farrer, Dermot Keogh, Terence Killeen, Seamus McGonagle, Douglas Sealy, Maurice P. Sweeney, and the staff of Trinity College Library, Dublin. The final word of thanks must go to my wife, Janet, for her patience and fortitude, and for the benefit of her unerring judgment.

You must become an ignorant man again
And see the sun again with an ignorant eye
And see it clearly in the idea of it.

*Wallace Stevens,*
*"Notes Toward a Supreme Fiction"*

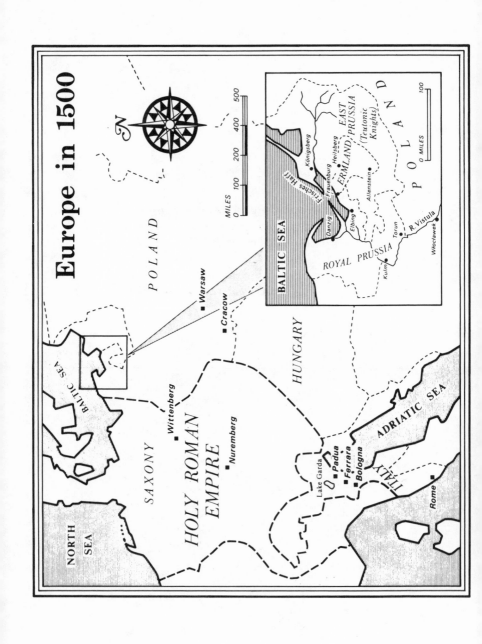

# Europe in 1500

POLAND

BALTIC SEA

N

MILES
0    100    200    400    500

NORTH
SEA

SAXONY

HOLY ROMAN
EMPIRE

Wittenberg

Nuremberg

HUNGARY

Lake Garda
Padua
Ferrara
Bologna

ITALY

ADRIATIC SEA

Rome

Warsaw

Cracow

POLAND

BALTIC SEA

Frisches Haff

Königsberg

Frauenburg
Heilsberg

ERMLAND

EAST
PRUSSIA
(Teutonic
Knights)

Allenstein

Danzig

Elbing

Torun

R. Vistula

Woclawek

Kulm

ROYAL PRUSSIA

P O L A N D

0   MILES   100

# I

---

*Orbitas Lumenque*

A t first it had no name. It was the thing itself, the vivid thing. It was his friend. On windy days it danced, demented, waving wild arms, or in the silence of evening drowsed and dreamed, swaying in the blue, the goldeny air. Even at night it did not go away. Wrapped in his truckle bed, he could hear it stirring darkly outside in the dark, all the long night long. There were others, nearer to him, more vivid still than this, they came and went, talking, but they were wholly familiar, almost a part of himself, while it, steadfast and aloof, belonged to the mysterious outside, to the wind and the weather and the goldeny blue air. It was a part of the world, and yet it was his friend.

*Look, Nicolas, look! See the big tree!*

Tree. That was its name. And also: the linden. They were nice words. He had known them a long time before he knew what they meant. They did not mean themselves, they were nothing in themselves, they meant the dancing singing thing outside. In wind, in silence, at night, in the changing air, it changed and yet was changelessly the tree, the linden tree. That was strange.

Everything had a name, but although every name was nothing without the thing named, the thing cared nothing for its name, had no need of a name, and was itself only. And then there were the names that signified no substantial thing, as linden and tree signified that dark dancer. His mother asked him who did he love the best. Love did not dance, nor tap the window with frantic fingers, love had no leafy arms to shake, yet when she spoke that name that named nothing, some impalpable but real thing within him responded as if to a summons, as

3

if it had heard its name spoken. That was very strange.

He soon forgot about these enigmatic matters, and learned to talk as others talked, full of conviction, unquestioningly.

The sky is blue, the sun is gold, the linden tree is green. Day is light, it ends, night falls, and then it is dark. You sleep, and in the morning wake again. But a day will come when you will not wake. That is death. Death is sad. Sadness is what happiness is not. And so on. How simple it all was, after all! There was no need even to think about it. He had only to be, and life would do the rest, would send day to follow day until there were no days left, for him, and then he would go to Heaven and be an angel. Hell was under the ground.

> Matthew Mark Luke and John
> Bless the bed that I lie on
> If I die before I wake
> Ask holy God my soul to take

He peered from behind clasped hands at his mother kneeling beside him in the candlelight. Under a burnished coif of coiled hair her face was pale and still, like the face of the Madonna in the picture. Her eyes were closed, and her lips moved, mouthing mutely the pious lines as he recited them aloud. When he stumbled on the hard words she bore him up gently, in a wonderfully gentle voice. He loved her the best, he said. She rocked him in her arms and sang a song.

> See saw Margery Daw
> This little chicken
> Got lost in the straw

*

He liked to lie in bed awake, listening to the furtive noises of the night all around him, the creaks and groans and abrupt muffled cracks which he imagined were the voice of the house complaining as, braced under the weight of the enormous darkness outside, it stealthily stretched and shifted the aching bones of its back. The wind sang in the chimney, the rain drummed on the roof, the linden tree tapped and tapped, tap tap tap. He was warm. In the room below his room his mother and father were talking, telling each other of their doings that

4

day abroad in the world. How could they be so calm, and speak so softly, when surely they had such fabulous tales to recount? Their voices were like the voice of sleep itself, calling him away. There were other voices, of churchbells gravely tolling the hours, of dogs that barked afar, and of the river too, though that was not so much a voice as a huge dark liquidy, faintly frightening rushing in the darkness that was felt not heard. All called, called him to sleep. He slept.

But sometimes Andreas in the bed in the corner made strange noises and woke him up again. Andreas was his older brother: he had bad dreams.

The children played games together. There was hide and seek, and hide the linger, jack stones and giant steps, and others that had no names. Katharina, who was older than Andreas, soon came to despise such childish frivolity. Andreas too grew tired of play. He lived in his own silent troubled world from whence he rarely emerged, and when he did it was only to pounce on them, pummelling and pinching, or twisting an arm, smiling, with eyes glittering, before withdrawing again as swiftly as he had come. Barbara alone, although she was the eldest of the four, was always glad of the excuse to abandon her gawky height and chase her little brother on all fours about the floor and under the tables, grinning and growling like a happy hound all jaws and paws and raggedy fur. It was Barbara that he loved the best, really, although he did not tell anyone, even her. She was going to be a nun. She told him about God, who resembled her strangely, an amiable, loving and sad person given to losing things, and dropping things. He it was, struggling to hold aloft so much, that fumbled and let fall their mother from out his tender embrace.

That was an awful day. The house seemed full of old women and the dreary sound of weeping. His father's face, usually so stern and set, was shockingly naked, all pink and grey and shiny. Even Katharina and Andreas were polite to each other. They paced about the rooms with measured tread, emulating their elders, bowing their heads and clasping their hands and speaking in soft stiff formal voices. It was all very alarming. His mother was laid out upon her bed, her jaw bound fast with a white rag. She was utterly, uniquely still, and seemed in this unique utter stillness to have arrived at last at a true and total definition of what she was, herself, her vivid self itself. Everything around her, even the living creatures coming and going, appeared vague and unfinished compared with her stark thereness. And yet she was dead, she was no longer his mother, who was in Heaven, so they told him. But if that was so, then what was this thing that remained? They took it away and buried it, and in time he forgot what it was that had puzzled him.

*

Now his father loomed large in his life. With his wife's death he had changed, or rather the change that her departure had wrought in the life of the household left him stranded in an old, discarded world, so that he trod with clumsy feet among the family's new preoccupations like a faintly comical, faintly sinister and exasperating ghost. The other children avoided him. Only Nicolas continued willingly to seek his company, tracking to its source the dark thread of silence that his father spun out behind him in his fitful wanderings about the house. They spent long hours together, saying nothing, each hardly acknowledging the other's presence, bathing in the balm of a shared solitude. But it was only in these pools of quiet that they were at ease together, and thrust into unavoidable contact elsewhere they were as strangers.

Despite the helplessness and pain of their public encounters, the father clung obstinately to his dream of a hearty man-to-man communion with his son, one that the town of Torun would recognise and approve. He explained the meaning of money. It was more than coins, O much more. Coins, you see, are only for poor people, simple people, and for little boys. They are only a kind of picture of the real thing, but the real thing itself you cannot see, nor put in your pocket, and it does not jingle. When I do business with other merchants I have no need of these silly bits of metal, and my purse may be full or empty, it makes no difference. I give my word, and that is sufficient, because my word is money. Do you see? He did not see, and they looked at each other in silence helplessly, baffled, and inexplicably embarrassed.

Nevertheless once a week they sallied forth from the big house in St Anne's Lane to display to the town the impregnable eternal edifice that is the merchant and his heir. The boy performed his part as best he could, and gravely paced the narrow streets with his hands clasped behind his back, while his insides writhed in an agony of shame and self-consciousness. His father, sabled, black-hatted, wagging an ornate cane, was a grotesque caricature of the vigorous bluff businessman he

6

imagined himself to be. The garrulous greetings—*Grüss Gott, mein-herr!* fine day! how's trade?—that he bestowed on friend and stranger alike in a booming public voice, fell clumsily about the streets, a horrible hollow crashing. When he paused to speak to an acquaintance, his sententiousness and grating joviality made the boy suck his teeth and grind one heel slowly, slowly, into the ground.

"And this is Nicolas, he is my youngest, but he has a nose already for the business, have you not, hey, what do you say, young scamp?"

He said nothing, only smiled weakly and turned away, seeking the consolation of poplars, and the great bundles of steely light above the river, and brass clouds in a high blue sky.

They made their way along the wharf, where Nicolas's fearful soul ventured out of hiding, enticed by the uproar of men and ships, so different from the inane babbling back there in the streets. Here was not a world of mere words but of glorious clamour and chaos, the big black barrels rumbling and thudding, winch ropes humming, the barefoot loaders singing and swearing as they trotted back and forth under their burdens across the thrumming gangplanks. The boy was entranced, prey to terror and an awful glee, discerning in all this haste and hugeness the prospect of some dazzling, irresistible annihilation.

His father too was nervous of the river and the teeming wharves, and hurried along in silence now, with his head bent and shoulders hunched, seeking shelter. The house of Koppernigk & Sons stood back from the quayside and contemplated with obvious satisfaction the frantic hither and thithering of trade below its windows; under that stony gaze even the unruly Vistula lay down meekly and flowed away. In the dusty offices, the cool dim caverns of the warehouses, the boy watched, fascinated and appalled, his father put on once more the grimacing mask of the man of consequence, and a familiar mingling of contempt and pity began to ache again within him.

Yet secretly he delighted in these visits. An obscure hunger fed its fill here in this tight assured little world. He wandered dreamily through the warren of pokey offices, breathing the crumbly odours of dust and ink, spying on inky dusty grey old men crouched with their quills over enormous ledgers. Great quivering blades of sunlight smote the air, the clamour of the quayside stormed the windows, but nothing could shake the stout twin pillars of debit and credit on which the house was balanced. Here was harmony. In the furry honeybrown gloom of the warehouses his senses reeled, assailed by smells and colours and textures, of brandy and vodka snoozing in casks, of wax and pitch, and tight-packed tuns of herring, of timber and corn and an orient of spices. Burnished sheets of copper glowed with a soft dark flame in their tattered wraps of sacking and old ropes, and happiness seemed a copper-coloured word.

It was from this metal that the family had its name, his father said, and not from the Polish *coper*, meaning horseradish, as some were spiteful enough to suggest. Horseradish indeed! Never forget, ours is a distinguished line, merchants and magistrates and ministers of Holy Church—patricians all! Yes, Papa.

*

The Koppernigks had originated in Upper Silesia, from whence in 1396 one Niklas Koppernigk, a stonemason by trade, had moved to Cracow and taken Polish citizenship. His son, Johannes, was the founder of the merchant house that in the late 1450s young Nicolas's father was to transfer to Torun in Royal Prussia. There, among the old German settler families, the Koppernigks laboured long and diligently to rid themselves of Poland and all things Polish. They were not entirely successful; the children's German was still tainted with a southern something, a faint afterglow of boiled cabbage as it were, that had troubled their mother greatly during her brief unhappy life. She was a Waczelrodt. The Waczelrodts it is true were Silesians just like the Koppernigks, having their name from the village of Weizenrodau near Schweidnitz, but apart from that they were something quite different from the Koppernigks: no stonemasons there, indeed no. There had been Waczelrodts among the aldermen and councillors of Münsterburg in the thirteenth century, and, a little later, of Breslau. Towards the end of the last century they had arrived in Torun, where they had soon become influential, and were among the governors of the Old City. Nicolas's maternal grandfather had been a wealthy man, with property in the town and also a number of large estates at Kulm. The Waczelrodts were connected by marriage with the Peckaus of Magdeburg and the von Allens of Torun. They had also, of course, married into the Koppernigks, late of Cracow, but that was hardly a connection that one would wish to boast of, as Nicolas's Aunt Christina Waczelrodt, a very grand and formidable lady, had often pointed out.

8

"Remember," his mother told him, "you are as much a Waczelrodt as a Koppernigk. Your uncle will be Bishop one day. Remember!"

★

Father and son returned weary and disgruntled from their outings, and parted quickly, with faces averted, the father to nurse in solitude his disappointment and unaccountable sense of shame, the son to endure the torment of Andreas's baiting.

"And how was business today, brother, eh?"

Andreas was the rightful heir, being the elder son. The notion elicited from his father one of his rare brief barks of laughter. "That wastrel? Ho no. Let him go for the Church, where his Uncle Lucas can find a fat prebend for him." And Andreas gnawed his knuckles, and slunk away.

Andreas hated his brother. His hatred was like a kind of anguish, and Nicolas sometimes fancied he could hear it, a high-pitched excruciating whine.

"The Turk is coming, little brother, he has invaded the south." Nicolas turned pale. Andreas smirked. "O yes, it is true, you know, believe me. Are you afraid? Nothing will stop the Turk. He impales his prisoners, they say. A big sharp stake right up your bum—like *that!* Ha!"

They walked to school and home again together. Andreas chose to be elaborately indifferent to Nicolas's meek presence beside him, and whistled through his teeth, and considered the sky, slowed up his pace abruptly to scrutinise some fascinating thing floating in a sewer or quickened it to lurch in mockery behind an unsuspecting cripple, so that, try as he might to anticipate these sudden checks and advances, Nicolas was forced to dance, smiling a puppet's foolish fixed smile, on the end of his capricious master's invisible leash. And the harder he tried to efface himself the fiercer became Andreas's scorn.

"You, creepy—do not creep behind me always!"

Andreas was handsomely made, very tall and slender, dark, fastidious, cold. Running or walking he moved with languorous negligent grace, but it was in repose that he appeared most lovely, standing by a window lost in a blue dream, with his pale thin face lifted up to the light like a perfect vase, or a shell out of the sea, some exquisite fragile thing. He had a way when addressed directly of frowning quickly and

9

turning his head away; then, poised thus, he seemed shaped in his beauty by the action of an ineradicable distress within him. In the smelly classrooms and the corridors of St John's School he floundered, a vulnerable aetherial creature brought low in an alien element, and the masters roared in his face and beat him, their stolid souls enraged by this enigma, who learned nothing, and trailed home to endure in silence, with his face turned away, the abuse of a disappointed father.

Gaiety took him like a falling sickness, and sent him whinnying mad through the house with his long limbs wildly spinning. These frantic fits of glee were rare and brief, and ended abruptly with the sound of something shattering, a toy, a tile, a windowpane. The other children cowered then, as the silence fluttered down.

He chose for friends the roughest brutes of boys St John's could offer. They gathered outside the school gates each afternoon for fights and farting contests and other fun. Nicolas dreaded that bored malicious crowd. Nepomuk Müller snatched his cap and pranced away, brandishing the prize aloft.

"Here, Nepomuk, chuck it here!"

"Me, Müller, me!"

The dark disc sailed here and there in the bitter sunlight, sustained in flight it seemed by the wild cries rising around it. A familiar gloom invaded Nicolas's soul. If only he could be angry! Red rage would have flung him into the game, where even the part of victim would have been preferable to this contemptuous detachment. He waited morose and silent outside the ring of howling boys, drawing patterns on the ground with the toe of his shoe.

The cap came by Andreas and he reached up and plucked it out of the air, but instead of sending it on its way again instanter he paused, seeking as always some means of investing the game with a touch of grace. The others groaned.

"O come on, Andy, throw it!"

He turned to Nicolas and smiled his smile, and began to measure up the distance separating them, making feints like a rings player, taking careful aim.

"Watch me land it on his noggin."

But catching Nicolas's eye he hesitated again, and frowned, and then with a surly defiant glance over his shoulder at the others he stepped forward and offered the cap to his brother. "Here," he mur-

10

mured, "take it." But Nicolas looked away. He could cope with cruelty, which was predictable. Andreas's face darkened. "Take your damned cap, you little snot!"

They straggled homeward, wrapped in a throbbing silence. Nicolas, sighing and sweating, raged inwardly in fierce impotence against Andreas, who was so impressively grown-up in so many ways, and yet could be so childish sometimes. That with the cap had been silly. *You must not expect me to understand you, even though I do!* He did not quite know what that meant, but he thought it might mean that the business of the cap had not really been silly at all. O, it was hopeless! There were times such as this when the muddle of his feelings for Andreas took on the alarming aspect of hatred.

They were no longer heading homeward. Nicolas halted.

"Where are we going?"

"Never mind."

But he knew well where they were going. Their father had forbidden them to venture by themselves beyond the walls. Out there was the New Town, a maze of hovels and steaming alleys rife with the thick green stench of humankind. That was the world of the poor, the lepers and the Jews, the renegades. Nicolas feared that world. His flesh crawled at the thought of it. When he was dragged there by Andreas, who revelled in the low life, the hideousness rolled over him in choking slimy waves, and he seemed to drown. "Where are we going? We are not to go down there! You know we are not supposed to go down there. Andreas."

But Andreas did not answer, and went on alone down the hill, whistling, toward the gate and the drawbridge, and gradually the distance made of him a crawling crablike thing. Nicolas, abandoned, began discreetly to cry.

\*

The room was poised, weirdly still. A fly buzzed and boomed tinily against the diamond panes of the window. On the floor a dropped book was surreptitiously shutting itself page by page, slowly. The beady eager eye of a mirror set in a gilt sunburst on the far wall contained another room in miniature, and another doorway in which there floated a small pale frightened face gaping aghast at the image of that stricken creature swimming like an eyelash come detached on the rim

11

of the glass. Look! On tiptoe teetering by the window he hung, suspended from invisible struts, an impossibly huge stark black puppet, clawing at his breast, his swollen face clenched in terrible hurt.

And here comes a chopper
To chop off his
head

He dropped, slack bag-of-bones, and with him the whole room seemed to collapse.

*"Children, your father is dead, of his heart."*

*

The reverberations of that collapse persisted, muted but palpable, and the house, bruised and raw from the shedding of tears, seemed to throb hugely in pain. Grief was the shape of a squat grey rodent lodged in the heart.

The more fiercely this grief-rat struggled the clearer became Nicolas's thinking, as if his mind, horrified by that squirming thing down there, were scrambling higher and higher away from it into rarer and rarer heights of chill bright air. His mother's death had puzzled him, yet he had looked upon it as an accident, in dimensions out of all proportion to the small flaw in the machine that had caused it. This death was different. The machine seemed damaged now beyond repair. Life, he saw, had gone horribly awry, and nothing they had told him could explain it, none of the names they had taught him could name the cause. Even Barbara's God withdrew, in a shocked silence.

*

Uncle Lucas, Canon Waczelrodt, travelled post-haste from Frauenburg in Ermland when the news reached him of his brother-in-law's death. The affairs of the Chapter of Canons at Frauenburg Cathedral were as usual in disarray, and it was not a good time to be absent for a man with his eye on the bishopric. Canon Lucas was extremely annoyed—but then, his life was a constant state of vast profound annoyance. The ravages wrought by the unending war between his wilfulness and a recalcitrant world were written in nerveknots on the grey map of his face, and his little eyes, cold and still above the nose thick as

12

a hammerhead, were those of the lean sentinel that crouched within the fleshy carapace of his bulk. He did not like things as they were, but luckily for things he had not yet decided finally how they should be. It was said that he had never in his life been known to laugh. His coming was the boom of a bronze gong marking the entry of a new order into the children's lives.

He strode about the house sniffing after discrepancies, with the four of them trotting in his wake like a flock of frightened mice, twittering. Nicolas was mesmerised by this hard, fascinatingly ugly, overbearing manager of men. His cloak, flying out behind him, sliced the air ruthlessly, as once Nicolas had seen him on the magistrate's bench in the Town Hall slicing to shreds the arguments of whining plaintiffs. In the strange, incomprehensible and sometimes cruel world of adults, Uncle Lucas was the most adult of all.

"Your father in his will has delivered you his children into my care. It is not a responsibility that I welcome, yet it is my duty to fulfil his wishes. I shall speak to each of you in turn. You will wait here."

He swept into the study and shut the door behind him. The children sat on a bench in the sanded hall outside, picking at their fingernails and sighing. Barbara began quietly to weep. Andreas tapped his feet on the floor in time to the rhythm of his worried thoughts. Sweat sprang out on Nicolas's skin, as always when he was upset. Katharina nudged him.

"You will be sent away, do you know that?" she whispered. "O yes, far far away, to a place where you will not have Barbara to protect you. Far, far away."

She smiled. He pressed his lips tightly together. He would not cry for her.

The time went slowly. They listened intently to the tiny sounds within, the rustle of papers, squeak of a pen, and once a loud grunt, of astonishment, so it sounded. Andreas announced that he was not going to sit here any longer doing nothing, and stood up, but then sat down again immediately when the door flew open and Uncle Lucas came out. He looked at them with a frown, as if wondering where it was that he had seen them before, then shook his head and withdrew again. The flurry of air he had left behind him in the hall subsided.

At last the summons came. Andreas went in first, pausing at the doorway to wipe his damp hands on his tunic and fix on his face an

13

ingratiating leer. In a little while he came out again, scowling, and jerked his thumb at Nicolas.

"You next."

"But what did he say to you?"

"Nothing. We are to be sent away."

O!

Nicolas went in. The door snapped shut behind him like a mouth. Uncle Lucas was sitting at the big desk by the window with the family papers spread before him. He reminded Nicolas of a huge implacable frog. A panel of the high window stood open on a summer evening full of white clouds and dusty golden light.

"Sit, child."

The desk was raised upon a dais, and when he sat on the low stool before it he could see only his uncle's head and shoulders looming above him like a bust of hard grey grainy stone. He was frightened, and his knees would not stay still. The voice addressing him was a hollow booming noise directed less at him than at an idea in Uncle Lucas's mind called vaguely Child, or Nephew, or Responsibility, and Nicolas could distinguish only the meaning of the words and not the sense of what was being said. His life was being calmly wrenched apart at the joints and reassembled unrecognisably in his uncle's hands. He gazed intently upward through the window, and a part of him detached itself and floated free, out into the blue and golden air. *Włocławek*. It was the sound of some living thing being torn asunder . . .

The interview was at an end, yet Nicolas still sat with his hands gripping his knees, quaking but determined. Uncle Lucas looked up darkly from the desk. "Well?"

"Please sir, I am to be a merchant, like my father."

"What do you say, boy? Speak up."

"Papa said that one day I should own the offices and the warehouses and all the ships and Andreas would go for the Church because you would find a place for him but I would stay here in Torun to tend the business, Papa said. You see," faintly, "I do not think I really want to go away."

Uncle Lucas blinked. "What age are you, child?"

"Ten years, sir."

"You must finish your schooling."

"But I am at St John's."

14

"Yes yes, but you will leave St John's! Have you not listened? You will go to the Cathedral School at Włocławek, you and your brother both, and after that to the University of Cracow, where you will study canon law. Then you will enter the Church. I do not ask you to understand, only to obey."

"But I want to stay here, please sir, with respect."

There was a silence. Uncle Lucas gazed at the boy without expression, and then the great head turned, like part of an immense engine turning, to the window. He sighed.

"Your father's business has failed. Torun has failed. The trade has gone to Danzig. He timed his death well. These papers, these so-called accounts: I am appalled. It is a disgrace, such incompetence. The Waczelrodts made him, and this is how he repays us. The house will be retained, and there will be some small annuities, but the rest must be sold off. I have said, child, that I do not expect you to understand, only to obey. Now you may go."

Katharina was waiting for him in the hall. "I told you: far far away."

*

The evening waned. He would not, could not weep, and his face, aching for tears, pained him. Anna the cook fed him sugar cakes and hot milk in the kitchen. He sat under the table. That was his favourite place. The last of the day's sunlight shone through the window on copper pots and polished tiles. Outside, the spires of Torun dreamed in summer and silence. Everywhere he looked was inexpressible melancholy. Anna leaned down and peered at him in his lair.

"Aye, master, you'll be a good boy now, eh?"

She grinned, baring yellowed stumps of teeth, and nodded and nodded. The sun withdrew stealthily, and a cloud the colour of a bruise loomed in the window.

"What is canon law, Anna, do you know?"

Barbara was to be sent to the Cistercian Convent at Kulm. He thought of his mother. The future was a foreign country; he did not want to go there.

"*Ach ja*, you be a good boy, *du, Knabe*."

*

The wind blew on the day that he left, and everything waved and waved. The linden tree waved. Goodbye!

*    *    *

Dearest Sister:
    I am sorry that I did not write to you before. Are you happy at the Convent? I am not happy here. I am not very unhappy. I miss you & Katharina & our house. The Masters here are very Cross. I have learned Latin very well & can speak it very well. We learn Geometry also which I like very much. There is one who is named Wodka but he calls himself Abstemius. We think that is very funny. There is another by name Caspar Sturm. He teaches Latin & other things. Does Andreas write to you? I do not see him very often: he goes with older fellows. I am very Lonely. It is snowing here now & very Cold. Uncle Lucas came to visit us. He did not remember my name. He tested me in Latin & gave me a Florin. He did not give Andreas a Florin. The Masters were afraid of him. They say he is to be the Bishop soon in Ermland. He did not say anything to me of that matter. I must go to Vespers now. I like Music: do you? I say Prayers for you & for everyone. We are going home for Christmas-tide: I mean to Torun. I hope that you are well. I hope that you will write to me soon & then I will write to you again.

Your Loving Brother:<br>Nic: Koppernigk

*

He was not very unhappy. He was waiting. Everything familiar had been taken away from him, and all here was strange. The school was a whirling wheel of noise and violence at the still centre of which he cowered, dizzy and frightened, wondering at the poise of those swaggering fellows with their rocky knuckles and terrible teeth, who knew all the rules, and never stumbled, and ignored him so completely. And even when the wheel slowed down, and he ventured out to the very rim, still he felt that he was living only half his life here at Włocławek, and that the other, better half was elsewhere, mysteriously. How otherwise to explain the small dull ache within him always, the ache

16

that a severed limb leaves throbbing like an imprint of itself upon the emptiness dangling from the stump? In the cold and the dark at five in the mornings he rose in the mewling dormitory, aware that somewhere a part of him was turning languidly into a deeper lovelier sleep than his hard pallet would ever allow. Throughout his days that other self crossed his path again and again, always in sunlight, always smiling, taunting him with the beauty and grace of a phantom existence. So he waited, and endured as patiently as he could the mean years, believing that someday his sundered selves must meet in some far finer place, of which at moments he was afforded intimations, in green April weather, in the enormous wreckage of clouds, or in the aetherial splendours of High Mass.

He found curiously consoling the rigours of discipline and study. They sustained him in those times when the mind went dead, after he had been trounced by the band of bullies that were Andreas's friends, or flogged for a minor misdemeanor, or when memories of home made him weep inside.

Lessons commenced at seven in the Great Hall after matins. At that grey hour nothing was real except discomfort, and there was neither sleep nor waking but a state very like hallucination between the two. The clatter and crack of boots on floorboards were the precise sounds that in the imagination chilled bones were making in their stiff sockets. Slowly the hours passed, sleep withdrew, and the morning settled down to endure itself until noon, when there was dinner in the refectory and then what they called play for an hour. The afternoons were awful. Time slackened to a standstill as the orbit of the day yawned out into emptiness in a long, slow, eccentric arc. The raucous babble of a dozen classes ranged about the room clashed in the stale thickening air, and the masters bellowed through the din in mounting desperation, and by evening the school, creeping befuddled toward sleep, knew that another such day was not to be borne. But day followed day with deathly inevitability, into weeks distinguished one from the next only by the dead caesura of the sabbath.

He learned with ease, perhaps too easily. The masters resented him, who swallowed down their hard-won knowledge in swift effortless draughts. It was as if they were not really teaching him, but were merely confirming what he knew already. Dimly he saw how deeply he thus insulted them, and so he feigned dull-wittedness. He watched cer-

17

tain of his classmates, and learned from them, to whom it came quite naturally, the knack of letting his lower lip hang and his eyes glaze over when some complexity held up the progress of a lesson; and sure enough the masters softened toward him, and at length to his relief began to ignore him.

But there were some not so easily fooled.

*

Caspar Sturm was a Canon of the Chapter of Włocławek Cathedral, to which the school was attached. He taught the *trivium* of logic and grammar and Latin rhetoric. Tall and lean, hard, dark, death-laden, he stalked through the school like a wolf, always alone, always seemingly searching. He was famous in the town for his women and his solitary drinking bouts. He feared neither God nor the Bishop, and hated many things. Some said he had killed a man once long ago, and had entered the Church to atone for his sin: that was why he had not taken Holy Orders. There were other stories too, that he was the King of Poland's bastard, that he had gambled away an immense fortune, that he slept in sheets of scarlet silk. Nicolas believed it all.

The school feared Canon Sturm and his moods. Some days his classes were the quietest in the hall, when the boys sat mute and meek, transfixed by his icy stare and the hypnotic rhythm of his voice; at other times he held riotous assembly, stamping about and waving his arms, roaring, laughing, leaping among the benches to slash with the whip he always carried at the fleeing shoulders of a miscreant. His fellow teachers eyed him with distaste as he pranced and yelled, but they said nothing, even when his antics threatened to turn their classes too into bedlam. Their forbearance was an acknowledgment of his wayward brilliance—or it might have been only that they too, like the boys, were afraid of him.

He chose his favourites from among the dullards of the school, hulking fellows bulging with brawn and boils who sprawled at their desks and grinned and guffawed, basking in the assurance of his patronage. He looked on them with a kind of warm contempt. They amused him. He cuffed and pummelled them merrily, and with cruel shafts of wit exposed their irredeemable ignorance, making them squirm before the class in stuttering sullen shame; yet still they loved him, and were fiercely loyal.

18

On Nicolas he turned a keen and quizzical eye. The boy blushed and bowed his head, embarrassed. There was something indecent in the way Caspar Sturm looked at him, gently but firmly lifting aside the mask and delving into the soft palpitating core of his soul. Nicolas clenched his fists, and a drop of sweat trickled down his breastbone. *You must not understand me!* The master rarely addressed him directly, and when he did there settled around them a private silence fraught with cloying unspeakable intimacies that neither would think of attempting to speak, and Canon Sturm stepped back and nodded curtly, as if he had satisfied himself once again of the validity of a conclusion previously reached.

"And here is Andreas, elder scion of the house of Koppernigk! Come, dolt, what can you tell us now of Tullius's rules for the art of memory, eh?"

*

He learned with ease, perhaps too easily: his studies bored him. Only now and then, in the grave cold music of mathematics, in the stately march of a Latin line, in logic's hard bright lucid, faintly frightening certainties, did he dimly perceive the contours of some glistening ravishing thing assembling itself out of blocks of glassy air in a clear blue unearthly sky, and then there thrummed within him a coppery chord of perfect bliss.

"Herr Sturm Herr Sturm!" the class cried, "a conundrum, Herr Sturm!"

"What! Are we here to learn or to play games?"

"Ach, Herr Sturm!"

"Very well, very well. Regard:"

In a room there are 3 men, A & B who are blindfold, & C who is blind. On a table in this room there are 3 black hats & 2 white hats, 5 hats in all. A 4th man enters: call him D. He, D, places a hat on each of the heads of A & B & C, and the 2 remaining hats he hides. Now D removes the blindfold from A, who thus can see the hats that B & C are wearing, but not the hat that he himself wears, nor the 2 hats that are hidden. D asks A if he can say what colour is the hat that he, A, is wearing? A ponders, and answers:

"No."

Now D removes the blindfold from B, who thus can see the hats that

A & C are wearing, but not the hat that he himself wears, nor the two hats that are hidden. D asks B if he can say what colour is the hat that he, B, is wearing? B ponders, hesitates, and answers:

"No."

Now: D cannot remove the blindfold from C, who does not wear a blindfold, and can see no hats at all, not white nor black, not worn nor hidden, for C, as said, is blind. D asks C if he can say what colour is the hat that he, C, is wearing? C ponders, smiles, and answers:

"Yes!"

"—Well, gentlemen," said Canon Sturm, "what is the colour of the blind man's hat, and how does he know it?"

The glass blocks sailed in silence through the bright air, and locked.

Done!

Harmonia.

"Well, young Koppernigk? You have solved it?"

Startled, Nicolas ducked his head and began scribbling feverishly on his slate. He was hot all over, and sweating, aghast to think that his face might have betrayed him, but despite all that he was ridiculously pleased with himself, and had to concentrate very hard on the thought of death in order to keep from grinning.

"Come, man," the Canon muttered. "Have you got it?"

"Not yet, sir, I am working on it sir."

"Ah. You are working on it."

And Caspar Sturm stepped back, and nodded curtly.

*

And then there was Canon Wodka. Nicolas walked with him by the river. It was the Vistula, the same that washed in vain the ineradicable mire of Torun—that is, the name was the same, but the name meant nothing. Here the river was young, as it were, a bright swift stream, while there it was old and weary. Yet it was at once here and there, young and old at once, and its youth and age were separated not by years but leagues. He murmured aloud the river's name and heard in that word suddenly the concepts of space and time fractured.

Canon Wodka laughed. "You have a clerkly conscience, Nicolas." It was true: what the world took for granted he found a source of doubt and fear. He would not have had it otherwise. The Canon's smile faltered, and he glanced at the boy timidly, tenderly, out of troubled eyes. "Beware these enigmas, my young friend. They exercise the mind, but they cannot teach us how to live."

Canon Wodka was an old man of thirty. He was startlingly ugly, a squat fat waddling creature with a globular head and pockmarked face and tiny wet red mouth. His hands were extraordinary things, brown and withered like the claws of a bat. Only his eyes, disconsolate and bright, revealed the sad maimed soul within. To the school he was a figure of rare fun, and Canon Sturm's boys loved to follow him at a lurch down the corridors, mocking his preposterous gait. Even his name, so perfectly inapt, conspired to make a clown of him, a role to which he seemed to have resigned himself, for it was in irony that he had taken the name Abstemius, and when thus addressed would sometimes cross his eyes and let his great head loll about in a travesty of drunkenness. Nicolas suspected that the Canon, despite his admonition, derived from the intricacies of pure playful thought the only consolation afforded by a life that he had never quite learned how to live.

He taught the *quadrivium* of arithmetic and geometry, astronomy and music theory. He was a very bad teacher. His was not the disciplined mind that his subjects required. It was too excitable. In the midst of a trigonometrical exposition he would go scampering off after Zeno's arrow, which will never traverse the 100 ells that separate the target from the bow because first it must fly 50 ells, and before that 25, and before that $12\frac{1}{2}$, and so on to infinity, where it comes to a disgruntled kind of halt. But the farther that the arrow did not go the nearer Nicolas drew to this poor fat laughable master. They became friends, cautiously, timidly, with many checks and starts, unwilling to believe in their good fortune, but friends they did become, and even when one day in the airy silence of the organ loft in the cathedral Canon Wodka put one of his little withered claws on Nicolas's leg, the boy stared steadily off into the gloom under the vaulted ceiling and began to talk very rapidly about nothing, as if nothing at all were happening.

In their walks by the river the Canon sketched the long confused history of cosmology. At first he was reluctant to implant new ideas in a young mind that he considered too much concerned already with abstractions, but then the wonder of the subject possessed him and he was whirled away into stammering starry heights. He spoke of the oyster universe of the Egyptians in which the Earth floated on a bowl of bitter

21

waters beneath a shell of glair, of the singing spheres of the Greeks, Pythagoras and Herakleides, of the Church Fathers whose Earth was a temple walled with air, and then of the Gnostic heresiarchs and their contention that the world was the work of fallen angels. Last of all he explained Claudius Ptolemy's theory of the heavens, formulated in Alexandria thirteen centuries before and still held by all men to be valid, by which the Earth stands immobile at the centre of all, encircled eternally in grave majestic dance by the Sun and the lesser planets. There were so many names, so many notions, and Nicolas's head began to whirl. Canon Wodka glanced at him nervously and put his finger to his own lips to silence himself, and presently began to speak earnestly, like one doing penance, of the glory of God and the unchallengeable dogma of Mother Church, and of the joys of orthodoxy.

But Nicolas hardly listened to all that. He knew nothing yet of scruples such as those besetting his friend. The firmament sang to him like a siren. Out there was unlike here, utterly. Nothing that he knew on earth could match the pristine purity he imagined in the heavens, and when he looked up into the limitless blue he saw beyond the uncertainty and the terror an intoxicating, marvellous grave gaiety.

Together they made a sundial on the south wall of the cathedral. When they had finished they stood and admired in silence this beautiful simple thing. The shadow crept imperceptibly across the dial as the day waned, and Nicolas shivered to think that they had bent the enormous workings of the universe to the performance of this minute and insignificant task.

"The world," he said, "is all an engine, then, after all, no more than that?"

Canon Wodka smiled. "Plato in the *Timaeus* says that the universe is a kind of animal, eternal and perfect, whose life is lived entirely within itself, created by God in the form of a globe, which is the most pleasing in its perfection and most like itself of all figures. Aristotle postulated as an explanation of planetary motion a mechanism of fifty-five crystalline spheres, each one touching and driving another and all driven by the primary motion of the sphere of the fixed stars. Pythagoras likened the world to a vast lyre whose strings as it were are the orbits of the planets, which in their intervals sing beyond human hearing a perfect harmonic scale. And all this, this crystalline eternal singing being, *this* you call an engine?"

"I meant no disrespect. Only I am seeking a means of understanding, and belief." He hesitated, smiling a little sheepishly at the lofty sound of that. "Herr Wodka—Herr Wodka, what do you believe?"

The Canon opened wide his empty arms.

"I believe that the world is *here*," he said, "that it exists, and that it is inexplicable. All these great men that we have spoken of, did they believe that what they proposed exists in reality? Did Ptolemy believe in the strange image of wheels within wheels that he postulated as a true picture of planetary motion? Do *we* believe in it, even though we say that it is true? For you see, when we are dealing with these matters, truth becomes an ambiguous concept. In our own day Nicolas Cusanus has said that the universe is an infinite sphere whose centre is nowhere. Now this is a *contradictio in adjecto*, since the notions of sphere and infinity cannot sensibly be put together; yet how much more strange is the Cusan's universe than those of Ptolemy or Aristotle? Well, I leave the question to you." He smiled again, ruefully. "I think it will give you much heartache." And later, as they walked across the cathedral close at dusk, the Canon halted, suddenly struck, and touched the boy lightly in excitement with a trembling hand. "Consider this, child, listen: all theories are but names, *but the world itself is a thing.*"

In the light of evening, the gathering gloom, it was as if a sibyl had spoken.

\*

On Saturdays in the fields outside the walls of the town Caspar Sturm instructed the school in the princely art of falconry. The hawks, terrible and lovely, filled the sunny air with the clamour of tiny deaths. Nicolas looked on in a mixture of horror and elation. Such icy rage, such intentness frightened him, yet thrilled him too. The birds shot into the kill like bolts from a bow, driven it seemed by a seeled steely anguish that nothing would assuage. Compared with their vivid presence all else was vague and insubstantial. They were absolutes. Only Canon Sturm could match their bleak ferocity. At rest they stood as still as stone and watched him with a fixed tormented gaze; even in flight their haste and brutal economy seemed bent to one end only, to return with all possible speed to that wrist, those silken jesses, those eyes. And their master, object of such terror and love, grew leaner, harder, darker, became something other than he was. Nicolas watched him watching his creatures and was stirred, obscurely, shamefully.

"Up sir! Up!" A heron shrieked and fell out of the air. "Up!" Monstrous hawklike creatures were flying on invisible struts and wires across a livid sky, and there was a great tumult far off, screams and roars, and howls of agony or of laughter, that came to him from that immense distance as a faint terrible twittering. Even when he woke and lay terror-stricken in a stew of sweat the dream would not end. It was as if he had tumbled headlong into some beastly black region of the firmament. He pulled at that blindly rearing lever between his legs, pulled at it and pulled, pulling himself back into the world. Dimly he sensed someone near him, a dark figure in the darkness, but he could not care, it was too late to stop, and he shut his eyes tight. The hawks bore down upon him, he could see their great black gleaming wings, their withered claws and metallic talons, their cruel beaks agape and shrieking without sound, and under that awful onslaught his self shrank together into a tiny throbbing point. For an instant everything stopped, and all was poised on the edge of darkness and a kind of exquisite dying, and then he arched his back like a bow and spattered the sheets with his seed.

He sank down and down, far, far down, and sighed. The beasts were all banished, and his inner sky was empty now and of a clear immaculate blue, and despite the guilt and the grime and the smell like the smell of blood and milk and decayed flowers, he felt afar a faint mysterious chiming that was at once everywhere and nowhere, that was a kind of infinite music.

He opened his eyes. In moonlight Andreas's pale thin unforgiving face floated above him, darkly grinning.

*

Now he became an insubstantial thing, a web of air rippling in red winds. He felt that he had been flayed of a vital protective skin. His surfaces ached, flesh, nails, hair, the very filaments of his eyes, yearning for what he could not name nor even properly imagine. At Mass he spied down from the choir loft on the women of the town kneeling in the congregation below him. They were hopelessly corporeal creatures. Even the youngest and daintiest of them in no way matched the

24

shimmering singing spirits that flew at him out of the darkness of his frantic nights. Nor was there any comfort to be had from the snivelling smelly little boys that came trailing their blankets through the dormitory, offering themselves in return for the consolation of a shared bed. What he sought was something other than ordinary flesh, was something made of light and air and marvellous grave gaiety.

Snow fell, and soothed the raw wound he has opened with his own hands. For three days it stormed in eerie silence, and then, on the fourth, dawn found the world transformed. It was in the absence of things that the change lay; the snow itself was hardly a presence, was rather a nothing where before there had been something, a pavement, a headstone, a green field, and the eye, lost in that white emptiness, was led irresistibly to the horizon that seemed immeasurably farther off now than it had ever been before.

Nicolas carried his numbed and lightened spirit up the winding stairs of the tower where Canon Wodka had his observatory, a little circular cell with a single window that opened out like a trapdoor on the sky. All tended upward here, so that the tower itself seemed on the point of flight. He climbed the seven wooden steps to the viewing platform, and as his head emerged into the stinging air he felt for a moment that he might indeed continue upward effortlessly, up and up, and he grew dizzy. The sky was a dome of palest glass, and the sun sparkled on the snow, and everywhere was a purity and brilliance almost beyond bearing. Through the far clear silence above the snowy fields and the roofs of the town he heard the bark of a fox, a somehow perfect sound that pierced the stillness like a gleaming needle. A flood of foolish happiness filled his heart. All would be well, O, all would be well! The infinite possibilities of the future awaited him. That was what the snow meant, what the fox said. His young soul swooned, and slowly, O, slowly, he seemed to fall upward, into the blue.

\*   \*   \*

In his fourth year at the University of Cracow he was ordered by Uncle Lucas to return at once to Torun: the Precentor of the Frauenburg Chapter was dying, and Uncle Lucas, now Bishop of the diocese, was bent on securing the post for his youngest nephew. Nicolas

25

made the long journey northwards alone through a tawny sad September. He was twenty-two. He carried little away with him from the Polish capital. Memories still haunted him of certain spring days in the city when the wind sang in the spires and washes of sunlight swept through the streets, and the heart, strangely troubled by clouds and birds and the voices of children, became lost and confused in surroundings that yesterday had seemed irreproachably familiar.

Andreas and he had lodged with Katharina and her husband, Gertner the merchant. Nicolas disliked that smug stolid household. Womanhood and early marriage had not changed his sister much. She was still, behind the mask of the young matron, a feline calculating child, cruel and greedy, tormented by an implacable discontent. Nicolas suspected her of adultery. She and Andreas fought as fiercely as ever they had done as children, but there was palpable between them now a new accord, forged by the sharing of secrets concealed from husband and brother alike. They united too in baiting Nicolas. His anxieties amused them, his shabbiness, his studiousness, his risible sobriety—amused them, yes, but disturbed them too, obscurely. He suffered their jibes in silence, smiling meekly, and saw, not without a certain satisfaction of which he tried but failed to feel ashamed, that indifference was the weapon that wounded them most sorely.

*

True, he had learned a great deal in Poland. After four years his head was packed with great granite blocks of knowledge; but knowledge was not perception. His mind, already venturing apprehensively along certain perilous and hitherto untrodden paths, required a lightness and delicacy of atmosphere, a sense of air and space, that was not to be had at Cracow. It was significant, he realised later, that the college on first sight had reminded him of nothing so much as a fortress, for it was, despite its pretensions, the main link in the defences thrown up by scholasticism against the tide of new ideas sweeping in from Italy, from England, and from Rotterdam. In his first year there he witnessed pitched bloody battles in the streets between Hungarian scholastics and German humanists. Although these student brawls seemed to him senseless and even comical, he could not help but see, in the meeting under the lowering mass of Wawel Rock of flaxen-haired northerners and the Magyars with their sullen brows and muddy complexions, something made tangible of that war of minds being waged across the continent.

The physical world was expanding. In their quest for a sea route to the Indies the Portuguese had revealed the frightening immensity of Africa. Rumours from Spain spoke of a vast new world beyond the ocean to the west. Men were voyaging out to all points of the compass, thrusting back the frontiers everywhere. All Europe was in the grip of an inspired sickness whose symptoms were avarice and monumental curiosity, the thirst for conquest and religious conversion, and something more, less easily defined, a kind of irresistible gaiety. Nicolas too was marked with the rosy tumours of that plague. His ocean was within him. When he ventured out in the frail bark of his thoughts he was at one with those crazed mariners on their green sea of darkness, and the visions that haunted him on his return from *terra incognita* were no less luminous and fantastic than theirs.

Yet the world was more, and less, than the fires and ice of lofty speculation. It was also his life and the lives of others, brief, pain-laden, irredeemably shabby. Between the two spheres of thought and action he could discern no workable connection. In this he was out of step with the age, which told him heaven and earth in his own self were conjoined. The notion was not seriously to be entertained, however stoutly he might defend it out of loyalty to the humanist cause. There were for him two selves, separate and irreconcilable, the one a mind among the stars, the other a worthless fork of flesh planted firmly in earthy excrement. In the writings of antiquity he glimpsed the blue and gold of Greece, the blood-boltered majesty of Rome, and was allowed briefly to believe that there had been times when the world had known an almost divine unity of spirit and matter, of purpose and consequence: was it this that men were searching after now, across strange seas, in the infinite silent spaces of pure thought?

Well, if such harmony had ever indeed existed, he feared deep down, deep beyond admitting, that it was not to be regained.

*

He took humanities, and also theology, as Uncle Lucas had directed. His studies absorbed him wholly. His ways became the set ways of the scholar. Old before his time, detached, desiccated and fussy, he

27

retreated from the world. He spoke Latin now more readily than German.

And yet it was all a deeply earnest play-acting, a form of ritual by which the world and his self and the relation between the two were simplified and made manageable. Scholarship transformed into docile order the hideous clamour and chaos of the world outside himself, endistanced it and at the same time brought it palpably near, so that, as he grappled with the terrors of the world, he was terrified and yet also miraculously tranquil. Sometimes, though, that tranquil terror was not enough; sometimes the hideousness demanded more, howled for more, for risk, for blood, for sacrifice. Then, like an actor who has forgotten his lines, he stood paralysed, staring aghast into a black hole in the air.

He believed in action, in the absolute necessity for action. Yet action horrified him, tending as it did inevitably to become violence. Nothing was stable: politics became war, law became slavery, life itself became death, sooner or later. Always the ritual collapsed in the face of the hideousness. The real world would not be gainsaid, being the true realm of action, but he must gainsay it, or despair. That was his problem.

*

Amongst the things he wished to forget from Cracow was his encounter with Professor Adalbert Brudzewski, the mathematician and astronomer. The memory of that mad mangled afternoon, however, was the ghost of a persistent giant with huge hairy paws that for years came at him again and again, laughing and bellowing, out of a crimson miasma of embarrassment and shame. It would not have been so bad if only Andreas had not been there to witness his humiliation. By rights he should not have been there: he had shown no interest whatever in Brudzewski or his classes until, after weeks of wheedling and grovelling, Nicolas had at last won a grudging invitation to the Professor's house—to his *house!*—and then he had announced in that languid way of his that he would go along too, since he had nothing better to do that day. Yet Nicolas made no protest, only shrugged, and frowned distractedly to show how little he cared in the matter, while in his imagination a marvellously haughty version of himself turned and told his brother briefly but with excoriating accuracy what a despicable hound he was.

28

*

Professor Brudzewski's classes were rigorous and very exclusive, and were, as the Professor himself was fond of pointing out, one of the main bases on which the university's impeccable reputation rested. Although he was of course a Ptolemeian, his recent cautious but by no means hostile commentary on Peurbach's planetary theory had raised some eyebrows among his fellow academics—brows which, however, he immediately caused to knit again into their wonted, lamentably low state by means of a few good thumps in defence of Ptolemaic dogma, delivered with malicious relish to the more prominent temples of suspect scholarship. The Peurbachs of the present day might come and go, but Ptolemy was unassailable on his peak, and Professor Brudzewski was there to say so, as often and as strenuously as he deemed it necessary so to do.

Nicolas had read everything the Professor had ever written on the Ptolemaic theory. Out of all those weary hours of wading through the dry sands of a sealed mind there had been distilled one tiny precious drop of pearly doubt. He could no longer remember where or when he had found the flaw, along what starry trajectory, on which rung of those steadily ascending ladders of tabular calculation, but once detected it had brought the entire edifice of a life's work crashing down with slow dreamlike inevitability. *Professor Brudzewski knew that Ptolemy was gravely wrong.* He could not of course admit it, even to himself; his investment was too great for that. This failure of nerve explained to Nicolas how it was that a mathematician of the first rank could stoop into deceit in order, in Aristotle's words, *to save the phenomena,* that is, to devise a theory grounded firmly in the old reactionary dogmas that yet would account for the observed motions of the planets. There were cases, such as the wildly eccentric orbit of Mars, that the general Ptolemaic theory could not account for, but faced with these problems the Professor, like his Alexandrian *magister* before him, leant all the weight of his prodigious skill upon the formulae until they buckled into conformity.

At first Nicolas was ashamed on the Professor's behalf. Then the shame gave way to compassion, and he began to regard the misfortunate old fellow with a rueful, almost paternal tenderness. He would help him! Yes, he would become a pupil, and in the classroom

29

take him gently in hand and show him how he might admit his folly and thereby make amends for the years of stubborness and wilful blindness. And there would be another but very different book, perhaps the old man's last, the crowning glory of his life, *Tractatus contra Ptolemaeus*, with a brief acknowledgment to the student—so young! so brilliant!—whose devastating arguments had been the thunderbolt that had struck down the author on his blithe blind way to Damascus. O yes. And though the text itself be forgotten, as surely it would be, generations of cosmologists as yet unborn would speak of the book with reverence as marking the first public appearance—so characteristically modest!—of one of the greatest astronomers of all time. Nicolas trembled, drunk on these mad visions of glory. Andreas glanced at him and smirked.

"You are sweating, brother, I can smell you from here."

"I do not have your calm, Andreas. I worry. I very much want to hear him lecture."

"Why? This stargazing and so forth, what good is it?"

Nicolas was shocked. What good?—the only certain good! But he could not say that, and contented himself with a smile of secret knowing. They passed under the spires of St Mary's Church. Spring had come to Cracow, and the city today seemed somehow airborne, an intricate aetherial thing of rods and glass flying in sunlight through pale blue space. Andreas began to whistle. How handsome he was, after all, how dashing, in his velvet tunic and plumed cap, with his sword in its ornate scabbard swinging at his side. He had carried intact into manhood the frail heart-breaking beauty of his youth. Nicolas touched him tenderly on the arm.

"I am interested in these things, you see," he said, "that is all."

He had done his brother no wrong that he could think of, yet he seemed to be apologising; it was a familiar phenomenon.

"You are interested—of course you are," Andreas answered. "But I imagine you are not entirely unmindful either that our dear uncle is watching our progress closely, eh?"

Nicolas nodded gloomily. "So: you think I am trying by being zealous to outflank you in his favour."

"What else should I think? You did not want me to come with you today."

"You were not invited!"

30

"Pah. You must understand, brother, that I know you, I know how you plot and scheme behind my back. I do not hate you for it, no—I only despise you."

"Andreas."

But Andreas had begun to whistle again, merrily.

*

Professor Brudzewski lived in a big old house in the shadow of St Mary's. The brothers were shown into the hall and left to wait, ringed round by oppressive pillars of silence stretching up past the gallery to the high ceiling with its faded frescos. They looked about them blandly, as if to impress on someone watching them the innocence of their intentions, only to discover with a start that they were indeed being watched by a dim figure behind the screens to the left. They turned away hurriedly, and heard at their backs a soft mad laugh and footsteps retreating.

They waited for a long time, apparently forgotten, while the hall came gradually to weird life around them. At first it was a matter of doors flying open to admit disembodied voices that shredded the silence, before closing again slowly with a distinct but inexplicable air of menace. Then, when they had wearied of assuming an expectant smile at each unfinished entrance, the voices began to be followed through the doorways by their owners, an oddly distracted, anonymous assortment of persons who did not stay, however, but merely passed through in small tight groups of two or three, murmuring, on their absorbed way elsewhere. These enigmatic pilgrims were to cross Nicolas's path throughout that day without ever giving up the secret of their mysterious doings.

The steward returned at last, a soft fat pale pear-shaped creature with a tiny voice and paddle feet and an immaculately bald white skull. He crooked a dainty finger at the brothers and led them into an adjoining room full of sudden sunlight from a high window. Briefly they glimpsed, as they entered by one door, a smiling girl in a green gown going out by another, leaving behind her trembling on the bright air an image of blurred beauty. Professor Brudzewski peered at them dubiously and said:

"Ah!"

He had a long yellowish face with a little pointed grey beard

31

clenched under the lower lip like a fang. His back was so grievously bent that his loose black robe, fastened tight at the throat, hung down to the floor curtainwise. Through a vent at the side was thrust a gnarled claw in which there was fixed, as a peg into a socket, the stout black stick that alone it seemed prevented him from collapsing in a little heap of dust and drapery and dry bones. This seeming frailty was deceptive: he was a quick-tempered cold old body who disliked the world, and tolerated it at best, or, when it made so bold as to accost him face to face, lashed out at it with high-pitched furious loathing.

There was a silence; it was plainly apparent that he had no idea who his guests were, and hardly cared. Nicolas felt his smile curdle into a sickly smirk. He could think of nothing to say. Andreas, clutching the hilt of his sword—which both brothers at once, wincing, suddenly remembered he was forbidden by college rules to wear in public—stepped forward with a clank.

"*Magister*! this is my brother, Nicolas Koppernigk, whom you know, of course; I am Andreas of that name. We come in humility to this veritable Olympus. Ha ha. Our uncle, Doctor Lucas Waczelrodt, Bishop of Ermland, sends greetings."

"Yes yes, quite so," the Professor muttered. "Quite so." He had not been listening. He looked past them with a frown to the doorway where three gentlemen had entered quietly, and stood now in a huddle, whispering. One was tall and thin, another short and fat, and the third, whose back was turned, was a middling sort with warts. They had a look about them of conspirators. Professor Brudzewski began to make a whirring noise under his breath. Abruptly he excused himself, set off rapidly crabwise for the door through which the green girl had gone, mumbled something that the brothers did not catch, and vanished. The conspirators hesitated, exchanging looks and hopping agitatedly from foot to foot, and then all together in a rush plunged after him, almost knocking over in their haste the steward returning with two incongruously jolly foaming mugs of beer, which he tenderly bestowed upon the guests in silence, with a mournful smile. Cloudshadow swooped into the room like a great dark bird.

After that for a long time the brothers drifted slowly about the house, somewhat dazed, jostled by flotsam. A strange distraught little man in cloak and hose with an absurd feather in his hat waylaid them in a corridor and launched without preamble into a bitter invective against the incompetence of the Chaldean cosmographers, who he seemed to feel had injured him personally in some mysterious way. Andreas slipped off, leaving Nicolas to stand alone, smiling and nodding helplessly, under a fine spray of spittle. At last the little man wound down, and, panting, departed, nodding furious approval of his own arguments. Nicolas turned, and turning caught at the edge of a canted mirror blazing with reflected sunlight a glimpse of green, that smile again, that girl! and all at once he knew her to be an emblem of light and elusive loveliness, a talisman whose image he might hold up against the malignant chaos of this ramshackle afternoon.

He hurried down the corridor, following the mirror's burning gaze, and turned a corner to find no girl, only the black stooped figure of the Professor tapping his way toward him.

"Ah, you!" the old man said peevishly. "Where have you been?" He frowned. "Were there not two of you? Well, no matter."

Nicolas launched forth at once upon the speech that for days he had been preparing. He stammered and sweated, beside himself in his eagerness to impress. Pythagoras! Plato! Nicolas Cusanus! The names of the glorious dead rolled out of his mouth and crashed together in the narrow corridor like great solid stone spheres. He hardly knew what he was saying. He felt that he had become entangled in the works of some dreadful yet farcical, inexorable engine. Herakleides! Aristotle! Regiomontanus! Bang! Crash! Clank! The Professor watched him carefully, as if studying a novel and possibly snappish species of rodent.

"Ptolemy, young man—you make no mention of Ptolemy, who has after all, as is well known, resolved for us the mysteries of the universe."

"Yes but but but *magister*, if I may say, is it not true, has it not been suggested, that there are certain, how shall I say, certain dispositions of the phenomena that nothing in Ptolemy will explain?"

The Professor smiled a wan and wintry smile, and tapped on the oaken tiles with his stick as if searching for a flaw in the floor.

"And what," he murmured, "might these inexplicable phenomena be?"

"O but I do not say that there are such mysteries, no no," Nicolas answered hastily. "I am asking rather."

This would not do, this faint-heartedness, it would not do at all. What was required now was a clear and fearless exposition of his views.

33

But what were his views? And could they be spoken? It was one thing to know that Ptolemy had erred, and that planetary science since his time had been a vast conspiracy aimed at saving the phenomena, but it was quite another to put that knowledge into words, especially in the presence of a prime conspirator.

The orbit of the afternoon had brought him back to his starting point in the hall. He was confused, and growing desperate. Things were not at all as he had imagined they would be. The little man with the feather in his cap, scourge of the Chaldeans, passed them by with a fierce look.

He could only say what was not, and not what was; he could only say: this is false, and that is false, ergo that other must be true of which as yet I can discern only the blurred outline.

"It seems to me, *magister*, that we must revise our notions of the nature of things. For thirteen hundred years astronomers have been content to follow Ptolemy without question, *like credulous women*, as Regiomontanus says, but in all that time they have not been able to discern or deduce the principal thing, namely the shape of the universe and the unchanging symmetry of its parts."

The Professor said: "Hum!" and flung open the door on the sunlit room and the high window. This time there was alas no green girl, only the ubiquitous trio of conspirators, each with a hand on another's shoulder—*Soft! See who comes!*—watching. The Professor advanced, shaking his head.

"I fail to understand you," he growled. "The principal thing, you claim, is to, what was it? to discern the shape of the universe and its parts. I do not understand that. How is it to be done? We are here and the universe, so to speak, is there, and between the two there is no sensible connection, surely?"

The room was high and wide, with rough white walls above half panelling, a ceiling with arched black beams and a checkered stone floor. There was a table and four severe chairs, and on the table a burnished copper bowl brimming with rose petals. A plaster relief on one wall depicted three naked women joined hand to shoulder in a sinuous circular dance of giving, receiving and returning. Below them on the floor a pearwood chest stood smugly shut, opposite an antique hourglass-shaped iron stove with a brass canopy. The conspirators began imperceptibly to advance. The window's stippled diamond panes gave

34

on to a little courtyard and a stunted cherry tree in bloom. Suddenly Nicolas was appalled by the blank anonymity of surfaces, the sullen, somehow resentful secretiveness of unfamiliar things whose contours have been rubbed and shaped by the action of unknown lives. Doubtless for others this room was strung with a shimmering web of exquisitely exact significances, perhaps it was so even for these three peculiar persons edging stealthily forward; but not for Nicolas. He thought: what can we know that is not of ourselves?

"Paracelsus says," he said, "that in the scale of things man occupies the centre, that he is the measure of all things, being the point of equilibrium between that which is great and that which is small."

Professor Brudzewski was staring at him.

"Paracelsus? Who is this? He is mad, surely. *God* is the measure of all things, and only *God* can comprehend the world. What you seem to suggest, young man, with your *principal thing*, smacks of blasphemy therefore."

"Blablablasphemy?" Nicolas bleated. "Surely not. Did you yourself not say that in Ptolemy we find the solution to the mysteries of the universe?"

"That was a manner of speaking, no more."

The door behind them opened and Andreas entered softly. Nicolas squirmed, drenched with sweat. The conspirators, without seeming to move, were yet bearing down upon him inexorably. He felt a dismayed sense of doom, like one who hears the ice shattering behind him as he careers with slow, mad inevitability out into the frozen lake.

"But *magister*, you said—!"

"Yes yes yes yes, quite—I know what I said." The old man glared at the floor, and gave it a whack with his stick—take *that*, you! "Listen to me: you are confusing astronomy with philosophy, or rather that which is called philosophy today, by that Dutchman, and the Italians and their like. You are asking our science to perform tasks which it is incapable of performing. Astronomy does not describe the universe as it is, but only as we observe it. That theory is correct, therefore, which accounts for our observations. Ptolemy's theory is perfectly, almost perfectly valid insofar as pure astronomy is concerned, *because it saves the phenomena*. This is all that is asked of it, and all that can be asked, in reason. It does not discern your principal thing, for that is not to be discerned, and the astronomer who claims otherwise will be hissed off the stage!"

"Are we to be content then," Nicolas cried, "are we to be content with mere abstractions? Columbus has proved that Ptolemy was mistaken as to the dimensions of the Earth; shall we ignore Columbus?"

"An ignorant sailor, and a Spaniard. Pah!"

"He has *proved* it, sir—!" He lifted a hand to his burning brow; calm, he must keep calm. The room seemed full of turbulence and uproar, but it was only the tumult within him dinning in his ears. Those three were still advancing steadily, and Andreas was at his back doing he did not wish to imagine what. The Professor swung himself on his stick in a furious circle around the table, so stooped now that it appeared he might soon, like some fabulous serpent, clamp his teeth upon his own nether regions and begin to devour himself in his rage. Nicolas, gobbling and clucking excitedly, pursued him at a hesitant hop.

"Proof?" the old man snapped. "Proof? A ship sails a certain distance and returns, and the captain comes ashore and agitates the air briefly with words; you call this *proof*? By what immutable standards is this a refutation of Ptolemy? You are a nominalist, young man, and you do not even know it."

"I a nominalist—*I*? Do you not merely say the name of Ptolemy and imagine that all contrary arguments are thus refuted? No no, *magister*; I believe not in names, but in things. I believe that the physical world is amenable to physical investigation, and if astronomers will do no more than sit in their cells counting upon their fingers then they are shirking their responsibility!"

The Professor halted. He was pale, and his head trembled alarmingly on its frail stalk of neck, yet he sounded more puzzled than enraged when he said:

"Ptolemy's theory saves the phenomena, I have said so already; what other responsibility should it have?"

Tell him. *Tell him.*

"Knowledge, *magister*, must become perception. The only acceptable theory is that one which *explains* the phenomena, which explains . . . which . . ." He stared at the Professor, who had begun to shake all over, while out of his pinched nostrils there came little puffs of an extraordinary harsh dry noise: he was laughing! Suddenly he turned, and pointed with his stick and asked:

"What do you say, young fellow? Let us hear your views."

Andreas leaned at ease by the window with his arms folded and his face lifted up to the light. A handful of rain glistened on the glass, and a breeze in silence shook the blossoms of the cherry tree. The unutterable beauty of the world pierced Nicolas's sinking heart. His brother pondered a moment, and then with the faintest of smiles said lightly:

"I say, *magister*, that we must hold fast to sanity and Aristotle."

It meant nothing, of course, but it sounded well; O yes, it sounded well. Professor Brudzewski nodded his approval.

"Ah yes," he murmured. "Just so." He turned again to Nicolas. "I think you have been too much influenced by our latterday upstarts, who imagine that they can unravel the intricacies of God's all-good creation. You spoke of Regiomontanus: I studied under that great man, and I can assure you that he would have scorned these wild notions you have put forth today. You question Ptolemy? Mark this: to him who thinks that the ancients are not to be entirely trusted, the gates of our science are certainly closed. He will lie before those gates and spin the dreams of the deranged about the motion of the eighth sphere, and he will get what he deserves for believing that he can lend support to his own hallucinations by slandering the ancients. Therefore take this young man's sound advice, and hold fast to sanity."

Nicolas in his dismay felt that he must be emitting a noise, a thin piercing shriek like that of chalk on slate. There was a distinct sensation of shock at the base of his spine, as if he had sat down suddenly without looking on the spot from whence a chair had been briskly removed. The three conspirators, crowding at his shoulder, regarded him with deep sadness. They were at once solicitous and sinister. The one with the warts kept his face turned away, unable to look full upon such folly. Andreas, laughing silently, said softly in his brother's ear:

"*Bruder, du hast in der Scheisse getreppen.*"

And the fat conspirator giggled. Behind the screens in the hall the secret watcher waited. It was of course—of course!—the green girl. The Professor peered at her balefully, and turning to the brothers he sighed and said:

"Gentlemen, you must forgive me my daughter. The wench is mad."

He shook his stick at her and she retreated, harlequinned by crisscross shadows, pursued by the conspirators scurrying on tiptoe, twittering, to the stairs, where the little man in the plumed hat waited among other, vaguer enigmas. All bowed and turned, ascended slowly into the gloom, and vanished.

Professor Brudzewski impatiently bade the brothers good day—but not before he had invited Andreas to attend his lectures. Grey rain was falling on Cracow.

"What?—spend my mornings listening to that old cockerel droning on about the planets and all that? Not likely, brother; I have better things to do."

*

Nicolas arrived in Torun at September's end. The house in St Anne's Lane received him silently, solicitously, like a fellow mourner. Old Anna and the other servants were gone now, and there was a new steward in charge, a surly fellow, one of the Bishop's men. He followed Nicolas about the house with a watchful suspicious eye. The sunny autumn day outside was all light and distance, and above the roofs and spires a cloud, a ship in air, sailed gravely at the wind's pace across a sky immensely high and blue. The leaves of the linden were turning.

"Build a fire, will you. I am cold."

"Yes, master. His Grace your uncle gave me to understand that you would not be staying?"

"No, I shall not be staying."

Uncle Lucas came that evening, in a black rage. He greeted Nicolas with a glare. The Frauenburg Precentor had been crass enough to die in an uneven-numbered month, when the privilege of filling Church appointments in the See of Ermland passed by Church law from the Bishop to the Pope.

"So we may forget it, nephew: I am not loved at Rome. Ach!" He beat the air vainly with his fists. "Another week, that was all! However, we must be charitable. God rest his soul." He fastened his little black eyes on Nicolas. "Well, have you lost your tongue?"

"My Lord—"

"Pray, do not grovel! You took no degree at Cracow. Four years."

"It was you that summoned me away, my Lord. I had not completed my studies."

"Ah." The Bishop paced about a moment, nodding rapidly, with his hands clasped behind his back. "Hmm. Yes." He halted. "Let me give

38

you some advice, nephew. Rid yourself of this rebellious streak, if you wish to remain in my favour. *I will not have it!* Do you understand?" Nicolas bowed his head meekly, and the Bishop grunted and turned away, disappointed it seemed with so easy a victory. He hoisted up his robe and thrust his backside to the fire. "Steward! Where is the whoreson? Which reminds me: I suppose your wastrel brother is also kicking his heels in Poland waiting for me to find him a soft post? What a family, dear God! It is from the father, of course. Bad blood there. And you, wretch, look at you, cowering like a kicked dog. You hate me, but you have not the courage to say it—O yes, it's true, I know. Well, you will be rid of me soon enough. There will be other posts at Frauenburg. Once I have secured you a prebend you will be off my hands, and my accounts, and after that I care not a whit what you do, I shall have fulfilled my responsibility. Take my advice and go to Italy."

"It—?"

"—Or wherever, it's no matter, so long as it is somewhere far off. And take your brother with you: I do not want him within an ass's roar of my affairs. Well, man, what are you grinning at?"

Italy!

*     *     *

On Easter Day in 1496 Canon Nicolas and his brother marched forth from Cracow's Florian Gate in the company of a band of pilgrims. There were holy men and sinners, monks, rogues, mountebanks and murderers, poor peasants and rich merchants, widows and virgins, mendicant knights, scholars, pardoners and preachers, the hale and the halt, the blind, the deaf, the quick and the dying. Royal banners fluttered in the sunlight against an imperial blue sky, and the royal trumpeters blew a brassy blast, and from high upon the fortress walls the citizens with cheers and a wild waving of caps and kerchiefs bade the wayfarers farewell, as down the dusty road into the plain they trudged. Southwards they were bound, over the Alps to Rome, the Holy City.

"He could have got us a couple of nags," Andreas grumbled, "damned skinflint, instead of leaving us to walk like common peasants."

Nicolas would not have cared had Bishop Lucas forced them to crawl to Italy. He was, for the first time in his life, so it seemed to him, free. A post had been found for him at last at Frauenburg; the Chapter at the Bishop's direction had granted him immediate leave of absence, and he had departed without delay for Cracow. He found that city strangely altered, no longer the forlorn gloomy terminus he had known during his university years, but a bustling waystation cheerful with travellers and loud with the uproar of foreign tongues. To be sure, the change was not in the city but in him, the traveller, who noticed now what the student had ignored, yet he chose to see his new regard for this proud cold capital as a sign that he had at last grown up into himself and his world, that he was at last renouncing the past and turning his face toward an intrepid manhood; it was all nonsense, of course, he knew it; but still, he was allowed for a few days at least to feel mature, and worldly-wise, and significant.

His newfound self-esteem, however tentative it was and prone to collapse into self-mockery, infuriated Andreas. No undemanding canonry had been secured for him. Wherever he turned Bishop Lucas's black shadow fell upon him like a blight. He was not going to Italy—he was being sent. And he had not even been provided with a horse to lift him above the common throng.

"I am almost thirty, and still he treats me like a child. What have I ever done to deserve his contempt? What have I done?"

He glared at Nicolas, daring him to answer, and then turned his face away, grinding his teeth in rage and anguish. Nicolas was embarrassed, as always in the presence of another's public pain. He wanted to walk away very quickly, he even imagined himself fleeing with head down, muttering, waving his arms like one pursued by a plague of flies, but there was nowhere to go that would be free of his brother's anger and pain.

Andreas laughed.

"And you, brother," he said softly, "feeding off me, eating me alive."

Nicolas stared at him. "I do not understand you."

"O get away, get away! You sicken me."

And so, lashed together by thongs of hatred and frightful love, they set out for Italy.

*

They equipped themselves with two stout staffs, good heavy jackets

40

lined with sheepskin against the Alpine cold, a tinderbox, a compass, four pounds of sailor's biscuit and a keg of salt pork. The gathering of these provisions afforded them a deep childish satisfaction. Andreas found in the Italian swordsmith's near the cathedral an exquisitely tooled dagger with a retracting blade that at the touch of a concealed lever sprang forward with an evil click. This ingenious weapon he kept in a sheath sewn for the purpose inside his bootleg. It made him feel wonderfully dangerous. Bartholemew Gertner, Katharina's husband, sold them a mule, and cheated them only a little on the deal, since they were family, after all. A taciturn and elderly beast, this mule carried their baggage readily enough, but would not bear the indignity of a rider, as they quickly discovered.

Nicolas could have bought them a pair of horses. Before leaving Frauenburg he had drawn lavishly on his prebend. But he kept his riches secret, and sewed the gold into the lining of his cloak, because he did not wish to embarrass his penniless brother, so he told himself.

Andreas gazed gloomily southwards. "Like common pig peasants!"

Forth from St Florian's Gate they marched into the great plain, behind them the cheering and the brassy blare of trumpets, before them the long road.

*

The weather turned against them. Near Braclav a windstorm rose without warning out of the plain and came at them like a great dark animal, howling. The inns were terrible, crawling with lice and rogues and poxed whores. At Graz they were fed a broth of tainted meat and suffered appalling fluxions; at Villach the bread was weevilled. A child died, fell down on the road screaming, clenched in agony, while its mother stood by and bawled.

Their number shrank steadily day by day, for many who had left with them from Cracow had been, like the brothers, merely travellers seeking protection and companionship on their way to Silesia or Hungary or South Germany, and by the time they reached the Carnic Alps they were no more than a dozen adults and some children, and even of that small band less than half were pilgrims. Old Felix, the holy man, smote the ground with his staff and inveighed against those worldly ones in their midst who were exploiting God's protection on this holy journey; it was their impiety that had led them all to misfortune. He

41

was a stooped emaciated ancient with a long white beard. On the women especially he fixed his burning eyes.

"It is sin that has brought us to this pass!"

Krack the murderer grinned.

"Ah give it a rest, grandpa."

He was a jolly fellow, Krack, and useful too, for he knew well the ways of the road, and could truss and roast a pilfered chicken very prettily. He was convinced that they were all fugitives like him, using the pilgrimage as a handy camouflage for flight. Their dogged protests of innocence hurt his feelings: had he not regaled them readily enough with the details of his own moment of glory? "Bled like a pig he did, howling murder and God-a-mercy. He was tough, I tell you, the old bugger—slit from ear to ear and still clutching his few florins as if they was his ballocks I was tearing off. Jesus!"

The men squabbled among themselves, and once there broke out a desperate fight with fists and cudgels in which a knife with a spring blade played no small part. There was trouble too with the womenfolk. A young girl, a crazed creature mortally diseased who lay at night with whatever man would have her, was set upon by the other women and beaten so severely that she died soon after. They left her for the wolves. Her ghost followed them, filling their nights with visions of blood and ruin.

And then one rainy evening as they were crossing a high plateau under a sulphurous lowering sky a band of horsemen wheeled down on them, yelling. They were unlovely ruffians, tattered and lean, deserters from some distant war. "Good holy Jesus poxed fucking Christ!" Krack muttered, gaping at them, and slapped his leg and laughed. They were old comrades of his, apparently. Their leader was a red-headed Saxon giant with an iron hook where his right hand had once been.

"We are crusaders, see," this Rufus roared, his carroty hair whipping in the yellow wind, "off to fight the infidel Turk. We need food and cash for the long journey before us. When you reach Rome you may tell the Pope you met with us: we're his men, fighting his cause, and he'll return with interest the donations you're going to make to us. Right, lads?" His fellows laughed heartily. "Now then, let's have you. Food I say, and whatever gold you've got, and anyone who tries to cheat us will have his tripes cut out."

42

Old Felix stepped forward.

"We are but poor pilgrims, friend. If you take what little we have you must answer to God for our deaths, for *certes* we shall not leave these mountains alive."

Rufus grinned. "Offer up a prayer, dad, and Jesus might send manna from heaven."

The old man shakily lifted his staff to strike, but Rufus with a great laugh drew his sword and ran him through the guts, and he sank to his knees in a torrent of blood, bellowing most terribly. Rufus wiped his sword on his sleeve and looked about. "Any other arguments? No?"

His men went among the travellers then like locusts, leaving them only their boots and a few rags to cover their backs. The brothers watched in silence their mule being driven off. Nicolas's suspiciously weighty cloak was ripped asunder, and the hoard of coins spilled out. Andreas looked at him.

"Friends," cried Rufus, "many thanks, and God go with you."

They mounted up, but paused and muttered among themselves, grinning, and then dismounted again and raped the woman and two young boys. It took a long time for all those heaps of wriggling white flesh to be skewered, screaming, in the mud. Old Felix died as night fell, lying supine on the ground in the rain with his horny bare feet splayed, like a large wooden effigy, crying: Ah! Ah! Krack, waving a cheery farewell, had gone off with his friends. Andreas said:

"All that money, and not a word; you cunt."

*

They would have perished surely, every one, had they not next day at dawn chanced upon a monastery perched on a rock high above a verdant valley. An old monk tending a vegetable garden outside the walls dropped his hoe and fled in terror at the sight of these walking dead who lifted up their frozen arms and mewled eerily. They could themselves hardly believe that they had survived. The night had been a kind of silvery icy death. They had spent it climbing blindly and in frantic haste, like possessed things, up the rocky slopes, watched by a huge impassive moon. Dawn had come in a flash of cold fire.

The monks of St Bernard received them kindly. One of the young boys died. Andreas, still brooding on that hidden trove of gold, would not speak to his brother. Nicolas passed his days out of doors, tramping the mountain paths in a monk's cloak and cowl, telling himself stories, muttering Latin verse, imagining Italy, trying to purge himself of the memory of rain and screaming, of rags stiff with brown blood, of Krack's smile. This country was unreal, this fiery icy Ultima Thule. He could not get his bearings here, everything was too big or too small, those impossible glittering mountains, the tiny blue flowers in the valley. Even the weather was strange, vast bluish brittle days of Alpine spring, fierce sun all light and little heat, transparent skies pierced by snowy peaks. The mountain goats clattered off with bells jangling at his approach, frightened by this staring alpenstocked dark parcel of pain and loathing. There was no forgetting. At night he was plagued by dreams whose sombre afterglow contaminated his waking hours, hung about him like a darkening of the air. He began to detect in everything signs of secret life, in flowers, mountain grasses, the very stones underfoot, all living, all somehow in agony. Thunderclouds flew low across the sky like roars of anguish on their way to being uttered elsewhere.

It was not the sufferings of the maimed and dead that pained him, but the very absence of that pain; he could not forget those terrible scenes, the blood and mud, the bundles of squirming flesh, but, remembering, he felt nothing, nothing, and this emptiness horrified him.

*

At Bologna, where they were to enrol at the university, the brothers parted company with the remnants of the pilgrimage. The representative at Rome of the Frauenburg Chapter, Canon Bernhard Schiller, had travelled north to meet them. He was a small grey cautious man.

"Well, gentlemen," he snapped, "welcome to Italy. You are late arriving. I hope you had a pleasant journey, for certainly it was a leisurely one."

They gazed at him. Andreas laughed. He said:

"We have no money."

"What!" The Canon's grey face turned greyer. In the end, however, he agreed to advance them a hundred ducats. "Understand, this is not my money, nor the Church's either; it is your uncle's. I have written to him today informing him of this transaction, and demanding an immediate refund." He permitted himself a bleak smile. "I trust you have ready for him a satisfactory explanation of your poverty? And why,

44

may I ask, are you got up in this monkish garb? Have you been gambling with clerics? A perilous pastime. Well, it is no business of mine. Good day."

Andreas watched with bitter amusement as Nicolas carefully counted his share of the ducats.

"Better get it sewed up quick, brother."

\*     \*     \*

At twilight through hot crowded noxious streets he strode, speculating furiously on the true dimensions of the universe. Dark glossy heads and almond eyes turned to follow him with curiosity and amusement as he flew past. Bologna was a city of grotesques and madmen, yet he did not go unnoticed, with his long cloak and stark fanatic face. What did he care for their opinion, this noisy, stupid people! Italy had been a great disappointment; he hated it, the heat, the stale inescapable smell, the infantile uproar, the indolence, the corruption, the disorder. He had imagined a proud blue sunlit, serene land. Hawkers shrieked in his face, wheedling and bullying, thrusting at him their wine, their sweetmeats, their blinded singing birds. A fat buffoon with a head like a gobbet of raw meat, jiggling a string of stinking sausages, opened the wet red hole of his mouth and crowed: *Bello, professore, bello, bello!* A leprous beggar extended a fingerless hand and whined. He fled around a corner and was struck full tilt by a blinding blast of light. The setting sun sat on the city wall, flanked by a pair of robbers freshly hung that morning, black blots against the gold. Suddenly he yearned for those still pale pearly, limpid northern evenings full of silence and clouds. Vile vapours rose up from below. He had stepped in dogmerd.

With a sinking heart he heard his name called from the courtyard of a tavern close by, but when he made to hurry on he was prevented by a grinning drab, black as pitch, who planted herself in his path, smacking her blubber lips. A roar of tipsy laughter gushed out of the tavern.

"Come join us, brother, in a cup of wine," Andreas called. He sat with a band of blades, good Germans all, his friends. "See, fellows, how pale and gaunt he looks. You are too much at the books."

They regarded him merrily, delighted with him, provider of fine sport. One said:

"Too much at the rod, more like."

"Aye, been galloping the maggot, have you, Canon?"

"Bashing the venerable bishop, eh?"

"Haw haw."

"O sit down!" Andreas snapped, flushed and petulant; drink did not agree with him very well. Nicolas had often wondered at his brother's uncanny knack of gathering about him the same friends wherever he went. The names varied, and the faces a little, but otherwise they were the same at Torun or Cracow or here in Bologna, idlers and whoremasters, pretender poets, rich men's sons with too much money, bullyboys all. There was of course this difference, that they got progressively older. Among this present lot there was not a one under thirty. Perennial students! Nicolas smiled wryly to himself: he was not so young that he could afford to scoff at others. Yet he *was* different, he knew it, a different species; why else did he fit so ill among them, perched here on the edge of this bench, hugging himself in a transport of embarrassment and repugnance, grinning like an idiot?

"Tell us, brother, who was that fair wench we spied you with just now? Likely you were discussing the motions of the spheres? Venus rising and suchlike?" Nicolas shrugged and squirmed, simpering foolishly; he was no match for his brother at this kind of cutting banter. Andreas turned to the others with his languorous smile. "He is very hot on stargazing, you know, the pearly orbs, the globes of night, and so forth."

A pimply fellow with straw-coloured locks and a wispy beard, the son of a Swabian count, took his sharp little nose out of his pintpot and leaned across the table seriously, and seriously said:

"Canon, have you heard tell of the unfortunate astronomer who got his sums mixed, and ended up with two planets where there should have been only one? Why, he made a ballocks of the orbit of Mars!"

There was more hawing and hohoing then, and more wine, and landlord! landlord! come fellow, a bowl of your best stewed tripe, for blind me but I have a longing for innards tonight. They left off baiting Nicolas. He was a poor foil for their wit, a poor punchbag. The last light of evening faded and the night came on apace, and stars, hesitant and dainty, glimmered in the trellis of vineleaves above their heads. A boy with a bunch of smoking tapers went among the tables. Here comes our young Prometheus, bringer of fire. What a sweet arse he has, look where he bends; here, boy, a ducat for your favours. The child backed off, smiling in fright. Music swelled in the street, wild caterwauling of fifes and the rattle of kettledrums, and a band of minstrels entered the courtyard in search of free wine. Nicolas grew dizzy in the noise and the smoke of the shaking rushlight. He drank. The Tuscan red was dark and tawny as old blood. Andreas mounted the table, wild-eyed and unsteady, roaring of freedom and rebirth, the new age, *l'uomo nuovo*. He staggered, clutching the air, and fell with a scream and a clatter into his brother's lap. Nicolas, suddenly stricken by sad helpless love, rocked in his arms this slack damp drunken lump, this grotesque babe, who leaned out over the table and gawked—*Ork!*—upon the straw-strewn floor a dollop of tripe and wine.

Later they were in a narrow ill-lit stinking street, and someone was lying in an open drain being strenuously kicked. The count's son stood by sniggering, until he was punched smartly out of the darkness by a disembodied fist and went down with a cry, gushing blood from a smashed nose. Nicolas found himself unaccountably on his knees in a low room or kind of little hut. The place was loud with grunting and moaning, and tangles of humped pale phosphorescent flesh writhed on the earthen floor. In the ghastly candlelight a woman lay on a pallet before him spreadeagled like an anatomical specimen, grinning and whimpering. She smelled of garlic and fish. He fell upon her with a moan and sank his teeth into her shoulder. It was a messy business, quickly done. Only afterwards did it strike him, when he put it to himself formally as it were, that he had at last relinquished his virginity. It had been just as he had imagined it would be.

*

Next morning he crept into the Aula Maxima bleared and crapulous, and late; his fellow students, elderly earnest young men, glared at him in disapproval and reproach. The Professor ignored him—what was a student's tardiness to Domenico Maria da Novara, astronomer, scholar of Greek, devotee of Plato and Pythagoras? Perched in his high pulpit he was as ever supremely, magisterially bored. The dry sombre voice strolled weary and indifferent through the lecture, pacing out the sentences as if they were so many ells of fallow land; only later would the significance and peculiar brilliance of his thought be made manifest, when their notes exploded slowly, like an unfolding myriad-

47

petalled flower, in the mean rooms and minds of his students. He was a cold queer fastidious man, tall and swart, in his middle years, with a cruel face like a sharp dark blade. At Bologna, where it was not uncommon for an arrogant lecturer to be humbled by a hail of brickbats, or even run through by a playful rapier, Novara commanded universal fear and respect.

"Koppernigk—a word, if I might." Nicolas halted in alarm. The class had ended, and the last of his fellows were shuffling out of the hall. He tried to smile, and leering waited, sick-shotten, quaking. The Professor descended thoughtfully from the pulpit, and on the last step stopped and looked at him. "I am told that you have been putting about some, how shall I say, some curious ideas. Is it so, hmm?"

"Forgive me, *maestro*, I do not understand."

"No?" Novara smiled thinly. They walked together down a sunlit corridor. Narrow stone arches to their right gave on to a paved courtyard and a marble statue with one arm raised in mysterious hieratic greeting; jagged shadows bristled under their feet. The Professor went on: "I mean of course astronomical ideas, speculations on the shape and size of the universe, that kind of thing. I am interested, you understand. They tell me that you have expressed doubts on certain parts of the Ptolemaic doctrine of planetary motion?"

"I have taken part, it is true, in some discussions, in the taverns, but I have done no more than echo what has been said already, many times, by you yourself among others." Novara pursed his lips and nodded. Something seemed to amuse him. Nicolas said: "I do not believe that I have anything original to say. I am a dabbler. And I am not well this morning," he finished wanly.

They strolled in silence for a time. The corridor was loud with the tramp of students, who eyed with furtive speculation this ill-assorted pair. Novara brooded. Presently he said:

"But your ideas on the dimensions of the universe, the intervals between planets, these seem to me original, or at least to promise great originality." Nicolas wondered uneasily how the man could have come to hear of these things. His encounter with Brudzewski in Cracow had taught him discretion. He had admitted taking part in tavern talk, but surely he had never been more than a silent sharer? Who then knew enough of his thinking to betray him? The Professor watched him sidelong with a calculating look. "What interests me," he said, "is whether or not you have the mathematics to support your theories?" There was of course one only who could have betrayed him; well, no matter. He was both pained and pleased, as if he had been caught in the commission of a clever crime. The few notions he had managed to put into words, gross ungainly travesties of the inexpressibly elegant concepts blazing in his brain, were suddenly made to seem far finer things than he had imagined by the attentions of the authoritative Novara.

"*Maestro*, I am no astronomer, nor a mathematician either."

"Yes." The Professor smiled again. "You are a dabbler, as you say." He seemed to think that he had made a joke. Nicolas grinned greyly. They came out on the steps above the sunny piazza. The bells of San Pietro began to ring, a great bronze booming high in the air, and flocks of pigeons blossomed into the blue above the golden domes. Novara mused dreamily on the crowds below in the square, and then abruptly turned and with what passed in him for animation said:

"Come to my house, will you? Come today. There are some people I think you might be interested to meet. Shall we say at noon? Until noon, then. *Vale*." And he went off quickly down the steps.

Well what—?

*

"Well, what happened?" Andreas asked.

"Where?"

"At Novara's!"

"O, that." They sat in the dining-hall of the German *natio*, where they lodged; it was evening, and beyond the grimy windows the Palazzo Communale brooded in late sunlight. The hall was crowded with crop-headed Germans at feed. Nicolas's head pained him. "I do not know what Novara wants with me, I am not his kind at all. There were some others there, Luca Guarico, Jacob Ziegler, Calcagnini the poet—"

Andreas whistled softly. "Well well, I am impressed. The cream of Italy's intellectuals, eh?" He smirked. "—And you, brother."

"And I, as you say. Andreas, have you been putting about those few things I told you of my ideas on astronomy?"

"Tell me what happened at Novara's."

"—Because I wish you would not; I would rather you would not do that."

49

"Tell me."

*

He was shown into a courtyard with orange bushes in earthenware pots; a fountain plashed, playing a faint cool music. The guests were gathered on the terrace, lolling elegantly on couches and dainty cane chairs, sipping white wine from long-stemmed goblets of Murano crystal and lazily conversing. Nicolas was reminded of those cages of pampered quail that were to be seen hanging from the porticoes of the better houses of the city. Diffident, ill at ease, acutely aware of his rawboned Prussian gracelessness, he stood mute and nervously smiling as the Professor introduced him. Novara was very much the patrician here, with his fine town house behind him. He affected a scissorsshaped lorgnon with which he made much play. This article, together with the brilliant light, the pools of violet shadow on the terrace, the sparkling glass, the watermusic and the perfume of the orange bushes, contrived to create an air of theatre. Elbing. Elbing? Nicolas wondered vaguely why he should suddenly have thought of that far northern town.

How did he like Italy? The climate, ah yes. And what subjects was he studying here? Indeed? There was a silence, and someone coughed behind gloved fingers. Their duty done, they turned back to the conversation that evidently his arrival had interrupted. Celio Calcagnini, a willowy person no longer in the first flower of youth, said languidly:

"The question, then, is what can be achieved? Bologna is not Firenze, and I think we all agree that our Don John Bentivoglio is not, and never could be, a Magnifico." All softly laughed and shook their heads; the jibe against the Duke of Bologna seemed to be a familiar one. "And yet, my friends," the poet continued, "we must work with the material to hand, however poor it is. The wise man knows that compromise is sometimes the only course—this is an excellent vintage, Domenico, by the way. I envy your cellar."

Novara, leaning at ease against a white pillar, lifted his glass and bowed sardonically. A sleek black hound, which Nicolas with a start noticed now for the first time, lay at the Professor's feet, sphinxlike, panting, with a fanged ferocious grin. Jacob Ziegler, astronomer of some repute and author of a recent much-admired work on Pliny, was a dark and brooding lean young blade with a pale long face and flashing eyes and a pencil-line moustache. He was exquisitely if a trifle foppishly attired in rubious silk and calfskin; a wide-brimmed velvet hat lay beside him like a great soft black exotic bird. The cane chair on which he sat crackled angrily as he leaned forward and cried:

"Compromise! Caution! *I tell you we must act!* Times do not change of themselves, but are changed by the actions of men. Bologna is not Firenze, just so; but what is Firenze? A town of fat shopkeepers besotted by soft living." He glanced darkly at Calcagnini, who raised his eyebrows mildly and toyed with the stem of his wineglass. "They gobble up art and science as they would sugared marchpane, and congratulate themselves on their culture and liberality. Culture? Pah! And their artists and their scientists are no better. A gang of panders, theirs is the task of supplying the pretty baubles to mask the running sores of the poxed courtesan that is their city. Why, I should a thousand times rather we were the outcasts that we are than be as they, pampered adorners of decadence!"

"Decadence," Novara softly echoed, gingerly tasting the word. Calcagnini looked up.

"A pretty speech, Jacob," he said, smiling, "but I think I resent your imputations. Compromise likes me no better than it does you, yet I know that there is a time for everything, for caution and for action. If we move now we can only make our state worse than it already is. And come to that, what, pray, would you have us do? The Bentivoglio rule in this city is unshakeable. There is peace here, while all Italy is in turmoil—O I know, I know you would not call it peace, but besottedness. Yet call it what you will, our citizens, like their fellows in Firenze, are well fed and therefore well content to leave things just as they are. That is the equation; it is as simple as that. You may harangue them all you wish, berate them for their decadence, but they will only laugh at you—that is, so long as you are no more than a crazy astronomer with your head in the clouds. Come down to earth and meddle in their affairs, then it will be another matter. Fra Girolamo, the formidable Savonarola, was cherished for a time by Firenze. The city writhed in holy ecstasy under his lash, until he began to frighten them, and then—why, then they burnt him. You see? No no, Jacob, there will be no *autos da fe* in Bologna."

Ziegler pouted, and a pretty flush spread upward from his cheeks to

51

his pale forehead. "Are you comparing us to that mad monk, that *creature*, who castigated Plato as a source of immorality? He deserved burning, I say!"

Calcagnini smiled again tolerantly.

"No, my dear Jacob," he murmured, "of course I make no such comparison. I am merely trying to demonstrate to you that precipitate and rash action on our part can lead us straight to ruin."

"—And further," Ziegler continued hotly, "why do you assume that the power of the Bentivoglios can be challenged only from within Bologna's walls?"

The hound shut its jaws with a wet snap and rose and loped leanly away. There was an awkward silence. Ziegler glared about him haughtily, flushed and defiant. "Well?" he asked, of no one in particular. Novara frowned at him with pursed lips, and very slightly shook his head in wordless mild reproof. A scrawny individual, rejoicing in the name of Nono, laughed squeakily.

"L-let us hear the results of L-Luca's l-l-labours!" he ventured brightly. The others paid no heed to him, being engrossed in disapproving silently of whatever indiscretion it was that the unrepentant Ziegler had committed, and Nono turned unhappily to Nicolas and said, very loudly and deliberately, as if addressing a stone-deaf idiot: "H-he has made a horosc-sc-scope of Cesare, you see. *Il Valentino*, as he is called, ha ha." Nicolas nodded, smiling hugely, miming extravagant gratitude and encouragement. "Bo-Bo-Borgia, that is," Nono finished lamely, and frowned, searching it seemed for that last elusive word, the stammerer's obsession, that surely would make all come marvellously clear.

Novara stirred. "Yes, Luca, tell us, what do the stars say of our young prince?"

Luca Guarico, he of the large head and hooked nose of a decayed Caesar, sighed fatly, and fatly shrugged. He was fat; he was that kind of fat that conjures up, in the goggling imaginations of thin fastidious men such as Nicolas, hideous and irresistible visions of quaking copulations, and monstrous labours in water closets, and helpless tears at the coming undone of a shoe buckle. He thrashed about briefly on the couch where he sat, and panting brought out from beneath his robes a wrinkled scrap of parchment.

"There is little to tell," he wheezed. "Had I the facts it would be easy, but I have not. A long life, certainly; good fortune at first, as befits—" he smiled gloomily "—the Pope's bastard. After his thirtieth year there will come a falling off, but that is not clear. He will conduct a victorious campaign in Lombardy and the Romagna, as that Sforza bitch will learn to her cost. He should beware the French, if Mars is to be trusted." He shrugged again apologetically and put away the parchment. "So."

"O brilliant, brilliant," Ziegler muttered, plucking fiercely at his moustache. Guarico looked at him. Calcagnini hastened to say:

"Jacob, you are so fiery today! As Luca has told us, he has not the necessary facts—and indeed we may ask, who can know the facts concerning that strange and secretive dynasty?"

Bland smiles were exchanged. Novara said:

"But Luca, do you have nothing that touches on our concerns?"

"I can tell you this," the fat man answered, and looked about him dourly, "this I can tell you: he will never sit on the throne of Peter."

There was the sense of a slow soft crash, and Ziegler sniggered bitterly.

"Well then," Novara murmured, "there is nothing for us there."

Suddenly they all relaxed, and looked at Nicolas, a little bashfully it seemed, like players awaiting his applause. He stared back blankly, baffled. He felt he must have missed something of deep significance. The servants carried on to the terrace small silver trays of choice comestibles, flaked game in aspic, chunks of melon, translucent cuts of the spiced ham of the region. He picked, not without a faint concealed amusement, at a portion of cold quail. The sun had shifted out of the square of sky above the courtyard, and the light there no longer crackled harshly, but was a solid cube of hot bluish brilliance. He was acutely aware of his foreignness, and longed for the cold north. This was not his world, this heat, these strident passions, this stale flat air that sat so heavily in his lungs, like someone else's breath; nothing touched him here, and he touched nothing. He was a little Prussia in the midst of Italy. An olive-skinned young dandy sitting opposite was eyeing him peculiarly, with a kind of knowing insolence.

Having eaten, the company retired from the terrace to a cool blue high-ceilinged lavish room, with an open archway at one end, and at the other wide windows giving on to a hazy sunlit distance of shimmering cypresses and olive-green hills. An air of expectancy was palpable, and presently the desultory talk stopped abruptly on the entrance of a strange distraught emaciated person with a lyre. He seemed the luckless bearer of a burden of intolerable knowledge, a seer cursed with unspeakable secrets. He stood by patiently, his blurred gaze fixed on some inner vision, while the servants reverently arranged a bank of cushions for him in the centre of the floor, then he settled himself with great care, crossing his pathetically skinny ankles, and began to sing in a weird piping voice. A breeze stirred the silken drapes at the windows, and billows of pale pearly light swayed across the shining floor. The black dog returned and lay down throbbing at Novara's feet with wet jaws agape. Nicolas felt vaguely alarmed, for what reason he did not know. The song was a sustained sinuous incomprehensible cry that the anguished singer seemed to spin out of his very substance, slowly, painfully, a thin silver thread of sound rippling and weaving hypnotically above the soft dark plashing of the lyre. The company sat rapt, listening with such intensity that it appeared they were in some way assisting in the making of this unearthly music.

At length the song ended, and the singer gazed about him with a lost forsaken look, fretfully fingering the lank yellow strands of his hair. The others rose and went to him quickly, cooing and whispering, solicitous as women. He was given a beaker of wine to drink but took only a sip, and then was helped away, mumbling and sighing. The room was left limp and somehow satiated, as after a debauch. Novara rose, and with a glance invited Nicolas to follow him. Together they went out under the archway with the black dog padding softly behind them. The singer sat alone in an antechamber, ravaged and desolate in the midst of a great light. He looked at them blankly out of his strange pale yellowish eyes, and could not answer when Novara spoke to him, and only shook his head a little and turned away. But he smiled at the dog knowingly, as one conspirator to another. They passed on, and Nicolas asked:

"What is he? Is he ill?"

Novara lifted the lorgnon and looked at him searchingly.

"You do not know? Did you not recognise that music? It was an Orphic hymn to the Sun. He knew Ficino, you see, at the Academy in Firenze. He is not ill, not with what you or I understand as illness. The ancient knowledge to which he is heir consumes him fiercely. Great passion, great wisdom, these cannot be lightly borne by mortal men."

Nicolas nodded, and said no more. All this was fraught with deep meaning, it seemed; it meant little to him.

They entered the library and walked among the cases of precious manuscripts and incunabula and priceless first editions from Germany and Venice. Novara caressed with his fingertips tenderly the polished spines. He was abstracted, and said little. A bent blade of sunlight from a narrow window clove the gloom. The silence throbbed. Novara produced a tiny gold key with which he unlocked a pearwood chest that Nicolas vaguely felt he had seen somewhere before. Here was the heart of the library, its true treasure, rare and exquisite copies of the *Corpus Hermeticum* along with Marsilio Ficino's translations and a host of commentaries and glosses. The Professor began gravely to expatiate on the celestial mysteries. He spoke of decans and angels, of talismans and sympathetic magic, of the *spiritus mundi* that rules the world in secret. A change came over him and he spoke as one possessed. He was, it seemed, something of a magus.

"Do you believe, Herr Koppernigk?" he asked suddenly.

"I do not know what I believe, *maestro*."

"Ah."

Nicolas had already heard of the strange aetherial philosophy of this Thrice-Great Hermes, Trismegistus the Egyptian, wherein the universe is conceived as a vast grid of dependencies and sympathetic action controlled by the seven planets, or Seven Governors as Trismegistus called them. It was all altogether too raddled with cabalistic obscurities for Nicolas's sceptical northern soul, yet he found deeply and mysteriously moving the gnostic's dreadful need to discern in the chaos of the world a redemptive universal unity.

"The link that bound all things was broken by the will of God," Novara cried. "That is what is meant by the fall from grace. Only after death shall we be united with the All, when the body dissolves into the four base elements of which it is made, and the spiritual man, the soul free and ablaze, ascends through the seven crystal spheres of the firmament, shedding at each stage a part of his mortal nature, until, shorn of all earthly evil, he shall find redemption in the Empyrean and be united there with the world soul that is everywhere and everything and eternal!" He fixed on Nicolas his burning gaze. "Is this not what you yourself have been saying, however differently you say it, however different your terms? Ah yes, my friend, yes, I think you do believe!"

Nicolas smiled nervously and turned away, alarmed by this man's sudden tentacled intensity. It was mad, all mad! yet when he imagined that fiery soul flying upward, aching upward into light, a nameless elation filled him, and that word glowed in his head like a talisman, that greatest of all words: *redemption*.

"I believe in mathematics," he muttered, "nothing more."

At that suddenly the Professor checked himself, his fire abated, and he was once again his former urbane studied self. "Exactly, my dear fellow," he said, smiling, "just my point!" And he touched his guest lightly on the shoulder and led him back to join the waiting company.

Luca Guarico, squatting on a delicate ebony and velvet couch, shifted his vast bulk to make a little space beside him which he patted with a pudgy hand in roguish invitation, and Nicolas had no choice but to lower himself with a shiver into the faintly perfumed puddle of warmth that the fat man had left behind him. Novara paced the floor deep in thought, tapping the folded lorgnon against a thumbnail. No one spoke. Nicolas suspected that Guarico was watching him, and he would not turn for fear of what frightful intimacies he might be forced to share by meeting those pinkish porcine eyes. The insolent dandy who had stared at him before was now deep in whispered dark confabulation with two others of his kind. Celio Calcagnini sighed a brief bored melody and considered the ceiling, peeling off his immaculate white linen gloves finger by finger. The fiery Ziegler gnawed his nails in a furious abstraction. Nicolas was suddenly beset out of the blue by a sense of general absurdity. He rose hastily, propelled to his feet by the force of a soft fart inadvertently let slip by Guarico, and at that moment Novara turned to him and said: "Herr Koppernigk . . ." He stopped, perplexed, finding his guest apparently on the point of fleeing. Nicolas leered apologetically and slowly subsided, while just above his head he fancied he could hear rumblings of muffled celestial merriment. "Herr Koppernigk," Novara continued, "I feel I am not wrong in thinking that you are one of us at heart. You have realised by now, of course, that this is no mere aimless gathering of friends; we are, you may say, men with a purpose. We marked how closely you attended to that brief exchange between Celio here and our dear impetuous Jacob, and so we suspect that you have some little notion of the nature of our purpose?"

"O yes," Nicolas said brightly, quite at a loss; finding himself stared at he beat an immediate retreat. "That is to say I feel I understand—"

"Yes yes, I see." Novara waved a languid hand and resumed his pacing. "Let me explain. I say we have a purpose, but from this you must not imagine that you have stumbled upon a nest of conspirators. No doubt in the north they tell terrible tales of us here in Italy, but I assure you, we have no stilettos under our cloaks, no poisons secreted in our signet rings. We are, simply, a group of men dissatisfied with the state of things, *frightened* by the state of things. The world, my dear friend, is flying headlong to disaster, driven thither by the corruption that is all too evident in Church and State. There is the decay of the aristocracy, and along with it the collapse of the manorial system. There is the diminution of the standards of education, so that mere tradesmen's sons are now allowed into our greatest univ . . ." He caught Nicolas's eye, and winced. "Ahem. In short, Herr *von* Koppernigk, there is the decadence of the age. Decadence. Ah. Is it not greatly to be feared? Is it not a plague, is it not worse than war? For decadence is the attendant midwife at a brute birth, and the beast that is being born, here, now, in this very city, is—I shudder to say it—"

"He m-means," piped Nono, eager as the clever boy in the classroom, "the c-concept of lullul lullul lu-liberty!"

Novara looked at him coldly. "Just so," he said, and turned away.

Calcagnini was still dreamily considering the ceiling, where pink plaster cherubs rioted in buttocky abandon.

"Ah, liberty," he murmured, smacking his lips delicately, "that *fearful* word." For the first time that day he turned his cool sardonic gaze directly on Nicolas, and smiled. "You see, my dear sir, we believe that when the people are allowed to entertain notions of individual freedom—nay when they are encouraged to it!— then begins the swift decline of civilised values."

At that for some reason Guarico chortled. Nicolas's heart sank into a quag of gloom. He was tired, he wanted to be elsewhere. His glass was full again, and already he had drunk too much. He shook his head and mumbled dully:

"I do not understand."

"The point is—" Novara began, but once again he was interrupted, this time by Ziegler who lunged forward and jabbed a trembling finger at Nicolas's breastbone, crying:

"The point is that the rot can be stopped! Yes yes, it can be stopped by a few determined men, a few good minds—*we*, sir, we can stop it!"

"How, pray?" Nicolas snapped. He disliked intensely this rabid young man, whose face under the force of his passion had turned a kind of furious purple.

"Jacob," Novara said softly. "Calm now, calm." He turned to Nicolas. "You see how strongly our feelings run? How should it be otherwise? We are, as Jacob has already remarked, outcasts in this city. O there is no conspiracy against us, no pressures are brought to bear on us, we are free to come and go, to congregate, to hatch plots even, if we wish; we are—" he shrugged "—free. But what does it signify, this objectless freedom? Only that we are not feared, because the times themselves ensure that men such as we shall not be heeded. In a bad age the wise man is scorned." He paused in his pacing and looked about him at the company with a fond melancholy smile. "Regard us, sir: we are scholars, we are philosophers and scientists and poets, but we are not activists. Yet now, here in Bologna and throughout Italy and all Europe, action is necessary. Who will act if we do not? As Platonists we know that justice and good government are possible only when power rests in the hands of the philosophers. Therefore we must have power. How are we to achieve it? Herr Koppernigk, let me be specific: we seek—" Calcagnini stirred nervously, but Novara disregarded him "—we seek, sir, firstly union between our city state and Rome, and beyond that, O far beyond that, a Europe united under papal rule. A new, strong and united Holy Roman Empire—that is our aim, no less than that."

Nicolas blinked. Calcagnini coughed drily.

"I think, Domenico," he murmured, "I think you have forgotten a most important thing." He looked at Nicolas. "We seek, yes, a Europe united, *but only under a Pope of our making*. His Holiness Alexander will not do, he will not do at all." A ripple of bitter amusement passed through the room. Novara nodded.

"Of course," he said, not without a trace of irritation, and bowed to the poet, "a most important point assuredly. A Pope, yes, of our making. We have even considered candidates; does that surprise you, Herr Koppernigk? We are in earnest, you see. We have for instance considered Alexander's bastard Cesare. Luca's horoscope, however, is not encouraging, and tends to confirm the grave doubts we have for some time been entertaining in that quarter. I think we must look elsewhere." And he looked with a smile upon Nicolas, who after a moment's reflection sat upright suddenly and said:

"O but you cannot imagine that I—I mean, surely not!"

They stared at him, and then Novara laughed somewhat uneasily.

"Ah," he said, "a joke; I see. I did not at first—very droll, yes."

Calcagnini joined his fingers at the tips and tapped that spire thoughtfully against his pursed lips, saying:

"We thought: What if we should discover that there is in Bologna a young churchman from the north, a scientist, whose uncle is Bishop of a Prussian princedom and a voice of no little significance in the affairs of Europe? And what if we should discover further that this young scientist is a thinker of potential greatness? Would he not be, to use a cold word, useful? These are strange times. The world is yielding up its secrets to those who know how to look for them. What if it should come to our ears that this young man has been cautiously expounding the outlines of a planetary theory which, if proved, should compel us to reconsider our conception of the nature of the physical world? We said: What if we were to provide for this astronomer certain facilities—a villa in the quiet of the provinces, say, and ample funds to enable him to spend two or three years in study and research—if, in short, we were to provide him with the means of perfecting this new theory of his? Now the Church, as we all know, is free apparently to indulge in all manner of fleshly vices, but it is not free to indulge in speculations that run contrary to dogma: for dogma is unassailable. And whose is the task of ensuring the inviolability of dogma? Why, it is the Pope's! Now, what if our young astronomer, at the end of this two or three years of seclusion, should travel to Prussia and present to his uncle the proofs of his new theory? It is well known that the Bishop of Ermland is no friend of Rome's, and especially not of Alexander, this bloated Borgia despot. Does it not seem likely that within a short time all Europe would be rife with reports of this new and apparently blasphemous theory? And Alexander would be forced to act. But the Bishop of Ermland is not the only enemy that the Pope has; his enemies are legion. In that battle, then, between a theory mathematically verified and vouched for beyond all doubt, and a bad Pope, who, we wondered, would be likely to win? It seemed to us that the only possible outcome would be a new conclave of the College of Cardinals; and thus the cause of the Church would be served, and our cause, and also of course, Herr

Koppernigk, yours. These are questions, you understand, that we have been putting to ourselves for some time past. We hoped that you might be able to help us to find the answers. Hmm?"

But Nicolas was engrossed in the wonderfully ridiculous image of himself and Bishop Lucas deep in dark discussion of a plot to bring down the Pope, and he said only:

"Sir, you do not know my uncle."

It was a poor reply to such a speech, but it hardly mattered, for the company, strangely, had lost all interest in him. The dandy and his friends, amid shrieks of laughter, were trying to force the hound to drink a goblet of wine. Novara stood by the window gazing vacantly at the far hills. Nicolas was reminded of an audience grown bored with a play. The singer had crept back into their midst with a tentative uncertain grin, no longer the mysterious priestly figure that their attentions·had made him seem before, but a soulful, sad, unloved and unlovely weird madman. Guarico had fallen asleep. Calcagnini smiled blearily, nodding. He was drunk. They were all drunk. Nicolas rose to go. The scrawny Nono, giggling and stammering and trembling all over, crept after him and made an inept and farcical attempt at seduction.

*

Andreas pushed his platter away and belched sourly. A scullion passed by their table, lugging a steaming urn, and he turned to watch her joggling haunches. Dreamily he said:

"They are all *Italians*, of course," and he smiled at his brother suddenly, icily. "Yes, bumboys all."

Nicolas went no more to Novara's house, and stayed away from his lectures. By Christmastide he had left Bologna forever.

*　　*　　*

The city crouched, sweating in fright, under the sign of the brooding bull. Talk of portents was rife. Blood rained from the sky at noon, at night the deserted streets shook with the thunder of unearthly hoofbeats and weird cries filled the air. A woman at Ostia come to her time brought forth an issue of rats. Some said it was the reign of Antichrist, and that the end was nigh. In February the Pope's son

Cesare returned victorious from the Romagna and rode in triumph with his army through the cheering streets. He was clad for the occasion all in black, with a collar of gold blazing at his throat. The entire army likewise was draped in black. It seemed, in the brumous yellowy light of that winter day, that the Lord of Darkness himself had come forth to be acclaimed by the delirious mob.

This was Rome, in the jubilee year of 1500.

*

The brothers had moved south to the capital on the instructions of Uncle Lucas: they were to act as unofficial ambassadors of the Frauenburg Chapter at the jubilee celebrations. It was a nebulous posting. They performed during that year only one duty that could have been considered in any way connected with diplomacy, when they dined at the Vatican as guests of a minor papal official, a smooth foxy cleric with a disconcerting wall-eyed stare, who desired, as far as the brothers could ascertain from his elaborately veiled insinuations, to be reassured that Bishop Lucas's loyalty to Rome was in no danger of being transferred to the King of Poland; and they might have made a serious blunder, inexperienced as they were in matters of such delicacy, had not the grey and cautious Canon Schiller, the representative of the Frauenburg Chapter, been there to guide them with astutely timed and enthusiastically administered kicks under the table.

It was with Schiller that they lodged, in a gloomy villa on the damp side of a hill near the Circo Massimo, where the food was stolidly Prussian and the air heavy with the odour of sanctity. Nicolas glumly accepted the discipline and arid rituals of the house; from his schooldays on he had been accustomed to that kind of thing, and expected nothing better. Andreas, however, chafed under Canon Schiller's watchful eye, in which there was reflected, all the way from Prussia, the light of a far fiercer, icier gaze. Lately he had become more morose than ever, his rages were redder, his fits of melancholia less and less amenable to the curative pleasures of student life. What had once in him been fecklessness was now a thirst for small destructions; his gay cynicism had turned into something very like despair. He complained vaguely of being ill. His face was drawn and pallid, eyes shot with blood, his breathing oddly thin and papery. He began to frequent the booths of astrologers and fortune tellers of the worst kind. Once even

61

he asked Nicolas to cast his horoscope, which Nicolas, appalled at the idea, refused to do, pleading not very convincingly a lack of skill. Uncle Lucas had secured a canonry at Frauenburg for Andreas, and for a time his finances flourished, but he was soon penniless again, and, worse, in the hands of the Jews. Nicolas watched helplessly his brother's life disintegrate; it was like witnessing the terrible slow fall into the depths of a once glorious marvellously shining angel.

Yet Andreas loved Rome. In that wicked wolf-suckled city his peculiar talents came briefly to full flower, nourished by the pervading air of menace and intrigue. He spoke the language of these scheming worldly churchmen, and it was not long before he had found his way into the cliques and cabals that abounded at the papal court. In the eyes of the world he was a firebrand, brilliant, careless, and hedonistic, destined for great things. Schiller cautioned him on the manner of his life. He paid no heed. He was by then treading waters deeper than that Canon could conceive of. But he was out over jagged reefs, and his light was being extinguished; he was drowning.

Nicolas detested the capital. It reminded him of an old tawny lion dying in the sun, on whose scarred and smelly pelt the lice bred and feverishly fed in final frantic carnival. He was shocked by what he saw of the workings of the Church. God had been deposed here, and Rodrigo Borgia ruled in his place. On Easter Sunday two hundred thousand pilgrims knelt in St Peter's Square to receive the blessing of the Pope; Nicolas was there, pressed about by the poor foolish faithful who sighed and swayed like a vast lung, lifting their faces trustingly toward the hot sun of spring. He wondered if perhaps the tavern prophets were right, if this was the end, if here today a last terrible blessing was being administered to the city and the world.

In July Lucrezia Borgia's husband, Alfonso Duke of Bisceglie, was savagely attacked on the steps of St Peter's; Cesare was behind the outrage, so it was whispered. The rumours seemed confirmed some weeks later when *Il Valentino's* man, Don Michelotto, broke into Alfonso's sickroom in the Vatican and throttled the Duke in his bed. Nicolas recalled a certain strange day in Bologna, and wondered. But of course it was altogether mad to think that Novara and his friends could be in any way involved in these bloody doings, or so at least the Professor himself insisted when one day, by chance, Nicolas met him on the street near the amphitheatre of Vespasian.

"No no!" Novara whispered hoarsely, glancing nervously about. "How can you imagine such a thing? In fact the Duke knew something of our views, and was not unsympathetic. Certainly we wished him no harm. It is too terrible, truly. And to think that we once considered this Cesare as . . . O, terrible!"

He was paying a brief visit to Rome on university business. Nicolas was shocked by his appearance. He was stooped and sallow, with dead eyes and trembling hands, hardly recognisable as the magisterial, cold and confident patrician he had lately been. He frowned distractedly and mopped his brow, tormented by the heat and the dust and the uproar of the traffic. He was dying. A slender bored young man got up in scarlet accompanied him, and stood by in insolent silence with one hand resting on his hip; his name was Girolamo. He smiled at Nicolas, who suddenly remembered where he had seen him before, and blushed and turned away only to find to his horror Novara watching him with tears in his eyes.

"You think me a fool, Koppernigk," he said. "You came to my house only to laugh at me—O yes, do not deny it, your brother told me how you laughed after running away from us that day. My scheming and my magic, I suppose they must have seemed foolish to you, whose concern is facts, computation, the laws of the visible world."

Nicolas groaned inwardly. Why were people, Andreas always, now Novara, so eager that he should think well of them? What did his opinion matter? He said:

"My brother lied; he is prone to it. Why should I laugh at you? You are a greater astronomer than I." This was horrible, horrible. "I left your house because I knew I could be of no use to you. What part could I play in your schemes—" he could not resist it "—I, a mere tradesman's son?"

Novara nodded, grimacing. The sun rained hammerblows on him. He had the look of a wounded animal.

"You lack charity, my friend," he said. "You must try to understand that men have need of answers, articles of faith, myths—lies, if you will. The world is terrible and yet we are terrified to leave it: that is the paradox that hurts us so. Does anything hurt you, Koppernigk? Yours is an enviable immunity, but I wonder if it will endure."

"I cannot help it if I am cold!" Nicolas cried, beside himself with rage and embarrassment. "And I have done nothing to deserve your

63

bitterness." But Novara had lost interest, and was shuffling away. The youth Girolamo hesitated between them, glancing with a faint sardonic smile from one of them to the other. Nicolas trembled violently. It was not fair!—even if he was dying, Novara had no right to cringe like this; his task was to be proud and cold, to intimidate, not to mewl and whimper, not to be weak. It was a scandal! "I never asked anything of you!" Nicolas howled at the other's back, ignoring the looks of the passers-by. "It was you that approached me. *Are you listening?*"

"Yes yes," Novara muttered, without turning. "Just so, indeed. And now farewell. Come, Girolamo, come."

The young man smiled languorously a last time, and with a small regretful gesture went to the Professor and took his arm. Nicolas turned and fled, with his fury clutched to him like a struggling captive wild beast. He was frightened, as if he had looked into a mirror and seen reflected there not his own face but an unspeakable horror.

He did not see Novara again. Once or twice their paths might have crossed, but time and circumstance happily intervened to keep them apart; happily, not only because Nicolas feared another painful scene, but also because he dreaded the possibility of being confronted again by the frightening image of himself he had glimpsed in the looking glass of that incomprehensible fit of naked fury. When he heard of the Professor's death he could not even remember clearly what the man had looked like; but by then he was in Padua, and everything had changed.

\*

That city at first made little impression on him, he was so busy searching for habitable lodgings, performing the complicated and exasperating rituals of enrolment at the university, choosing his subjects, his professors. He had also to cope with Andreas, who by now was badly, though still mysteriously, ill, and full of spleen. Early in the summer the brothers travelled to Frauenburg, their leave of absence having expired. They had asked by letter for an extension, but Bishop Lucas had insisted that they should make the request in person. The extra leave was granted, of course, and after less than a month in Prussia they set out once more for Italy.

Nicolas paused at Kulm to visit Barbara at the convent. She had not changed much in the years since he had seen her last; in middle age she was still, for him, the ungainly girl who had played hide and seek with him long ago in the old house in Torun. Perhaps it was these childhood echoes that made their talk so stilted and unreal. There was between them still that familiar melancholy, that tender hesitant regard, but now there was something more, a faint sense of the ridiculous, of the ponderous, as if they were despite their pretensions really children playing at being grown-ups. She was, she told him, Abbess of the convent now, in succession to their late Aunt Christina Waczelrodt, but he could not grasp it. How could Barbara, his Barbara, have become a person of such consequence? She also was puzzled by the elaborate dressing-up that he was trying to pass off as his life. She said:

"You are becoming a famous man. We even hear talk of you here in the provinces."

He shook his head and smiled. "It is all Andreas's doing. He thinks it a joke to put it about that I am formulating in secret a revolutionary theory of the planets."

"And are you not?"

Summer rain was falling outside, and a pallid, faintly flickering light entered half-heartedly by the streaming windows of the high hall where they sat. Even in her loose-fitting habit Barbara was all knees and knuckles and raw scrubbed skin. She looked away from him shyly. He said:

"I shall come again to see you soon."

"Yes."

*

When he returned to Padua he found Andreas, though sick and debilitated already from the Prussian journey, preparing to depart for Rome. "I can abide neither your sanctimonious stink, brother, nor this cursed Paduan smugness. You will breathe easier without me to disgrace you before your pious friends."

"I have no friends, Andreas. And I wish you would not go."

"You are a hypocrite. Do not make me spew, please."

However much he tried not to be, Nicolas was glad of his brother's going; now perhaps at last, relieved of the burden of Andreas's intolerable presence, he would be permitted to become the real self he had all his life wished to be.

But what was that mysterious self that had eluded him always? He could not say. Yet he was convinced that he had reached a turning point. Those first months alone in Padua were strange. He was neither happy nor sad, nor much of anything: he was neutral. Life flowed over him, and under the wave he waited, for what he did not know, unless it was rescue. He applied himself with energy to his studies. He took philosophy and law, mathematics, Greek and astronomy. It was in the faculty of medicine, however, that he surfaced at last, like a spent swimmer flying upward into light, in whose aching lungs the saving air blossoms like a great dazzling yellow flower.

*

"Signor Fracastoro?"

The young man turned, frowning. "*Si*, I am Fracastoro."

How handsome he was, how haughty, with those black eyes, that dark narrow arrogant face; how languidly he sprawled on the bench among the twittering band of dandies, with his long legs negligently crossed. The lecture hall was putrid with the stink of a dissected corpse, the gross gouts and ganglia of which two bloodstained attendants were carting away, but he was aristocratically indifferent to that carnage, and only now and then bothered to lift to his face the perfume-soaked handkerchief whose pervasive musky scent was the unmistakable trademark of the medical student. He was dressed with casual elegance in silk and soft leather, booted and spurred, with a white linen shirt open on the frail cage of his chest; he had come late to the lecture that morning, flushed and smiling, bringing with him into the fetid hall a crisp clean whiff of horses and sweet turf and misty dawn meadows. He was all that Nicolas was not, and Nicolas, sensing imminent humiliation, cursed himself for having spoken.

"We met last year in Rome, I think," he said. "You were with Professor Novara."

"O?"

Fracastoro's friends nudged each other happily, and gazed at Nicolas with bland sardonic seriousness, trying not to laugh; they too could see humiliation coming.

"Yes yes, in Rome, and before that in Bologna, at the Professor's house." He was beginning to babble. Someone sniggered. "I remember it well. You tried to make a drunkard of Novara's dog, ha ha. Ha."

The young man raised an eyebrow. "Yes? A dog, you say? Extraordinary. Certainly I do not remember that."

Nicolas sighed. Blast you, you young prig. Life is dreadful, really. He stepped back, trying not to bow.

"A mistake," he muttered. "Forgive me."

"But wait, wait," Fracastoro said, "this Novara, it seems to me I do know the man, vaguely." He lifted a slender hand to his brow. "Ah yes, a mathematician, is he not?—much given to mysticism? Yes, I know him. Well?"

"You do not remember our meeting."

"No; but I may do so, if I concentrate. Do you have news of the Professor?"

"No, no, I merely—it is no matter."

"But—?"

"No matter, no matter." And he fled, pursued by laughter.

*

They met again some days later, in the vegetable market, of all places, at dawn. Lately Nicolas had begun to suffer from sleeplessness, and went out often at night to walk about the city and bathe his feverishly spinning brain in the chill dark air. He developed a fondness for the market especially; the colours, the clamour, the heavy honeyed smell of ripeness, all conspired to cheat of its bleakness that inhuman hour before first light. He was leaning on the damp parapet of the Ponte San Giorgio, idly watching the upriver barges like great ungainly whales unloading their produce in the bluish gloom of the wharf below, when a voice said at his shoulder:

"Koppernigk, is it not?"

He was wrapped in a dun cloak, and his long fair swathe of hair was hidden under a battered old black slouch hat; even in such dull apparel he could not be less than elegant. He was smiling a little, not looking at Nicolas, but musing on the still-dark distance beyond the city walls, saying silently, as it were: come, cut me now if you wish, and so have some small revenge. But Nicolas just as silently declined the offer, and suddenly the Italian laughed softly and said:

"Nicolas Koppernigk—you see? I have been concentrating."

Nicolas with a faint smile inclined his head in acknowledgment. "Signor Fracastoro."

The other looked at him directly then, and laughed again.

"O please," he said, "my friends call me that; *you* may call me Girolamo. Shall we walk this way a little?" They left the bridge and crossed the open piazza, where the fishwives were hurling amiable abuse from stall to stall. "But tell me, what brings you here at this strange hour?"

Nicolas shrugged. "I do not sleep well. And you?"

"Wine and women, I fear, keep me from my bed. I am for home now after a misspent night." It was meant as a boast. He was at that age, not quite twenty yet, when the youth he had been and the man he was becoming both held sway at once, so that in the same breath he could slip disconcertingly from hard cold derisive cynicism into simple silliness. Now he said: "You disappointed Novara greatly, you know, by not taking seriously his grand schemes to save the world. Ah, poor Domenico!"

They both laughed, a little spitefully, and Nicolas, suddenly stared at out of the sky by the Professor's pained reproachful eyes, said hastily:

"But they are not without significance, his preoccupations."

"No, of course; but it is all mere talking. He is too much in love with magic, and despises action. I mean that natural magic for him is all centaurs and chimaeras. Now I, however, understand it in general as the science which applies the knowledge of hidden forms to the production of wonderful operations." He glanced out quickly from under the downturned brim of his black hat with a candid questioning look, but it was impossible to know if he was being sincere or otherwise. "What do you say, friend?"

But Nicolas only shrugged and murmured warily:

"Perhaps, perhaps . . ."

He did not know what to make of this young man; he did not trust him, and did not trust himself, and so determined to go cautiously, even though he could not see where trust came into it, except that he knew he did not care to be made a fool of again. It was all odd, this meeting, this dreamlike morning, these dim figures hurrying here and there and crying out in the gloom. They entered a narrow alleyway given over entirely to the trade in cagebirds. Cascades of bright mad music drenched the dark air. Coming out at the other end they found themselves abruptly in a deserted square. The sky was of a deep illyrian blue, lightening rapidly now to the east, and the towers of the city were tipped with gold.

"May I offer you breakfast?" said Fracastoro. "My rooms are close by."

He lived in a tumbledown palazzo near the Basilica of St Anthony, the family home of an elderly count who had long ago fled to a villa in the Dolomites for the sake of his ailing lungs. "My uncle, you know," he said, and winked. They ascended through the shabby splendours of gilt and tempera and stained marble statuary to the fourth floor, where a kind of rambling lair, stretching through five or six large rooms, had been scooped out of the dust and genteel wreckage deposited by years of neglect. Here, under the sagging canopy of a vast four-poster, they came upon a young man asleep in a tangle of soiled sheets. He was naked, his limbs sprawled in touchingly childish abandon, tacked down firmly, as it were, like some exotic specimen, by the enormous erection that reared grotesquely out of his jet-black bush. Fracastoro barely glanced at him, but in passing picked up a tortured shirt from the floor and flung it at his head, crying:

"Up up up! Come!"

The main room was a general disorder of books and clothes and empty wine bottles. Most of the furniture was draped in dustsheets. Here and there amidst the clutter the skeleton of a former glory was visible in richly patterned panelling and polished marble pillars, gold-embroidered drapes, an inlaid rosewood spinet delicate and tentative as a deer. Magnificent arched windows framed a triptych of the airy architecture of St Anthony's soaring motionless against an immaculate blue sky. Fracastoro looked about him, and with a shrug waved his hand in a vague helpless gesture of apology. How many generations of aristocratic breeding had been necessary, Nicolas wondered, to produce that patrician indifference and ease? He shrank back into his black cloak, a lean grey troubled soul suddenly aching with envy of this young man's confidence and carelessness, his disdain for the trivial trappings of the world. They stood a while in silence by the window, gazing out at the sunlit city and listening to the morning noises that rose to them from the street below, the rattle of cane shutters, rumbling of the watercart, the breadman's harsh cry. Nothing happened, they said nothing, but forever afterwards, even when much else had faded, Nicolas was to remember that moment with extraordinary vividness as marking the true beginning of their friendship.

There was a sound behind them, and Girolamo turned and said:

"Ah, here you are, you dreadful dog."

It was the handsome young man from the bedroom. He stood in the doorway clad only in his shirt, scratching his head and gazing at them blearily. His name was Tadziu or Tadzio, Nicolas did not catch it clearly; it hardly mattered, since he was never to see him again. After that first morning he disappeared mysteriously, and Girolamo did not mention him save once, a long time afterwards. They spoke together rapidly now in a dialect that Nicolas did not understand, and the boy shrugged and went away. Girolamo turned to his guest with a smile. "I must apologise: apparently there is no food. But we shall have something presently." He began to glance idly through a disorderly mass of papers overflowing a small ornate table, looking up at Nicolas now and then with a quizzical, faintly amused expression, seeming each time about to speak but yet remaining silent. At last he laughed, and throwing up his hands said helplessly:

"I do not know what to say!"

Nicolas would not look at him; he knew what he meant.

"Nor I," he murmured, confused and suddenly happy. "Nor I!"

Tadziu or Tadzio returned then, with a steaming loaf of bread under his arm, and in one hand a magnum of champagne, in the other a platter covered with a napkin which Girolamo lifted gingerly to reveal a greasy mess of griddle cakes. "O disgusting, disgusting!" he cried, laughing, and they sat down and began to eat. Girolamo's handsome young friend bent on Nicolas bitterly a dark unwavering glare. But Nicolas refused to be intimidated; he had been light-headed already from lack of sleep, but now the champagne and the warm brown stink of the bread and the griddle cakes befuddled him entirely. He was happy.

"Come," said Girolamo, "tell us your famous theory of the planets."

Yes, yes, he was happy!

*

But happiness was an inadequate word for the transformation that he underwent that summer—for it was no less than a transformation. His heart thawed. A great soft inexpressible something swelled within him, and there were moments when he felt that this rapture must burst

70

forth, that his cloak would fly open to reveal a huge grotesque foolish gaudy flower sprouting comically from his breast. It was ridiculous, but that was all right; he dared to be ridiculous. He fell in love with the city, its limpid mornings, burning noons, evenings in the piazzas loud with birds, that city fraught now with secret significances. Never again without a unique pang of anguished tenderness would he walk through the market, or stand upon the Ponte San Giorgio at dawn, or smell at the streetcorner stalls the rank humble pungency of frying griddle cakes.

Yet behind all this fine frenzy there was the fear that it could destroy him, for surely it was a kind of sickness. In his studies he thought he might find an antidote. He read Plato in the Greek, and reread Nicolas Cusanus and Ptolemy's *Almagest*, which last by now he almost knew by heart. He took up again those texts to which Novara had introduced him, and plunged once more into the thickets of the translation of Trismegistus that Ficino had made for Lorenzo de' Medici. But it was useless, he could not concentrate, and rushed out and strode through the deserted noonday streets under the throbbing plane trees, distraught and alarmed, until his legs of their own volition brought him to the Palazzo Antonini and that disordered room overlooking the basilica, where Girolamo smiled at him sleepily and said:

"Why, my friend, what is it? You look quite crazed."

"I am too old for this, too old!"

"For what?"

"All this: you, Italy, everything. Too old!"

"An old greybeard you are, yes, of twice ten years and eight! Come, uncle, sit here. You should not go out in the sun, you know."

"It is not the sun!"

"No; you are altogether too much a Prussian, too sceptical and cold. You must learn to treasure yourself more dearly."

"Nonsense."

"But—"

"Nonsense!"

Girolamo stretched himself and yawned.

"Very well, uncle," he mumbled, "but it is siesta time now," and he laid his head down on the couch beside his friend and smiling fell asleep at once. Nicolas gazed at him, and wrung his hands. I am besotted with him, besotted!

71

He was captive to a willing foolishness. Those concerns that up to now he had held to be serious, and worthy of serious considerations, he had with lunatic lightheartedness abandoned; but they had not abandoned him, no, they waited in the outer darkness, gnashing their teeth, ready to come back at him and have a fourfold revenge, he knew it. He knew, but could not care. Had he not liberated himself at last from the pinched mean hegemony of the intellect? Had he not at last set free the physical man that all his life had waited within him for release? The senses now would have their day; they deserved it. Yet strangely, the body whose bonds he had cast off seemed not to know what to do with its newfound liberty. Like a starved stark loony released after years in the dungeons, it reeled about drunkenly in the unaccustomed light, sweating and dribbling, tripping over itself, a gangling spidery pale fork of flesh and fur, faintly repellent, faintly comical, wholly absurd.

Absurd, absurd: he remembered Ferrara particularly, and the day of his conferring.

*

It was for reasons of economy—or stinginess, according to Girolamo —that Nicolas chose to take his doctorate in canon law other than at Padua, for even the most solitary of graduates would find himself surrounded by hitherto unknown friends when the conferring ceremony, and more especially the lavish banquet he would be expected to provide afterwards, were at hand. Nicolas had no intention of allowing a gang of sots to stupefy themselves with drink at his expense, and therefore, although it was a far less prestigious institution than Padua, and he had never studied there, he applied for graduation to the University of Ferrara, and was accepted, and in the autumn of the year travelled south accompanied by Girolamo.

The ritual of conferring took a full week to complete. It was a horrible business. The promoter assigned to him by the college was one Alberti, a harassed apologetic canon lawyer with a limp and a wild fuzz of prematurely grey hair that stood out from his narrow skull like an exclamation of alarm. During a class of his once a student had been stabbed to death while he lectured on oblivious. Nicolas liked him; he was of the same sad endearing tribe as Abstemius of Włocławek.

"Well now, Herr Kupperdik, here is the drill. Firstly I take you before an assembly of doctors to whom you will swear that you have been through the proper course et cetera, which ha ha you have, I take it? The reverend gentlemen will set you two passages of law, and we retire together to study them. It is all a sham, of course, since I know already what the passages will be—I should be a poor promoter if I didn't, eh, Herr Kopperdyke? Anyway, after a decent absence we return, the doctors question you, they ballot, and you are made a licentiate. All that remains then is for you to take the public examination for your full doctorate, but that is merely a formality after the oral test, which as I said is really a formality also. And there you are: *Doctor Popperdink!* Nothing to it!"

But of course it was not so simple. Alberti got the set passages mixed, and coached Nicolas, with admirable diligence, in those intended for another graduate, and on the day of the inquisition Nicolas spent a frantic hour in a hot antechamber, while the doctors fretted next door, trying to memorise the new answers and at the same time block out the distracting apologies of his mortified promoter. The examiners, however, seemed to have had some experience already of Alberti's organisational powers. It was apparent that they cared less about the indifferent quality of Nicolas's performance than they did about the fact that the ritual had not been strictly adhered to. They voted, mumbling among themselves, fixed Alberti with a crushing glare, and having announced the result of the examination rose and swept away amid an outraged rustling of gowns. Nicolas, drenched with sweat, closed his eyes and lowered his burning face gently into his hands. His promoter leapt at him and began to thump him on the back in a transport of relief, almost knocking him off his chair. "Congratulations, my dear fellow, congratulations!" Throughout, Nicolas had been able to think of one thing only: the reception he would get from Uncle Lucas if he returned to Ermland without his doctorate. "Herr Poppernik? Are you unwell?"

Girolamo laughed, of course, when he heard of the affair, and then sat in silence, pale and distant, while Nicolas poured over him the scalding bitter brew of the day's pent-up frustration and rage. And that night along with Alberti they went down to the stews and got vilely drunk in the company of a band of shrieking whores.

The week rolled on inexorably, like a giant engine gone out of control and disintegrating, flinging bits of itself in all directions, bombarding Nicolas, the innocent bystander, with spokes and broken ratchets and gouts of thick black oil. On Sunday the contraption exploded finally, with a deafening report. Arriving at the cathedral for the conferring, he halted in the porch, horror-stricken. "Jesus, what's this?" The place was full of students, hundreds of them, they were even squatting on the steps of the high altar. Alberti turned to him with a bland enquiring smile. "Yes, *Doctor?*" He had taken to using that title at every opportunity, with a proprietary rib-nudging roguishness that made Nicolas want to strike him very hard with his fist.

"This crowd!" he cried. "What does it mean? I came to Ferrara to avoid just this kind of thing!"

Alberti was puzzled; a true Italian, he thrived on crowds and clamour.

"But the students always come to hear the orations," he said mildly. "It is the custom."

"God!"

Girolamo was studiously inspecting the architecture, with the solemn look of one shaking inwardly with laughter. He was got up for the occasion in a quilted scarlet doublet and tight black hose, with a long white plume to his cap; like a damned peacock, Nicolas thought bitterly. Now without turning Girolamo murmured:

"It is for the comic possibilities that they come, I imagine?"

Alberti nodded enthusiastically. "*Si, si*, the comedy, just so."

"*God*," Nicolas groaned again, and, wrapping his gown about him tightly, plunged up the aisle to the pulpit. On the narrow steps he trod upon the liripipe dangling from his neck and almost throttled himself. A sea of rapturous expectant faces greeted him as he peered apprehensively over the brim of the pulpit. Someone at the back of the nave whistled a piercing heraldic flourish, provoking an uproar of catcalls and applause. Nicolas fished about under his gown for the text of his oration. For one appalling moment he thought . . . but no, he had not left it behind, it was there, though in a dreadful jumble that his shaking hands at once made worse.

"*Reverendissimi . . .*"

The rest of his opening address was drowned by shouts and a stamping of feet, and he stopped, quite lost. Alberti and Girolamo, sitting below him, leaned forward with their hands cupped around their mouths and together cried: "*They cannot hear you!*" After a time

74

some semblance of order returned, and he stuck out his neck like an enraged tortoise and hurled his text at them as if it were an execration. His argument was a defence of the canonical interdict on marriage between a widow and her brother-in-law; it was a purely formal declaration of an accepted doctrine, upon which his audience in like formality was meant to challenge him, but he suspected, rightly as it happened, that these turbulent students had no intention of playing by the rules. Even before he had finished, a dozen of them or more were on their feet, howling abuse at him and at each other amid a general hilarity. He tried to discern even some halfway sensible objection to the contents of his text, but in vain, for his tormentors were mouthing merely nonsense, or obscenities, or both at once, and like a large rag doll being fought over by children he bounced about in the pulpit, throwing up his arms, grinning, opening and closing his mouth in mute helplessness and pain. Never in his life had he known such an exquisite agony of embarrassment.

At length they lost interest in him, and as the uproar subsided and they began to look about for the entrance of a fresh victim, he scrambled shakily down from the pulpit. He was grabbed at once by a pair of burly vestrymen with cruelly barbered skulls, who marched him off smartly to a side altar and thrust him into the master's chair. There he was presented with the cap, the book and the gold ring and the graduate's diploma, and Alberti, with the lunatic intensity of a father crazed with pride, his wild hair bristling, advanced limping and planted on his cheek a tacky garlic-scented kiss of peace.

*"Ave magister!"* he cried; and then, unable to restrain himself, he added rapturously: *"Doctor* Peppernik!"

As if from a distance Nicolas looked in anguished amusement at himself, a dazed grotesque figure with cap askew, full of irredeemable foolishness, a lord of misrule propped upon a pretender's throne. Italy had done this to him, Italy and all that Italy signified. Girolamo came forward to kiss him, but he turned his cheek away.

*       *       *

The weather was bad that spring, rain and gales for weeks and the muttering of thunder in the mountains. Great fortresses of black cloud rumbled westward ceaselessly, and Lake Garda boiled in leaden rage. This tumult in the air seemed to Nicolas an omen, though what it might signify he could not say. He arrived with Girolamo at the villa at dusk, wet and weary and dispirited. The big old timber and stone house was set among tall cypresses on a steep hill overlooking Incaffi and the lake. It had the look of money about it. There was a spacious courtyard paved with rough-cut marble, and busts of the Caesars set on marble plinths; wide stone steps swept up to a pillared entrance. He had expected something far more modest than this.

"Will your family be here?" he asked, unable to conceal his apprehension.

"Why no," said Girolamo, "they are in Verona. They live there. We do not agree, and so I seldom see them. This is my house."

"O."

The Italian laughed. "Come now, my friend, do not look so alarmed. There will be no one here but you and I."

"I did not think you were so—"

"—Rich? Does it trouble you?"

"No; why should it?"

"Then for God's sake stop cringing!" he snapped, and slapping his riding gloves against his thigh he turned and strode up the steps to the vestibule, where the servants were gathered to welcome their master. There was a dozen of them or more, from young girls to grey old men. They looked at Nicolas in silence stonily, and all at once he was acutely aware of his shabbiness, his cracked boots and few poor bits of baggage, the decrepit mare trying not to fall over out in the courtyard behind him. We know your kind, those eyes told him, we have seen you come and go many times before, in different versions but all essentially the same. And he wondered how many others there had been . . .

Girolamo impatiently performed his signorial duty, pacing up and down the line of attentive servants with a fixed false smile, questioning each one in turn in a detached formal voice on their health and that of their parents or children. And what news of the estate? Everything was in order? Splendid, splendid. Nicolas looked on with envy. At twenty, Girolamo had the ageless self-assurance of the aristocrat. He dropped his wet cloak and gloves on the floor, from whence they were immediately and reverently snatched up by one of the maids, and throwing himself down into a chair he motioned the steward, a bent old gouty brute, to help him off with his boots. He looked up at Nicolas and smiled faintly.

"Well, my friend?" he said.

"What?"

"*Caro Nicolo.*"

They sat down in a richly appointed dining-room to an elaborate veal and champagne supper. A candelabrum of Venetian glass glistened above their heads, its gaudy splendours reflected deep in the dark pool of the polished table on which there sailed a fleet of hand-crafted gold and silver serving dishes. The room was hushed, suspended in stillness, except where their bone knives and delicate forks stabbed and sliced the silence above their plates with tiny deft ferocity. Everywhere that Nicolas looked he encountered the Fracastoro monogram, intricately graven in goldleaf on the dishes and the cruets, woven into the napkins, even carved on the facings and reredos of the vast black marble fireplace.

"Tell me," he said, "how many such establishments as this do you keep up?"

"O, not many; the apartments in Verona, where my books are, and a house in Rome. And of course there is a hunting lodge in the mountains, which we must visit, if the weather clears. Why do you ask?"

"Curiosity."

"Are you still brooding on my unsuspected wealth? It is not so great as you seem to imagine. You are too easily impressed."

"Yes."

"Are you glad you came here?"

"Yes."

"Is that all you can say?"

"What would you have me say? Indeed, my liege, my humble thanks, sweet lord, I am overwhelmed." He ground his teeth. "Forgive me, I am tired from the journey, and out of sorts. Forgive me."

Girolamo gazed at him mildly, more in curiosity it seemed than anger or hurt.

"No, it is my fault," he said. "I should not have brought you here. We were happier on neutral ground—or should I say, we were *happy?*" He smiled. "For we are not happy now, are we?"

"Does happiness seem to you the greatest good?"

At that the Italian laughed. "Come, Nicolas, none of your sham philosophising, not with me. Do you hate me for my wealth and privilege?"

"Hate?" He was genuinely shocked, and a little frightened. "I do not hate you. I . . . do not hate you. I am happy to be here, in your—"

"Then do you love me?"

He was sweating. Girolamo continued to gaze at him, with fondness, and amusement, and regret.

"I am happy to be here, in your house; I am grateful, I am glad we came." He realised suddenly that even yet they did not call each other *thou*. "Perhaps," he stammered, "perhaps the weather will clear tomorrow . . ."

*

But the weather did not clear, in the world nor in the villa. Nicolas stormed, wrapped in a black silence. His rage had no one cause, not that he could discover, but bubbled up, a poisonous vapour, out of a mess of boiling emotions. He felt constantly slighted, by Girolamo, by the smirking servants, even by the villa itself, whose sumptuous sybaritic splendours reminded him that it was accustomed to entertaining aristocrats, while he was what Novara had said, a mere tradesman's son. Yet was he in reality being thus sorely scorned? Was he not, in discerning, indeed in cultivating this contempt all round him, merely satisfying some strange hunger within him? It was as if he were being driven to add more and more knots to a lash wielded by his own hand. It was as if he were beating himself into submission, cleansing himself, preparing himself: but for what? He hungered, obscenely, obscurely, as under the lash his flesh flinched, went cold and dead, and at last out of a wracked humiliated body his mind soared slowly upward, into the blue.

Now he saw at last how the plot had been hatching in secret for years, the plot that had brought him without his willing it to this moment of recognition and acceptance; or rather, he had not been brought, had not been made to move at all, but had simply stood and waited while the trivia and the foolishness were shorn away. The Church had offered him a quiet living, the universities had offered academic success, Italy had even offered love. Any or all of these gifts might have seduced him, had not the hideousness intervened to demonstrate the poverty of what they had to offer. At Frauenburg among the doddering canons he had been appalled by the stink of celibacy and clerkly caution. Ferrara had been a farce. Now Italy was making of him an anguished grimacing clown. The Church, academe, love: nothing. Seared and purified, shorn of the encumbering lumber of life, he stood at last like a solitary pine that stands in a wilderness of snow, aching upward fiercely into the sky of fire and ice that was the true concern of the essential selfhood that had eluded him always until now. Beware of these enigmas, Canon Wodka had warned him, for they cannot teach us how to live. But he did not wish to live, not by lessons that the world would teach him.

He had often before retreated into science as a refuge from the ghastliness of life; thus, he saw now, he had made a plaything of science, by demanding from it comfort and consolation. There would be no more of that, no more play. Here was no retreat, but the conscious accepting, on its own terms, of a cold harrowing discipline. Yet even astronomy was not the real issue. He had not spent his life pursuing a vision down the corridors of pain and loneliness in order merely to become a stargazer. No: astronomy was but the knife. What he was after was the deeper, the deepest thing: the kernel, the essence, the true.

*

Rain fell without cease. The world streamed. Lamps were lit at noon, and a great fire of pine logs burned day and night in the main hall. Outside, black phantom cypresses shuddered in the wind.

"The villagers have gone back to the old ways," Girolamo said. "Christ-come-lately is abandoned, and the ancient cults are revived. Now they are praying to Mercury to carry their appeals to the gods of fair weather."

They were at table. They dined now four or five times a day. Eating had become a sullen joyless obsession: they fed their guts incessantly in a vain effort to dull the pangs of a hunger that no food would assuage. The tender flesh of fish was as ash in Nicolas's mouth. He was pained by Girolamo's gentle puzzled attempts to reach out to him across the chasm that had opened between them, but it was a vague pain, hardly much more than an irritant, and becoming vaguer every day. He nodded absently. "Curious."

"What? What is curious? Tell me."

"O, nothing. They are praying to Mercury, you say; but I am thinking that Mercury is the Hermes of the Greeks, who in turn is the Egyptian Thoth, whose wisdom was handed down to us, through the priests of the Nile, by Hermes Trismegistus. Therefore by a roundabout way your villagers are praying to that magus." He looked up mildly. "Is that not curious?"

"The fisherfolk cannot work in this weather," Girolamo said. "Three of their men have been lost on the lake."

"Yes? But then fishermen are always being drowned. It is, so to speak, what they are for. All things, and all men, however humble, have their part to play in the great scheme."

"That is somewhat heartless, surely?"

"Would you not say *honest*, rather? This sudden concern of yours comes strangely from one who lives by the labour of the common people. Look at this fish here, so impeccably prepared, so tastefully arranged: has it not occurred to you that those fishermen may have perished so that you might sit down to this splendid dinner?"

Guido, the stooped steward, paused in his quaking progress around the table and peered at him intently. Girolamo had turned pale about the lips, but he smiled and said only:

"Do I deserve this, Nicolas, really?—Guido, you may go now, thank you." The old man departed with a dazed look, shocked and amazed it seemed at the suggestion that his master should concern himself with *housekeeping*. Girolamo's hand trembled as he poured the wine. "Must you make a fool of me before the servants?"

Nicolas put down his knife and laughed. "You see? You are less anxious for the fate of fishermen than for the good opinion of your servants!"

"You twist everything I say, everything!" Suddenly the Italian's poise had collapsed entirely, and for a moment he was a spoilt petulant boy. Nicolas, intensely gratified, smiled with his teeth. He watched the other closely, with a kind of detached curiosity, wondering if he might be about to break down and weep in fury and frustration. But Girolamo did not weep, and sighed instead and murmured: "What do you want from me, Nicolas, more than I have already given?"

"Why nothing, my dear friend, nothing at all." But that was not true: he wanted something, he did not know precisely what, but something large, vivid, outrageous—violence perhaps, terrible insult, a hideous blood-boltered wounding that would leave them both whimpering in final irremediable humiliation. Both, yes. There must be no victor. They must destroy each other, that is, that part of each that was in the other, for only by mutual destruction would he be freed. He understood none of this, he was too crazed with rage and impatience to try to understand, nevertheless he knew it to be valid. Frantically he cast about for a further weapon to thrust into the shuddering flesh. "My theory is almost complete, you know," he said, shouted almost, with a kind of ghastly constricted cheerfulness.

Girolamo glanced up uneasily. "Your theory?"

"Yes yes, my theory of planetary motion, my refutation of Ptolemy. Ptolemy . . ." He seemed to gag on the name. "Have I not told you about it? Let me tell you about it. Ptolemy, you see—"

"Nicolas."

"—Ptolemy, you see, misled us, or we misled ourselves, it hardly matters which, into believing that the *Almagest* is an explanation, a representation—*vorstellung*, you know the German term?—for what is real, but the truth is, the truth is that Ptolemaic astronomy is nothing so far as existence is concerned; it is only convenient for computing the nonexistent." He paused, panting. "What?"

Girolamo shook his head. "Nothing. Tell me about your theory."

"You do not believe it, do you? I mean you do not think that I am capable of formulating a theory which shall reveal the eternal truths of the universe; you do not believe that I am capable of greatness. *Do you?*"

"Perhaps, Nicolas, it is better to be good than great?"

*"You do not believe!—"*

"—I believe that if there are eternal truths, and I am not convinced of it, then they can only be known, but not expressed." He smiled. "And I believe that you and I should not fight."

"You! You you you— I amuse you, do I not? I am kept for the fine sport I provide: what matter if it rain, Koppernigk will cut a merry caper and keep us in good spirits." He had leapt up from the table, and was prancing furiously about the room in what indeed looked like a grotesque comic dervish dance of pain and loathing. "O, he's a jolly fellow, old Koppernigk, old Nuncle Nick!" Girolamo would not look at him, and at last, trembling, he sat down again and held his face in his hands.

81

They were silent. Greenish rainlight draped them about. The trees beyond the window throbbed and thrashed. Presently Girolamo said:

"You wrong me, Nicolas; I have never laughed at you. We are made differently. I cannot take the world so seriously as you do. It is a lack in me, perhaps. But I am not the dunderhead you like to think me. Have you ever, once, shown even the mildest interest in *my* concerns? I am a physician, that I take seriously. My work on contagion, the spread of diseases, this is not without value. Medicine is a science of the tangible, you see. I deal with what is here, with what ails men; if I were to discover thereby one of your eternal truths, why, I think I should not notice having done it. Are you listening? I express it badly, I know, but I am trying to teach you something. But then, I suppose you cannot believe that I am capable of teaching you anything. It is no matter. Do you want to know what I am currently embarked upon? I am writing a poem—yes, a poem—dealing with the pox! But you do not want to know, do you? Remember, Nicolas, the morning we met in the market place in Padua? I told you I was returning from a debauch; not so. I had gone there to study the methods of sanitation, or I should say the lack of such, in the meat market. Yes, laugh—" It had been hardly a laugh, rather a hollow retching noise. "—How prosaic, you will say, how comic even. That is why I lied to you that morning. You wanted me to be a rake, a rich wastrel, something utterly different from yourself: a happy fool. And I obliged you. I have been lying ever since. So you see, Nicolas, you are not the only one who fears to be thought dull, who is afraid to be ridiculous." He paused. "Love . . ." It was as if he were turning up the word gingerly with the toe of his shoe to see what outlandish things might be squirming underneath. "You drove Tadzio away." There was no trace of accusation in his tone, only sadness, and a faint wonderment. Nicolas, still cowering behind his hands, ground his teeth until they ached. He was in pain, he thought it was pain, until late that night when the word was redefined for him, and *pain* took on a wholly new meaning. Girolamo's door was ajar, and there were sounds, awful, vaguely familiar. The scene was illuminated by the faint flickering light of an untrimmed lamp, and in a mirror on the far wall all was eerily repeated in miniature. Girolamo with his long legs splayed was sitting on the edge of the bed with his head thrown back and his lips open in an O of ecstasy, a grotesque and yet mysteriously lovely stranger, his blurred gaze fixed sightlessly on the shadowy ceiling. Ah! he cried softly, Ah! and suddenly his body seemed to buckle, and reaching out with frenzied fingers he grasped by the hair the serving girl kneeling before him and plunged his shuddering cock into her mouth. Look! The girl squirmed, moaning and gagging. Girolamo twined his legs about her thighs. Thus, locked together in that monstrous embrace like some hideous exhibit in a bestiary, they began to rock slowly back and forth, and with them the whole room seemed to writhe and sway crazily in the shaking lamplight. Nicolas shut his eyes. When he opened them again it was finished. Girolamo gazed at him with a look of mingled desolation and defiance, and of utter finality. The slattern turned away and spat into the darkness. Nicolas retreated, and closed the door softly.

\*

Nothing less than a new and radical instauration would do, if astronomy was to mean more than itself. It was this latter necessity that had obsessed him always, and now more than ever. Astronomy was entirely sufficient unto itself: it saved the phenomena, it explained the inexistent. That was no longer enough, not for Nicolas at least. The closed system of the science must be broken, in order that it might transcend itself and its own sterile concerns, and thus become an instrument for verifying the real rather than merely postulating the possible. He considered this recognition, of the need to restate the basic function of cosmography, to be his first contribution of value to science; it was his manifesto, as it were, and also a vindication of his right to speak and be heard.

A new beginning, then, a new science, one that would be objective, open-minded, above all honest, a beam of stark cold light trained unflinchingly upon the world as it is and not as men, out of a desire for reassurance or mathematical elegance or whatever, wished it to be: that was his aim. It was to be achieved only through the formulation of a sound theory of planetary motion, he saw that clearly now. Before, he had naturally assumed that the new methods and procedures must be devised first, that they would be the tools with which to build the theory; that, of course, was to miss the essential point, namely, that the birth of the new science must be preceded by a radical act of creation. Out of nothing, next to nothing, disjointed bits and scraps, he would have to weld together an explanation of the phenomena. The enormity

83

of the problem terrified him, yet he knew that it was that problem and nothing less that he had to solve, for his intuition told him so, and he trusted his intuition—he must, since it was all he had.

Night after night in the villa during that tempestuous spring he groaned and sweated over his calculations, while outside the storm boomed and bellowed, tormenting the world. His dazed brain reeled, slipping and skidding in a frantic effort to marshal into some semblance of order the amorphous and apparently irreconcilable fragments of fact and speculation and fantastic dreaming. He knew that he was on the point of breaking through, he knew it; time and time over he leapt up from his work, laughing like a madman and tearing his hair, convinced that he had found the solution, only to sink down again a moment later, with a stricken look, having detected the flaw. He feared he would go mad, or fall ill, yet he could not rest, for if he once let go his fierce hold, the elaborate scaffolding he had so painfully erected would fall asunder; and also, of course, should his concentration falter he would find himself sucked once more into the quag of that other unresolved problem of Girolamo.

And then at last it came to him, sauntered up behind him, as it were, humming happily, and tapped him on the shoulder, wanting to know the cause of all the uproar. He had woken at dawn out of a coma of exhaustion into an immediate, almost lurid wakefulness. It was as if the channels of his brain had been sluiced with an icy drench of water. Involuntarily he began to think at once, in a curiously detached and yet wholly absorbed fashion that was, he supposed later, a unique miraculous objectivity, of the two seemingly unconnected propositions, which he had formulated long before, in Bologna or even earlier, that were the solidest of the few building blocks he had so far laid for the foundation of his theory: that the Sun, and not Earth, is at the centre of the world, and secondly that the world is far more vast than Ptolemy or anyone else had imagined. The wind was high. Rain beat upon the window. He rose in the dawning grey gloom and lifted aside the drapes. Clouds were breaking to the east over a sullen waterscape. Calmly then it came, the solution, like a magnificent great slow golden bird alighting in his head with a thrumming of vast wings. It was so simple, so ravishingly simple, that at first he did not recognise it for what it was.

He had been attacking the problem all along from the wrong direction. Perhaps his training at the hands of cautious schoolmen was to blame. No sooner had he realised the absolute necessity for a creative leap than his instincts without his knowing had thrown up their defences against such a scandalous notion, thrusting him back into the closed system of worn-out orthodoxies. There, like a blind fool, he had sought to arrive at a new destination by travelling the old routes, had thought to create an original theory by means of conventional calculations. Now in this dawn, how or why he did not know, his brain, without his help or knowledge, as it were, had made that leap that he had not had the nerve to risk, and out there, in the silence and utter emptiness of the blue, had done all that it was necessary to do, had combined those two simple but momentous propositions and identified with impeccable logic the consequences of that combining. Of course, of course. Why had he not thought of it before? If the Sun is conceived as the centre of an immensely expanded universe, then those observed phenomena of planetary motion that had baffled astronomers for millennia became perfectly rational and necessary. Of course! The verification of the theory, he knew, would take weeks, months, years perhaps, to complete, but that was nothing, that was mere hackwork. What mattered was not the propositions, but the combining of them: *the act of creation*. He turned the solution this way and that, admiring it, as if he were turning in his fingers a flawless ravishing jewel. It was the thing itself, the vivid thing.

He crawled back to bed, exhausted now. He felt like a very worn old man. The shining clarity of a moment ago was all gone. He needed sleep, days and days of sleep. However, no sooner had he laid down than he was up again, scrabbling eagerly at the drapes. He thrust his face against the stippled glass, peering toward the east, but the clouds had gathered again, and there was to be no sun, that day.

*

Girolamo and he said their farewells in a filthy little inn by the lakeshore; it seemed best to part on neutral ground. They could think of nothing to say, and sat in silence uneasily over an untouched jar of wine amid the reek of piss and the rancid catty stink of spilt beer. Through a tiny grimed window above their heads they watched the thunderclouds massing over the lake.

"*Caro Nicolo.*"

"My friend."

But they were only words. Nicolas was impatient to be away. He was returning to Prussia; Italy had been used up. Go! he told himself, go now, and abruptly he rose, wearing his death's-head grin. Girolamo looked up at him with a faint smile. "Farewell then, uncle." And as Nicolas turned, something of the past came back, and he realised that once, not long ago, there had been nothing in the world more precious than this young man's reserved, somehow passionately detached presence by his side. He went out quickly, into the wind and the gauzy warm rain, and mounted up. Riding away from Incaffi was like riding away from Italy herself. He was leaving behind him a world that had begun and ended, that was complete, and immune to change. What had been, was still, in his memory. Someday, fleeing from some extremity of anguish or of pain, his spirit would return to this bright place and find it all intact. The ghostly voices rose up at his back. *Do thyself no harm!* they cried, *for we are all here!*

# II
_____

## *Magister Ludi*

Waterborne he comes, at dead of night, sliding sleek on the river's gleaming back, snout lifted, sniffing, under the drawbridge, the portcullis, past the drowsing sentry. Brief scrabble of claws on the slimed steps below the wall, brief glint of a bared tooth. In the darkness for an instant an intimation of agony and anguish, and the night flinches. Now he scales the wall, creeps under the window, grinning. In the shadow of the tower he squats, wrapt in a black cloak, waiting for dawn. Comes the knocking, the pinched voice, the sly light step on the stair, and how is it that I alone can hear the water dripping at his heels?

*One that would speak with you, Canon.*

No! No! Keep him hence! But he will not be denied. He drags himself into the corner where night's gloom still clings, and there he hangs, watching. At times he laughs softly, at others lets fall a sob. His face is hidden in his cloak, all save the eyes, but I recognise him well enough, how would I not? He is the ineffable thing. He is ineluctable. He is the world's worst. Let me be, can't you!

*

Canon Koppernigk arrived at Heilsberg as night came on, bone-weary, wracked by fever, a black bundle slumped in the saddle of the starved nag that someone somewhere along the way had tricked him into buying. He had set out from Torun that morning, and travelled without pause all day, fearful of facing, prostrate in a rat-infested inn, the gross fancies conjured up by this sickness boiling in his blood. Now he could hardly understand that the journey was over, hardly knew where he was. It seemed to him that, borne thither on the surge and sway of waters, he had run aground on a strange dark shore. There were stars already, but no moon, and torches smoking high up on the walls. Off to the left a fire burned, tended by still figures, some squatting wrapt in cloaks and others with halberds leaning at watch. The river sucked and slopped, talking to itself as it ran. All this appeared disjointed and unreal. It was as if in his sickness he could apprehend only the weird underside of things, while the real, the significant world was beyond his fevered understanding. A rat, caught in a chance reflection of fire-light from the river, scuttled up the slimed steps below the wall and vanished.

He was shaken roughly, and heard himself, as from a great distance, groan. Maximilian, his manservant, gnawing an onion, scowled up at him, mumbling.

"What? What do you say?" The servant only shrugged, and gestured toward the gate. A peasant's cart with a broken axle straddled the drawbridge. In the half-light it had the look of a huge malign frog. "Go on, go on," the Canon said. "There is room enough."

But they were forced to pass perilously close to the edge. He peered down at the glittering black water, and felt dizzy. How fast it runs! The carter was belabouring with a stick in mute fury the impassive mule standing trapped between the shafts. Max blessed the fellow gravely, and sniggered. From this hole in the gate-tower a sentry shambled sleepily forth.

"State your business, strangers."

Max, the good German, waxed immediately indignant, to be addressed thus loutishly in the outlandish jabber of a native Prussian, a barbarian, beneath contempt. Imperiously he announced: "Doctor Copernicus!" and made to march on. The Prussian poked him perfunctorily in the belly with his blunt lance.

"Nicolas Koppernigk," the Canon said hastily, "liegeman to our Lord Bishop. Let us pass now, please, good fellow, and you shall have a penny." Max looked up at him, and he perceived, not for the first time and yet with wonder still, the peculiar mixture of love and loathing his servant bore for him.

In the deserted courtyard his horse's hoofs rang frostily and clear upon the flagstones. The hounds began to bay. He lifted his throbbing eyes to the pillared arches of the galleries, to the lowering mass of the castle keep faintly slimed with starlight, and thought how like a prison the place appeared. Heilsberg was intended to be his home now; not even Prussia itself was that, any longer.

"Max."

"*Ja, ja,*" the servant growled, stamping off. "I know—the Bishop must not be disturbed. I know!"

Then there were lights, and voices close by in the darkness, and a decrepit half-blind old woman came and led him inside, scolding him, not unkindly, as though he were an errant child. He had not been expected until the morrow. A fire of birchwood burned on the hearth in the great main hall, where a pallet had been laid for him. He was glad to be spared the stairs, for his limbs were liquid. The fever was mounting again, and he trembled violently. He lay down at once and pulled his cloak tight about him. Max and the old woman began to bicker. Max was jealous of her authority.

"Master, she says your nuncle must be summoned, with you sick and arriving unexpected."

"No no," the Canon groaned, "please, no." And, in a whisper, with a graveyard laugh: "O keep him hence!"

The old woman babbled on, but he closed his eyes and she went away at last, grumbling. Max squatted beside him and began to whistle softly through his teeth.

"Max—Max I am ill."

"Aye. I seen it coming. And I warned you. Didn't I say we should have stopped at Allenstein for the night? But you would none of it, and now you're sicker than a dog."

"Yes yes, you were right." Max was a good cure for self-pity. "You were quite right." He could not sleep. Even his hair seemed to pulse with pain. The sickness was a keepsake of Italy; he smiled wryly at the thought. Long shadows pranced like crazed things upon the walls. A dog came to sniff at him, its snout fastidiously twitching, but Max growled, and the creature pricked up its ears and loped away. Canon Koppernigk gazed into the fire. The flames sang a little song whose melody was just beyond grasping. "Max?"

"Aye."

Still there: a lean bundle of bones and sinew crouched in the firelight, staring narrowly at nothing. The hound returned and settled down unmolested beside them, licked its loins with relish, slept. The

Canon touched the soiled coarse fur with his fingertips. Suddenly he was comforted by common things, the fire's heat, this flea-bitten dog, Max's bitter regard, and beyond these the campfire too, and the watchers about it, the peasant's cart, the poor fastidious mule, even that rat on the steps: enduring things, brutish and bloody and warm, out of which, however dark and alien the shore, the essential self assembles a makeshift home.

Later that night Bishop Lucas came and looked at him, and shook his great head gloomily. "A fine physician I have appointed!"

\*

That title meant little. He was no true medic. He had not sufficient faith in the art of healing, nor in himself as a healer. At Padua they had taught him to cut up corpses very prettily, but that would have made him a better butcher than physician. Yet he had accepted the post without protest. On returning from Italy he had gone straight to Frauenburg, thinking to take up his duties as a canon of the Chapter; but he was not ready yet for that life, Italy was too much in his blood, and having secured with ease yet another, this time indefinite, leave of absence he had drifted to Torun. Katharina and her husband after protracted negotiations had bought from the Bishop the old house in St Anne's Lane, and had moved there from Cracow. He should have known better than to go to them, of course. The company of his shrewish sister and her blustering mate irked him; they for their part made him less than welcome. He had engaged Max more as an ally than a servant, for he was a match indeed for that ill-tempered sullen household.

Then word came from the Bishop: Canon Nicolas was summoned at once to Heilsberg as physician-in-residence at the castle, that he might thus, however inadequately, repay the expense of his years of Italian studies.

He liked the job well enough. Medicine was a means of concealment, whereby he might come at his true concerns obliquely and by stealth: to unsuspecting eyes there was not much difference between a star table and an apothecary's prescription, a geometrical calculation and a horoscope. But although he was free to work, he felt that he was trapped at Heilsberg, trapped and squirming, a grey old rat. He was thirty-three; his teeth were going. Once life had been an intense bright dream awaiting him elsewhere, beyond the disappointment of ordinary days, but now when he looked to that place once occupied by that gorgeous golden bowl of possibilities he saw only a blurred dark something with damaged limbs swimming toward him. It was not death, but something far less distinguished. It was, he supposed, failure. Each day it came a little nearer, and each day he made its coming a little easier, for was not his work—that is, his true work, his astronomy—a process of progressive failing? He moved forward doggedly, line by painful line, calculation by defective calculation, watching in mute suspended panic his blundering pen pollute and maim those concepts that, unexpressed, had throbbed with limpid purity and beauty. It was barbarism on a grand scale. Mathematical edifices of heart-rending frailty and delicacy were shattered at a stroke. He had thought that the working out of his theory would be nothing, mere hackwork: well, that was somewhat true, for there was hacking indeed, bloody butchery. He crouched at his desk by the light of a guttering candle, and suffered: it was a kind of slow internal bleeding. Only vaguely did he understand the nature of his plight. It was not that the theory itself was faulty, but somehow it was being contaminated in the working out. There seemed to be lacking some essential connection. The universe of dancing planets was out there, and he was here, and between the two spheres mere words and figures on paper could not mediate. Someone had once said something similar: who was that, or when? What matter! He dipped his pen in ink. He bled.

And yet, paradoxically, he was happy, if that was the word. Despite the pain and the repeated disappointments, despite the emptiness of his grey life, there was not happiness anywhere in the world to compare with his rapturous grief.

But there was more to his post at Heilsberg than tending to the Bishop's boils and bowels and fallen arches: there was politics also. At sixty, and despite his numerous ailments, Bishop Lucas was more vigorous far than the nephew nearly half his age. A hard cold prince, a major man, he devoted the main part of his prodigious energies to the task of extricating Ermland from the monstrous web of European political intrigue. The Canon was not long at the castle before he discovered that, along with physician, secretary and general factotum, he was to be his uncle's co-conspirator as well. He was appalled. Politics baffled him. The ceaseless warring of states and princes seemed to him insane. He wanted no part in that raucous public world, and yet, aghast, like one falling, he watched himself being drawn into the arena.

He began to be noticed, at Prussian Diets, or on the autumn circuit of the Ermland cities, hanging back at the Bishop's side. He cultivated anonymity, yet his pale unsmiling face and drab black cloak, his silence, his very diffidence, served only to surround him with an aura of significance. Toadies and leeches sought him out, hung on his heels, waylaid him in corridors, grinning their grins, baring their sharp little teeth, imagining that they had in him a sure channel to the Bishop's favour. He took the petitions that they thrust at him on screwed-up bits of paper, and bent his ear intently to their whisperings, feeling a fool and a fraud. He could do nothing, he assured them, in a voice that even to him sounded entirely false, and realised with a sinking heart that he was making enemies across half of Europe. Pressures from all sides were brought to bear on him. His brother-in-law Bartholemew Gertner, that fervent patriot, stopped speaking to him after the Canon one day during his stay at Torun had refused to declare himself, by inclination if not strictly by birth, a true German. Suddenly he was being called upon to question his very nationality! and he discovered that he did not know what it was. Bishop Lucas, however, resolved that difficulty straightway. "You are not German, nephew, no, nor are you a Pole, nor even a Prussian. You are an Ermlander, simple. Remember it."

And so, meekly, he became what he was told to be. But it was only one more mask. Behind it he was that which no name nor nation could claim. He was Doctor Copernicus.

*

Bishop Lucas knew nothing of that separate existence—or if he did, for there was little that went on at the castle without his knowledge, he chose to ignore it. He had lofty plans for his nephew. These he never spoke of openly, however, believing seemingly that they were best left to become apparent of themselves in the fullness of time, of which there was ample, he knew, for he had yet to be convinced that one day he would, like lesser men, be compelled to die. He was torn between his innate obsession with secrecy on one hand, and on the other the paramount necessity of dinning into the Canon's wilfully dull-witted skull, by main force if that would do it, the niceties of political intrigue. Diplomacy and public government were all right, any fool could conduct himself with skill and even elegance there, but the scheming and conniving by which the world was really run, these were a different matter, requiring intensive and expert coaching. But the trouble was that he did not entirely trust his nephew. The Canon sometimes had a look, hard to identify, but worrying. It was not simple stupidity, surely, that made his jaw hang thus, that misted over his rather ratty eyes with that peculiar greyish film?

"—Your head is in the clouds, nephew. Come back to earth!" The Canon started, hastily covering up the papers he had been working on, and peered over his shoulder with a wan apprehensive smile. Bishop Lucas looked at him balefully. I'll tell the dolt nothing; let him flounder! "I said: there is a guest expected. Are you going deaf?"

"No, my lord, I heard you well enough. I shall be down presently. I have some . . . some letters to finish."

The Bishop had turned to go, but now he came back, glowering menacingly. A born bully, he was well aware that his power over others depended on his determination to let pass no challenge, however faint-hearted. "Letters? What letters?" He was decked out all in purple, with purple gloves, and carried the mitre and staff tucked negligently under a fat arm. He was at once alarming and faintly comic. The Canon wondered uneasily why he had found it necessary personally to climb to this high room atop a windy tower merely to summon his nephew to dinner: it must be an important guest indeed. "*Now*, man—come!"

They hurried down dark stairways and rank damp passages. A storm was bellowing about the castle like a demented bull. The great entrance doors stood wide open, and in the porch a muffled faceless crowd of clerics and petty officials huddled by flickering torchlight, muttering. The night outside was a huge black spinning cylinder of wind and rain. Faintly between gusts there came the noise of riders approaching and the shrill blast of a trumpet. A ripple of excitement passed through the porch. Hoofbeats clattered across the courtyard, and suddenly dark mounted figures loomed up in the swirling darkness. Then there were many voices at once, and one that rang above all others, saying:

"Sennets and tuckets, by Christ!—and look here, a damned army awaiting us."

95

The Canon heard his uncle beside him moan faintly in anger and dismay, and then they were both confronted abruptly by a stone-grey face with staring eyes and a beard streaming rain.

"Well Bishop, now that you have announced our coming to every German spy in Prussia, I suppose we can leave off this blasted disguise, eh?"

"Your majesty, forgive me, I thought—"

"Yes yes yes, enough."

There was a scuffling in the porch, and the Canon glanced behind him to see the welcoming party with difficulty sinking to its knees in homage. Some few fell over in the crush, clutching wildly, amid stifled hilarity. Bishop Lucas juggled with the mitre and staff and proffered awkwardly the episcopal ring to be kissed. His Majesty looked at it. The Bishop whirled on his nephew and snarled:

"Bend your knee, churl, before the King of Poland!"

*

In the Hall of Knights above the nine great tables a thousand candles burned. First came hounds and torch-bearers and gaudy minstrels, and then the Bishop with his royal guest, followed by the Polish nobles, those hard-eyed horsemen, and at last the common household herd, pushing and squabbling and yelping for its dinner. A sort of silence fell as grace was offered. At the *amen* the Bishop sketched a hasty blessing on the air and ascended the dais to the *mensa princeps*, where he seated himself with the King on his right hand and the Canon on his left, and with heavy jowls sunk on his breast cast a cold eye upon the antics of the throng. He was still brooding on his humiliation in the porch. Jugglers and mountebanks pranced and leaped, spurred on by the shrieks of Toad the jester, a malignant stunted creature with a crazed fixed grin. Sandalled servants darted to and fro with fingerbowls and towels, and serving maids carried platters of smoking viands from the fire, where an uproar of cooks was toiling. A ragged cheer went up: one of the tumblers had fallen, and was being dragged away, writhing. Toad made a droll joke out of the fellow's misfortune. Then an ancient rhymester with a white beard tottered forth and launched into an epic in praise of Ermland. He was pelted with crusts of bread. Come, Toad, a song!

96

See how he flies up, O, pretty young thrush
Heigh ho! sing willow
Here's a health to the bird in the bush

Clamour and meat! Brute bliss! King Sigismund laughed loud and long, clawing at his tangled black beard.

"You keep a merry table, Bishop!" he cried. His temper was greatly improved. He had cast off his sodden disguise of linsey cloak and jerkin ("Who would mistake us for a peasant anyway!"), and was dressed now in the rough splendour of cowhide and ermine. That Jagellon head, however, lacking its crown, was still a rough-hewn undistinguished thing. Only the manner, overbearing, cruel and slightly mad, proclaimed him royal. He had made the long hard journey from Cracow to Prussia in wintertime, disguised, because he, like the Bishop, was alarmed by the resurgence of the Teutonic Knights. "Aye, very merry."

But Bishop Lucas was in no mood for pleasantries, and he shrugged morosely and said nothing. He was worried indeed. The Knights, once rulers of all Prussia and now banished to the East, were again, with the encouragement of Germany, pushing westward against Royal Prussia, whose allegiance to the Jagellon throne, however unenthusiastic, afforded Poland a vital foothold on the Baltic coast. At the centre of this turbulent triangle stood little Ermland, sore pressed on every side, her precarious independence gravely threatened, by Poland no less than by the Knights. Something would have to be done. The Bishop had a plan. But from the start, from that stormy arrival tonight, he had felt that things were going somehow awry. Sigismund played at being a boor, but he was no fool. He was crazed, perhaps, but cunningly so. His Ambassador was whispering in his ear. The Bishop's brow darkened.

"I am a plain man," he growled, "a priest. I believe in plain speaking. And I say that the Knights are a far greater threat to Poland than to our small state."

The Ambassador left off whispering, and squirmed unhappily in his chair. The Bishop and he were old enemies. He was a sour little man with an absurd moustache and sallow high-boned cheeks: a Slav. His one secret concern was to protect his prospects of a coveted posting out of the backwoods of Ermland to Paris, city of his dreams (where within a year he was to be throttled by a berserk in a brothel).

"Yes yes, Lord Bishop," he ventured, "but is it not possible that we might treat with these unruly Knights in some way other than by open, and, I might add, dangerous, confrontation? I have great faith in diplomacy." He simpered. "It is something I am not unskilled in."

Bishop Lucas bent on him a withering look. "Sir, you may know diplomacy, but you do not know the Cross. They are a vile rapacious horde, and cursed of God. *Infestimmus hostis Ordinis Theutonici!* The time is not long past when they held open season against our native Prussians, and slaughtered them for sport."

King Sigismund looked up, suddenly interested. "Did they?" His expression grew wistful, but then he recollected himself, and frowned. "Yes, well, for our part we see only one real threat, that is, the Turk, who is already at our southern border. What do you say of *that* vile horde, Bishop?"

It was just the opening that the Bishop needed to reveal his plan, yet, because his too intense hatred of the Knights threw him off, or because he underestimated the King and his crawling Ambassador, for whatever reason, his judgment faltered, and he bungled it.

"Is it not plain," he snapped, "what I have in mind? Are not the Knights, supposedly at least, a crusading order? I say send, or lure, or force them, whatever, to your southern frontiers, that they may defend those territories against the Infidel." There was a silence. He had been too precipitate, even the Canon saw it. He began to see it himself, and hastened to retrieve the situation. "They want to fight?" he cried, "— then let them fight, and if they are destroyed, why, the loss shall not be ours." But he had succeeded only in making things worse, for now there arose before the horrified imaginations of the Poles the vision of a Turkish army flushed with victory, blooded as it were, swarming northwards over the mangled corpse of one of Europe's finest military machines. Ah no, no. They avoided his fiercely searching eye; they seemed almost embarrassed. Of course they had known beforehand the nature of his scheme, but knowing was not the thing. The Canon watched his uncle covertly, and wondered, not without a certain malicious satisfaction, how it came that such an expert ritualist had stumbled so clumsily—for ritual *was* the thing.

"A jolly fellow, Bishop, that fool of yours," King Sigismund said. "Sing up, sirrah! And let us have more wine here. This Rhenish is damned good—the only good that's ever come out of Germany, I say. Ha!"

All dutifully laughed, save the Bishop, who sat and glared before him out of a purple trance of fury and chagrin. The Ambassador eyed him craftily, and smoothly said:

"I think, my lord, that we must consider in greater detail this problem of the Knights. Your solution seems a little too—how should I say?—too simple. Destroy the Turk or be destroyed, these appear to be the only alternatives you foresee, but rather might not the Cross destroy Poland? Ah no, Bishop, I think: no."

Bishop Lucas seemed about to bite him, but instead, plucking at himself in his agitation, he turned abruptly to the King and made to speak, but was prevented by a steward who came running and whispered urgently in his ear. "Not now, man, not . . . what? . . . *who?*" He whirled on the Canon, the wattles of red fat at his throat wobbling. "You! you knew of this."

The Canon reared away in fright, shaking his head. "Of what, my lord, knew of what?"

"The whoreson! Go to him, go, and tell him, tell him—" The table was agog. "—Tell him if he is not gone hence by dawn I'll have his poxed carcase strung up at the castle gate!"

Through passageways Canon Nicolas scurried, tripping on his robe in the darkness and moaning softly under his breath. Something from long ago, from childhood, ran in his head, over and over: *The Turk impales his prisoners! The Turk impales his prisoners!* In the flickering torchlight under the porch a dark figure waited, wrapt in a black cloak. The wind bellowed, whirled all away into the swirling tunnel of the tempest, Turks and Toad, sceptre and Cross, crusts, dust, old rags, a battered crown: all.

"You!"

"Yes, brother: I."

*     *     *

Bishop Lucas's decline began mysteriously that night of Andreas's arrival at Heilsberg. It was not that he fell ill, or that his reason failed, but a kind of impalpable though devastating paralysis set in that was eventually to sap his steely will. The King of Poland, crapulous and monumentally irritated, would hear no more talk of the Knights, and left before morning with his henchmen, despite the weather. The Bishop stood puzzled and querulous, wracked by impotent rage and buffeted by black rain, watching his hopes for the security of Ermland depart with the royal party into storm and darkness. Of any other man it would have been said that he was growing old, that he had met his match in the King and his Ambassador, but these simple reasonings were not sufficient here. Perhaps for him also a dark something had lain in wait, whose vague form was suddenly made hideous flesh in Andreas's coming.

"Has that bitch's bastard gone yet?"

"No, my lord. My lord he is ill, you cannot send him away."

"Cannot? Cannot I now!" He was flushed and shaken, and bobbed about in his rage like a large inflated bladder. "Go find him, you, in whatever rathole he is skulking, and tell him, tell him—*ach!*"

The Canon climbed the tower to his cell, where his brother sat on the edge of the bed with his cloak thrown over his shoulders, eating a sausage.

"You have been speaking with the Bishop, I can see," he said. "You are sweating." He laughed, a faint thin dry scraping sound. Now in the candlelight his face was horrible and horribly fascinating, worse even than it had seemed at first sight in the ill-lit porch, a ghastly ultimate thing, a mud mask set with eyes and emitting a frightful familiar voice. He was almost entirely bald above a knotted suppurating forehead. His upper lip was all eaten away on one side, so that his mouth was set lop-sidedly in what was not a grin and yet not a snarl either. One of his ears was a mess of crumbled white meat, while the other was untouched, a pinkish shell that in its startling perfection appeared far more hideous than its ruined twin. The nose was pallid and swollen, unreal, dead already, as if there, at the ravaged nostrils, Death the Jester had marked the place where when his time came he would force an entry. With such damage, the absence of blood was an unfailing surprise. "I think, brother, our uncle loves me not."

The Canon nodded, unable to speak. He felt sundered, as if mind and body had come apart, the one writhing here in dazed helpless horror, the other bolt upright there on the floor, a thing of sticks and straw, nodding like a fairground dummy. A dome of turbulent darkness, held aloft only by the frail flame of the candle, pressed down upon the little room. He drew up a chair and very slowly sat. He told himself that *this* was not Andreas, could not be, was a phantom out of a dream. But it was Andreas, he knew it. What surprised him was that he was not surprised: had he known all along, without admitting it, the nature of his brother's illness? Suddenly his sundered halves rushed together with a sickening smack, and he wrung his hands and cried:

"Andreas, Andreas, how have you come so low!"

His brother looked at him, amused and gratified by his distress, and lightly said:

"I had suspected, you know, that you would not fail to notice some little change in me since last we met. Have I aged, do you think? Hmm?"

"But what—what—?"

But he knew, only too well. Andreas laughed again.

"Why, it is the pox, brother, the *Morbus Gallicus*, or as your dear friend Fracastoro would have it in his famous verses, *Syphilis*, the beautiful boy struck down by the gods. A most troublesome complaint, I assure you."

"O Christ. Andreas."

Andreas frowned, if that was what to call this buckling of his maimed face.

"I'll have none of your pity, damn you," he said, "your mealy-mouthed concern. I am brought low, am I? You cringing clown. Rather I should rot with the pox than be like you, dead from the neck down. I have lived! Can you understand what that means, you, death-in-life, Poor Pol, can you? When I am dead and in the ground I shall not have been brought so low as you are now, brother!"

Into the globe of light in which they sat dim shapes were pressing, a crouched chair, the couch, a pile of books like clenched teeth, mute timid things, lifeless and yet seemingly alive, aching toward speech. The Canon looked about, unable to sustain the weight of his brother's burning eyes, and wondered vaguely if these things among which he lived had somehow robbed him of some essential presence, of something vivid and absolutely vital, in order to imbue themselves with a little vicarious life. For certainly (Andreas was right!) he was in a way dead, cold, beyond touching. Even now it was not Andreas really that he pitied, but the pity itself. That seemed to mean something. Between the object and the emotion a third something, for him, must always

101

mediate. Yes, that meant something. He did not know what. And then it all drifted away, those paradoxical fragments of almost-insight, and he was back in the charnel house.

"Why do you hate me so?" he asked, not in anger, nor even sadness much, but wonderingly, with awe.

Andreas did not answer. He fished up from under his cloak a soiled piece of cheese, looked at it doubtfully, and put it away. "Is there wine?" he growled. "Give it here." And the ghost of the imperious headstrong bright beautiful creature he had once been appeared briefly in the furry yellow light, bowed haughtily, and was gone. He produced a length of hollow reed, and turning away with the fastidious stealth of a wounded animal, inserted one end of it between his lips and sucked up a mouthful of wine. "I suppose you think it only justice," he mumbled, "that I have no longer a mouth with which to drink? You always disapproved of my drinking." He wiped his lips carefully on his wrist. "Well, enough of this poking in the past—let us speak of present things. So you have sold yourself to Nuncle Luke, eh? For how much, I wonder. Another fat prebend? I hear he has given you a canonry at Breslau: rich pickings there, I daresay. Still, hardly enough to buy you whole, I should have thought. Or has he promised you Ermland, the bishopric? You'll have to take Holy Orders for that. Well, say nothing, it's no matter. You'll rot here, as surely as I will, elsewhere. Perhaps I shall return to Rome. I have friends there, influence. You do not believe me, I see. But that is no matter either. What else can I tell you?— ah yes: I am a father." Suddenly his eyes glittered, bright with spite. The Canon flinched. "Yes, the bitch that dosed me redeemed herself somewhat by dropping a son. Imagine that, brother: a son, a little Andreas! That burns your celibate soul, doesn't it?"

O yes, it burned him, burned him badly, worse than he would ever have suspected it could do. Andreas's aim was uncanny: he felt as dry as a barren woman. He said:

"Where is he now, your son?"

Andreas took another sip of wine, and looked up, grinning in anguish. "Hard to say where he might be; in Purgatory, I expect, seeing that he was so grossly got. He could not live, not with such parents, no." He sighed, and glanced about the darkling room abstractedly, then groped under his cloak again and brought up this time a raw carrot with the stalk still on. "I asked your fellow to filch me some food, and look what he brought, the dog."

"*Max?*" the Canon yelped, "was it Max? Did he see your . . . did he see you clearly? He will tell the Bishop how things are with you. Andreas."

But Andreas was not listening. He let fall the carrot from his fingers, and gazed at it where it lay on the floor as if it were all hope, all happiness lost. "Our lives, brother, are a little journey through God's guts. We are soon shat. Those hills are not hills but heavenly piles, this earth a mess of consecrated cack, in which we sink at the end." He grinned again. "Well, what do you say to that? Is it not a merry notion? The world as God's belly: there is an image to confound your doctors of astronomy. Come, drink some wine. Why do I hate you? But I do not. I hate the world, and you, so to speak, are standing in the way. Come, do take some wine, we might as well be drunk. How the wind blows! Listen! Ah, brother, ah, I am in pain."

A bitter cold invaded the Canon's veins. He had emerged on the far side of grief and horror into an icy plain. He said:

"You cannot stay here, Andreas. Max will surely tell the Bishop how things are. He knows you are sick, but not how badly, how . . . how obviously. He will drive you out, he has threatened already to have you hanged. You must go now, tonight. I shall send Max with you to the town, he will find lodgings for you." And in the same dry measured tone he added: "Forgive me."

Andreas had taken up his ebony cane and was leaning on it heavily, rocking back and forth where he sat. He was drunk.

"But tell me what *you* think of the world, brother," he mumbled. "Do you think it a worthy place? Are we incandescent angels inhabiting a heaven? Come now, say, what do you think of it?"

The Canon grimaced and shook his head. "Nothing, I do not think. Will you go now, please?"

"*Christ!*" Andreas cried, and lifted the stick as if to strike. The Canon did not stir, and they sat thus, with the weapon trembling above them. "Tell me, damn you! Tell me what you think!"

"I think," Canon Koppernigk said calmly, "that the world is absurd."

Andreas lowered the stick, and nodded, smiling, it was almost a smile, almost blissful. "That is what I wanted you to say. Now I shall go."

He went. Max found a hole for him to hide in. The Bishop, believing, wishing to believe, that he had left the country, let it be known that he wanted to hear no more mention of him. But such rage and pain as Andreas's could not easily be erased. His coming had contaminated the castle, and some malign part of his presence persisted, a desolation, a blackening of the air. The Canon visited him once. He lay in darkness in a shuttered garret and would not speak, pretending to be asleep. The crown of his skull, all that was visible of him above the soiled blanket, scaly with scurf and old scabs and stuck with patches of scant hair, was horrid and heart-rending. Downstairs the innkeeper leered with ghastly knowing. He wiped his hands on his apron before taking the coins the Canon offered.

"You must give him better food. None of your slops, mind. Send to the castle for supplies if you must. Do not tell him that I spoke to you, that I gave you money."

"O aye, your honour, mum's the word. And I'll do that with the prog."

"Yes." He looked at the cowering ingratiating fellow, and saw himself. "Yes."

*

Church business took him with his uncle to Cracow. For once he was glad of that long weary journey. As they travelled southwards over the Prussian plain he felt the clutch of that dread phantom in the garret weaken, and at last fall away.

In Cracow he spent at Haller's bookshop what little time the Bishop would allow him away from his secretarial duties. Haller was publishing his Latin translations from the Byzantine Greek of Simocatta's *Epistles*. It was a poor dull book. The sight of the text, mysteriously, shockingly naked on the galley proofs, nauseated him. *If thou wouldst obtain mastery over thy grief, wander among graves* . . . O! But the text was unimportant. What mattered was the dedication. He was out to woo the Bishop.

He enlisted in this delicate task the help of an old acquaintance, Laurentius Rabe, a poet and wandering scholar who had taught him briefly here at Cracow during his university days. Rabe, who affected on occasion the grandiloquent latinised name of Corvinus, was a spry

104

old man with spindly legs and a plump chest and watery pale blue eyes. He liked to dress in black, and sported proudly still the liripipe of the graduate. He was no raven, despite the name, but resembled some small quick fastidious bird, a swallow, perhaps, or a swift. A jewel glittered at the tip of his sharp little beak.

"I would have some verses, you see," the Canon said, "to flatter my uncle. I should be grateful to you."

They stood together amid the crash and clatter of the caseroom at the rear of Haller's. Rabe nodded rapidly, rubbing his chilblained fingers together like bundles of dry twigs.

"Of course, of course," he cried, in his pinched voice. "Tell me what you require."

"Some small thing merely, a few lines." Canon Nicolas shrugged. "Something, say, on Aeneas and Achates, something like that, loyalty, piety, you know. The verse is no matter—"

"O."

"—But most importantly, you must put in some mention of astronomy. I plan to produce a small work on planetary motion, a mere outline, you understand, of something much larger that I have in train. This preliminary *commentariolus* is a modest affair, but I fear controversy among the schoolmen, and therefore I must have the support of the Bishop, you see." He was babbling, beset by embarrassment and nervousness. He found it unaccountably obscene to speak to others of his work. "Anyway, you know how these things go. Will you oblige me?"

Rabe was flattered, and for the moment, quite overcome, he could say nothing, and continued to nod, making faint squeaking noises under his breath. He was preparing one of his ornate speeches. The Canon had not time for that.

"Excuse me," he said hastily, "I must speak to Haller." The printer approached between the benches, a big stolid silent man in a leather apron, scratching his beard with a thick thumb and studying a sheet of parchment. "*Meister* Haller, I wish to put in some verses with the dedication: can you do that?"

Haller frowned pensively, and then nodded.

"We can do that," he said gravely.

Rabe was watching the Canon with a gentle, somewhat crestfallen questioning look.

"You have changed, my dear Koppernigk," he murmured.

"What?"

"You have become a public man."

"Have I? Perhaps so." What can he mean? No matter. "You will do this favour for me, then? I shall pay you, of course."

He turned his attention to the galleys, and when he looked again Rabe was gone. He had the distinct, vaguely troubling impression that the old man had somehow been folded up and put neatly but unceremoniously away: closed, as it were, like a dull book. He shook his head impatiently. He had not the time to worry over trivia.

★

He had all the time in the world. There was no hurry. He knew in his heart that the Bishop would be about as much impressed with the *Commentariolus* on Doctor Copernicus's planetary theory (did it not sound somehow like the name of a patent medicine put out by some quack?) as he would be with dreary Simocatta. Or he might be so impressed as to forbid publication. The times were inauspicious. In Germany the Church was under attack, while the humanists were everywhere execrated—and translating Simocatta could be, the Canon supposed, considered a humanist pursuit, however laughable the notion seemed to him. Bishop Lucas had troubles in plenty abroad without exposing himself to the accusation of laxity in his own house. One scandalous nephew was enough.

"What am I to do with him!" he roared, drumming on his forehead with his fists. "Come, you are my physician, advise me how to rid myself of this sickness that is your blasted brother."

"He is sick, my lord," Canon Nicolas said quietly. "We must try to be charitable."

"Charity? *Charity?* Christ in Heaven, man, don't make me spew. How can I be charitable to this . . . this . . . this defilement, this weeping sore? You have seen him: he is rotting, the beast is rotting on his feet! Jesus God, if they should hear of this scandal at Rome—"

"He tells me he has influence at the Vatican, my lord."

"—Or in Königsberg! O!" He sat down suddenly, appalled. "If they hear of it in Königsberg, what will they not make of it, the Knights. Something must be done. I will be rid of him, nephew, mark it, I will be rid of him."

106

They were in the library, a large high cold stone hall that in former times had been the garderobe, where now the business of the castle, and all Ermland, was conducted. The furnishings were scant, some uninviting chairs, a prie-dieu, an incongruously dainty Italian table, the vast desk at the side of which the Canon sat on a low stool with pen and slate before him. One wall was draped with a vast tapestry, out of which, as from some elaborate puzzle, the Bishop's flat stern face in various disguises peered with watchful mien, while in the middle distance, incidentally as it were, was depicted the martyrdom of St Stephen. A seven-branched candelabrum shed a brownish underwater light. Nervous petty officials summoned here over the years had left their mark on the air, a vague mute sense of distress and guilt and failure. It was Bishop Lucas's favourite room. He snuffed up great lungfuls of that rank air, puffed himself up on it. In these latter days he left the library only to eat and sleep. He was safe here, while outside the pestilence raged, that plague of the spirit made tangible in Andreas's coming. They had returned from Cracow to find him entrenched at the castle, determined, with hideous cheerfulness, not to be dislodged this time. Max had made him very comfortable in his master's tower, where he passed the time waiting for their return by reading the notes and preliminary drafts of the Canon's secret book . . . A climate of doom descended on Heilsberg.

The Bishop began pacing again, a bell-like bundle of fear and frustration in his long voluminous purple robe, banging and booming angrily. He halted at the narrow mullioned window and stood staring out with his fists clasped behind him. Hoarfrost was on the glass, and a pale moon like a fat cheesy skull gleamed above a snowbound land.

"I might have him murdered," he mused. "Can you find me an assassin that we can trust?" He turned, glowering. "Can you?"

Canon Nicolas closed his eyes wearily. "My lord, your letter to King Sigismund—"

"Damn King Sigismund! I have asked you a question."

"You are not in earnest, surely."

"Why not? Would he not be better off dead? He is dead already, except that his black heart out of spite persists in beating."

"Yes," the Canon murmured, "yes, he is dead already."

"Just so. Therefore—"

"He is my brother!"

"—Yes, and he is my nephew, my sister's son, my blood, and I would happily see his throat cut if I knew it could be quietly done."

"I cannot believe—"

"What? What can you not believe? He is anathema, *and I will be rid of him.*"

The Canon frowned. "Then, Bishop, you will be rid of me also."

His uncle slowly approached and stood over him, peering at him with interest. He seemed gratified, as if he derived a certain grim satisfaction from the thought that the long list of injuries done him by a filthy world were here being neatly rounded off.

"So you will betray me also, will you?" he said briskly. "Well well, so it has come to this. After all I have done for you. Well. And where, pray, will you go?"

"To Frauenburg."

"Ha! And rot there, among the cathedral mice? You are a fool, nephew."

But the Canon was hardly listening, engrossed as he was in contemplation of this new unrecognisable self that had suddenly from nowhere risen up, waving fists in defiance and demanding an apocalypse. Yet he was calm, quite, quite calm. It was of course the logical thing to do; yes, he would leave Heilsberg, there was no avoiding that command, it sang in the wires of his blood, a great black chord. He would embrace exile, would give it all up, for Andreas. It would be the final irrefutable proof of his regard for his brother. And there would be no need for words. Yes. Yes. He looked about him, blinking, bemused by the joy and dismay warring in his confused heart. It was all so simple, after all. The Bishop threw up his hands and lumbered off.

"*Fool!*"

*

Andreas laughed. "Fool you are, brother. Think you can escape me by hiding among the holy canons?"

"He is talking of assassination, Andreas."

"What of it! A dagger in the throat is not the worst thing that can befall me. O go away, you. Your false concern is sickening. You would like nothing better than to see me dead. I know you, brother, I *know* you." The Canon said nothing. What there was to say could not be said. No need for words? Ah! He turned to go, but Andreas plucked him

108

slyly by the sleeve. "Our nuncle will be interested to know how you have occupied yourself all these years under his patronage, do you not think?"

"I ask you, say nothing to him of this work of mine. You should not have read my papers. It is all foolery, a pastime merely."

"O, but you are too modest. I feel it is my duty to acquaint him with these very interesting theories which you have formulated. A heliocentric universe! He will be impressed. Well, what do you say?"

"I cannot prevent you from betraying me. It hardly matters now. Heed me, Andreas, and leave Heilsberg, or he will surely do you grievous injury."

Andreas grinned, grinding his teeth.

"You do not understand," he said. "*I want to die!*"

"Nonsense. It is revenge that you want."

They were startled by that, the Canon no less than Andreas, who stepped back with an offended look.

"What do you know of it?" he muttered sulkily. "Go on, scuttle off to your pious friends at Frauenburg." But as the Canon went down the stairs the door flew open behind him and Andreas appeared, framed against the candlelight like a dangling black spider, crying: "Yes! Yes! I will be revenged!"

*

Canon Koppernigk set out for Frauenburg by night, a cloaked black figure slumped astride a drooping mare. He was alone. Max had elected to stay and serve Andreas. That was all right. They might try, but they would not take everything from him, no. If the sentry were to accost him now he would announce himself fiercely, would bellow his name and impress it like a seal upon the waxen darkness for all Heilsberg to hear: *Doctor Copernicus!* But the sentry was asleep.

*     *     *

Day up there on the Baltic broke in storms of petrified fire. He had never seen such dawns. They were excessive, faintly alarming, not at all to his taste. He had come to detest extremes. The sky here was altogether too vast, too high, and too much given to empty tempestuous displays. It was all surface. He preferred the sea, whose hidden deeps communicated a sense of enormous grey calm. But sometimes the sea too disturbed him, when by a trick of tide or light it rose up in his window, humped, slate-blue, like the back of some waterborne brute, menacing and ineluctable.

He had asked for the tower at the north-west corner of the cathedral wall. The Frauenburg Chapter thought him mad. It was a grim bare place, certainly, but it suited him. There were three whitewashed rooms set squarely one above the other. From the second floor a door led out to a kind of platform atop the wall. This would do for an observatory, affording as it did an open view of the great plain to the south, and north and west across the narrow freshwater lake called the Frisches Haff to the Baltic beyond, and of the stars by night. For furniture he had a couch to sleep on, a table, two chairs, a lectern. That second chair troubled him in its suggestion of the possibility of a guest, but he allowed it stay, knowing that perfection is not of this world. Anyway, the desk far outweighted in garishness any number of chairs. It was his father's desk from Torun, which he had asked Katharina to let him have, as a keepsake. A big solid affair of oak, with drawers and brass fittings and a top inlaid with worn green leather, it fitted ill in that stark cell, but it was a part of the past, and in time he grew accustomed to it. He felt that to have left the rooms entirely bare would have been preferable, but he was not a fanatic. It was only that he had perceived in this grey stone tower, this least place, an image of his deepest self that furniture, possessions, comforts, only served to blur. He was after the thing itself now, the unadorned, the stony thing.

The Chapter demanded little of him. His fifteen fellow canons considered him a dull dog. They lived in the grand style, with servants and horses and estates outside the walls. His tower to them was a mark of incomprehensible and suspect humility. Yet they treated him with studied deference. He supposed they were afraid of him, of what he represented: he was, after all, the Bishop's nephew. He had not the interest to reassure them on that score. Anyway, their fright kept them at a welcome distance—the last thing he wanted was companionship. On his arrival at Frauenburg he was immediately, with indecent haste almost, appointed Visitator, a largely honorary title thrust on him in the hope apparently of mollifying for the moment the hunger for advancement that the canons imagined must be gnawing at this stark alarming newcomer. He compelled himself to attend all Chapter meet-

110

ings, and sat, without ever uttering a word, listening diligently to endless talk of tithes and taxes and Church politics. Easier to bear were the daily services at the cathedral. As a canon without Holy Orders he was called on to be present, but not of course to officiate. Unlike the Chapter sessions, where his mute brooding presence was patently resented, in church his reticence was ideally matched, was absorbed even, by God's huge stony silence.

Only rarely did he travel beyond the environs of Frauenburg. He liked the town. It was old, sleepy, safe, it reminded him of his birthplace; it was enough. Once he journeyed to Torun and called upon the Gertner household, and to Kulm to see Barbara at the convent. Neither visit was a success. Barbara and he still could not cope with each other as adults, and Katharina . . . was still Katharina. He resolved to venture forth no more, and gently refused the invitations of his colleagues to accompany them on their frequent roistering rounds of the diocese. He had at last, so it seemed to him, come to a dead halt. The waves of the world broke in storm and clamour far above the pool of stillness in which he floated.

*

But he was not left entirely unmolested. Ripples slithered down and stirred the filth at the bottom of his pool. He heard of the death of Rabe, poor Corvinus, on the very day that the copy of the Simocatta translations that he had sent to Bishop Lucas was returned, unread and unremarked, from Heilsberg. Then Max appeared one evening, sheepish and sullen; Andreas, he said, had gone back to Italy, with twelve hundred Hungarian gold florins in his belt, entrusted to him for ecclesiastical purposes by the Frauenburg Chapter.

"*What!*" The Canon stared. "What are you saying? Was he here? When was he here?"

Max shrugged. "Aye, he was here. They gave him the gold. He's gone off. Said I could go to the devil. Your nuncle gave him monies too, to be rid of him. A bad lot, your brother, if you'll permit me say it, master."

The Canon sat down. "Twelve hundred gold florins!" That was bad, but worse, far worse, was that Andreas had been in Frauenburg and no one had thought to warn him. (Warn? He turned the word this way and that, scrutinising it.)

*

He was not to have peace, that much was clear. No matter how far he
fled he would be followed. Mysterious emissaries were sent to him,
cunningly disguised. The most innocent-seeming stranger, or even
someone he thought he knew, might suddenly by a look, a word,
deliver the secret message: *beware*. He had rid his life of everything
that could have brought him comfort, but evidently that was not
enough, renunciation was not enough. Was passivity, then, his crime?
He set himself to work on behalf of the Chapter, accepting only the
most servile and distasteful of tasks. He wrote letters, collected rents,
drew up reports that no one read; he rode the length and breadth of the
diocese to deal with minute matters, frenziedly, like a deckhand racing
about a sinking ship vainly plugging leaks that opened again as soon as
they were stanched. Now the Chapter became finally convinced that
he was a lunatic. He negotiated, almost on his knees, with sneering
officials from Cracow and Königsberg. And he treated the sick. Even
they sometimes to his horror revealed a treacherous knowing.

It was strange: the people had such faith in him. They sent him their
sickest, their hopeless cases, leprous children, wasting brides, the old.
He could do nothing, yet he continued doggedly to advise and admonish, making passes in the air, frowning under the weight of a wholly
spurious wisdom. The more outlandish his treatment, and more grotesque the ingredients of the potions he poured down their throats, the
more satisfied they seemed. Why, some even recovered! He gained
quite a reputation throughout Ermland. Yet not for a moment did he
doubt that he was a fake.

There was a young girl, Alicia her name, she could not have been
more than fifteen, a slender delicate child. She was brought to him one
day in April. The air was drenched with sun and rain, cloudshadows
skimmed the bright Baltic. She wore a green gown. The tower did not
know what to do with her: such loveliness was more than those grim
grey stones could cope with. Her father was an over-dressed faintly ridiculous fat man, a fodder merchant and a member of the town council.
He owned a wooden house within the walls and a vineyard in the
suburbs. His people, he said, hailed from Lower Saxony, a fact which
he seemed to consider impressive. He let it be known that he could
read, and also write; he carefully avoided meeting the Canon's eye
directly. The mother was a large sad timid woman in black, with a

112

broad pale face all puffed and wrinkled as if perpetually anticipating tears. They were both elderly. Alicia had come, they confided, a gift from God, just when they had at last given up all hope of issue; and they looked at each other shyly, in wonder, and then at their daughter with such anguished tenderness that the Canon was forced to turn away, the celibate's bitterness rising in him like bile.

"Why have you come to me?"

"She is not well, Father, we think," the merchant answered. He hesitated, and looked to his wife. She wrung her pale heavy hands, and her lips trembled. She said:

"She has a . . . a rash, Father, and there is a flux—"

"Please, do not call me Father, I am not a priest." He had meant to be kind, to put them at their ease, but succeeded only in intimidating them further. He was himself uneasy. He wanted to walk out quickly now and abandon this fat fodder merchant and his sorrowful wife and ailing daughter, to escape. A handful of bright rain clattered against the window. The sea sparkled. He disliked springtime, unsettling season. With a thumb and finger under her chin he lifted the child's face and studied it silently for a moment. A faint blush spread upwards from her slender inviolate throat. She was afraid of him also. Or was she? It seemed to him that he detected fleetingly in those exquisite velvety dark eyes a cold and calculating sardonic look, piercing and familiar. He stepped away from her, frowning.

"Come," he said. The mother moaned faintly in distress and made as if to touch her daughter. Alicia did not look at her. "Come, child, do not be afraid."

He led her up the narrow stairs to his observatory. (The sick were suitably cowed by the astrolabe and quadrant and all those dusty tomes.) Today however it was not the patient who was the most apprehensive, but the physician. The girl's strange closed silence was disturbing. She seemed to be turned inward somehow, away from the world, as if she were the carrier of a secret that made her inner self wholly sufficient, as if she were the initiate of a cult.

"Where have you this rash, child?"

Still she said nothing, but stood a moment apparently debating within herself, then leaned down quickly and lifted up the hem of her skirts. He was not surprised; he was appalled, even frightened, yes, but not surprised. A carrier she was, certainly. Now he knew the cult into which she had been initiated. How strange: the sun was on the Baltic, the lindens were in bud, and water and air and earth trembled with the complicity of the awakening season's fire, and yet this young girl was infected. Once again he was struck by the failure of things and times to connect. The world was there, Alicia was here, and between the two the chasm yawned. She was watching him out of those blank exquisite eyes without fear or shame, but with a kind of curiosity. There, between seraphic face and that dreadful flower blossoming in secret inside her young girl's frail thighs, was yet another failure of connection.

"What man have you been with?" he asked.

She let fall the hem of her gown and with prim little swooping movements smoothed the wrinkles carefully out of the green silk.

"No man," she said. "I have been with no man, Father."

"Odysseus then," the Canon murmured, and was vaguely shocked at himself for making a joke at such a time. He could think of nothing else to say. He took her hand and felt her heart-breaking frailty. "Ah child, child." There was nothing to be said, nor done. The sense of his failure struck him like a hammerblow.

The parents stood as he had left them, poised, like ships becalmed, waiting for wonders. They had only to look at him and they knew. They had known already, in their hearts. The silence was frightful. The Canon said: "I suggest—" but the merchant and his wife both began to speak at once, and then stopped in confusion. The mother was weeping effortlessly.

"There is a young man, Father," she said. "He wishes to marry our Alicia." Her face suddenly crumpled, and she wailed: "O he is a fine boy, Father!"

"We—" the merchant began, puffing up his chest, but he could not go on, and looked about the room, baffled and lost, as if searching for some solid support that he knew was not to be found, not here nor anywhere. "*We!*—"

"My sister is Abbess of the Cistercian Convent at Kulm," the Canon said quickly. "I can arrange for your daughter to go there. She need not take the vow, of course, unless you wish it. But the nuns will care for her, and perhaps—" Stop! Do not! "—Perhaps in time, when she is cured . . . when she . . . perhaps this young man . . . Ach!" He could bear this no longer. They knew, they all knew: the child's groin was crawling with crabs, she was poxed, she would never marry, would probably not live to be twenty, they knew that! Why then this charade? He advanced on them, and they retreated before him as if buffeted by the wind of his dismay and rage. The girl did not even glance at him. He wanted to shake her, or clasp her in his arms, to throttle her, save her, he did not know what he wanted, and he did nothing. When the door was opened a solid block of sunlight fell upon them, and all hesitated a moment, dazzled, and then mother and daughter turned away into the street. The merchant suddenly stamped his foot.

"It is witchcraft," he gasped, "I know it!"

"No," the Canon said. "There is no witchery here. Go now and comfort your wife and child. I shall write today to Kulm."

But the merchant was not listening. He nodded distractedly, mechanically, like a large forlorn doll.

"The blame must fall somewhere," he muttered, and for the first time looked directly at the Canon. "It must fall somewhere!"

Yes, yes: somewhere.

*

The ripples increased in intensity, became waves. Rumours reached him that he was being talked of at Rome as the originator of a new cosmology. Julius II himself, it was said, had expressed an interest. The blame must fall somewhere: he heard again that voice on the stairs shrieking of revenge. An unassuageable constriction of fear and panic afflicted him. Yet there was nowhere further that he could flee to. Lateral drift was all that remained.

Suddenly one day God abandoned him. Or perhaps it had happened long before, and he was only realising it now. The crisis came unbidden, for he had never questioned his faith, and he felt like the bystander, stopped idly to watch a brawl, who is suddenly struck down by a terrible stray blow. And yet it could not really be called a crisis. There was no great tumult of the soul, no pain. The thing was distinguished by a lack of feeling, a numbness. And it was strange: his faith in the Church did not waver, only his faith in God. The Mass, transubstantiation, the forgiveness of sin, the virgin birth, the vivid truth of all *that* he did not for a moment doubt, but behind it, behind the ritual, there was for him now only a silent white void that was everywhere and everything and eternal.

He confessed to the Precentor, Canon von Lossainen, but more out of curiosity than remorse. The Precentor, an ailing unhappy old man, sighed and said:

"Perhaps, Nicolas, the outward forms are all that any of us can believe in. Are you not being too hard on yourself?"

"No, no; I do not think it is possible to be too hard on oneself."

"You may be right. Should I give you absolution? I hardly know."

"Despair is a great sin."

"Despair? Ah."

*

He ceased to believe also in his book. For a while, in Cracow, in Italy, he had succeeded in convincing himself that (what was it?) the physical world was amenable to physical investigation, that the principal thing could be deduced, that the thing itself could be said. That faith too had collapsed. The book by now had gone through two complete revisions, rewritings really, but instead of coming nearer to essentials it was, he knew, flying off in a wild eccentric orbit into emptiness; instead of approaching the word, the crucial Word, it was careering headlong into a loquacious silence. He had believed it possible to say the truth; now he saw that all that could be said was the saying. His book was not about the world, but about itself. More than once he snatched up this hideous ingrown thing and rushed with it to the fire, but he had not the strength to perform that ultimate act.

Then at last there came, mysteriously, a ghastly release.

It was a sulphurous windy evening in March when Katharina's steward arrived to summon him to Torun, where his uncle the Bishop was lying ill. He rode all night through storm and rain into a sombre yellowish dawn that was more like twilight. At Marienburg a watery sun broke briefly through the gloom. The Vistula was sullen. By nightfall he had reached Torun, exhausted, and almost delirious from want of sleep. Katharina was solicitous, and that told him, if nothing else would, that the situation was serious.

Bishop Lucas had been to Cracow for the wedding of King Sigismund. On the journey home he had fallen violently ill, and being then closer to Torun than Heilsberg had elected to be taken to the house of his niece. He lay now writhing in a grey sweat in the room, in the very bed where Canon Nicolas had been born and probably conceived. And

116

indeed the Bishop, mewling in pain and mortal fright, seemed himself a great gross infant labouring toward an agonised delivery. He was torn by terrible fluxions, that felt, he said, as if he were shitting his guts: he was. The room was lit by a single candle, but a greater ghastly light seemed shed by his rage and pain. The Canon hung back in the shadows for a long time, watching the little changing tableau being enacted about the bed. Priests and nurses came and went silently. A physician with a grey beard shook his head. Katharina put a cross into her uncle's hands, but he fumbled and let it fall. Gertner picked his nails.

*"Nicolas!"*

"Yes, uncle, I am here."

The stricken eyes sought his vainly, a shaking hand took him fiercely by the wrist. "They have poisoned me, Nicolas. Their spies were at the palace, everywhere. O Jesus curse them! O!"

"He is raving now," Katharina said. "We can do nothing."

The Canon paced about the dark house. It was changed beyond all recognition. It looked the same as it had always done, yet everything that he rapped upon with his questioning presence gave back only a dull sullen silence, as if the living soft centre of things had gone dead, had petrified. The deathwatch had conferred a lawless dispensation, and weird scenes of licence met him everywhere. In the little room that as a child he had shared with Andreas a pair of hounds, a bitch and her mate, reared up from the bed and snarled at him, baring their phosphorescent fangs in the darkness. Under a disordered table in the dining-hall he found his servant Max, and Toad, the Bishop's jester, drunk and asleep, wrapped in a grotesque embrace, each with a hand thrust into the other's lap. A stench like the stench of stagnant waters hung on the stairs. There was laughter in the servants' quarters and the sounds of stealthy merrymaking. His own fingers when he lifted them to his face smelled of rot. He sat down by a dead fire in the solar and fell into a kind of trance between sleep and waking peopled by blurred phantoms.

In the dead hour before dawn he was summoned to the sickroom. There was in the globe of light about the bed that sense of suspended animation, of a finger lifted to lips, preparatory to the entrance of the black prince. Only the dying man himself seemed unaware that the moment was at hand. He hardly stirred at all now, and yet he appeared

117

to be frantically busy. Life had shrunk to a swiftly spinning point within him, the last flywheel turning still as the engine approached its final collapse. The Canon was prey to an unshakeable feeling of incongruousness, of being inappropriately dressed, of being, somehow, all wrong. Suddenly the Bishop's eyes flew open and stared upward with an expression of astonishment, and in a strong clear voice he cried: "No!" and all in the sickroom went utterly still and silent, as if fearing, like children in a hiding game, that to make a sound would mean being called forth to face some dreadful forfeit. "No! Keep him hence!" But the dark visitor would not be denied, and, battered and shapeless, an already indistinct pummelled soiled sack of pain and bafflement, Bishop Lucas Waczelrodt blundered into the darkness under the outstretched black wing of that enfolding cloak. The priest anointed his forehead with holy chrism. Katharina sobbed. Gertner looked up, frowning. The Canon turned away.

"Send at once to Heilsberg, tell them their Bishop is dead."

The bells spoke.

*

Revolted by the pall of fake mourning put on by the house, Canon Nicolas slipped out by the servants' passageway into the garden. The morning, sparkling with sun and frost, seemed made of finely wrought glass. The garden had been let go to ruin, and it was with difficulty that memory cleared away the weeds and rubbish and restored it to what it had been once. Here were the fruit bushes, the little paved path, the sundial—yes, yes, he remembered. As a child he had played here happily, soothed and reassured by the familiarity of the ramshackle: weathered posts, smouldering bonfires, unaccountably amiable backs of houses, the gaiety of cabbages. And when he was older, how many mornings such as this had he stood here in chill brittle sunlight, rapt and trembling at the thought of the infinite possibilities of the future, dreaming of mysterious pale young women in green gowns walking through dewy grass under great trees. He passed through a gap in the tumbledown paling into the narrow lane that ran behind the gardens. Brambles sprouted here at the base of a high white wall. A faint, sweetish, not altogether unpleasant tang of nightsoil laced the air. An old woman in a black cloak with a basket of eggs on her arm passed him by, bidding him *Grüss Gott* out of a toothless mouth. An

extraordinary stealthy stillness reigned, as if an event of great significance were waiting for him to be gone so that it could occur in perfect
solitude. The night, the candles and the murmuring, the wracked
creature dying on the bed, all that was immensely far away now,
unreal. Yet it had been as much a part of the world as this sunlight and
stillness, those pencil-lines of blue smoke rising unruffled into the paler
blue: was all this also unreal, then? He turned, and stood for a long
time gazing toward the linden tree. It was to be cut down, so Gertner
had said. It was old, and in danger of falling. The Canon nodded once,
smiling a little, and walked back slowly through the resurrected
garden to the house.

\*      \*      \*

He could not in honesty mourn his uncle's death. There was guilt,
of course, regret at the thought of opportunities lost (perhaps I
wronged him?), but these were not true feelings, only empty rituals,
purification rites, as it were, performed in order that the ghost might
be laid; for death, he now realised, produces a sudden nothingness in
the world, a hole in the fabric of the world, with which the survivors
must learn to live, and whether the lost one be loved or hated makes no
difference, that learning still is difficult. He was haunted for a long
time by a kind of ferocious implacable absence stamped unmistakably
with the Bishop's seal.

Then, inevitably, came the feeling of relief. Cautiously he tested the
bars of his cage and found them not so rigid as they had been before.
He even began to look a little more kindly on his work, telling himself
that after all what he considered a poor flawed thing the world would
surely think a wonder. He completed the *Commentariolus*, and, at
once appalled and excited by his own daring, had copies made of it by a
scribe in the town which he quietly distributed among the few scholars
he considered sympathetic and discreet. Then, with teeth gritted, he
awaited the explosion that would surely be set off by the seven axioms
which together formed the basis of the theory of a sun-centred universe. He feared ridicule, refutations, abuse; most of all he feared in-
volvement. He would be dragged out, kicking and howling, into the
market place, he would be stood on a platform like a fairground exhibit

119

and invited to expound proofs. It was ridiculous, horrible, not to be borne! Again he began to wonder if he would be well advised to destroy his work and thus have done with the whole business. But his book was all he had left—how could he burn it? Yet if they should come, sneering and snarling and bellowing for proof, smash down his door and snatch the manuscript from his hands, dear God, what then?

It was not the academics that he feared most (he felt he knew how to handle them), but the people, the poor ordinary deluded people ever on the lookout for the sign, the message, the word that would herald the imminent coming of the millennium and all that it entailed: liberty, happiness, redemption. They would seize upon his work, or a mangled version of it more like, with awful fervour, beside themselves in their eagerness to believe that what he was offering them was an explanation of the world and their lives in it. And when sooner or later it dawned upon them that they had been betrayed yet again, that here was no simple comprehensive picture of reality, no new instauration, then they would turn on him. But even that was not the point. O true, he had no wish to be reviled, but far more important than that was his wish not to mislead the people. They must be made to understand that by banishing Earth and man along with it from the centre of the universe, he was passing no judgments, expounding no philosophy, but merely stating what is the case. The game of which he was master could exercise the mind, but it would not teach them how to live.

He need not have worried. There was no explosion, no one came. There was not even a tapping at his door. The world overlooked him. It was just as well. He was relieved. He had given them the *Commentariolus*, the preface as it were, and they had taken no notice. Now he could finish writing his book in peace, unmolested by idiots. For surely they were all idiots, if they could ignore the challenge he had thrown down at their feet, idiots and cowards, that they would not see the breathtaking splendour and daring of his concepts—he would show them, yes, yes! And sullenly, consumed by disappointment and frustration, he sat down to his desk, to show them. The great spheres wheeled in a crystal firmament in his head, and when (rarely, rarely!) he looked into the night sky, he was troubled by a vague sense of recognition that puzzled him until he remembered that it was that sky, those cold white specks of light, that had given form to his mind's world. Then the familiar feeling of dislocation assailed him as he strove in vain to discern a connection between the actual and the imagined. Inevitably, inexplicably, Andreas's ravaged face swam into view, slyly smiling—Constellation of Syphilis!—blotting out all else.

\*

"One that would speak with you, Canon."

Canon Koppernigk looked up frowning and shook his head vehemently in silent refusal. He did not wish to be disturbed. Max only shrugged, and with a brief sardonic bow withdrew. Even before his visitor appeared the Canon knew from that inimitable respectful light step on the stairs who it was. He sighed, and put away carefully into a drawer the page of manuscript on which he had been working.

"My dear Doctor, forgive me, I hope I do not disturb you?" Canon Tiedemann Giese was a good-humoured, somewhat stout, curiously babyish fresh-faced man of thirty. He had a large flaxen head, an incongruously stern hooked nose, squarish useless hands, and wide innocent eyes that managed to bestow a unique tender concern on even the least thing that they encountered. Although he came of an aristocratic line, he disapproved of the opulent lives led by his colleagues in the Chapter, a disapproval that he expressed—or paraded, as some said—by dressing always in the common style in smocks and breeches and stout sensible riding boots. His academic achievements were impressive, yet he was careful to wear his learning lightly. By some means he had got hold of a copy of the *Commentariolus*, and although he had never mentioned that work directly, he let it be known, by certain sly remarks and meaningful looks that made Canon Koppernigk flinch, that he had been won over entirely to the heliocentric doctrine. Canon Giese was one of the world's innate enthusiasts.

"Please sit," Canon Koppernigk said, with a wintry smile. "There is something I can do for you?"

Giese laughed nervously. He was the younger of the two by some seven years only, yet his manner in Canon Koppernigk's presence was that of a timid but eager bright schoolboy. With desperate nonchalance he said:

"Just passing, you know, and I thought I might call in to . . ."

"Yes."

Giese's discomfited eye slid off and wandered about the cell. It was low and white, white everywhere: even the beams of the ceiling were

121

white. On the wall behind the desk at which the Doctor sat was fixed an hourglass in a frame, his wide-brimmed hat hanging on a hook, and a wooden stand holding a few medical implements. Set in a deep embrasure, a small window with panes of bottled glass gave on to the Frisches Haff and the great arc of the Baltic beyond. The rickety door leading on to the wall was open, and out there could be seen the upright sundial and the triquetrum, a rudimentary crossbow affair over five ells tall for measuring celestial angles, a curiously distraught-looking thing standing with its frozen arms flung skywards. Was it with the aid of these poor pieces only, Giese wondered, that the Doctor had formulated his wonderful theory? A gull alighted on the windowsill, and for a moment he gazed thoughtfully at the bird's pale eye magnified in the bottled glass. (Magnified?—but no, no, a foolish notion . . .)

"I too have some interest in astronomy, you know, Doctor," he said. "Of course, I am merely a dabbler, you understand. But I think I know enough to recognise greatness when I encounter it, as I have done, lately." And he leered. Canon Koppernigk's stony expression did not alter. He was really a peculiar cold closed person, difficult to touch. Giese sighed. "Well, in fact, Doctor, there *is* a matter on which I wished to speak to you. The subject is, how shall I say, a delicate one, painful even. Perhaps you know what I am referring to? No?" He began to fidget. He was seated on a low hard chair before the Doctor's desk. It was on occasions such as this that he heartily regretted having accepted the position of Precentor of the Frauenburg Chapter, which had fallen to him on Canon von Lossainen's accession to the bishopric following the death of Lucas Waczelrodt: he was not cut out for this kind of thing, really. "It is your brother, you see," he said carefully. "Canon Andreas."

"O?"

"I know that it must be a painful subject for you, Doctor, and indeed that is why I have come to you personally, not only as Precentor, but as, I hope, a friend." He paused. Canon Koppernigk raised one eyebrow enquiringly, but said nothing. "The Bishop, you see, and indeed the Chapter, all feel that, well, that your brother's presence, in his lamentable condition, is not . . . that is to say—"

"Presence?" said the Doctor. "But my brother is in Italy."

Giese stared. "O but no, Doctor, no; I assumed that you—have you

122

not been told? He is here, in Frauenburg. He has been here for some days now. I assumed he would have called on you. He is not—he is not well, you know."

*

He was not well: he was a walking horror. In the years since the Canon had seen him last he had surrendered his own form to that of his disease, so that he was no longer a man but a *memento mori* only, a shrivelled twisted hunchbacked thing on whose ruined face was fixed a death's-head grin. All this the Canon learned at second hand, for his brother kept away from him, not out of tact, of course, but because he found it amusing to haunt him from a distance, by proxy as it were, knowing how much more painful it would be that others should carry word of his disgraceful doings into the fastness of the Canon's austere white tower. He lodged at a kip down in the stews (where else would have him?), but flaunted his frightful form by day in the environs of the cathedral, where he terrified the town's children and their mothers alike; and once even, one Sunday morning, he came lurching up the central aisle during High Mass and knelt in elaborate genuflexion at the altar rails, behind which poor ailing Bishop von Lossainen sat in horror-stricken immobility on his purple throne.

It was not long, of course, until there began to be talk of black magic, of vampirism and werewolves. Crosses appeared on the doors of the town. A young girl, it was said, had been found in the hills with her throat torn open. By night a black-cloaked demon haunted the streets, and howling and eerie laughter was heard in the darkness. Toto the idiot, who had the gift of second sight, was said to have seen a huge bird with the pinched violet face of a man fly low over the roofs on All Souls' Eve, shrieking. Hysteria spread through Frauenburg like the pest, and throughout that sombre smoky autumn small groups of grim-faced men gathered at twilight on street corners and muttered darkly, and mothers called their children home early from play. The Jews outside the walls began discreetly to fortify their houses, fearing a pogrom. Things could not continue thus.

The first snow of winter was falling when the canons met in the conference hall of the chapterhouse, determined finally to resolve the situation. They had already decided privately on a course of action, but a general convocation was necessary to put an official seal upon it. The

123

meeting had a further purpose: Canon Koppernigk had so far remained entirely aloof from the problem, as if his brother were no concern of his, and the Chapter, outraged at his silence and apparent indifference, was determined that he should be made to bear his share of responsibility. Indeed, feeling among the canons ran so high that they were no longer quite clear in their minds as to which of the brothers deserved the harsher treatment, and some were even in favour of banishing both and thus having done with that troublesome tribe for good and ever.

The Canon arrived late at the chapterhouse, wrapped up against the cold and with his wide-brimmed hat pulled low. A thin forbidding figure in black, he moved slowly down the hall and took his place at the table, removed his hat, his gloves, and having crossed himself in silence folded his hands before him and lifted his eyes to the bruisedark sky looming in the high windows. His colleagues, who had fallen silent as he entered, now stirred themselves and glanced morosely about the table, dissatisfied and obscurely disappointed; they had somehow expected something of him today, something dramatic and untoward, a yell of defiance or a grovelling plea for leniency, even threats perhaps, or a curse, but not this, this *nothingness*—why, he was hardly here at all!

Giese at the head of the table coughed, and, continuing the address that Canon Nicolas's coming had interrupted, said:

"The situation then, gentlemen, is delicate. The Bishop demands that we take action, and now even the people press for the afflicted Canon's, ah, departure. However, I would counsel against too hasty or too severe a solution. We must not exaggerate the gravity of this affair. The Bishop himself, as we know, is not well, and therefore may not be expected perhaps to take a perfectly reasoned view on these matters—"

"*Is he saying that von Lossainen has the pox?*" someone enquired in a loud whisper, and there was a subdued rumble of laughter.

"—The people, of course," Giese continued stoutly, "the people as ever are given to superstitious and hysterical talk, and should be ignored. We must recognise, gentlemen, that our brother, Canon Andreas, is mortally afflicted, but that he has not willed this terrible curse upon himself. We must, in short, try to be charitable. Now—"

While before he had simply not looked at Canon Koppernigk, now he began elaborately and with tight-lipped sternness not to look at him, and fidgeted nervously with the sheaf of papers before him on the table. "—I have canvassed opinion generally among you, and certain proposals have emerged which are, in my opinion, somewhat extreme. However, these proposals are ... the proposals ... ah ..." Now he looked at the Canon, and blanched, and could not go on. There was silence, and then the Danziger Canon Heinrich Snellenburg, a big swarthy truculent man, snorted angrily down his nostrils and declared:

"It is proposed to break all personal connections with the leper, to demand that he account for the sum of twelve hundred gold florins entrusted to him by this Chapter, to seize his prebend and all other revenues, and to grant him a modest annuity on condition that he takes himself off from our midst immediately. That, Herr Precentor, gentlemen, is what is proposed." And he turned his dark sullen gaze on Canon Koppernigk. "If these are dissenting voices, let them be heard now."

The Canon was still watching the snow swirling greyly against the window. All waited in vain for him to speak. He seemed genuinely indifferent to the proceedings, and somehow that genuineness annoyed the Chapter far more than pretence would have done, for they could at least have understood pretence. Had the man no ordinary human feelings whatever? He said nothing, only now and then drummed his fingers lightly, thoughtfully, on the edge of the table. But even if he would not speak they were yet determined to have some response of him, and so, with unspoken unanimity, they agreed that his silence should be taken as a protest. Canon von der Trank, an aristocratic German with the thin nervous look about him of a whippet, pursed up his wide pale pink lips and said:

"Whatever it is that we do, gentlemen, certainly we must do something. The matter must be dealt with, there must be a quick clean end to the present intolerable situation. The Precentor gives it as his opinion that the measures we have proposed are too extreme. He tells us that this—" his sharp fastidious nose twitched at the tip "—this *person* did not will upon himself the disease that afflicts him, yet we may ask whose will, if not his, was involved? All are aware of the nature of his malady, which he contracted in the bawdyhouses of Italy. We are urged to be charitable, but our charity and our care must be ex-

125

tended firstly to the faithful of this diocese: them we have the duty to protect from this outrageous source of scandal. And further, there is the reputation of this Chapter to be considered. This is the very sort of thing that the monk Luther will be delighted to hear of, so that he may add it as another strand to the whip with which he lashes the Church. Therefore I say let us hear no more talk of charity and caution. Our duty is clear—let us perform it. The leper must be declared anathema and driven hence without delay!''

A rumble of yeas followed this address, and all with set jaws glared at Giese grimly, who squirmed, and mopped his forehead, and turned a beseeching gaze on Canon Koppernigk.

"What do you think, Doctor? Surely you wish to make some reply?"

The Canon took his eyes reluctantly from the darkling window and glanced about the table. Snellenburg, you owe me a hundred marks; von der Trank, you hate me because I am a tradesman's son and yet cleverer than you; Giese—poor Giese. What does it matter? Lately he had begun to feel that he was somehow fading, that his physical self was as it were evaporating, becoming transparent; soon there would remain only a mind, a sort of grey ghostly amoeba spinning silently in the dead air. What does it matter? He turned away. How softly the snow falls! "I think," he murmured, "that it would be foolish to worry overmuch as to what Father Luther thinks of us or says. He will go the way all others of his kind have gone, and will be forgotten with the rest."

They stared at him, nonplussed. Did he think this was some kind of religious discussion? Had he even been listening? For a long time no one spoke, and then Canon Snellenburg shrugged and said:

"Well, if the fellow's own brother will not even say a word in his defence!—"

"Please, please gentlemen," Giese cried, as if convinced that the table was about to rise up and attack the Canon with fists. "Please! Doctor, I wonder if you realise fully what is being proposed? The Chapter intends to strip your brother of all rights and privileges whatever, to—to cast him out, like a beggar!"

But Canon Koppernigk paid no heed. Look at them! First they blamed me because he is my brother, now they despise me because I will not defend him. Wait, Snellenburg, just wait, I will have my hundred marks of you! Just then he found an unexpected and

126

unwanted ally, when another of the canons, one Alexander Sculteti, a scrawny fellow with a red nose, stood up and delivered himself of a rambling and disjointed defence of Canon Andreas to which nobody listened, for Sculteti was a reprobate who kept a woman and a houseful of children at his farm outside the walls, and besides, he was far from sober. Canon Koppernigk took up his hat, and wrapping his cloak about him went out into the burgeoning darkness and the snow.

*

As if he had been waiting for a signal, Andreas visited his brother for the first time on the very day that he heard of the Chapter's decision to banish him. For a man so grievously maimed he negotiated the stairs of the tower with surprising stealth, and all that could be heard of his coming was his laboured breathing and the light fastidious tapping of his stick. He was indeed in a bad way now, but what shocked the Canon most were the signs of ageing that even the damage wrought by the disease could not outweigh. The few swatches of hair remaining on his skull had turned a yellowish grey, and his eyes that had once flashed fire were weary and rheumy and querulous. His uncanny intuition, however, had not forsaken him, for he said:

"Why do you stare so, brother—did you expect me to have become whole again? I am nearing fifty, I do not have long more, thank God."

"Andreas—"

"Do not *Andreas* me; I have heard what plans the Chapter has in store for me. And now—wait!—you are going to tell me how on your knees you pleaded my cause, spoke of my sterling work at Rome on behalf of little Ermland, how I have taken up the banner in the crusade against the Teutonic Knights passed on to me by our dear late uncle— eh, brother, eh, are you going to tell me that?"

The Canon shook his head. "I know nothing of your doings, and so how should I plead such mitigation?"

Andreas glanced at him quickly, surprised despite himself at the coldness of his brother's tone. "Well, it's no matter," he growled. He eyed morosely the bare white walls. "Still stargazing, are you, brother?"

"Yes."

"Good, good. It's well to have some pastime." He sat down slowly at the Canon's desk and folded his ravaged hands on the knob of his stick.

127

His mouth, all eaten away at the corners, was fixed in a horrid leer. Extraordinary, that one could be so damaged and still live. It was spleen and spite, surely, that kept him going. He gazed through the bottled windowpanes at the blurred blue of the Baltic. "I will not be made to go," he said. "I will not be kicked out, like a dog. I am a canon of this Chapter, I have rights. You cannot compel me to go, whatever you do, and you may tell the holy canons that. I shall leave Frauenburg, yes, Prussia, I shall return to Rome, happily, but only when the interdict against me is lifted, and when my prebend and all my revenues are restored. Until then I shall remain here, frightening the peasants and drinking the blood of their daughters." Suddenly he laughed, that familiar dry scraping sound. "I am quite flattered, you know, by this unwonted notoriety. Is it not strange, that I had to begin visibly to rot before I could win respect? Life, brother, life is very odd. And now good day; I trust you will communicate my terms to your colleagues? I feel the message will carry more weight, coming from you, who are so intimately involved in the affair."

Max had been listening outside the door, for he entered at once unbidden, with the ghost of a grin on his lean face. At the foot of the stairs he and Andreas stopped and whispered together briefly; seemingly they had patched up their Heilsberg quarrel. The Canon shivered. He was cold.

*

The battle dragged on for three months. Chapter sessions grew more and more frantic. At one such meeting Andreas himself made an appearance, stumbled drunk into the conference hall and sat laughing among the outraged canons, mumbling and dribbling out of his ruined mouth. At length they panicked, and gave in. The seizure of his prebend was withdrawn, and he was granted a higher annuity. On a bleak day in January he left Frauenburg forever. He did not bid his brother goodbye, at least not in any conventional way; but Max, the Canon's sometime servant, went with him, saying he was sick of Prussia, only to return again that same night, not by road, however, but floating facedown on the river's back, a bloated gross black bag with a swollen purplish face and glazed eyes open wide in astonishment, grotesquely dead.

It rose up in the east like black smoke, stamped over the land like a ravening giant, bearing before it a brazen mask of the dark fierce face of Albrecht von Hohenzollern Ansbach, last Grand Master of the brotherhood of the Order of St Mary's Hospital of the Germans at Jerusalem, otherwise called the Teutonic Knights. Once again they were pushing westward, determined finally to break the Polish hold on Royal Prussia and unite the three princedoms of the southern Baltic under Albrecht's rule; once again the vice closed on little Ermland. In 1516 the Knights, backed up by gangs of German mercenaries, made their first incursions across the eastern frontier. They plundered the countryside, burnt the farms and looted the monasteries, raped and slaughtered, all with the inimitable fervent enthusiasm of an army that has had its bellyful of peace. It was not yet a fully fledged war, but a kind of sport, a mere tuning up for the real battle with Poland that was to come, and hence the bigger Ermland towns were left unmolested, for the present.

In November of that turbulent year Canon Koppernigk was appointed Land Provost, and transferred his residence to the great fortress of Allenstein, lying some twenty leagues south-east of Frauenburg in the midst of the great plain. It was an onerous and exacting post, but one with which, during the three years that he held it, he proved himself well fitted to cope. His duties included the supervision of Allenstein as well as the castle at nearby Mehlsack and the domains in those areas; he supervised also the collection of the tithes paid to the Frauenburg Chapter by the two towns and the villages and estates roundabout. At the end of each year he was required to submit to the Chapter a written report of all these affairs, a task to which he applied himself with scrupulous care and, indeed, probity.

But above all else he was responsible for ensuring that the areas under his control were fully tenanted. With the rise of the towns, the land over the previous hundred years had become steadily more and more depopulated, but now, with the Knights rampaging across the frontier, driving all before them, the exodus from the land to the urban centres had quickened alarmingly. Without tenants, so the Frauenburg Chapter reasoned, there would be no taxes, but beyond that immediate danger was the fear that the very fabric of society was unravelling. As long ago as 1494 the Prussian ordinances had imposed restrictions upon the peasants that had effectively made serfs of them—but what ordinance could hold a farmer locked to a burnt-out hovel and ravaged fields? During his three years as Provost, Canon Koppernigk dealt with seventy-five cases of resettlement of abandoned holdings, but even so he had barely scratched the surface of the problem.

Those were difficult and demoralising years for him, whose life hitherto had been lived almost entirely in the lofty empyrean of speculative science. Along with the rigours of his administrative duties came the further and far more wearying necessity of holding at arm's length, so to speak, the grimy commonplace world with which those duties brought him into unavoidable contact. For it *was* necessary to fend it off, lest it should contaminate his vision, lest its pervasive and, one might say, stubborn seediness should seep into the very coils of his thought and taint with earthiness the transcendant purity of his theory of the heavens. Yet he could not but feel for the plight of the people, whose pain and anguish was forever afterwards summed up for him in the memory of the corpse of a young peasant woman that he came upon in the smouldering ruins of a plundered village the name of which he did not even know. As he expressed it many years later to his friend and colleague Canon Giese: "The wench (for indeed she was hardly more than a child) had been tortured to death by the soldiery. I shall not describe to you, my dear Tiedemann, the state in which they had left her, although the image of that poor torn thing is burned ineradicably upon my recollection. They had worked on her for hours, laboured over her with infinite care, almost with a kind of obscene love, if I may express it thus, in order to ensure her as agonising a death as it was possible for them to devise. I realised then, perhaps (to my shame I say it!) perhaps for the *first time*, the inexpendable capacity for evil which there is in man. How, I asked myself then (I ask it now!), how can we hope to be redeemed, that would do such things to our fellow creatures?"

As well as Land Provost, he was also for a time head of the *Bro-teamt*, or Bread Office, at Frauenburg, in which capacity he had charge over the Chapter's bakeries and the malt and corn stores, the brewery, and the great mill at the foot of Cathedral Hill. Repeatedly he held the post of Chancellor, supervising the Chapter's records and correspondence and legal paperwork. Briefly too he was *Mortuarius*, whose task it was to administer the numerous and often considerable sums willed to the Church or donated by the families of the wealthy dead.

Along with these public duties, he was being called upon in another sphere, that of astronomy, to make himself heard in the world. His fame was spreading, despite the innate humility and even diffidence which had kept him silent for so long when others far less gifted than he were agitating the air with their empty babbling. Canon Bernhard Wapowsky of Cracow University, a learned and influential man, requested of him an expert opinion on the (defective, defective!) astronomical treatise lately put out by the Nuremberger, Johann Werner, a request with which Canon Koppernigk readily complied, glad of the opportunity to take a swipe at that proud foolish fellow who had dared to question Ptolemy. Then came a letter from Cardinal Schönberg of Capua, one of the Pope's special advisers, urging the learned Doctor to communicate in printed form his wonderful discoveries to the world. All this, of course, is not to mention the invitation that had come to him in 1514, by way of Canon Schiller in Rome (no longer the representative of the Frauenburg Chapter, but domestic chaplain to Leo X, no less), to take part in a Lateran Council on calendar reform. Canon Koppernigk refused to attend the council, however, giving as excuse his belief that such reform could not be carried out until the motions of the Sun and Moon were more precisely known. (One may remark here, that while this account—*ipse dixit*, after all!—of his unwillingness to accept what was most probably an invitation from the Pope himself, must be respected, one yet cannot, having regard to the date, and the stage at which we know the Canon's great work then was, help suspecting that the *learned Doctor*, to use Cardinal Schönberg's mode of address, was using the occasion to drop a careful hint of the revolution which, thirty years later, he was to set in train in the world of computational astronomy.)

Thus, anyway, it can be seen that, however unwillingly, he had become a public man. The Chapter was well pleased with him, and welcomed him at last as a true colleague. Some there were, it is true, who did not abandon their suspicions, remembering his extraordinary and unaccountable behaviour at the time of the distasteful affair of his outrageous brother's banishment. Among that section of the Chapter,

131

which included of course Canons Snellenburg and von der Trank, it was never finally decided whether the Doctor should be regarded as a villain because of his connection with the *poxed Italian* (as von der Trank, his pale sharp aristocratic nose a-twitch, had dubbed Andreas), or as a cold despicable brute who would not even rise to the defence of his own brother. While that kind of thing may be dismissed as the product merely of envy and spite, nevertheless there *was* something about Canon Koppernigk—all saw it, even the kindly and all-forgiving Canon Giese—a certain lack, a transparence, as it were, that was more than the natural aloofness and other-worldliness of a brilliant scientist. It was as if, within the vigorous and able public man, there was a void, as if, behind the ritual, all was a hollow save for one thin taut cord of steely inexpressible anguish stretching across the nothingness.

*

The spring of 1519 saw the sudden collapse of the political and military situation in the southern Baltic lands. Sigismund of Poland, perhaps at last recognising the truth of Bishop Waczelrodt's contention years before that the Cross represented a very real threat to his kingdom, summoned Grand Master Albrecht to Torun for peace talks. Albrecht refused to negotiate directly, and Poland immediately mobilised and marched on Prussia. Total war seemed inevitable. The Knights now suggested that the Bishop of Ermland should mediate between themselves and Sigismund. Bishop von Lossainen's health, however, was by this time seriously in decline. The Frauenburg Chapter, therefore, knowing well that little Ermland would be the theatre for the coming war, decided that in the Bishop's stead the Precentor, Canon Tiedemann Giese, along with Land Provost Koppernigk, should travel at once to Königsberg and attempt to reconcile the warring parties.

Were the wrong men chosen for the task? Precentor Giese thought so, afterwards. He had, he supposed, gone to Königsberg too inno· cently, with too much trust in the essential worthiness of men, and so had failed where a hard cold scheming fellow might have succeeded. Or was it that in his heart he had known all along that the mission was doomed to failure, and this knowledge had affected his ability to negotiate? Well well, who could say? From the start he had not believed that Albrecht, although a Lutheran, could be so black as he was painted. It

132

was said that he was irredeemably wicked, a monster, worse even than Hungary's infamous Vlad Drakulya the Impaler. But no, the good Precentor could not believe that. When he told his companion so, as they rode eastward through dawn mists along the coast at the head of their escort of Prussian mercenaries, Canon Koppernigk looked at him queerly and said:

"I would agree with you that likely he is no worse nor better than any other prince—but they are all bad."

"You are right, Doctor, perhaps, and yet . . ."

"Well?"

"You are right, yes, quite right. Ahem."

Precentor Giese was a little afraid of Canon Koppernigk; or perhaps that is too strong—perhaps a better word would be nervous, he was a little nervous of him, yes. There was at times a certain silent intensity, or ferocity even, about the man that alarmed those who came close to him, not that many were allowed to do so, of course, come close, that is. This morning, hunched in the saddle with his hat pulled low and his cloak wrapped about him to the nose so that only the eyes were visible, staring keenly ahead into the mist, he seemed more than ever burdened with a secret intolerable knowledge. Maybe it was this stoical air the Canon had of a man marked out for special suffering that made Giese's heart ache with sympathy and concern for his friend, if he, Giese, could call him, the Canon, a friend, as he was determined to do, justified or not.

But friendship aside, was it wise of the Chapter, Giese could not help wondering, to have sent the Canon with him on this delicate mission? He, the Canon, had always been something of a recluse, despite his public duties (which of course he fulfilled with impeccable et cetera), had always held the world at arm's length, as it were, and while this aspect of his character was not in any way a fault, indeed was only to be expected of one engaged in such important and demanding work as he was, it did mean that he was, so to say, unpractised in the subtleties of diplomacy, that he was, in fact, quite tactless, although it could be said that this very tactlessness, if that was what it was, was no more than evidence of a charming innocence and lack of guile. Well, not innocence perhaps . . . Canon Giese glanced at the dark figure in the saddle beside him: no, definitely not innocence.

O dear! The Precentor sighed. It was all very difficult.

They arrived at Königsberg as night came on. Their escort was allowed no further than the city gates. Albrecht's castle was a vast grim fortress on a hill. The two emissaries were led into a large white and gold hall. Crowds milled about here, soldiers, diplomats, clerics, ornate women, all going nowhere purposefully. Canon Koppernigk stood in silence waiting, wrapt in his black cloak, with his hat still on. Precentor Giese fidgeted. A band of courtiers, some armed, marched swiftly into the hall and wheeled to a halt. Grand Master Albrecht was a small quick reptile-like man with a thin dark face and pointed ears lying flat against his skull. His heavy quilted doublet and tight breeches gave him the look of a well-fed lizard. A gold medallion bearing the insignia of the Order hung by a heavy chain on his breast. (It was said that he was impotent.) He smiled briefly, displaying long yellow teeth.

"Reverend gentlemen," he said in German, "welcome. This way, please."

They all turned and marched smartly out of the hall, cutting a swathe through the obsequious crowd. Candles burned in a marble corridor. Their boots crashed on the cold stone. They wheeled into a small chamber hung with maps and a huge portrait of the Grand Master standing in an heroic pose before his massed army. Albrecht sat down at an oaken desk, while his party took up positions behind him with folded arms. Flunkeys came forward bearing chairs, and Albrecht with a quick gesture invited the Canons to sit. A silken diplomat leaned down and whispered in his ear. He nodded rapidly, pursing his mouth, and then looked up and said:

"We demand an oath of allegiance from the Bishop of Ermland and the Frauenburg Chapter. Mark, this is a condition of negotiation, not of settlement. We are prepared to speak to Poland through you only when we are assured of your loyalty." There was no bluster, no threat, only a brisk statement of fact. He was almost cheerful. He grinned. "Well?"

Precentor Giese was astounded. He had come to negotiate, not to take delivery of an ultimatum! He chose to disbelieve his ears.

"My dear sir," he said, "I fear you misunderstand the situation. Ermland is a sovereign princedom, and owes allegiance to its Prince-Bishop and clergy and none other. It was you yourself, you will recall, who requested us to mediate. Now—"

Albrecht was shaking his head.

"No no," he said gently, "no. It is you, I think, Herr Canon, who has misunderstood how matters are. Ermland is a small weak province. You wish to believe, or you wish *me* to believe, that you are, so to speak, an honest broker who observes matters with utter dispassion. But this war will be fought on your fields, in the streets of your towns and villages. Even if we fail to defeat Poland, as we may well fail, and even if we do not capture Royal Prussia, which is also possible I regret to say, nevertheless we shall certainly take Ermland. Sigismund will not protect you. Therefore why not join with us now and thus avoid a deal of . . . unpleasantness? Men who are anxious to win the favour of a prince present themselves to him with the possessions they value most: since you wish to win my favour in these negotiations, and since obviously you value loyalty most dearly, should you not in that case swear to be loyal to us?"

"But this is preposterous!" Giese cried, looking about him indignantly for support. He met only the cold eyes of the Grand Master's men ranged silently behind the desk. "Preposterous," he said again, but faintly.

Albrecht lifted his hands in a gesture of regret.

"Then there is nothing more to say," he said. There was a silence. He turned his sardonic faintly humorous gaze now for the first time on Canon Koppernigk, and his eyes gleamed. "Herr Canon, we are honoured by your presence. The fame of Doctor Copernicus is not unknown even in this far-flung province. We have heard of your wonderful theory of the heavens. We are eager to hear more. Perhaps you will dine with us tonight?" He waited. "You do not speak."

The Canon had turned somewhat pale. Giese was watching him expectantly. Now this insolent knight would receive the kind of answer he deserved! But, in a voice so low it could be hardly heard, Canon Koppernigk said only:

"There is nothing more to say."

Albrecht bowed his head, smiling thinly. "I meant, of course, Herr Canon, when I said what you have just echoed, that there is nothing more to say in these—ha—negotiations. On other, more congenial topics there is surely much we can discuss. Come, my dear Doctor, let us take a glass of wine together, like civilised men."

Then followed that curious exchange that Precentor Giese was to remember ever afterwards with puzzlement and grave misgiving. Canon Koppernigk grimaced. He seemed in some pain.

"Grand Master," he said, "you are contemplating waging war for the sake of sport. What is Ermland to you, or Royal Prussia? What is Poland even?"

Albrecht had been expecting something of the sort, for he answered at once:

"They are glory, Herr Doctor, they are posterity!"

"I do not understand that."

"But you do, I think."

"No. Glory, posterity, these are abstract concepts. I do not understand such things."

"You, Doctor?—you do not understand abstract concepts, you who have expressed the eternal truths of the world in just such terms? Come sir!"

"I will not engage in empty discussion. We have come to Königsberg to ask you to consider the suffering that you are visiting upon the people, the greater suffering that war with Poland will bring."

"The people?" Albrecht said, frowning. "What people?"

"The common people."

"Ah. The common people. But they have suffered always, and always will. It is in a way what they are for. You flinch. Herr Doctor, I am disappointed in you. The common people?—pah. What are they to us? You and I, *mein Freund*, we are lords of the earth, the great ones, the major men, the makers of supreme fictions. Look here at these poor dull brutes—" His thin dark hand took in the silent crowd behind him, the flunkeys, Precentor Giese, the painted army. "—They do not even understand what we are talking about. But *you* understand, yes, yes. The people will suffer as they have always suffered, meanly, mewling for pity and mercy, but only you and I know what true suffering is, the lofty suffering of the hero. Do not speak to me of the people! They are the brutish mask of war, but war itself is that which they in the ritual of their suffering express but can never comprehend, for their eyes are ever on the ground, while you and I look up, ever upward, into the blue! The people—peasants, soldiers, generals—they are my tool, as mathematics is yours, by which I come directly at the true, the eternal, the real. Ah yes, Doctor Copernicus, you and I—you and I! The generations may execrate us for what we do to their world, but we and those rare ones like us shall have made them what they are . . !" He broke off then and dabbed with a silk kerchief at the corners of his thin mouth. He had a smug drained sated look about him, that the troubled Precentor found himself comparing to that of a trooper fastening up his breeches after a particularly brutal and gratifying rape. Canon Koppernigk, his face ashen, rose in silence and turned to go. Albrecht, in the tone he might have used to remark upon the weather, said: "I had your uncle the Bishop poisoned, you know." The crowd behind him stirred, and Giese, halfway up from his chair, sat down again abruptly. Canon Koppernigk faltered, but would not turn. Albrecht said lightly, almost skittishly, to his hunched black back: "See, Doctor, how shocked they are? But *you* are not shocked, are you? Well then, say nothing. It is no matter. Farewell. We shall meet again, perhaps, when the times are better."

As they went down the hill from the castle, borne through the gleaming darkness on a river of swaying torches, Precentor Giese, confused and pained, tried to speak to his friend, but the Doctor would not hear, and answered nothing.

*

At dead of night to the castle of Allenstein they came, a hundred men and horse, Poland's finest, bearing the standard of their king before them, thundered over the drawbridge, under the portcullis, past the drowsing sentry into the courtyard and there dismounted amidst a great clamour of hoofs and rattling sabres and the roars of Sergeant Tod, a battle-scarred tough old soldier with a heart of stoutest oak. "Right lads!" he boomed, "no rest for you tonight!" and dispatched them at once to the walls. "Aw for fuck's sake, Sarge!" they groaned, but jumped to their post with alacrity, for each man knew in his simple way that they were here not only to protect a lousy castle and a pack of cringing bloody Prussians, but that the honour of Poland herself was at stake. Their Captain, a gallant young fellow, scion of one of the leading Polish families, covered with his cloak the proud glowing smile that played upon his lips as he watched them scramble by torchlight to the battlements, and then, pausing only to pinch the rosy cheek of a shy serving wench curtseying in the doorway, he hurried up the great main staircase with long-legged haste to the Crystal Hall where Land

137

Provost Koppernigk was deep in urgent conference with his be-
leaguered household. He halted on the threshold, and bringing his
heels together smartly delivered a salute that his commanding officer
would have been proud to witness.

The Canon looked up irritably. "Yes? What is it now? Who are
you?"

"Captain Chopin, Herr Provost, at your service!"

"Captain *what?*"

"I am an officer of His Gracious Majesty King Sigismund's First
Royal Cavalry, come this night from Mehlsack with one hundred of
His Highness's finest troops. My orders are to defend to the last man
this castle of Allenstein and all within the walls." ("O God be praised!"
cried several voices at once.) "Our army is on the march westward and
expects to engage the foe by morning. The Teutonic Knights are at
Heilsberg, and are bombarding the walls of the fortress there. As you
are aware, Herr Provost, they have already taken the towns of Gutt-
stadt and Wormditt to the north. A flanking assault on Allenstein is
expected hourly. These devils and their arch fiend Grand Master
Albrecht must be stopped—and they shall be stopped, by God's blood!
(Forgive a soldier's language, sire.) You will recall the siege of Frauenburg, how they fired the town and slaughtered the people without
mercy. Only the bravery of your Prussian mercenaries prevented them
from breaching the cathedral wall. Your Chapter fled to the safety of
Danzig, leaving to you, Herr Provost, the defence of Allenstein and
Mehlsack. However, in that regard, I must regretfully inform you now
that Mehlsack has been sacked, sire, and—"

But here he was interrupted by the hasty entrance of a large dark
burly man attired in the robes of a canon.

"Koppernigk!" cried Canon Snellenburg (for it is he), "they are
bombarding Heilsberg and it's said the Bishop is dead—" He stopped,
catching sight of the proud young fellow standing to attention in his
path. "Who are you?"

"Captain Chopin, sire, at your—"

"Captain *who?*"

Zounds! the Captain thought, are they all deaf? "I am an officer of
His Gracious—"

"Yes yes," said Snellenburg, waving his large hands. "Another
damned Pole, I know. Listen, Koppernigk, the bastards are at Heils-

138

berg. They'll be here by morning. What are you going to do?"

The Land Provost looked mildly from the Canon to the Captain, at his household crouched about the table, the secretaries, whey-faced clergy, minor administrators, and then to the frightened gaggle of servants ranged expectantly behind him. He shrugged.

"We shall surrender, I suppose," he said.

"For God's sake—!"

"Herr Provost—!"

But Canon Koppernigk seemed strangely detached from these urgent matters. He stood up from the table slowly and walked away with a look of infinite weary sadness. At the door, however, he halted, and turning to Snellenburg said:

"By the way, Canon, you owe me a hundred marks."

"*What?*"

"Some years ago I loaned you a hundred marks—you have not forgotten, I trust? I mention it only because I thought that, if we are all to be destroyed in the morning, we should make haste to set our affairs in order, pay off old scores—I mean debts—and so forth. But do not let it trouble you, please. Captain, good night, I must sleep now."

\*

The Knights did not attack, but instead marched south-west and razed the town of Neumark. Two thousand three hundred and forty-one souls perished in that onslaught. In the first days of the new year Land Provost Koppernigk sat in what remained of Neumark's town hall, recording in his ledger, in his small precise hand, the names of the dead. It was his duty. An icy wind through a shattered casement at his back brought with it a sharp tang of smoke from the smouldering wreckage of the town. He was cold; he had never known such cold.

\*   \*   \*

Frau Anna Schillings had that kind of beauty which seems to find relief in poor dress; a tall, fine-boned woman with delicate wrists and the high cheekbones typical of a Danziger, she appeared most at ease, and at her most handsome, in a plain grey gown with a laced bodice, and, perhaps, a scrap of French lace at the throat. Not for her the frills and flounces, the jewelled slippers and horned capuchons of the day. This attribute, this essential modesty of figure as well as of spirit, was now more than ever apparent, when circumstances had reduced a once lavish wardrobe to just one such gown as we have described. And it was in this very gown, with a dark cape wrapped about her shoulders against the cold, and her raven-black hair hidden under an old scarf, that she arrived in Frauenburg with her two poor mites, Heinrich and little Carla, at the beginning of that fateful year (how fateful it was to be she could not guess!), 1524.

As the physical woman prospered in misfortune, so too the spiritual found enhancement in adversity. Not for Frau Schillings the tears and tantrums with which troubles are most commonly greeted by the weaker sex. *It is life, and one must make the best of it:* such was her motto. This stoical fortitude had not always been easy to maintain: her dear Papa's early death had awakened her rudely from the happy dreaming of early girlhood; then there had been Mama's illness in the head. Nor was marriage the escape into security and happiness that she had imagined it would be. Georg . . . poor, irresponsible Georg! She could not, even now, after he had gone off with those ruffians and left her and the little ones to fend for themselves as best they might—even now she could not find it in her heart to hate him for his wanton ways. There was this to be said for him, that he had never struck her, as some husbands were only too prone to do; or at least he had never beaten her, not badly, at any rate. Yes, she said, with that gentle smile that all who knew her knew so well, yes, there are many worse than my Georg in the world! And how dashing and gay he could be, and even, yes, how loving, when he was sober. Well, he was gone now, most likely for good and ever, and she must not brood upon the past; she must make a new life for herself, and for the children.

War is a thing invented by men, and yet perhaps it is the women who suffer most in times of strife among nations. Frau Schillings had lost almost everything in the dreadful war that was supposed to have ended—her home, her happiness, even her husband. Georg was a tailor, a real craftsman, with a good sound trade among the better Danzig families. Everything had been splendid: they had nice rooms above the shop, and money enough to satisfy their modest needs, and then the babies had come, first Heinrich and, not long after, little Carla—O yes, it was, it was, splendid! But then the war broke out, and Georg got that mad notion into his head that there was a fortune to be made in tailoring for the mercenaries. She had to admit, of course, that he might be right, but it was not long before he began to talk wildly of the need to *follow the trade*, as he put it, meaning, as she realised with dismay, that they should become some kind of camp-followers, trailing along in the wake of that dreadful gang of ragamuffins that the Prussians called an army. Well she would have none of that, no indeed! She was a spirited woman, and there was more than one clash between herself and Georg on the matter; but although she was spirited, she *was* also a woman, and Georg, of course, had his way in the end. He shut up shop, procured a wagon and a pair of horses, and before she knew it they were all four of them on the road.

It was a disaster, naturally. Georg, poor dreamer that he was, had imagined war as a kind of stately dance in which two gorgeously (and expensively!) caparisoned armies made ritual feints at each other on crisp mornings before breakfast. The reality—grotesque, absurd, and hideously cruel—was a terrible shock. His visions of brocaded and beribboned uniforms faded rapidly. He spent his days patching breeches and bloodstained tunics. He even took to cobbling—he, a master tailor!—for the few pennies that were in it. He grew ever more morose, and began drinking again, despite all his promises. He struck Carla once, and frequently shook poor Heinrich, who was not strong, until his teeth rattled. It could not continue thus, and one morning (it was the birthday of the Prince of Peace) Frau Schillings awoke in the filthy hovel of an inn where they had lodged for the night to find that her husband had fled, taking with him the wagon and the horses, the purse with their few remaining marks, and even hers and the children's clothes—everything! The innkeeper, a venal rough brute, told her that Georg had gone off with a band a deserters led by one Krock, or Krack, some awful brutish name like that, and would she be so good now as to pay him what was owed for herself and the brats? She had no money? Well then, she would have to think of a way of paying him in kind then, wouldn't she? It is a measure of the woman's—we do not hesitate to say it—of the woman's *saintliness* that at first she did not understand what the beastly fellow was suggesting; and when he had told her precisely what he meant, she gave vent to a low scream and burst immediately into tears. Never!

As she lay upon that bed of shame, for she was forced in the end to allow that animal to have his evil way with her, she reflected bitterly that all this misfortune that had befallen her was due not to Georg's frailty, not really, but to a silly dispute between the King of Poland and that dreadful Albrecht person. How she despised them, princes and politicians, despised them all! And was she not perhaps justified? Are not our leaders sometimes open to accusations of irresponsibility on a scale far greater than ever the poor Georg Schillingses of this world may aspire to? And you may not say that this contempt was merely the bitter reaction of an empty-headed woman searching blindly for some symbol of the world of men which she might blame for wrongs partly wrought by her own lack of character, for Anna Schillings had been educated (her father had wanted a son), she could read and write, she knew something of the world of books, and could hold her own in logical debate with any man of her class. O yes, Anna Schillings had opinions of her own, and firm ones at that.

Those weeks following Georg's departure constituted the worst time that she was ever to know. How she survived that awful period we shall not describe; we draw a veil over that subject, and shall confine ourselves to saying that in those weeks she learned that there are abroad far greater and crueller scoundrels than that concupiscent innkeeper we have spoken of already.

She did survive, she did manage somehow to feed herself and the little ones, and after that terrible journey across Royal Prussia into northern Ermland, after that *via dolorosa*, she arrived, as we have said, at Frauenburg in January of 1524.

*

The best and truest friend of her youth, Hermina Hesse, was housekeeper to one of the canons of the Cathedral Chapter there. Hermina had been a high-spirited, self-willed girl, and although the years had smoothed away much of her abrasiveness, she was still a lively person, full of well-intentioned gaiety and given to gales of laughter at the slightest provocation. She had never been a beauty, it is true: her charms were rather of the homely, reassuring kind; but it was certainly *not* true to say, as some had said, that she looked and spoke like a beer waitress, that her life was a scandal and her eternal soul irretrievably lost. That kind of thing was put about by the "stuffed shirts", as she called them (with a defiant toss of the head that was so familiar)

142

among the Frauenburg clergy; as if *their* lives were free of taint, besotted gang of sodomites that they were! Was she to blame if the good Lord had blessed her with an abundant fruitfulness? Did they expect her to disown her twelve children? Disown them! why, she loved them just as much and more than any so-called respectable married matron could love her lawful offspring, and would have fought for them like a wildcat if anyone had dared (which no one did!) to try to take them away from her. Scandal, indeed—pah!

The two friends greeted each other with touching affection and tenderness. They had not met for . . . well, for longer than they cared to remember.

"Anna! Why Anna, what has happened?"

"O my dear," said Frau Schillings, "my dear, it has been so awful, I cannot tell you—!"

Hermina lived in a pleasant old white stone house on a hectacre of land some three leagues south of Frauenburg's walls. Certainly it was a well-appointed nest, but was it not somewhat isolated, Frau Schillings wondered aloud, when they had sat down in the pantry to a glass of mulled wine and fresh-baked poppyseed cake? The wine was wonderfully cheering, and the warmth of the stove, and the sight of her friend's familiar beaming countenance, comforted her greatly, so that already she had begun to feel that her agony of poverty and exile might be at an end. (And indeed it was soon to end, though not at all in the manner she expected!) Her little ones were making overtures in their shy tentative way to the children of the house. O dear! She felt suddenly near to tears: it was all so—so *nice*.

"Isolated, aye," Hermina said darkly, breaking in upon Frau Schillings's tender reverie. "I am as good as banished here, and that's the truth. The Canon has rooms up in the town, but I am kept from there—not by him, of course, you understand (he would not dare attempt to impose such a restriction on *me!*), but by, well, *others*. However, Anna dear, my troubles are nothing compared with yours, I think. You must tell me all. That swine Schillings left you, did he?"

Frau Schillings then related her sorry tale, in all its awful starkness, neither suppressing that which might shock, nor embellishing those details that indicated the quality of her character: in a word, she was brutally frank. She spoke in a low voice, with eyes downcast, her fine brow furrowed by a frown of concentration; and Hermina Hesse, that

143

good, kind, plump, stout-hearted, ruddy-cheeked woman, that pillar of fortitude, that light in the darkness of a naughty world, smiled fondly to herself and thought: Dear Anna! scrupulous to a fault, as ever. And when she had heard it all, all that heart-breaking tale, she took Frau Schillings's hands in hers, and sighed and said:

"Well, my dear, I am distressed indeed to hear of your misfortune, and I only wish that there was some way that I could ease your burden—"

"O but there is, Hermina, there is!"

"O?"

Frau Schillings looked up then, with her underlip held fast in her perfectly formed small white teeth, obviously struggling to hold back the tears that were, despite her valiant efforts, welling in her dark eyes.

"Hermina," said she, in a wonderfully steady voice, "Hermina, I am a proud person, as you well know from the happy days of our youth, as all will know who know anything at all of me; yet now I am brought low, and I must swallow that pride. I ask you, I beg of you, please—"

"Wait," said Hermina, patting the hands that still lay like weary turtle doves in her own, "dear Anna, wait: I think I know what you are about to say."

"Do you, Hermina, do you?"

"Yes, my poor child, I know. Let me spare you, therefore; let *me* say it: you want a loan."

Frau Schillings frowned.

"O no," she said, "no. Why, what can you think of me, to imagine such a thing? No, actually, Hermina, dearest Hermina, I was wondering if you could spare a room for myself and the children for a week or two, just to tide us over until—"

Hermina turned away with a pained look, and began to shake her head slowly, but at just that awkward moment they were interrupted by the sound of hoofbeats outside, and presently there entered by the rickety back door Canon Alexander Sculteti, a low-sized man in black, blowing on his chilled fists and swearing softly under his breath. He was thin, and had a red nose and small watchful eyes. He caught sight of Frau Schillings and halted, glancing from her to Hermina with a look of deep suspicion.

"Who's this?" he growled, but when Hermina began to explain her friend's presence, he waved his arms impatiently and stamped away

144

into the next room, thrusting a toddler roughly out of his path with a swipe of his boot. He was not a pleasant person, Frau Schillings decided, and certainly she had no intention of begging *him* for a place to stay. And yet, what was she to do if Hermina could not help her? Grey January weather loomed in the window. O dear! Hermina winked at her encouragingly, however, and followed the Canon into the next room, where an argument began immediately. Despite the noise that the children made (who now, having become thoroughly acquainted, seemed from the sounds to be endeavouring to push each other down the stairs, the dear little rascals), and even though she went so far as to cover her ears, she could not help hearing *some* of what was said. Hermina, although no doubt fighting hard on her friend's behalf, spoke in a low voice, while Canon Sculteti on the other hand seemed not to care who heard his unkind remarks.

"Let her stay here?" he yelled, "so that the Bishop can be told that I have installed another tart?" (O! Frau Schillings's hands flew to her mouth to prevent her from crying out in shame and distress.) "Woman, are you mad? I am in trouble enough with you and these damned brats. Do you realise that I am in danger not only of losing my prebend, but of being *excommunicated?* Listen, here is a plan—" He interrupted himself with a high-pitched whinny of laughter. "—Here is what to do: send her to Koppernigk—" (What was that name? Frau Schillings frowned thoughtfully . . .) "—He's in bad need of a woman, God knows. Ha!"

Summoning up all her courage, Anna Schillings rose and went straight into the room where they were arguing, and in a cold, dignified voice asked:

"Is this *Nicolas* Koppernigk that you speak of?"

Canon Sculteti, standing in the middle of the floor with his hands on his hips, turned to her with an unpleasant, sardonic grin. "What's that, woman?"

"I could not help overhearing—you mention the name Koppernigk: is this Canon Nicolas Koppernigk? For if so, then I must tell you that he is my cousin!"

*

Yes, she was a cousin to the famous Canon Koppernigk, or Doctor Copernicus, as the world called him now. Theirs was a tenuous

145

connection, it is true, on the distaff side, but yet it was to be the saving of Anna Schillings. She had never met the man, although she had heard talk of him in the family; there had been some scandal, she vaguely remembered, or was that to do with his brother . . ? Well, it was no matter, for who was *she* to baulk at a whiff of scandal?

Their first meeting was unpromising. Canon Sculteti took her that very night to Frauenburg (and was knave enough to make a certain suggestion on the way, which of course she spurned with the contempt it deserved); she left the children in the care of Hermina, for, as Sculteti in his coarse way put it, they did not want to frighten."old Koppernigk" to death with the prospect of a readymade family. The town was dark and menacing, bearing still the marks of war, burnt-out houses and crippled beggars and the smell of death. Canon Koppernigk lived in a kind of squat square fortress in the cathedral wall, a cold forbidding place, at the sight of which, in the slime of starlight, Frau Schillings's heart sank. Sculteti rapped upon the stout oak door, and presently a window above opened stealthily and a head appeared.

"Evening, Koppernigk," Sculteti shouted. "There is one here that would speak with you urgently." He sniggered under his breath, and despite the excited beating of her heart, Frau Schillings noted again what a lewd unpleasant man this Canon was. "Kin of yours!" he added, and laughed again.

The figure above spoke not a word, but withdrew silently, and after some long time they heard the sound of slow footsteps within, and the door opened slowly, and Canon Nicolas Koppernigk lifted a lighted candle at them as if he were fending off a pair of demons.

"Here we are!" said Sculteti, with false joviality. "Frau Anna Schillings, your cousin, come to pay you a visit. Frau Schillings—Herr Canon Koppernigk!" And so saying he took himself off into the night, laughing as he went.

*

Canon Koppernigk, then in his fifty-first year, was at that time laden heavily with the responsibilities of affairs of state. On the outbreak of war between the Poles and the Teutonic Knights, the Frauenburg Chapter almost in its entirety had fled to the safety of the cities of Royal Prussia, notably Danzig and Torun; he, however, had gone into the very midst of the battlefield, so to speak, to the castle of Allenstein,

146

where he held the post of Land Provost. Then, after the armistice of 1521, he had in April of that year returned to Frauenburg as Chancellor, charged by Bishop von Lossainen (rumours of whose death in the siege of Heilsberg had happily proved unfounded) with the task of reorganising the administration of the province of Ermland, a task that at first had seemed an impossibility, since under the terms of the armistice the Knights retained those parts of the princedom which their troops were occupying at the close of hostilities. There was also the added difficulty of the presence in the land of all manner of deserter and renegade, who spread lawlessness and disorder through the countryside. However, by the following year the Land Provost had succeeded to such a degree in restoring normalcy that his faint-hearted colleagues could consider it safe enough for them to creep out of hiding and return to their duties.

Even yet the demands of public life did not slacken, for with the death at last, in January of 1523, of Bishop von Lossainen, the Chapter was compelled to take up the reins of government of the turbulent and war-torn bishopric; once again the Chapter turned to Canon Koppernigk, and he was elected Administrator General, which post he held until October, when a new Bishop was installed. In all this time he had been working on a detailed report of the damage wrought by the war in Ermland, which he was to present as a vital document in the peace talks at Torun. Also he had drawn up an elaborate and complex treatise setting forth means whereby the debased monetary system of Prussia might be reformed, which had been requested of him by the King of Poland. Nor was he spared personal sorrow: shortly after hearing of the death at Kulm of his sister Barbara, he received news from Italy that his brother Andreas had succumbed finally to that terrible disease which for many years had afflicted him. Small wonder then, with all this, that Canon Koppernigk appeared to Frau Schillings a reserved and distracted, cold, strange, solitary soul.

On that first night, when Sculteti abandoned her as he would some ridiculous and tasteless practical joke on his doorstep, the Canon stared at her, with a mixture of horror and bafflement, as if she were an apparition out of a nightmare. He backed away from her up the dark narrow stairs, still holding the candle at arm's length like a talisman brandished in the face of a demon. In the observatory he put his desk between himself and her. For the second time that day, Frau

Schillings related her tale of woe, haltingly, with many omissions this time, holding her hands clasped upon her bodice. He watched her with a kind of horrified fascination, but she could plainly see that he was not taking in the half of what she said. He seemed to her a kindly man, for all his reserve.

"I'll not mince words, Herr Canon," she said. "I have begged, I have whored, and I have survived; but now I have nothing left. You are my last hope. Refuse me, and I shall perish."

"My child," he began, and stopped, helpless and embarrassed. "My child . . ."

Moonlight shines through the arched window; the candle flickers. The books, the couch, the desk, all crouch like enchanted creatures frozen in the midst of a secret dance, and those strange ghostly instruments lift their shrouded arms into the shadows starward, mysterious, hieratic and inexplicable things. All fade; the dark descends.

*   *   *

*Nicolas Koppernigk, Canonicus: Frauenburg*

    Rev. Sir: I presume to write to you, remembering our many interesting conversations of some years ago, when we met at Cracow. I was then adviser to the Polish King, & you, as I recall, were secretary to your late uncle, His Grace Bishop Waczelrodt: on whose death may I be permitted now to offer you belated condolences. I admired the man greatly (although I knew him not at all), & would hear more of his life & works. His death was indeed a tragedy for Ermland, as events have proved. I dearly hope that your many public duties do not keep you from that great task which you are embarked upon. Many wonderful reports of your theories come to me, especially from Cardinal Schönberg at Rome, whom I think you know. You are fortunate indeed to have such allies, who surely will stand you in good stead against the bellowing of ignorant schoolmen & those others that you have outraged by the daring of your concepts. For myself, I have so little power at my command that I hesitate to assure you that you have my best wishes for your great & important work, which I pray God to bless, in the name of Truth. I hesitate, as I have said: yet who can know but that even the friendship of one so humble as myself may not at some future date prove useful? The Church in these perilous days, I fear, shall not for long be able to sustain that generous liberality which hitherto She was wont to extend to Her ministers (a liberality, I might add, for which I myself have been grateful on more than one occasion!). Dark times are coming, Herr Canon: we are all under threat. However, it is my conviction that, so long as we maintain strict vigilance over our lives, & do not leave ourselves open to accusations of corruption & lewdness by the Lutherans, we shall be safe, no matter how *revolutionary* our notions. I pray you, sir, regard me as your most devoted friend.

*ex Löbau, 11 November, 1532*
*+Johannes Dantiscus*
*Bishop of Kulm*

*

*Tiedemann Giese, Visitator: at Allenstein*
Dear Giese: I have had a letter from Dantiscus, which I enclose herewith: please tell me what you think of it, & how I should reply. I do not trust the man. He has a daughter in Spain, they say. Perhaps our own Bishop has asked him to write to me thus? I suspect a conspiracy against me. Destroy this letter, but send back the other, with your suggestions as to how I should proceed. I am not well: a catarrh of the stomach, & my bowels do not move, as usual. I think I shall not reply to him. Please say what I am to do.

*ex Franenburg, 16 December, 1532*
*Nic: Koppernigk*

*

*Johannes Dantiscus, Bishop of Kuim Löbau*
I have Your Rev. Lordship's letter, full of humanity & favour, in which he reminds me of that familiarity with Your Rev. Lordship which I contracted in my youth: which I know to have remained just as vigorous up to now. As for the information you required of me, how long my uncle, Lucas Waczelrodt of blessed memory, had lived: he lived 64 years, 5 months; was Bishop for 23 years; died on the last day but one of March, *anno Christi* 1512. With him came to an end a

149

family whose insignia can be found on the ancient monuments in Torun. I recommended my obedience to Your Rev. Lordship.

*ex Frauenburg, 11 April, 1533*
*Nic: Koppernigk: Canonicus*

\*

*Johannes Dantiscus, Bishop of Kulm: Löbau*

My Lord: I write to you on behalf of one that is dear to us both: *id est* Doctor Nicolas Copernicus, the astronomer, & Canon of this Chapter. As you are aware, the Frauenburg canons shall assemble this month for the purpose of electing a Bishop to the throne of Ermland, following the lamented death of Our Rev. Lordship Mauritius Ferber. The list of candidates, decided upon, as is the custom, by His Royal Highness Sigismund of Poland, comprises four names: Canons Zimmermann, von der Trank, & Snellenburg: the fourth name you know, of course. While it is not my wish to attempt to influence the course of this lofty affair, I feel it my duty humbly to suggest that one of these names, that of Canon Heinrich Snellenburg, be removed from the list, in order to protect the Chapter from ridicule, & the Polish throne (whose interests I hold as closely to my heart as does Your Rev. Lordship) from accusations of gross misjudgment. Your Lordship knows the manner of man it is that I speak of here. Canon Snellenburg is not a great sinner: but the very pettiness of his misdemeanours (unpaid debts et cetera) surely must exclude him from consideration as a candidate for this highest of offices. Therefore I suggest that he be removed forthwith from the list, his name to be replaced by that of Canon Nicolas Koppernigk. The Rev. Doctor, need I say, does not aspire to so high an office as the Bishopric of Ermland (and is not aware of this petition, be assured of that): yet even to name him a candidate would, I feel, & I think I am not alone in this opinion, be an indication, however subtle, of the high regard in which the Rev. Doctor is held both by the Church & the Polish throne: it would also, of course, be a means of arming him against his enemies, who are, alas, legion. Doctor Copernicus is an old man now, & in ill-health. He does not sleep well, & is plagued by hallucinations: sometimes he speaks of dark figures that hide in the corners of his room. All this indicates how he feels himself threatened & mocked by a hostile world. Your Rev. Lordship's generous praise for his great work (which even yet he refuses to

150

publish, for fear of what reaction it may provoke!) is not universally echoed: not long ago, the Lutheran Rector of the Latin School at Elbing, one *Ludimagister* Gnapheus, ridiculed the master's astronomical ideas (or those debased versions of them that this Gnapheus in his ignorance understands) in his so-called comedy, *Morosophus*, or *The Wise Fool*, which was performed publicly in that city as a carnival farce. (However, in this respect, as the Rev. Doctor himself remarked, Master Gnapheus has obviously never heard of the divine Cusan's great work, *De docta ignorantia*, or he would have seen the irony of choosing for his scurrilous farce the title that he did!) As another example of how the Doctor is persecuted, Your Rev. Lordship will forgive me, I hope, for mentioning this absurd but painful incident: Some ten years ago, a young girl was brought to him here in order that, in his capacity as physician, he might treat her for an unspeakable disease which the child had contracted we know not how. He could do nothing, of course, for the disease was already far advanced. The girl has since died at the Cistercian Convent in Kulm, & now her father, mad with grief no doubt, has begun to put it about that the Rev. Doctor is to blame for the tragedy, for the girl said, so the father claims, that when he was examining her he cast a spell upon her, making passes with his hands & speaking a strange word that she could not understand et cetera. The accusation is absurd, of course, but Your Lordship will understand how these things go; matters have come to such a pass that the sick will no longer trust themselves to his care. However, I fear that by now I have begun to stretch Your Lordship's patience with my ramblings. Let me close by saying that, having considered all these factors which I have mentioned, Your Lordship will recognise that our beloved Canon Nicolas deserves whatever honours it may be in our power to bestow upon him—& deserves also whatever small comforts, of the spirit *or of the flesh*, that he is himself able to wrest from a cruel world.

> *ex Frauenburg, 10 September, 1537*
> *Tiedemann Giese: Canonicus*

*

*Tiedemann Giese, Bishop of Kulm: Löbau*
  Lord Bishop: Disturbing reports continue to reach me regarding the Rev. Doctor & this matter of the woman, Anna Schillings. It is

suggested that he keeps her as his *focaria*, & that she fulfils *all duties* attaching to such a position, being housekeeper & also concubine. I obliged you, my Lord, by substituting his name for that of Snellenburg on the King's List, despite the grave reservations which I entertained at the time, for I confess that the substitution of the name of one sinner by that of another did not recommend itself to me as a wise act: however, I did so because of the high regard I had for the Doctor's work, if not for his character. Now I think that I should have been swayed not by your arguments & entreaties, but by my own feelings. Anyway, the matter is past: I mention it only so that you may now repay this favour by speaking to him, & encouraging him to put away this woman. *He must yield.* There is more at stake now than the reputation of the Frauenburg Chapter. He maintains close friendship with Sculteti: that is bad. Admonish him that such connections & friendships are harmful to him, but do not tell him that the warning originates from me. I am sure that you know that Sculteti has taken a wife, & is suspected of atheism.

*ex Heilsberg, 4 July, 1539*
*+ Johannes Dantiscus*
*Bishop of Ermland*

\*

*Johannes Dantiscus, Bishop of Ermland: Heilsberg*
My dear Lord Bishop: Doctor Nicolas is staying with us briefly here, along with a young disciple. I have spoken earnestly to the Rev. Doctor on the matter, according to Your Most Rev. Lordship's wish, & have set the facts of the matter plainly before him. He seemed not a little disturbed that although he had unhesitatingly obeyed the will of Your Rev. Lordship, malicious people still bring trumped-up charges of secret meetings, & so forth. For he denies having seen that woman since he dismissed her. I have certainly ascertained that he is not as much affected as many think. Moreover, his advanced age & his never-ending studies readily convince me of this, as well as the worthiness & respectability of the man: nevertheless I urged him that he should shun even the appearance of evil, & this I believe he will do. But again I think that it would be as well that Your Rev. Lordship should not put too much faith in the informer, considering that envy attaches so easily

152

to men of worth, & is unafraid even of troubling Your Most Rev. Lordship. I commend myself et cetera.

*ex Löbau, 12 August, 1539*
*+ Tiedemann Giese*
*Bishop of Kulm*

*

*Johannes Dantiscus, Bishop of Ermland: Heilsberg*

Your Grace . . . As regards the Frauenburg wenches, Sculteti's hid for a few days in his house. She promised that she would go away together with her children. Sculteti remains in his curia with his *focaria*, who looks like a beer waitress tainted with every evil. The woman of Doctor Nicolas sent her baggage ahead to Danzig, but she herself stays on at Frauenburg . . .

*ex Allenstein, 20 October, 1539*
*Heinrich Snellenburg: Visitator*

*

*Nicolas Koppernigk: Frauenburg*

Sir: I write to you directly in the hope that you may be made to understand the peril into which you have delivered yourself by your stubborn refusal to yield upon the matter of the woman, Anna Schillings. Surely you realise how great are the issues at stake? If it were merely a matter of this *focaria*, I should not be so intemperate as to hound you thus, but it is more than that, much more, as you must know. On my recommendation, Canon Stanislas Hosius was nominated candidate for the office of Precentor of the Frauenburg Chapter. I shall dare to be frank, my dear Doctor: I do not like Hosius, I do not like what he represents. He is a fanatic. You & I, my friend, are children of another age, a finer & more civilised age: but that age is past. Some years ago I warned you that dark times were coming: that darkness is upon us now, & its avatars are Canon Hosius and his ilk—the inquisitors, the fanatics. I do not like him, as I have said, yet I appointed him to a canonry at Frauenburg, & would see him Precentor: for, like him or not, I must accept him. For Ermland, the future is one of two choices: this province must become either Prussian & Lutheran, or Polish & Catholic. There is no third course. The autonomy of which your uncle was the architect & guardian is about to be taken from us. The choice, then, is clear: whatever our feelings regard-

153

ing Poland, we must bow to the Jagellon throne, or perish. Now, the Frauenburg Chapter, foolishly allowing itself to be misled by forces who have not the good of Ermland, nor Frauenburg, at heart, has elected the unspeakable Sculteti to be Precentor, thereby thwarting my carefully laid plans. This is intolerable. Do those damned clerics among whom you have chosen to live not realise that Sculteti is backed by that faction at the Papal Court which imagines that Ermland can be brought under the direct control of Rome? Even if this were feasible, which it is not, Rome rule would spell disaster for all of us. *We must cleave to Poland!* It is the only course. I must have Hosius: & the corollary of that need is that I must destroy Sculteti. I shall use whatever weapons against him that I can find. The scandalous manner of his life is one such weapon, perhaps the most lethal. I trust that these revelations, which I am foolish to commit to paper, will make clear why, for so many years, I have striven to force you to be rid of this woman. This shall be my last warning; ignore it, & you shall be in grave danger of going down along with Sculteti when he falls. That is all I have to say. *Vale.*

> *ex Heilsberg, 13 March, 1540*
> *+ Johannes Dantiscus*
> *Bishop of Ermland*

*

*Johannes Dantiscus, Bishop of Ermland: Heilsberg*

*Reverendissime in Christo Pater et Domine Clementissime!* I have received Your Rev. Lordship's letter. I understand well enough Your Lordship's grace & good will toward me: which he has condescended to extend not only to me, but to other men of great excellence. It is, I believe, certainly to be attributed not to my merits, but to the well-known goodness of Your Rev. Lordship. Would that some time I should be able to deserve these things. I certainly rejoice, more than can be said, to have found such a Lord & Patron.

I have done what I neither would nor could have left undone, whereby I hope to have given satisfaction to Your Rev. Lordship's warning.

> *ex Frauenburg, 3 July, 1540*
> *Your Rev. Lordship's most devoted*
> *Nicolas Copernicus*

154

*

*Tiedemann Giese, Bishop of Kulm: Löbau*

My dear Tiedemann: Sculteti has been expelled from the Chapter, & banished by Royal Edict. He will go to Rome, I think, as do all outcasts. His *focaria*, the Hesse woman, has disappeared. What a lot of trouble she caused! It occurs to me that our *Frauenburg* is aptly named. I have issued yet another edict of my own against Frau Schillings, but she refuses to go. I am touched, truly, by her devotion to a sick old man, & have not the heart to make her understand that it would be altogether best if she were to go. Anyway, where would she go to? So I await, without great interest, Dantiscus's next move. Do I seem calm? I am not. I am afraid, Tiedemann, afraid of what the world will think to do to me that it has not done already: the filthy world that will not let me be, that comes after me always, a black monster, dragging its damaged wings in its wake. Ah, Tiedemann . . .

*ex Frauenburg, 31 December, 1540*

*

Waterborne he comes, at dead of night, sliding sleek on the river's gleaming back, snout lifted, sniffing, under the drawbridge, the portcullis, past the drowsing sentry. Brief scrabble of claws on the slimed steps below the wall, brief glint of a bared tooth. In the darkness for an instant an intimation of agony and anguish, and the night flinches. Now he scales the wall, creeps under the window, grinning. In the shadow of the tower he squats, wrapt in a black cloak, waiting for dawn. Comes the knocking, the pinched voice, the sly light step on the stair, and how is it that I alone can hear the water . . ?

# III

———

*Cantus Mundi*

I, Georg Joachim von Lauchen, called Rheticus, will now set down the true account of how Copernicus came to reveal to a world wallowing in a stew of ignorance the secret music of the universe. There are not many who will admit that if I had not gone to him, the old fool would never have dared to publish. When I arrived in Frauenburg I was little more than a boy (a boy of genius, to be sure!), yet he recognised my brilliance, that was why he listened to me, yes. Princes of Church and State had in vain urged him to speak, but *my* arguments he heeded. To you, now, he is Copernicus, a titan, remote and unknowable, but to me he was simply Canon Nicolas, preceptor and, yes! friend. They say I am mad. Let them. What do I care for a jealous world's contumely? They drove me out, denied me my fame and honoured name, banished me here to rot in this Godforgotten corner of Hungary that they call Cassovia—yet what of it? I am at peace at last, after all the furious years. An old man now, yes, a forlorn and weary wanderer come to the end of the journey, I am past caring. But I don't forgive them! No! *The devil shit on the lot of you.*

*

My patron, the Count, is a noble gentleman. Cultured, urbane, brilliant, generous to a fault, he reminds me in many ways of myself when I was younger. We speak the same language—I mean of course the *language of gentlemen*, for in Latin it's true he is a little . . . rusty. Not like Koppernigk, whose schoolman's Latin was impeccable, while for the rest, well, his people were, after all, in trade. The Count saw in me one of his own kind, and welcomed me into the castle here (as house physician) when the others chose to forget me and the great work I have done. He dismisses with characteristic hauteur the vile slanders they fling at me, and laughs when they whisper to him behind their hands that I am mad. The Count, unfortunately, *is* mad, a little. It comes from the mother's side, I think: bad blood there without a doubt. Yes, I must exercise more caution, for he is capricious. Be less arrogant in his presence, grovel now and then, yes yes. Still, he needs me, we both know that. What, I ask, without me, would he do for the conversation, the intellectual stimulation, which save him from going altogether out of his mind? This country is populated with swineherds and witches and cretinous priests. I was a new star in his sparse firmament. Anyway, why should I worry?—the world is full of Counts, but there is only one Doctor Rheticus. It is not, the world, I mean, full of Counts, so go easy. What was I . . ? Copernicus, of course. Forty years ago— forty years!—I came to him.

Frauenburg: that hole. It clings to the Baltic coast up there at the outermost edge of the earth, and someday please God it will drop off, like a scab. My heart sank when first I beheld that grey fortress wall. It was 1539, summer supposedly, although the rain poured down, and there was a chill white wind off the sea. I remember the houses, like clenched fists, bristling within the gates. *Clenched* is the word: that was Frauenburg, clenched on its own ignorance and bitterness and Catholicism. Was it for this I had abandoned Wittenberg, the university, my friends and confraters? Not that Wittenberg was all that much better, mind you, but the meanness was different; in the corridors of the university they were still jabbering about freedom and change and redemption, parroting the Reformer's raucous squawks, but behind all that fine talk there lurked the old terror, the despair, of those who know full well and will not admit it that the world is rotten, irredeemable. In those days I believed (or had myself convinced that I did) that we were on the threshold of the New Age, and I took part with gusto in the game, and jabbered with the best of them. How could I do otherwise? At twenty-two I held the chair of mathematics and astronomy at the great University of Wittenberg. When the world favours you so early and so generously, you feel it your duty to support its pathetic fictions. I am inside the gates of Frauenburg.

Once inside the gates of Frauenburg, then, I went straightway to the cathedral, dragging my bags and books behind me through the sodden streets. From the cathedral I was directed to the chapterhouse, where I encountered no little difficulty in gaining entry, for they speak a barbaric dialect up there, and furthermore the doorkeeper was deaf. At length the fellow abandoned all attempt to decode my immaculate German, and grudgingly let me into a cavernous dark room where bloodstained idols, their Virgin and so forth, peered eerily out of niches in the walls. Presently there came a sort of scrabbling at the door, and an aged cleric entered crabwise, regarding me suspiciously out of the corner of a watery eye. I must have seemed a strange apparition there in the gloom, grinning like a gargoyle and dripping rain on his polished floor. He advanced apprehensively, keeping firmly between us the big oak table that stood in the middle of the room. His gaze was uncannily like that of the statues behind him: guarded, suspicious, hostile even, but ultimately indifferent. When I mentioned the name of Copernicus I thought he would take to his heels (was the astronomer then a leper even among his colleagues?), but he concealed his consternation as best he could, and merely smiled, if that twitch could be called a smile, and directed me to—where?—the cathedral. I held my temper. He frowned. I had been to the cathedral already? Ah, then he was afraid he could not help me. I asked if I might wait, in the hope that he whom I sought might in time return here. O! well, yes, yes of course, but now that he thought of it, I might perhaps enquire at the house of Canon Suchandsuch, at the other end of the town, for at this hour the Herr Doctor was often to be found there. And I was bustled out into the streets again.

Do you know what it is like up there in the grey north? Now I have nothing against rain—indeed, I think of it as a bright link between air and angels and us poor earthbound creatures—but up there it falls like the falling of dusk, darkening the world, and in that wet gloom all seems stale and flat, and the spirit aches. Even in spring there is no glorious drenching, as there is elsewhere, when April showers sweep through the air like showers of light, but only the same dull thin drip drip drip, a drizzle of tangible *accidie*, hour after hour. Yet that day I marched along regardless through those mean streets, my feet in the mire and my head swathed in a golden mist, ah yes, it has been ever

161

thus with me: when I set my mind on something, then all else disappears, and today I could see one thing only, the historic confrontation (for already I pictured our meeting set like a jewel in the great glittering wheel of history) between von Lauchen of Rhaetia and Doctor Copernicus of Torun. But the Herr Doctor was proving damnably elusive. At the house of Canon Suchandsuch (the name was Snellenburg, I remember it now), the dolt of a steward or whatever he was just looked at me peculiarly and shook his thick head slowly from side to side, as if he felt he was dealing with a large lunatic child.

I ferreted him out in the end, never mind how. I've said enough to demonstrate the lengths he would go to in order to protect himself from the world. He lived in a tower on the cathedral wall, a bleak forbidding eyrie where he perched like an old ill-tempered bird, beak and talons at the ready. I had my foot in the door before the housekeeper, Anna Schillings, his *focaria*, that bitch (more of *her* later) could slam it in my face—and I swear to God that if she had, I would have burst it in, brass studs, hinges, locks and all, with my head, for I was desperate. I dealt her a smile bristling with fangs, and she backed off and disappeared up the narrow stairs, at the head of which she presently reappeared and beckoned to me, and up there in the half dark (it's evening now) before a low arched door she abandoned me with a terrible look. I waited. The door with a squeak opened a little way. A face, which to my astonishment I recognised, peered around it cautiously, and was immediately withdrawn. There were some furtive scuffling sounds within. I knocked, not knowing what else to do. A voice bade me come in. I obeyed.

*

At my first, I mean my second—third, really—well, my first as it were *official* sight of him, I was surprised to find him smaller than I had anticipated, but I suppose I expected him to be a giant. He stood at a lectern with his hands on the open pages of a bible, I think it was a bible. Astronomical instruments were laid out on a table near him, and through the open window at his back could be seen the Baltic and the great light dome of the evening sky (rain stopped, cloud lifting, the usual). His expression was one of polite enquiry, mild surprise. I forgot the speech I had prepared. I imagine my mouth hung open. It was the same old man that had met me at the chapter-house, that is, he was

Copernicus, I mean they were one and the same—yes yes! the same, and here he was, gazing at me with that lugubrious glazed stare, pretending he had never set eyes on me before now. Ach, it depresses me still. Did he imagine I would not recognise him in this ridiculous pose, this stylised portrait of a scientist in his cell? He did not care! If his carefully composed expression was not free of a faint trace of unease, that uneasiness sprang from concern for the polish of his performance and not from any regard for me, nor from shame that his contemptible trick had been discovered. He might have been masquerading before a mirror. *Copernicus did not believe in truth.* He had no faith in truth. You are surprised? Listen—

O but really, all this is unworthy of me, of the subject. Two of the greatest minds of the age (one, at least, was great, *is* great) met that day, and I describe the momentous occasion as if it were a carnival farce. It is all gone wrong. The rain, the difficulty of finding him, that absurd pose, I did not intend to mention any of this trivia. Why is it not possible to speak of things calmly and accurately? My head aches. I could never achieve the classic style; one must have a grave turn of mind for that, a sense of the solemn pageantry of life, an absolutely unshakeable faith in the notion of order. Order! Ha! I must pause here, it is too late, too dark, to continue. The wolves are howling in the mountains. After such splendours, my God, how have I ended up in this wilderness? My head!

*

Now, where was I? Ah, I have left poor Canon Nicolas petrified all night before his lectern and his bible, posing for his portrait. He was in sixty-sixth year, an old man whose robes, cut for a younger, stouter self, hung about him in sombre folds like a kind of silt deposited by time. His face—teeth gone in the slack mouth, skin stretched tight on the high northern cheekbones—had already taken on that blurred, faded quality that is the first bloom of death. Thus must my own face appear now to others. Ah . . . He wore no beard, but the morning blade, trembling in an unsteady grip, had left unreaped on his chin and in the deep cleft above the upper lip a few stray grizzled hairs. A velvet cap sat upon his skull like a poultice. This, surely, was not that Doctor Copernicus, that great man, whom I had come to Frauenburg to find! The eyes, however, intense and infinitely clever, and filled with what I can only call an exalted cunning, identified him as the one I sought.

Nor was his observatory what I had thought it would be. I had expected something old-fashioned, it's true, a cosy little lair full of scholarly clutter, books and manuscripts, parchments crawling with complex calculations, all this draped in the obligatory membrane of vivid dust. Also, unaccountably, I had expected warmth, thick yellow warmth, like a species of inspirational cheese, in which would be embedded in his mellow old age the master, a jolly old fellow, absent-minded and unworldly, but sharp, sharp, putting the finishing touches to his masterpiece preparatory to unleashing it upon an unsuspecting world. The room I was in, however, was straight out of the last century, if not the one before, and more like an alchemist's cell than the workroom of a great modern scientist. The white walls were bare as bone, the beamed ceiling too. I saw no more than a handful of books. The instruments on the table had the self-conscious look of things that have been brought out for display. The window let in a hard merciless light. And the cold! Science here was not the cheerful, confident quest for certainties that *I* knew, but the old huggermugger of spells and talismans and secret signs. A leering death's-head and a clutch of dried batwings would not have surprised me. The air reeked of the chill sweat of guilt.

I did not take in all this detail at once—although it was all registered in my sense of shock—for at first I was distracted by waiting for him to offer some excuse, or at least explanation, regarding our prior meeting. When I realised, to my surprise and puzzlement (remember, I did not know him yet as I was to come to know him later), that he had no intention of doing so, I knew there was nothing for it but to play, as best I could, the part of the simpering idiot that obviously he considered me to be. In the circumstances, then, something dramatic was required. I crossed the room, I *bounded* across the room, and with my face lifted in doglike veneration I genuflected before him, crying:

"*Domine praeceptor!*"

Startled, he backed away from me, mumbling under his breath and trying not to see me, but I hobbled after him, still on one knee, until a corner of the table nudged him in the rear and he jumped in fright and halted. The instruments on the table, quivering from the collision, set up a tiny racket of chiming and chattering that seemed in the sudden silence to express exactly the old man's panic and confusion. You see?

You see? How can I be expected to be grave?

"Who are you?" he demanded petulantly, and did not bother to listen when I told him my name a second time. "You are not from the Bishop, are you?" He watched me carefully.

"No, *Meister*, I know no Bishop, nor king nor prince; I am ruled only by the greatest of lords, which is science."

"Yes yes, well, get up, will you, get up."

I rose, and rising suddenly remembered the words of my speech, which I delivered, in one breath, at high speed. Very flowery. *Sat verbum.*

Throughout that meeting we moved in circles about the room in a slow stealthy chase, he leading, keeping well out of my reach for fear I might attempt a sudden assault, and I following hard upon his heels uttering shrill cries of adoration and entreaty, throwing my arms about and tripping over the furniture in my excitement. We communicated (communicated!) in a kind of macaronic jabber, for whereas I found German most natural, the Canon was wont to lapse into Latin, and no sooner did I join him than we found ourselves stumbling into the vernacular again. O, it was great fun, truly. He was singularly unimpressed by my academic pedigree; his face took on a look of frank horror when it dawned upon him that I was a Lutheran—holy God, one of *them!* What would the Bishop say? But hold hard, Rheticus, hold hard now, you must be fair to him. Yes, I must be fair to him. I cannot in fairness blame a timorous cleric, who desired above all *not to be noticed*, for his dread at the arrival in his tower fortress of a firebrand from Protestant Wittenberg. Three months previous to my coming, the Bishop, Dantiscus the sleek, had issued an edict ordering all Lutherans out of Ermland on pain of dispossession or even death, and shortly thereafter he was to issue another, calling for all heretical—meaning Lutheran, *natürlich*—books and pamphlets to be burned in public. A nice gentleman, Dantiscus the bookburner: I shall have some more to say of him presently.

(In fairness to *myself*, I must add that Wittenberg considered Copernicus at best a madman, at worst the Antichrist. Luther himself, in one of those famous after-dinner harangues, amid the belches and the farts, had sneered at the notion of a heliocentric universe, thus displaying once again his unfailing discernment; so also had Melanchton mocked the theory—even Melanchton, my first patron! Therefore you

165

see that the *Meister* was less than popular where I came from, and I was granted leave of absence to visit him only because of who and what I was, and not because the Wittenberg authorities approved of the Ermlander's theories. I wanted to make that point clear, for the sake of accuracy.)

So, as I have said, he was not impressed et cetera—indeed, so unimpressed was he, that he seemed not even fully aware of my presence, for he kept on as it were sliding away from me, as though avoiding a distasteful memory, picking at his robe with agitated fingers and grimacing to himself. He was not thinking of me, but of the *consequences* of me, so to speak (*What will the Bishop say!*). I was profoundly disappointed, or rather, I was aware that something profoundly disappointing was occurring, for I myself, the essential I, was hardly there. That is not very clear. No matter. Doctor Copernicus, who before had represented for me the very spirit incarnate of the New Age, was now revealed as a cautious cold old brute obsessed with appearances and the security of his prebend. Is it possible to be disconcerted to the point of tears?

And yet there was something that told me all was not lost, that my pilgrimage might not have been in vain: it was a faint uncertainty in his look, a tiny tension, as if there were, deep within him, a lever longing to be pressed. I had brought gifts with me, fine printed editions of Ptolemy and Euclid, Regiomontanus and others, O, there must have been a dozen volumes in all, which I had had rebound (at a cost I do not care even now to recall), with his initials and a pretty monogram stamped in gold on the spines. These books I had cunningly dispersed throughout my luggage for fear of brigands, so that now when I remembered them and fell upon my bags in a final frantic burst of hope, they fell, diamonds amid ashes, out of a storm of shirts and shoes and soiled linen, and *There!* I cried, and *There!* near to tears, challenging him to find it in his cold heart to reject this ultimate token of homage.

"What are you doing?" he said. "What are these?"

I gathered the books in my arms and struggled to my feet. "For you—for you, *domine praeceptor!*"

Hesitantly he lifted the *Almagest* from atop the pile, and, with many a suspicious backward glance in my direction, took it to the window; I thought of an old grey rat scuttling off with a crust. He held the book close to his nose and examined it intently, sniffing and crooning, and the harsh lines of his face softened, and he smiled despite himself, biting his lip, old *pleased* grey rat, and click! I could almost hear that lever dip.

"A handsome volume," he murmured, "handsome indeed. And costly too, I should think. What did you say your name was, Herr . . ?"

And then, I think, I did weep. I recall tears, and more groans of adoration, and I on my knees again and he shooing me off, though with less distaste than before, I fancied. Behind him the clouds broke for a moment over the Baltic, and the sun of evening suddenly shone, a minor miracle, and I remembered that it was summer after all, that I was young, and the world was before me. I left him soon after that, with an invitation to return on the morrow, and staggered in blissful delirium into the streets, where even the leaden twilight and the filth in the sewers, the mud, the red gaping faces of the peasants, could not dampen my spirits. I found lodgings at an inn below the cathedral wall, and there partook of a nauseating dinner, that I remember in detail to this day, and, to follow, had a fat and extremely dirty, curiously androgynous whore.

*    *    *

I was up and about early next morning. Low sun on the Frisches Haff, the earth steaming faintly, wind freshening, the narrow streets awash with light and loud with the shrill cries of hawkers—aye, and my poor head splitting from the effects of that filthy poison which they dare to call wine. At the tower the bitch Schillings greeted me with another black look, but let me in without a word. The Canon was waiting for me in the observatory, in a state of extreme agitation. I had hardly crossed the threshold before he began to babble excitedly, and came at me waving his hands, forcing me to retreat before him. It was yesterday in reverse. I tried to make sense of what he was saying, but the fumes of last night's revels had not yet dispersed, and phlegm not blood lay sluggish in my veins, and I could grasp only a jumble of words: Kulm . . . the Bishop . . . Löbau . . . the castle . . . *venite!* We were leaving Frauenburg. We were going to Löbau, in Royal Prussia. Bishop Giese was his friend. He was Bishop of Kulm. We would stay with him at Löbau Castle. (What did it mean?) We were leaving that

167

morning, that minute—now! I shambled off in a daze and collected my belongings from the inn, and, when I returned, the Canon was already in the street, struggling into a brokendown hired carriage. I think if I had not arrived just then he would have left without giving me a second thought. The Schillings stuck out her fierce head at the door, the Canon groaned faintly and shrank back against the fusty seat, and as we moved off the *focaria* yelled after us like a fishwife something about being gone when we returned—on hearing which, I may add, I brightened up considerably.

There is a kind of lockjaw that comes with extreme embarrassment; I fell prey to that condition as we rattled through the streets of Frauenburg that morning. I may have been young, innocent I may have been, but I could guess easily enough the reason for our haste and the manner of our departure. It was not without justification, after all, that Luther had vilified Rome for its hypocrisy and its so-called celibacy, and no doubt now Bishop Dantiscus had instituted yet another drive against indecency among his clergy, as the Catholics were forever doing in those early days of the schism, eager to display their reforming zeal to a sceptical world. Not that I cared anything for that kind of nonsense; it was not the state of affairs between Canon Nicolas and the Schillings that troubled me (it did not trouble me much, at any rate), but the spectacle of Doctor Copernicus in the street, in public, involved in a sordid domestic scene. I could not speak, I say, and turned my face away from him and gazed out with such fierce concentration at drab Ermland passing by that it might have been the wonders of the Indies I beheld. Ah, how intolerant the young are of the frailties of the old! The Canon was silent also, until we reached the plain, and then he stirred and sighed, and there was a world of weariness in his voice when he asked:

"Tell me, young man, what do they say of me at Wittenberg?"

*

That dreary Prussian plain, I remember it. Enormous clouds, rolling down from the Baltic, kept pace with us as we were borne slowly southwards, their shadows stepping hugely across the empty land. Strange silence spread for miles about us, as if everything were somehow turned away, facing off into the limitless distance, and the muted clamour of our passage—creak of axles, monotonous thudding of

168

hoofs—could not avail against that impassive quiet, that indifference. We met not a soul on the road, if road it could be called, but once, far in the distance, a band of horsemen appeared, galloping laboriously away, soundlessly. Through the narrow slit opposite me I could see the driver's broad back bouncing and rolling, but as the hours crawled past it ceased to be a human form, and became a stone, a pillar of dust, the wing of some great bird. We passed through deserted villages where the houses were charred shells and dust blew in the streets, and the absence of the hum of human concourse was like a hole in the air itself. Thus do we voyage in dreams. Once, when I thought the Canon was asleep, I found him instead staring at me fixedly; another time when I turned to him he smiled a cunning and inexplicably alarming smile. Confused and frightened, I looked away hurriedly, out at the country-side revolving slowly around us, but there was no comfort for me there. The plain stretched away interminably, burnished by the strange brittle sunlight, and the wind sang softly. We might have been a thousand leagues from anywhere, adrift in the sphere of the fixed stars. He was still smiling, the old sorcerer, and it seemed to me that the smile said: this is my world, do you see? there is no Anna Schillings here, no gaping peasants, no bloodied statues, no Dantiscus, only the light and the emptiness, and that mysterious music high in the air which you cannot hear but which you know is there. And for the first time then I saw him whole, no longer the image of him I had carried with me from Wittenberg, but Copernicus himself—*it*self—the true thing, a cold brilliant object like a diamond (not like a diamond, but I am in a hurry), now all at once vividly familiar and yet untouchable still. It is not vouchsafed to many men to know another thus, with that awful clarity; when it comes, the vision is fleeting, the experience lasts only an instant, but the knowledge gleaned thereby remains forever. We reached Löbau, and in the flurry of arrival I felt that I was indeed waking from a dream. I waited for the Canon to acknowledge all that had happened out on the plain (whatever it was!), but he did not, would not, and I was disappointed. Well, for all I know, the old devil may have put a spell on me out there. But I shall always remember that eerie journey. Yes.

*

Löbau Castle was an enormous white stone fortress on a hill, its towers and turrets looking down over wooded slopes to the huddled roofs of the town. The air up there was crisp with the smell of spruce and pine. I might almost have been back in Germany. We drew into the courtyard and were greeted by an uproar of servants and grooms and hysterical dogs. A grizzled old fellow in a leather jerkin and patched breeches came to receive us. I took him for a steward or somesuch, but I was wrong: it was Bishop Giese himself. He greeted the Canon with grave solicitude. He hardly glanced at me, until, when he offered me the ring to kiss, I shook his hand instead, and that provoked a keen look. The two of them moved away together, the Canon shuffling slowly with bowed head, the Bishop supporting him with a gentle hand under his elbow, and the Canon groaned:

"Ah, Tiedemann, troubles, troubles . . ."

I was left to fend for myself, of course, as usual, until one of the serving lads took pity on me. He bounced up under my nose with a saucy grin smeared on his face, Raphaël he was called, hardly more than a child, a pretty fellow with an arse on him like a peach, O, I knew what he was about!—Raphaël, indeed: some angel. But I followed him willingly enough, and not without gratitude. As he scampered along before me, babbling and leering in his childish way, it occurred to me that I should have a chat with him in private, before I left, about the joys of matrimony and so on, and warn him of the tribulations in store for him if he continued to lean in the direction he so obviously leaned, at such a tender age. Had I only known what tribulations were in store for *me* on his account!

*

And so began our strange sojourn at Löbau. Throughout that long summer we remained there. The magical spell, the first touch of which I had felt out on the empty Prussian plain, settled over all that white castle on its peak, where we, as in an enchanted sleep, wandered amidst the luminous order and music of the planets, dreaming miraculous dreams. Luther had scoffed at Copernicus, calling him *the fool who wants to turn the whole science of astronomy upside down*, but Luther should have kept to theology, for in the sweat of his worst nightmare he could not have imagined what we would do during those months at Löbau. We turned the whole universe upon its head. *We*, I say *we*, for without me he would have kept silent even into the silence of the grave.

He had intended to destroy his book: how many of you knew *that?*
How very skilfully I am telling this tale.

*

Bishop Giese. Bishop Giese was not quite the crusty old pedant I had
expected. He was no gay dog, to be sure, but he was not without a certain . . . how shall I say, a certain sense of irony—better call it that
than humour, for none of those northerners knows how to laugh. In his
attitude toward the Canon, a blend of awe and solicitude and an occasional, helpless exasperation that yet was never less than amiable, he
revealed a loyal and gentle nature. He was something of an astronomer, and possessed a bronze armillary sphere for observing equin-
oxes, and a mighty gnomon from England, which I envied. However, it
was with an enthusiasm plainly forced that he displayed these and
other instruments, and I suspect he kept them chiefly as evidence of the
sincerity of his interest in the Canon's work. He was nearing sixty at
the time of which I speak, had been a canon of the Frauenburg Chapter, and was destined one day to take Danticus's place in the Bishopric
of Ermland. Of middle height, not stout but not gaunt either, he was
one of those middling men who are the unacknowledged proprietors of
the world. He was decent, unassuming, diligent—in short, a *good
man.* I loathed him, I still do. He suffered from the ague, which he had
contracted in the course of his duties somewhere in the wilds of that
enormous bog which is Prussia; Canon Nicolas, playing at medicine
(as I do now!), had for some time been treating him for the affliction,
hence, officially at least, our presence at Löbau. But it was not on the
Bishop alone that the Canon's skill was to be lavished . . .
    On the evening of our arrival, after I had lain down briefly to sleep, I
awoke drenched in sweat and prey to a nameless panic. My teeth chattered. I rose and for a long time wandered fitfully about the castle,
wringing my hands and moaning, lost and frightened in those unfamiliar stone corridors and silent galleries. I knew, but would not acknowledge it, what this mood of mounting urgency and alarm
presaged. All my life I have been subject to prolonged bouts of melancholia, which at their most severe bring with them fainting fits and
crippling pains, even temporary blindness sometimes, and a host of
other lesser demons to plague me. But worst of all is the heartache, the
*accidie.* More than once I have near died of it, and hard to bear indeed

171

would be the fear that at the last the ghost might abandon me in the midst of that drear dark, but, thankfully, my stars have laid in store for me an easier, finer end. The attack that came on that evening was one of the strangest that I have ever known, and was to endure, muted but always there, throughout my stay at Löbau. I have spoken already of enchantment: was it perhaps no more than the effect of viewing the events of that summer through the membrane of melancholy?

Dinner at the castle was always a wearisome and repellent ritual, but on that first evening it was torment. The company gathered and disposed itself hierarchically in a vast hall, whose stained-glass windows trapped the late sunlight in its muddy tints and checked its rude advance into the pious gloom so beloved of popish churchmen. Amid the appalling racket of bells and music and so forth the Bishop entered, in full regalia, and took his place at the head of the highest table. Slatterns with red hands and filthy heels bore in huge trays of pork and baskets of black Prussian bread and jars of wine, and then the uproar began in earnest as the doltish priests and leering clerks stuck their snouts into the prog, gulping and snorting and belching, flinging abuse and gnawed bones at each other, filling the smoky air with shrieks of wild laughter. A bout of fisticuffs broke out at one of the lower tables. In the face of it all, the Bishop, enthroned on my left, maintained a placid mien—and why not? By the standards of the Roman Church his dining-room was a model of polite behaviour. Yes, to him, to them all, everything was just splendid, and I alone could see the ape squatting in our midst and hear his howls. Even if they had seen him, they would have taken him for a messenger from God, an archangel with steaming armpits and blue-black ballocks, and sure enough, after a few prayers directed by the company toward the ceiling, the poor brute would have been pointing a seraphic finger upward in a new annunciation (the Word made Pork!). Thus does Rome transform into ritual the horrors of the world, in order to sustain the fictions. I hate them all, Giese with his mealy-mouthed hypocrisy, Dantiscus and his bastards, but most of all of them I hate—ah but bide, Rheticus, bide! The Bishop was speaking to me, some polite rubbish as usual, but the bread was turning to clay in my mouth, and the plate of meat before me had the look of an haruspex's bowl of entrails, signifying doom. I could no longer bear to remain in that hall. I rose with a snarl, and fled.

Soulsick and weary, I lay awake for hours by the window of the rathole I had been allotted as a room. Out on the plain faint lights flickered. The sky was eerily aglow. In those northern summers true darkness never falls, and throughout the white nights a pallid twilight endures from dusk to dawn. I longed for kindly death. My eyes ached, my arsehole was clenched, my hands stank of wax and ashes. Here in this barbarous clime was no place for me. Tears filled my eyes, and flowed in torrents down my cheeks. All of my life seemed in that moment inexplicably transfigured, a blackened and useless thing, and there was no comfort for me anywhere. I held my face in my hands as if it were some poor, wounded, suffering creature, and bawled like a baby.

There came a tapping, which I heard without hearing, thinking it was the wind, or a deathwatch beetle at work, but then the door opened a little way and the Canon cautiously put in his head and peered about. He wore the same robe that he had travelled in, a shapeless black thing, but on his head now there was perched an indescribably comic nightcap with a tassle. In his trembling hand he carried a lamp, the quaking light of which sent shadows leaping up the walls like demented ghosts. He seemed surprised, and even a little dismayed, to find me awake. I suspect he had come to spy on me. He mumbled an apology and began to withdraw, but then hesitated, remembering, I suppose, that I was not after all an article of furniture, and that a living creature wide awake and weeping might think himself entitled to an explanation as to why an elderly gentleman in a funny cap should be peering into his room at dead of night. With an impatient little sigh he shuffled in and closed the door behind him, put down the lamp with exaggerated deliberation, and then, carefully averting his gaze from my tears, he spoke thus:

"Herr von Lauchen, Bishop Giese tells me you are ill, or so he thought, when you fled his table so precipitately; and therefore I have come in order to ask if I might be of some assistance. The nature of your ailment is quite plain: Saturn, malign star, rules your existence, filled, as it has been, I'm sure, with gainful study, abstract thought, and deep reflection, which feed the hungry mind, but sap the will, and lead to melancholy and dejection. Nothing will avail you, sir, until, as Ficino recommends, you entrust yourself into the care of the Three Graces, and cleave to things under their rule. First, remember, even a single yellow crocus blossom, Jupiter's golden flower, may bring relief; also, the light of Sol, of course, is good, and green fields at dawn—or anything, in fact, that's coloured green, the shade of Venus. Do this, *meinherr*, shun all things saturnine, surround yourself instead with influences conducive to health and joy and spirits fine, and illness never more shall your defences breach. Ahem . . . The Bishop seated you by his side at table: an honour, sir, extended only to the very few. To rise in haste, as you did, is a slur. Perhaps at Wittenberg you have adopted Father Luther's table manners, and hence the reason why you so disrupted the Bishop's table. But please understand that here in Prussia we do things differently. *Vale.*—The dawn comes on apace, I see."

He waited, with head inclined, as though he fancied that his voice, of its own volition as it were, might wish to add something further; but no, he was quite done, and taking up his lamp he prepared to depart. I said:

"I shall be leaving today."

He stopped short in the doorway and peered at me over his shoulder. "You are leaving us, Herr von Lauchen, already?"

"Yes, *Meister*, for Wittenberg; for home."

"O."

He pondered this unexpected development, sinking into himself like a puzzled old snail into its carapace, and then, mumbling, he wandered away in an introspective trance, with those ghostly shadows prancing about him. Fool that I was, I should have packed my bags and fled there and then, while all the castle was abed, and left him to publish his book or not, burn it, wipe himself with it, whatever he wished. I even imagined my going, and wept again, with compassion for that stern sad figure which was myself, striding away into a chill sombre dawn. I had come to him in a prentice tunic, humbly: I, Rheticus, doctor of mathematics and astronomy at the great school of Wittenberg, and he had dodged me, ignored me, preached at me as if I were an errant choirboy. I should have gone! But I did not go. I crawled instead under the blankets and nursed my poor forlorn heart to sleep.

\*     \*     \*

I can see it now, of course, how cunning they were, the two of them, Giese and the Canon, cunning old conspirators; but I could not see it then. I woke late in the morning to find Raphaël beside me, with honey and hot bread and a jug of spiced wine. The food was welcome, but the mere presence of the lithesome lad would have been sufficient, for it broke a fast far crueller than belly-hunger—I mean the fasting from the company of youth and rosy cheeks and laughing eyes, which I had been forced to observe since leaving Wittenberg and coming among these greybeards. We spent a pleasant while together, and he, the shy one, twisted his fingers and shifted from foot to foot, chattering on in a vain effort to stem his blushes. At length I gave him a coin and sent him skipping on his way, and although the old gloom returned once he was gone, it was not half so leaden as before. Too late I remembered that sober talk I had determined to have with him; the matter would have to be dealt with. An establishment of clerics, all men—and Catholics at that!—was a perilous place for a boy of his . . . his youth and beauty. (I was about to say innocence, but in honesty I must not, even though I know that thereby I banish the word from the language, for if it is denied to him then it has no meaning anymore. I speak in riddles. They shall be solved. My poor Raphaël! they destroyed us both.)

*

I rose and went in search of the Canon, and was directed to the *arboretum*, a name which conjured up a pleasant image of fruit trees in flower, dappled green shade, and little leafy paths where astronomers might stroll, discussing the universe. What I found was a crooked field fastened to a hill behind the castle, with a few stunted bushes and a cabbage patch—and, need I say, no sign of the Canon. As I stamped away, sick of being sent on false chases, a figure rose up among the cabbages and hailed me. Today Bishop Giese was rigged out again in his peasant costume. The sight of those breeches and that jerkin irritated me greatly. Do these damn Catholics, I wondered, never do else but dress up and pose? His hands were crusted with clay, and when he drew near I caught a strong whiff of horse manure. He was in a hearty mood. I suppose it went with the outfit. He said:

"*Grüss Gott*, Herr von Lauchen! The Doctor informs me that you are ill. Not gravely so, I trust? Our Prussian climate is uncongenial, although here, on Castle Hill, we are spared the debilitating vapours of the plain—which are yet not so bad as those that rise from the

Frisches Haff at Frauenburg, eh, *meinherr?* Ho ho. Let me look at you, my son. Well, the nature of your ailment is plain: Saturn, malign star . . ." And he proceeded to parrot verbatim the Canon's little sermon in praise of the Graces. I listened in silence, with a curled lip. I was at once amused and appalled: amused that this clown should steal the master's words and pretend they were his own, appalled at the notion, which suddenly struck me, that the Canon may not after all have been mocking me, but may have been actually serious about that fool Ficino's cabalistic nonsense! O, I know well the baleful influence which Saturn wields over my life; I know that the Graces are good; but I also know that a hectacre of crocuses would not have eased my heartsickness one whit. *Crocuses!* However, as I was to discover, the Canon neither believed nor disbelieved Ficino's theories, no more than he believed nor disbelieved the contents of any of the score or so set speeches with which he had long ago armed himself, and from which he could choose a ready response to any situation. All that mattered to him was the saying, not what was said; words were the empty rituals with which he held the world at bay. Copernicus did not believe in truth. I think I have said that before.

Giese put his soiled hand on my arm and led me along a path below the castle wall. When he had finished his dissertation on the state of my health, he paused and glanced at me with a peculiar, thoughtful look, like that of an undertaker speculatively eyeing a sick man. The last remaining patches of the morning's mist clung about us like old rags, and the slowly ascending sun shed a damp weak light upon the battlements above. The world seemed old and tired. I wanted to find the Canon, to wrest from him his secrets, to thrust fame upon his unwilling head. I wanted *action*. I was young. The Bishop said:

"You come, I believe, from Wittenberg?"

"Yes. I am a Lutheran."

My directness startled him. He smiled wanly, and nodded his large head up and down very rapidly, as though to shake off that dreaded word I had uttered; he withdrew his hand carefully from my arm.

"Quite so, my dear sir, quite so," he said, "you are a Lutheran, as you admi- as you say. Now, I have no desire to dispute with you the issues of this tragic schism which has rent our Church, believe me. I might remind you that Father Luther was not the first to recognise the necessity for reform—but, be that as it may, we shall not argue. A man must live with his own conscience, in that much at least I would agree with you. So. You are a Lutheran. You admit it. There it rests. However, I cannot pretend that your presence in Prussia is not an embarrassment. It is—O not to me, you understand; the world pays scant heed to events here in humble Löbau. No, Herr von Lauchen, I refer to one who is dear to us both: I mean of course our *domine praeceptor*, Doctor Nicolas. It is to him that your presence is an embarrassment, and, perhaps, a danger even. But now I see I have offended you. Let me explain. You have not been long in Prussia, therefore you cannot be expected to appreciate the situation prevailing here. Tell me, are you not puzzled by the Doctor's unwillingness to give his knowledge to the world, to publish his masterpiece? It would surprise you, would it not, if I were to tell you that it is not doubt as to the validity of his conclusions that makes him hesitate, nothing like that, no—but fear. So it is, Herr von Lauchen: *fear*."

He paused again, again we paced the path in silence. I have called Giese a fool, but that was only a term of abuse: he was no fool. We left the castle walls behind, and descended a little way the wooded slope. The trees were tall. Three rabbits fled at our approach. I stumbled on a fallen bough. The pines were silvery, each single needle adorned with a delicate filigree of beaded mist. How strange, the clarity with which I remember that moment! Thus, even as the falcon plummets, the sparrow snatches a last look at her world. Bishop Giese, laying his talons on my arm again, began to chant, I think that is the word, in Latin:

"Painful is the task I must perform, and tell to one—from Wittenberg!—of the storm of envy which surrounds our learned friend. *Meinherr*, I pray you, to my tale attend with caution and forbearance, and don't feel that in these few bare facts you see revealed a plot hatched in the corridors of Rome. This evil is the doing of one alone: do you know the man Dantiscus, Ermland's Bishop (Johannes Flachsbinder his name, a Danzig sop)? Copernicus he hates, and from jealousy these many years he has right zealously persecuted him. Why so? you ask, but to answer you, that is a task, I fear, beyond me. Why ever do the worst detest the best, and mediocrities thirst to see great minds brought low? It is the world. Besides, this son of Zelos, dim-witted churl though he be, thinks Prussia has but room for one great mind—that's his! The fellow's moon mad, *certes*. Now, to achieve his aims, and ruin our *magister*, he defames his name, puts it about he

177

shares his bed with his *focaria*, whom he has led into foul sin to satisfy his lust. My friend, you stare, as though you cannot trust your ears. This is but one of many lies this Danziger has told! And in the eyes of all the world the Doctor's reputation is destroyed, and mocking condemnation, he believes, would greet his book. Some years ago, at Elbing, ignorant peasants jeered a waxwork figure of Copernicus that was displayed in a carnival farce. Thus Dantiscus wins, and our friend keeps silent, fearing to trust his brilliant theories to the leering mob. And so, *meinherr*, the work of twoscore years lies fallow and unseen. Therefore, I beg you, do not leave us yet. We must try to make him reconsider—*but hush! here is the Doctor now. Mind, do not say what secrets I have told you!*—Ah Nicolas, good day."

We had left the wood and entered the courtyard by a little low postern gate. Had Giese not pointed him out, I would not have noticed the Canon skulking under an archway, watching us intently with a peculiar fixed grin on his grey face. Out of new knowledge, I looked upon him in a new light. Yes, now I could see in him (so I thought!) a man enfettered, whose every action was constrained by the paramount need for secrecy and caution, and I felt on his behalf a burning sense of outrage. I would have flung myself to my knees before him, had there not been still vivid in my mind the memory of a previous genuflection. Instead, I contented myself with a terrible glare, that was meant to signify my willingness to take on an army of Dantiscuses at his command. (And yet, behind it all, I was confused, and even suspicious: what was it exactly that they required of me?) I had forgotten my declared intention of leaving that day; in fact, I had said it merely to elicit some genuine response from that nightcapped oracle in my chamber, and certainly I had not imagined that this thoughtless threat would provoke the panic which apparently it had. I determined to proceed with care—but of course, like the young fool that I was, I had no sooner decided on caution than I abandoned it, and waded headlong into the mire. I said:

"*Meister*, we must return to Frauenburg at once! I intend to make a copy of your great work, and take it to a printer that I know at Nuremberg, who is discreet, and a specialist in such books. You must trust me, and delay no longer!"

In my excitement I expected some preposterously dramatic reaction from the Canon to this naked challenge to his secretiveness, but he merely shrugged and said:

"There is no need to go to Frauenburg; the book is here."

I said:

"But but but but but—!"

And Giese said:

"Why Nicolas—!"

And the Canon, glancing at us both with a mixture of contempt and distaste, answered:

"I assumed that Herr von Lauchen did not journey all the way from Wittenberg merely for amusement. You came here to learn of my theory of the revolutions of the spheres, did you not? Then so you shall. I have the manuscript with me. Come this way."

We went all three into the castle, and the Canon straightway fetched the manuscript from his room. The events of the morning had moved so swiftly that my poor brain, already bemused by illness, could not cope with them, and I was in state of shock—yet not so shocked that I did not note how the old man vainly tried to appear unconcerned when he surrendered to me his life's work, that I did not feel his trembling fingers clutch at the manuscript in a momentary spasm of misgiving as it passed between us. When the deed was done he stepped back a pace, and that awful uncontrollable grin took hold of his face again, and Bishop Giese, hovering near us, gave a kind of whistle of relief, and I, fearing that the Canon might change his mind and try to snatch the thing away from me, rose immediately and made off with it to the window.

## DE REVOLUTIONIBUS ORBIUM MUNDI
### *—for mathematicians only—*

*

How to express my emotions, the strange jumble of feelings kindled within me, as I gazed upon the living myth which I held in my hands, the key to the secrets of the universe? This book for years had filled my dreams and obsessed my waking hours so completely that now I could hardly comprehend the reality, and the words in the crabbed script seemed not to speak, but to sing rather, so that the rolling grandeur of the title boomed like a flourish of celestial trumpets, to the accompaniment of the wordly fiddling of the motto with its cautious

179

admonition, and I smiled, foolishly, helplessly, at the inexplicable miracle of this music of Heaven and Earth. But then I turned the pages, and chanced upon the diagram of a universe in the centre of which stands Sol in the splendour of eternal immobility, and the music was swept away, and my besotted smile with it, and a new and wholly unexpected sensation took hold of me. It was sorrow! sorrow that old Earth should be thus deposed, and cast out into the darkness of the firmament, there to prance and spin at the behest of a tyrannical, mute god of fire. I grieved, friends, for our diminishment! O, it was not that I did not already know that Copernicus's theory postulated a heliocentric world—everyone knew that—and anyway I had been permitted to read Melanchton's well-thumbed copy of the *Commentariolus*. Besides, as everyone also knows, Copernicus was not the first to set the Sun at the centre. Yes, I had for a long time known what this Prussian was about, but it was not until that morning at Löbau Castle that I at last realised, in a kind of fascinated horror, the full consequences of this work of cosmography. Beloved Earth! he banished you forever into darkness. And yet, what does it matter? The sky shall be forever blue, and the earth shall forever blossom in spring, and this planet shall forever be the centre of all we know. I believe it.

*

I read the entire manuscript there and then; that is not of course to say that I read every word: rather, I opened it up, as a surgeon opens a limb, and plunged the keen blade of my intellect into its vital centres, thus laying bare the quivering arteries leading to the heart. And there, in the knotted cords of that heart, I made a strange discovery . . . but more of that presently. When at last I lifted my eyes from those pages, I found myself alone. The light was fading in the windows. It was evening. The day had departed, with Giese and Copernicus, unnoticed. My brain ached, but I forced it to think, to seek out a small persistent something which had been lodging in my thoughts since morning, biding its time. It was the memory of how, when in the courtyard I challenged him to surrender the manuscript to me, Copernicus had for an instant, just for an instant only, cast off the timorous churchman's mask to reveal behind it an icy scorn, a cold, cruel arrogance. I did not know why I had remembered it, why it seemed so significant; I was not even sure that I had not imagined it; but it troubled

180

me. *What is it they want me to do?* Go carefully, Rheticus, I told myself, hardly knowing what I meant . . .

I found Copernicus and Giese in the great hall of the castle, seated in silence in tall carved chairs on either side of the enormous hearth, on which, despite the mildness of the evening, stacked logs were blazing fiercely. The windows, set high up in the walls, let in but little of the evening's radiance, and in the gloom the robes of the two still figures seemed to flow and merge into the elaborate flutings of the thrones on which they sat, so that to my bruised perception they appeared limbless, a pair of severed heads, ghastly in the fire's crimson glow. Copernicus had put himself as close to the blaze as he could manage without risking combustion, but still he looked cold. As I entered the arc of flickering firelight, I found that he was watching me. I was weary, and incapable of subtlety, and once again I ignored my own injunction to go carefully. I held up the manuscript and said:

"I have read it, and find it is all I had expected it would be, more than I had hoped; will you allow me to take it to Nuremberg, to Petreius the printer?"

He did not answer immediately. The silence stretched out around us until it seemed to creak. At length he said:

"That is a question which we cannot discuss, yet."

At that, as though he had been given a signal, the Bishop stirred himself and put an end to the discussion (discussion!). Had I eaten? Why then, I must! He would have Raphaël bring me supper in my room, for I should retire, it was late, I was ill and in need of rest. And, like a sleepy child, I allowed myself to be led away, too tired to protest, clutching the manuscript, baba's favourite toy, to my breast. I looked back at Copernicus, and the severed head smiled and nodded, as if to say: sleep, little one, sleep now. My room looked somehow different, but I could not say in what way, until next morning when I noticed the desk, amply stocked with writing implements and paper, which they installed without my knowing. O the cunning!

*

A thought, which I find startling, has occurred to me, viz. that I was happy at Löbau Castle, perhaps happier than I had ever been before, or would be again. Is it true? Happiness. *Happiness.* I write down the word, I stare at it, but it means nothing. Happiness; how strange.

When the world, which is populated for the most part by fools and hypocrites, talks of being happy, really it is talking about no more than the gratification of hunger—hunger for love, or revenge, money, suchlike—but that cannot be what I mean. I have never loved anyone, and if I had money I would not know what to do with it. Revenge, of course, is another matter; but it will not make me *happy*. At Löbau, certainly, I knew nothing of revenge, did not even suspect that one day I would desire it. What am I talking about? I cannot understand myself, these ravings. Yet the thought will not go away. *I was happy that summer at Löbau*. It is like a kind of message, sent to me from I do not know where; a cipher. Well then, let me see if I can discover what it was that made me happy, and then maybe I shall understand what this happiness meant.

*

Quickly the days acquired a rhythm. In the mornings I was awakened by the sombre tolling of the castle bell, signifying that in the chapel the Bishop was celebrating Mass. The thought of that strange secret ritual of blood and sacrifice being enacted close at hand in the dim light of dawn was at once comical and grotesque, and yet mysteriously consoling. After Mass came Raphaël, sleepy-eyed but unfailingly gay, to feed and barber me. He was such a pleasant creature, and was happy to chatter or keep silent as my mood demanded. Even his silence was merry. I tried repeatedly to elicit from him a precise description of his duties in the Bishop's household, for it was apparent that he held a privileged position, but his answers were always vague. It occurred to me that he might be old Giese's bastard. (Perhaps he was? I hope not.) Sometimes I had him accompany me when I went forth to take the air in the woods below the walls, but after that he was banished from my side and warned not to appear again with his distracting ways till evening, for I had work to do.

The astronomer who studies the motions of the stars is surely like a blind man, who, with only the staff of mathematics to guide him, must make a great, endless, hazardous journey that winds through innumerable desolate places. What will be the result? Proceeding anxiously for a while, and groping his way with his staff, he will at some time, leaning upon it, cry out in despair to Heaven, Earth and all the gods to aid him in his anguish. Thus, day after day, for ten weeks, beset by illness and, worse, uncertainty regarding the purpose of my labours, I struggled with the intricacies of Copernicus's theory of the movements of the planets. This second reading of the manuscript was very different from the first deceptive glance, when, entranced by music, I went straight to the heart of the work, and cheerfully ignored the details. Ah, the details! Crouched at my desk, with my head in my hands, I did furious battle with them, moaning and muttering, weeping, laughing sometimes even, uncontrollably. I remember in particular the trouble caused me by the orbit of Mars, the warlord. That planet is a *cunt!* It nearly drove me insane. One day, despairing of ever comprehending the mystery of its orbit, I rose and dashed in frantic circles about the room, crashing my head against the walls. At length, when I had knocked myself near senseless, I sank to the floor with laughter booming in my ears, and a mocking voice—I swear it came from the fourth sphere itself!—roared at me: *Good, Rheticus, very good! You have found what you sought, for just as you have whirled about this room, just so does Mars whirl in the heavens!*

As if all this were not enough, I spent the evenings, when I should have been resting, locked in endless circular arguments with Copernicus, trying to persuade him to publish. These battles took place after dinner in the great hall, where a third carved throne had been provided for me before the fire. I say battles, but assaults would be a better word, for while I attacked, Copernicus merely cowered behind the ramparts of a stony silence, apparently untouchable. A remote grey figure, he sat huddled in the folds of his robe, staring before him, his jaw clenched tight as a gintrap. No matter how hot the fire, he was always cold. It was as if he generated coldness out of some frozen waste within him. Only when my pleading reached its fiercest intensity, when, beside myself with messianic fervour, I leaped to my feet and roared frantic exhortations at him, waving my arms, only then did his stolid defences show a trace of weakness. His head began to jerk from side to side, in a clockwork frenzy of refusal, while that ghastly grin spread wider and wider, and the sweat stood out on his brow, and, like a girl teasing herself with thoughts of rape, he peered down into the depths of the abyss into which I was inviting him to leap, hugging himself in horrified, panic-stricken glee. Sometimes, even, he was pressed so far that he spoke, but only in order to throw an obstacle in the path of my merciless advance, and then he was always careful to seize on some minor point of my argument, steering well clear of the main issue. Thus, when I put it to him that he had a duty to publish, if only to demonstrate the errors in Ptolemy, he shook a trembling finger at me and cried:

"We must follow the methods of the ancients! Anyone who thinks they are not to be trusted will squat forever in the wilderness outside the locked gates of our science, dreaming the dreams of the deranged about the motions of the spheres—and he will get what he deserves for thinking he can support his own ravings by slandering the ancients!"

Giese, for his part, liked to think of himself as the wise old mediator in these one-sided debates, and waded in now and again with some inane remark, which obviously he considered immensely learned and persuasive, and to which Copernicus and I attended in a painful polite silence, before continuing on as if the old clown had never opened his mouth. But he was happy enough, so long as he was allowed to say his piece, for, like all his breed, he saw no difference between words and actions, and felt that when something was said it was as good as done. He was not the only spectator on the battlefield. As the weeks went by, word spread through the castle, and even to the town and beyond, that free entertainment was being laid on each evening in the great hall, and soon we began to draw an audience of clerics and castle officials, fat burghers from the town, travelling charlatans on diplomatic missions to the See of Kulm, and God knows what all. Even the servants came creeping in to hear this wild man from Wittenberg perform. At first it disturbed me to have that faceless, softly breathing mass shifting and tittering behind me in the gloom, but I grew accustomed to it, in time. In fact, I began to enjoy myself. In the magic circle of the firelight, immured in the impregnable fortress high above the plain, I felt that I had been lifted out of the world of ordinary men into some rarefied aetherial sphere, where nothing that was soiled could touch me, where I touched nothing soiled. Outside it was summer, the peasants were working in the fields, emperors were waging wars, but here there was none of that, all that, blood and toil, things growing, slaughter and glory, bucolic pleasures, men dying—in short, life, no, none of that. For we were angels, playing an endless, celestial game. And I was happy.

—And if that is what is meant by happiness, *then I want none of it.*

\*    \*    \*

I am getting on, getting on, yes indeed; I am at Löbau still. My arguments won through in the end, and although it was in his own way, to be sure, and on his own terms, Copernicus capitulated. The first hint that he was ready to negotiate in earnest came when one evening he began out of the blue to babble excitedly about a plan, which he knew, he said, would meet with my enthusiastic approval. I must not think that his unwillingness to publish his modest theories sprang from contempt for the world; indeed, as I well knew (I did?), he bore a great love for ordinary men, and had no wish to leave them in ignorance *de rerum natura* if there was any way in which he could enlighten them. Also, he had a responsibility toward science, and the improvement of scientific method. Having regard to all this, then, he proposed to draw up astronomical tables, with new rules for plotting star courses, which would be an invaluable aid not only to astronomers but also to sailors and map-makers and so forth; these, when he had prepared them, I could take to my printer at Nuremberg. However, I should understand one thing clearly, that while the computational tables would have new and accurate rules, *there would be no proofs.* He was well aware that his theory, on which the tables would be founded, would, if published, overturn the accepted notions regarding the movements of the spheres, and would therefore cause a hideous commotion, and he was not prepared *to lend his name* to the causing of such disturbance (my italics). Pythagoras held that the secrets of science must be reserved for the few, for the initiates, the wise ones, and Pythagoras was an ancient, and he was right. So: new rules, yes, *but no proofs to support them.*

This would not do, of course, and well he knew it, for as soon as I began to put forward my objections he hurriedly agreed, and said yes, it was a foolish notion, he would abandon it. (I confess that, to this day, I still do not understand why he put forward this nonsensical plan only to relinquish it at once, unless he merely wished to signal to me, in his usual roundabout way, that he was now prepared to compromise.) The subject was closed then, which small detail was not, however, going to deter Giese from voicing *his* objections, the formulation of which, I suppose, cost him a mighty effort that he was fain to see wasted.

"But Doctor," he said, "these tables would be an incomplete gift to the world, unless you reveal the theory on which they are based, as Ptolemy, for whom you have such high regard, was always careful to do."

To that, Copernicus, who had once more retreated dreamily into himself, made an extraordinary answer. He said:

"The Ptolemaic astronomy is nothing, so far as existence is concerned, but it is convenient for computing the inexistent."

But having said it, he recollected himself, and pretended, by assuming an expression meant to indicate bland innocence but which merely made him look a halfwit, that he was unaware of having put forward a notion which, if he believed it to be true, made nonsense of his life's work (for, remember, whatever they may say about it now, his theory was based entirely upon the Ptolemaic astronomy—was indeed, as he pointed out himself, no more than a revision of Ptolemy, at least in its beginnings). So profound an admission was it, that at the time I failed to grasp its full significance, and only felt its black brittle wing brush my cheek, as it were, as it flew past. However, I must have perceived that something momentous had occurred, that part of the ramparts had collapsed, for immediately I was on my feet and crying:

"Let me take the manuscript, let me go to Nuremberg. We must act now, or forever keep silent—trust me!"

He did not answer at once. It seems to me now, although I am surely mistaken, that there was a vast audience in the hall that evening, for the silence was enormous, the kind of silence which only comes when the multitude for a moment, its infantile attention captured, stops yelping and goggles with mouth agape at some gaudy, gimcrack wonder. Even Giese held his peace. Copernicus was smiling. I don't mean grinning, not that grin, but a real smile, faint, quite calm, and full of cunning. He said:

"You say that I must trust you, and of course I do, indeed I do; but the journey to Nuremberg is long, and hazardous in these times, and who can say what evils might not befall you on the way? What if you should lose the manuscript in some misadventure, if it should be stolen, or destroyed? All would be lost then, all my work. This book has been thirty years in the writing."

What was he about? He watched me with cold amusement (I swear it was amusement!) as I wriggled like a stranded fish in my search for the correct, the only answer to the riddle he had set me. This was different to all that had gone before; this was in earnest. With great care I said:

"Then I shall make a copy of the manuscript, and take it with me, while you retain the original. That way, the safety of the book is assured, and also its publication. I see no further difficulty."

"But you might lose the copy, might you not, and what then? Rather, here is a plan: go now to Nuremberg, and there write down an *account* of the book from memory, which I have no doubt you could do with ease, and publish *that*."

"But it has already been done!" I cried. "You yourself have written an account, in the *Commentariolus*—"

"That was nothing, worse than nothing, full of errors. You must write an accurate account. You see the advantages for us both in this: your name shall gain prominence in the world of science, while the way shall have been prepared for the publication later of my book. You shall be a kind of—" he smiled again "—a kind of John the Baptist, the one who goes before."

He had won, and he knew it. I bowed my head, signifying defeat.

"I agree," I said. "I shall write this account, if it is in my power."

Ah, his smile, that little smile, how well I remember it! He said:

"This is a splendid plan, I think. Do you agree?"

"Yes, yes—but when will you publish *De revolutionibus?*"

"Well, when I consider the matter, I see no need to publish, if you ensure that your account is sufficiently comprehensive."

"But your book? Thirty years?"

"The book is unnecessary."

"And you intend—?"

"To destroy it."

"*Destroy it?*"

"Why, yes."

How simply and cheerfully it was said! How convincing it sounded!

*

Thus was conceived my *Narratio prima*, which in the thirty-six years since its publication has gained such fame (for *him*, not for me, whose work it was!). I have not given here a strictly literal account of how I was inveigled into writing it, but have contented myself with showing how cunningly he worked upon my youthful enthusiasm and my gullibility in order to achieve his own questionable ends. That nonsense about going at once to Nuremberg and writing the account from memory was only a part of the trap, of course, a condition on which he could without harm concede, and thereby appear gracious. Anyway,

187

he had to concede, for I had no intention of leaving his side, having heard him threaten (a threat which, I confess, I did not take seriously—but still . . .) to burn his book.

I began the writing that very night. Copernicus's book is built in six parts, each part more intricate, more difficult than the one before. By that time I was thoroughly familiar with the first three, had some grasp of the fourth, and only a general idea of the last two—but I managed, I managed, and the *Narratio prima*, as you may judge, while it is not so elegant as I would wish, is yet a brilliant piece of work. Who else—I ask it in all modesty—who else could have made such a compressed, succinct account, in so short a time, of that bristling mesh of astronomical theory, who else but I? And was I aided in my herculean labours by the *domine praeceptor*? I was not! Each evening, when I had finished work for the day, he came with some flimsy excuse and took away from me the precious manuscript. Did he think I was going to eat it? And how he dithered, and fussed and fretted, and plucked at my sleeve in his nervousness, hedging me about with admonitions and prohibitions. I must not mention him by name, he said. Then how could I proceed? A theory without a theorist? Was I to claim the work as my own? Ah, *that* made him bethink himself, and he went away and thought about it for a day or two, and came back and said that if I must name him, then let me call him only *Doctor Nicolas of Torun*. Very well—what did I care? If he wanted to be dubbed Mad Kaspar, or Mandricardo the Terrible, it was all one to me. So I wrote down my title thus:

*To the Most Illustrious Dr Johannes Schöner, a First Account of the Book of Revolutions by the Most Learned & Excellent Mathematician, the Reverend Father, Doctor Nicolas of Torun, Canon of Ermland, from a Young Student of Mathematics.*

What a start it must have given old Schöner (he taught me in mathematics and astronomy at Nuremberg) to find himself the unwitting target, so to speak, of this controversial work. The dedication was a piece of cunning, for Schöner's name could not but lend respectability to an account which, I knew, would stir up the sleeping hive of academic bees and set them buzzing. Also, for good measure, and in the hope of placating Dantiscus somewhat, I appended the *Encomium*

*Borussiae*, that crawling piece in praise of Prussia, its intellectual giants, its wealth in amber and other precious materials, its glorious vistas of bog and slate-grey sea, which had me wracking my brain for pretty metaphors and classical allusions. And since I had decided to print at Danzig, that city being but a day's ride away, instead of at Nuremberg, and since the Mayor there, one John of Werden, had invited me to visit him, I did not let the opportunity pass to devote a few warm words to the city and the lusty Achilles that it had for Mayor.

The *Narratio prima* was completed on the 23rd of September, in 1539. By then I had returned with Copernicus to Frauenburg. Although I cannot say that I was overjoyed to find myself once more in that dreary town, I was relieved nevertheless to be away from that fool Giese, not to mention that magicked castle of Löbau. (Leaving Raphaël was another matter, of course . . .) Alone with Copernicus in his cold tower, at least the issues were clear, I mean I could see clearly the chasm that lay between his horror of change and my firm faith in progress. But I shall deal with that subject later. Did I say we were alone in the tower—how could I forget that other presence planted in our midst like some dreadful basilisk, whose sullen glare followed my every movement, whose outraged silence hung about us like a shroud? I mean Anna Schillings, frightful woman. She did not fulfil her threat to be gone when we returned, and was there waiting for us grimly, with her arms folded under that enormous chest. O no, Anna, I have not forgotten you. She cannot have been very much younger than Copernicus, but she possessed a vigour, fuelled by bitterness and spite, which belied her years. Me she loathed, with extraordinary passion; she was jealous. I would not have put it past her to try to do me in, and I confess that, faced with those bowls of greenish gruel on which she fed us, the thought of poison oftimes crossed my mind. And speaking of poisoning, I suspect Copernicus may have considered ridding himself thus of this troublesome woman: I remember watching him concocting some noisome medicine which he had prescribed for one of her innumerable obscure complaints, grinding the pestle, and grinding it, with a wistful, horrid little smile, as though he were putting out eyes. Of course, he would not have dreamed of daring so bold a solution. Anyway, most like he feared even more than the harridan herself the prospect of her ghost coming back to haunt him.

189

He insisted that I lodge with him in the tower. I was flattered, until I realised that he wanted me near him not for love of my company, but so that he would have an ally against the Schillings. In truth, however, I must admit I was not of much use to him in that respect. O I could handle her, no question of that, she soon learned to beware the edge of my tongue, but when she could get no good of me she redoubled her efforts on the unfortunate Copernicus, and fairly trounced him; so that my presence in fact exacerbated his problems. Whenever she drew near he winced, and sank into the carapace of his robe, as though fearing that his ears were about to be boxed. Well, I had little sympathy for him. He had only to take his courage in his hands (what a curious phrase that is) and kick her out, or poison her, or denounce her as a witch, and all would have been well. What, anyway, was the hold she had on him? Apparently he had rescued her from a knocking shop, or so they said; she was a cousin of some sort. I confess it made me feel quite nauseous to ponder the matter, but I surmised that some cuntish ritual, performed years before when they were still capable of that kind of thing, had subjected him to her will. I have seen it before, that phenomenon, men turned into slaves by the tyranny of the twat. Women. I have nothing against them, in their place, but I know that they have only to master a few circus tricks in bed and they become veritable Circes. Ach, leave it, Rheticus, leave it.

When I say I had little sympathy for him in his plight, I do not mean that I was indifferent. The *Narratio prima* was completed, and I was ready to set off for Danzig, and after Danzig it was imperative that I return to Wittenberg, for I had already overstretched my term of leave; all this would mean that I could not be back in Frauenburg before the beginning of the following summer. By then, God knows what disasters would have occurred. Copernicus was an old man, far from robust, and his will was crumbling. Dantiscus had renewed his campaign, and almost by the week now he sent letters regarding Anna Schillings, bristling with threats under a veneer of sweetness and hypocritical concern for the astronomer's reputation; each letter, I could see it in Copernicus's stricken grey countenance, further jeopardised the survival of the manuscript. I knew, remembering what Giese had said that day in the pine wood below the walls of Löbau, that when Dantiscus spoke of his duty to extirpate vice from his diocese et cetera, he was in fact speaking of something else entirely: viz. his burning jealousy of Copernicus. Would the *Meister's* nerve hold until I returned, or, alone against the Schillings's bullying and in the face of Dantiscus's threats, would he burn his book, and bolt for the safety and silence of his burrow? It was a risk I could not take. If the Schillings could not be got rid of—and I despaired early of shifting that grim mass of flesh and fury—then the one for whom she was a weapon must be persuaded that the war he was waging was already lost. (Another riddle—solution follows.) I made a last, token effort to wrest the manuscript from the old man's clutches, but he only looked at me, mournfully, accusingly, and spoke not a word; I packed my bags and bade farewell to Frauenburg.

*       *       *

I shall not dwell upon my stay at Danzig. The Mayor, mine host, Fat Jack of Werden, was a puffed-up boorish burgher, whose greatest love, next to foodstuffs, that is, was the making of sententious speeches in praise of himself. He was pleased as punch to have as his guest that most exotic of beasts, a Lutheran scholar from Germany, and he missed no opportunity of showing me off to his friends, and, more especially, to his enemies. O, I had a rollicking time in Danzig. Still, the printer to whom I brought the manuscript of the *Narratio* was a civil enough fellow, and surprisingly capable too, for a jobber, I mean, out there in the wilds. The first edition came off his presses in February of 1540. Copies were sent to Frauenburg, and also to Löbau Castle, whence Giese dispatched one to the Lutheran Duke Albrecht of East Prussia at Königsberg—a shrewd move, as I was later to discover, which nevertheless annoyed Copernicus intensely, there being an old grudge there. A piece of shrewdness of my own was well rewarded, when my good friend Perminius Gassarus, on receipt of the copy I sent him, immediately brought out a second edition at Basle, which he financed out of his own pocket, thereby sparing me no little expense. For it was a costly business, this publishing, and, despite what they may say, I got no help, not a penny, from that old skinflint at Frauenburg, for whose benefit it was all done. Remember, these volumes to the Duke et cetera were delivered gratis (although Perminius, to my secret amusement, not only repaid my gift in the manner already recorded,

191

but also sent me a gold piece, the fool), and as well as to Giese and of course Copernicus himself, copies went also to Schöner, and Melanchton, and to many other scholars and churchmen—including Dantiscus, in whose presence, at Heilsberg Castle, I first saw my own book in print . . .

*

Yes, it was at Heilsberg that I saw the *Narratio prima* between boards for the first time. Here is how it came about. Having found the printer trustworthy, I left the completion of the work in his hands, packed my bags, said goodbye to Fat Jack and his household, and set out on the long trek to Heilsberg. I must have been out of my mind to make that hideous journey for the sake of one undeserving of the effort, whose only thanks was a peevish outburst of abuse. But as I have said more than once before, I was young then, and not half so wise as I am now. Howsoever, despite the delicate state of my health, and the foul vapours of that Prussian marsh in winter, not to mention the appalling conditions in which I had to travel (lame horses, lousy inns, so on), I reached Heilsberg at the beginning of March, not too much the worse for wear. Impetuous as ever, I went straightway to the castle and demanded to see the Bishop. I had forgotten, of course, that you do not simply walk up to these papist princelings and grasp them warmly by the arm, O no, first the formalities must be observed. Well, I shall not go into all that. Suffice it to say that it was some days before I made my way at last one morning through the gate into the vast courtyard. There I was met by a cringing cleric, a minor official with ill-shaven jowls, who inspected me with furtive sidelong glances, the tip of his chapped red nose twitching, and informed me that the Bishop had just returned from the hunt, but nevertheless had graciously agreed to receive me without further delay. As we made our way toward the sanctum, we passed by a low cart, drawn up under one of the arched stone galleries of the courtyard, on which was flung the morning's kill, a brace of boar, one of them still whimpering in agony, and a poor torn doe lying in a mess of her own guts. Whenever now I think of Dantiscus, I think first of that steaming, savaged flesh.

I had expected him to be another Giese, a pompous old fool, thick as pigshit, a petty provincial with no more style to him than an oxcart, but I was mistaken. Johannes Flachsbinder was four-and-fifty when I met him, a vigorous, striking man who wore well his weight of years. Although he was but the son of a Danzig beer brewer, he carried himself with the grace of an aristocrat. In his time he had been a soldier, scholar, a diplomat and a poet. He had travelled throughout Europe, to Araby and the Holy Land. Kings and emperors he listed among his friends, also some of the leading scientists and explorers of the age. His amorous adventures were famous, in legend as well as in his own verses, and there was hardly a corner of the civilised world that could not boast a bastard of his. A daughter, got by a Toledan noblewoman, was his favourite, so it was said, and on this brat he continued to lavish love and money, for all that Rome might say. He feared no one. At the height of the Lutheran controversy he maintained close connections with the foremost Protestants, even while the Pope himself was hurling thunderbolts at their heads. Yes, Dantiscus was a brilliant, fearless and elegant man. And a swine. And a fraud. And a lying, vindictive cunt.

In a blue and gold hall I found him, breakfasting on red wine and venison, surrounded by a gaudy crowd of huntsmen and toadies and musicians. If I thought Giese's peasant garb ridiculous, this fellow's outfit was farcical: he was clad in velvet and silk, kneeboots of soft leather, a belt inlaid with silver filigree, and—I do not lie!—a pair of close-fitting purple gloves. A prince, one of those Italian dandies, would have been daring indeed to be seen out hunting in such foppery—but a Prussian Bishop! How odd it is, the value which these Romish churchmen attach to mere show; without it, silk and so forth, they feel naked, apparently. Yet the apparel, and the music, and the Florentine splendour of the hall, could not disguise the true nature of this hard pitiless autocrat. He was a burly, thickset man, balding, with a gleaming high forehead, a great beak of a nose, and eyes of palest blue, like those of some strange vigilant bird. As I entered he rose and bowed, smiling blandly, but the glance with which he swept me was keen as a blade. His manner was warm, urbane, with just a hint of haughtiness, and all the while that he talked or listened, that faint smile continued to play about his mouth and eyes, as though some amusing, slightly ridiculous incident were taking place behind me, of which I was ignorant, and to which he was too tactful to draw attention. O, a polished fellow. He took his seat again, and, with a magisterial gesture, bade me sit beside him. He said:

193

"Herr von Lauchen, we are honoured. In these remote parts we are not often visited by the famous—O yes, indeed, I have heard of you, although I confess I had not imaged you to be so young. May I enquire what matter it is that brings you here to Heilsberg?"

He had kept me waiting three days for an audience: I was not impressed by his honeyed words. I bent on him a level gaze and said:

"I came, Bishop, to speak with you."

"Ah yes? I am flattered."

"Flattered, sir? I fail to see why you should feel so. I have not come on this journey, to this . . . this place, to flatter anyone."

That put a dent in his urbanity. It is not every day that a Bishop is spoken to thus. His smile disappeared so swiftly, I swear I heard the swish of its going. However, he was not at a loss for long; he chuckled softly, and rising said:

"My dear sir, that suits me well! I dislike flatterers. But come now, come, and I shall show you something which I think will interest you."

The company rose as we left the hall, and at the door Dantiscus bethought himself, and turned with an impatient frown, meant I'm sure to win my Lutheran approval, and daubed upon the air a negligent blessing. In silence we climbed up through the castle to his study, a long low room with frescoed walls, again in blue and gold, situated in a tower in the north-west wing, where a window gave on to what I realised must be the selfsame expanse of sky which Copernicus commanded from his tower way off in Frauenburg. I was startled, and for a moment quite confused, for here was the very model of an observatory that, before coming to Prussia, I had imagined Copernicus inhabiting. The place was stocked with every conceivable aid to the astronomer's art: globes of copper and bronze, astrolabes, quadrants, a kind of triquetrum of a design more intricate than I had ever seen, and, in pride of place, a representation of the universe exquisitely worked in gold rods and spheres, at which I gaped with open mouth, for it was based upon the Copernican theory as propounded in the *Commentariolus*. Dantiscus, smiling, pretended not to notice my consternation, but went to a desk by the window and from a drawer took out a book and handed it to me. Another shock: it was the *Narratio prima*, crisp as a loaf and smelling still of the presses and the binding room. Now the Bishop could contain himself no longer, and laughed outright. I sup-

194

pose my face was something to laugh at. He said:

"Forgive me, my friend, it is too bad of me to surprise you thus. I suppose this is the first you have seen of your book in print? Tiedemann Giese—whom you know, I think?—was kind enough to send me this copy. The messenger arrived with it only yesterday, but I have been through it in large part, and find it fascinating. The clarity of the work, and the firm grasp of the theory, are impressive."

Giese! who frothed at the mouth when he spoke the name of Dantiscus; who had warned me of this man's treachery, of his plot against Copernicus and how he had for years tormented our *domine praeceptor*; this very Giese had sent, on his own initiative, this most extraordinary of gifts to our arch enemy. Why? From nowhere, the words came to my mind: *what is it they require of me?* But then I chided myself, and put away the formless suspicions that had begun to stir within me. To be sure, there must be a simple explanation. Probably old bumbling Giese, imagining himself a cunning devil, had thought the attempt to melt this hard heart worth the hiring of a messenger to carry his gift post-haste to Heilsberg. I was not a little affected by the fancy, and wondered if my first impression of Tiedemann Giese had been mistaken, if he was not, after all, a kind and thoughtful fellow, anxious only to further my *magister's* fortunes. O Rheticus, thou dolt! The Bishop was still talking, and as he talked he moved among his instruments, laying his hands upon them lightly, as if they were the downy heads of his bastards he were caressing. He said:

"This room, you know, was once the Canon's, when he was secretary to his late uncle, my predecessor, here at Heilsberg. I am but an amateur in the noble science of astronomy, yet I possess, as you see, some few instruments, and when I came here first, and was seeking a place to house them, it seemed only fitting that I should choose this little cell, resonant as it is, surely, with echoes of the great man's thoughts. I feel I chose wisely, for these echoes, do you not think, might touch the musings of a humbler soul such as I, and perhaps inspire them?"

No, I thought nothing of the sort; the place was dead, a kind of decorated corpse; it had forgotten Copernicus, the mark of whose grey presence had been painted over with these gaudy frescoes. I said:

"Sir, I am glad you have brought up the subject of my *domine praeceptor*, Doctor Copernicus, for it is of him that I wish to speak to you."

195

He paused in his pacing, and turned upon me again his keen, careful glance. He seemed about to speak, but hesitated, and instead bade me continue. I said:

"Since his Lordship, Bishop Giese, has been in communication with you, he will, perhaps, have told you that I, along with Doctor Copernicus, have spent some months past at the Bishop's palace at Löbau. What he will not have told you, I fancy, is the purpose of our visit there." Here I turned away from him, so as not to have to meet his eyes during what came next; for I am not a good liar, it shows in my face, and I was about to lie to him. "We travelled to Löbau, sir, to discuss in peace and solitude the imminent publication of the Doctor's book, *De revolutionibus orbium mundi*, a work which you may already have heard some mention of."

He seemed not to notice the sarcasm of that last, for he stared at me for a moment, and then, to my astonishment and indeed alarm, he made a rush at me with outstretched arms. I confess he gave me a fright, for he was grinning like a maniac, which made that great beak of a nose of his dip most horribly, until the tip of it was almost in peril from those big bared teeth, and for an instant it seemed as though he were about to fall upon and savage me. However, he only clapped his hands upon my shoulders, crying:

"Why, sir, this is splendid news!"

"Eh?"

"How have you managed to persuade him? I may tell you, I have for years been urging him to publish, as have many others, and without the least success, but here *you* come from Wittenberg and win him round immediately. Splendid, I say, splendid!"

He stepped back then, evidently realising that this shouting and back-slapping was not seemly behaviour for a Bishop, and smiled his little smile again, though somewhat sheepishly. I said:

"It is good to find you so apparently pleased to hear this news."

He frowned at the coldness of my tone. "Indeed, I am very pleased. And I say again, you are to be congratulated."

"Many thanks."

"Pray, no thanks are due."

"Yet, I offer them."

"Well then, thanks also."

"Sir."

"Sir."

We disengaged, and shook our blades, but I, making a sudden advance, dealt him a bold blow.

"I have been told, however, Bishop, that Rome would not be likely to greet with great enthusiasm the making public of this work. Have I been misinformed?"

He looked at me, and gave a little laugh. He said:

"Let us have some wine, my friend."

Thus ended the first round. I was not displeased with my performance so far; but when the wine arrived, like a fool I drank deep, and very soon I was thinking myself the greatest swordsman in the world. That wine, and the hubris it induced, I blame for my subsequent humiliation. Dantiscus said:

"My dear von Lauchen, I begin to see why you have come to Heilsberg. Can it be, you think me less than honest when I say, hearing the news you bring with you today, that I am overjoyed? O, I well know the Canon thinks I hate him, and would, though God knows why, prevent him, if I could, from publishing his book. All this, I see, he has told you. But, my friend, believe me, he is mistaken, and does me grave injustice. To these his charges, I reply just this—come, let me fill your cup—has he forgot how I, this six years past, have ever sought to have him speak, and publicise his theory? *Meinherr* von Lauchen, truth to tell, I am weary of the man, and cannot help but feel rebuffed when you arrive here and reveal that winning his agreement took but a word from you!"

I shrugged, and said:

"But what, my Lord, about this Schillings woman, eh? It's said you accuse him of taking her to bed—and she his cousin! I think, my friend, instead of love you bear him malice."

He hung his head.

"Ah, that. Distasteful business, I agree. But, *Meinherr*, as Bishop of this See, it is my solemn duty to ensure that Mother Church's clergy shall abjure all vice. What can I do? The man insists on keeping in his house this cousin-mistress. And anyway, the matter is deeper than you know, as I, if you will listen, shall quickly show. First, the times are bad; the Church, my friend, fears all that Luther wrought, and must defend her tarnished reputation. Second, it's not the learned Doctor Nicolas at whom my shot is mainly aimed, but one Sculteti, Canon of

Frauenburg also—a treacherous fellow, this one. Not only does he live in sin, but also he plots against the Church here, and puts out false reports. Besides, he's involved with the Germans—ahem! More wine? But this is not germane to my intention, which is that you should know I love the learned Doctor, and would go to any lengths to spare him pain. And please! do not think evil of our Church. All these . . . these petty matters all are due to badness in the times. They are but passing madness, and will pass, while certain to endure is the Canon's masterwork, of this I'm sure. And now, my friend, a toast: to you! to us! and to *De revolutionibus!*"

I drained my cup, and looked about me, and was vaguely surprised to find that we had left the tower, and were standing now in the open air, on a high balcony. Below us was the courtyard, filled with searing lemon-coloured light; odd foreshortened little people hurried hither and thither about their business in a most humorous fashion. Something seemed to have gone wrong with my legs, for I was leaning all off to one side. Dantiscus, looking more than ever like a besotted Italianate princeling, was still talking. Apparently I had stopped listening some time before, for I could not understand him now very well. He said:

"Science! Progress! Rebirth! The New Age! What do you say, friend?"

I said:

"Yesh, O yesh."

And then there was more wine, and more talk, and music and a deal of laughter, and I grew merrier and merrier, and thought what a capital fellow after all was this Dantiscus, so civilised, so enlightened; and later I was feasted amid a large noisy company, which I addressed on divers topics, such as Science! and Progress! and the New Age! and all in all made an utter fool of myself. At dawn I awoke in a strange room, with a blinding ache in my head, and longing for death. I crept away from the castle without seeing a soul, and fled Heilsberg, never to return.

What was I to think now, in sickeningly sober daylight, of this Dantiscus, who had plied me with drink and flattery, who had feasted me in his hall, who had toasted the success of a publication for which, so Giese would have it, he wished in his heart nothing but abject failure? After much argument with myself, I decided that despite all he was a scoundrel—had he not ordered a burning of books? had he not threatened Lutherans with fire and the rack? had he not hounded without mercy my *domine praeceptor*? No amount of wine, nor flattery, nor talk of progress, could obliterate those crimes. O knave! O viper! O yesh.

*

Before I leave this part of my tale, there is something more I must mention. To this day I am uncertain whether or not what I am about to relate did in reality take place. On the following day, when I was well out on my flight from Heilsberg, and was wondering, in great trepidation, if Dantiscus, finding me gone without a word, might think to send after me, and drag me back to another round of drinking and carousing, suddenly, like some great thing swooping down on me out of a sky that a moment before had been empty, there came into my head the memory, I call it a memory, for convenience, of having seen Raphaël yesterday at the castle—Raphaël, that laughing lad from Löbau! He had been in the courtyard, surrounded by that lemon-coloured sunlight and the hither and thithering figures, mounted on a black horse. How clearly I remembered him!—or imagined that I did. He had grown a little since last I had seen him, for he was at that age when boys shoot up like saplings, and was very elegantly got up in cap and boots and cape, quite the little gentleman, but Raphaël for all that, unmistakably, I would have known him anywhere, at any age. I see it still, that scene, the sunlight, and the rippling of the horse's glossy blue-black flanks, the groom's hand upon the bridle, and the slim, capped and crimson-caped, booted, beautiful boy, that scene, I see it, and wonder that such a frail tender thing survived so long, to bring me comfort now, and make me young again, here in this horrid place. Raphaël. I write down the name, slowly, say it softly aloud, and hear aetherial echoes of seraphs singing. Raphaël. I have tears still. Why was he there, so far from home? The answer, of course, was simple, viz. the boy had brought my book from Löbau. Yet was there not more to it than that? I called his name, too late, for he was already at the gate, on his way home, and Dantiscus, taking me by the arm, said: *friend, you should be careful,* and gave me a strange look. What did he mean? Or did he speak, really? Did I imagine it, all of it? Was it a dream, which I am dreaming still? If that is so, if it was but a delusion spawned by a

199

mind sodden with drink, then I say the imagining was prophetic, in a way, as I shall demonstrate, in its place.

*     *     *

I returned home then to Wittenberg, only to find to my dismay that it was no longer home. How to explain this strange sensation? You know it well, I'm sure. The university, my friends and teachers, my rooms, my books, all were just as when I had left them, and yet all were changed. It was as if some subtle blight had contaminated everything I knew, the heart of everything, the essential centre, while the surface remained sound. It took me some time to understand that it was not Wittenberg that was blighted, but myself. The wizard of Frauenburg had put his spell on me, and one thing, one only thing, I knew, would set me free of that enchantment. After my ignominious flight from Heilsberg, all interest in Copernicus's work had mysteriously abandoned me, despite the lie I had told Dantiscus regarding the imaginary triumph I had scored at Löbau; for I had now no intention of continuing my campaign to force Copernicus to publish. I say that interest in his work abandoned me, and not vice versa, for thus it happened. I had no hand in it: simply, all notion of returning to Frauenburg, and joining battle with him again, all that just departed, and was as though it had never been. Had some secret sense within me perceived the peril that awaited me in Prussia? If so, that warning sense was not strong enough, for I was hardly back in Wittenberg before I found myself in correspondence with Petreius the printer. O, I was vague, and wrote that he must understand that there was no question now of publishing the main work; but I was, I said, preparing a *Narratio secunda* (which I was not), and since it would contain many diagrams and tables and suchlike taken direct from *De revolutionibus*, it was necessary that I should know what his block-cutters and type-setters were capable of in the matter of detail et cetera. However, despite all my caution and circumlocutions, Petreius, with unintentional and uncanny good aim, ignored entirely all mention of a second *Narratio*, and replied huffily that, as I should know, his craftsmen were second to none where scientific works were concerned, and he would gladly and with confidence contract to put between boards Copernicus's great treatise, of which he had heard so many reports.

200

Although this pompous letter angered and disturbed me, I soon came to regard it as an omen, and began again to toy with the idea of returning to Frauenburg. Not, you understand, that I was ready to go rushing off northwards once more, with cap in hand, and panting with enthusiasm, to make a fool of myself as I had done before, O no; this time if I journeyed it would be for my own purposes that I would do so, to find my lost self, as it were, and rid myself of this spell, so as to come home to my beloved Wittenberg again, and find it whole, and be at peace. Therefore, as soon as I was free, I set out with a stout heart, by post-carriage, on horseback, sometimes on foot, and arrived at Frauenburg at summer's end, 1540, and was relieved to find Copernicus not yet dead, and still in possession, more or less, of his faculties. He greeted me with a characteristic display of enthusiasm, viz. a start, an owlish stare, and then a hangman's handshake. The Schillings was still with him, and Dantiscus, need I say it, was still howling for her to be gone. For a long time now he had been using Giese to transmit his threats. Sculteti, Copernicus's ally in the affair of the *focariae*, whom Dantiscus had mentioned, had it seemed been expelled by the Chapter, and had flown to Italy. This departure, along with Dantiscus's increasingly menacing behaviour, had forced Copernicus to make a last desperate effort to get rid of her, but in vain. There had been a furious argument (smashed crockery, screams, pisspots flying through windows and striking passers-by: the usual, I suppose), which had ended with the *Mädchen* packing up her belongings and sending them off, at great expense (the Canon's), to Danzig, where some remnant of her tribe kept an inn, or a bawdyhouse, I forget which. However, it seems she considered this so to speak symbolic departure a sufficiently stern rebuke to Copernicus for his ill nature, and in reality had no intention of following after her chattels, which in due time returned, like some awful ineluctable curse. So we settled down, the three of us, in our tower, where life was barely, just barely, tolerable. I kept out of the way of the Schillings, not for fear of her, but for fear of *throttling* her; between the two of us the old man cowered, mumbling and sighing and trying his best to die. Soon, I could see, he would succeed in doing that. Death was slinking up behind him, with its black sack at the ready. I would have to work quickly, if I were to snatch his book from him before he took it with him into that suffocating darkness. Yet, if his body was weakening, his mind was still capable of withholding, in an iron grip, that for which I had come: the decision to publish.

*

I stayed with him for more than a year, tormented by boredom and frustration, and an unrelenting irritation at the impossible old fool and his ways. He agreed that I might make a copy of the manuscript, and that at least was some occupation; the work might even have calmed my restless spirit, had he not insisted on reminding me every day that I must not imagine, merely because he had relented thus far, that he would go farther, and allow me to take this copy to Petreius. So that there was little more for me in this scribbling than aching knuckles, and the occasional, malicious pleasure of correcting his slips (I crossed out that nonsensical line in which he speculated on the possibility of elliptical orbits—*elliptical orbits*, for God's sake!). Various other small tasks which I performed, to relieve the tedium, included the completion of a map of Prussia, which the old man, in collaboration with the disgraced Sculteti, had begun at the request of the previous Bishop of Ermland. This, along with some other trivial things, I sent off to Albrecht, Duke of Prussia, who rewarded me with the princely sum of one ducat. So much for aristocratic patronage! However, it was not for money I had approached this Lutheran Duke, but rather in the hope that he might use on my behalf his considerable influence among German churchmen and nobles, who I feared might make trouble should I win Copernicus's consent, and appear in their midst with a manuscript full of dangerous theories clutched under my arm. The Duke, I found, was more generous with paper and ink than he had been with his ducats; he sent letters to Johann Friedrich, Elector of Saxony, and also to the University of Wittenberg, mentioning how impressed he had been with the *Narratio prima* (*clever* old Giese!), and urging that I should be allowed to publish what he called *this admirable book on astronomy*, meaning *De revolutionibus*. There was some confusion, of course; there always is. Albrecht, like Petreius, apparently had found it inconceivable that I should be so eager to publish the work of another, and therefore he assumed that I was attempting some crafty ruse whereby I hoped to put out my own theories in disguise; did I think to fool the Duke of Prussia? thought haughty Albrecht, and put down in his letters what to him was obvious: that the work was all my own. The cretin. I had no end of trouble disentangling that mess, while

202

at the same time keeping these manoeuvres hidden from the Canon, who was wont to spit at the mention of the name of Grand Master Albrecht, as he insisted on calling him.

This was not the only little plot I had embarked upon in secret—*and* in trepidation, for I was mortally afraid that if he found out, Copernicus would burn the manuscript on the instant. Yet I had lapses, when my caution, which I had learned from him, deserted me. One day, shortly after my return to Frauenburg, I told him in a rash moment of frankness of my visit to Dantiscus. It was one of the rare occasions when I witnessed colour invade the ghastly pallor of his face. He flew into a rage, and gibbered, spraying me copiously with spit, yelling that I had no right to do such a thing, that I had *no right!* I was, he said, as bad as Giese, that damned meddler, who had sent the *Narratio prima* to Heilsberg even after he had been expressly warned not even to consider doing such a thing. What was surprising about this outburst was not so much the fury as the fear which I could plainly see, skulking behind the bluster; true, he had cause to be wary of Dantiscus, but this show of veritable terror seemed wholly excessive. What he feared, of course, although I could not know it then, was that I might have said something to Dantiscus that would ruin the plot which the Canon and Giese had been working out against me for years in secret—but wait, I am impetuous; wait.

There were other things that puzzled and surprised me. For instance, I discovered another aspect of his passion for secrecy: the Schillings knew so little of his affairs that she thought his astronomical work a mere pastime, a means of relaxing from the rigours of his true calling, which was, so she believed, medicine! And this woman shared his house, his bed!

And yet, perhaps he did regard astronomy as merely a plaything; I do not know, I do not know, I could not understand the man, I admit it. I was then, and I am still, despite my loss of faith, one of those who look to the future for redemption, I mean redemption from the world, which has nothing to do with Christ's outlandish promises, but with the genius of Man. We can do anything, overcome anything. Am I not a living proof of this? They schemed against me, tried to ruin me, and yet I won, although even yet they will not acknowledge my victory. What was I saying . . .? Yes: I look to the future, live in the future, and so, when I speak of the present, I am as it were looking backward, into

203

what is, for me, already the past. Do you follow that? Copernicus was different, very different. If he believed that Man could redeem himself, he saw in—how shall I say—in *immobility* the only possible means toward that end. His world moved in circles, endlessly, and each circuit was a repetition exactly of all others, past and future, to the extremities of time: which is no movement at all. How, then, could I be expected to understand one whose thinking was so firmly locked in the old worn-out frame? We spoke a different language—and I do not mean his Latin against my German, although that difference, now that I think about it, represents well enough the deeper thing. Once, when we were walking together on the little path within the cathedral wall, which he paced each day, gravely, at a fixed hour and a fixed pace, as though performing a penance rather than taking the air, I began to speak idly of Italy, and the blue south, where I spent my youth. He heard me out, nodding the while, and then he said:

"Ah yes, Italy; I also spent some time there, before you were born. And what times they were! It seemed as though a new world was on the point of birth. All that was strong and youthful and vigorous revolted against the past. Never, perhaps, have the social authorities so unanimously supported the intellectual movement. It seemed as though there were no conservatives left among them. All were moving and straining in the same direction, authority, society, fashion, the politicians, the women, the artists, the *umanista*. There was a boundless confidence abroad, a feverish joy. The mind was liberated from authority, was free to wander under the heavens. The monopoly of knowledge was abolished, and it was now the possession of the whole community. Ah yes."

I was of course astonished to hear him speak thus, astonished and filled with joy, for this, *this* was that Copernicus whom I had come to Frauenburg to find, and had not found, until now; and I turned to him with tears in my eyes, and began to yelp and caper in a paroxysm of agreement with all that he had said. Too late I noticed that small grey grin, the malicious glint in his look, and realised that I had fallen, O arse over tip, into a trap. He drew back, as one draws back from a slavering lunatic, and considered me with a contempt so profound it seemed near to nauseating him. He said:

"I was speaking less than seriously, of course. Italy is the country of death. You remind me sometimes of my late brother. He also was given to jabbering about progress and renascence, the new age whose dawn was about to break. He died in his beloved Italy, of the pox."

It was not the words, you understand, but the tone in which they were spoken, that seemed to gather up and examine briefly all that I was, before heaving it all, blood and bones and youth and tears and enthusiasm, back upon the swarming midden-heap of humanity. He did not hate me, nor even dislike me; I think he found me . . . distasteful. But what did I care? It is true, when I came to him first there was no thought in my head of fame and fortune for myself; I had one desire only, to make known to the world the work of a great astronomer. Now, however, all that had changed. I was older. He had aged me a decade in a year. No longer was I the young fool ready to fall to his knees before some manufactured hero; I had realised myself. Yet perhaps I should be grateful to him? Was it not his contempt that had forced me to look more closely at myself, that had allowed me to recognise in the end that I was a greater astronomer than he? Yes! yes! far greater. Sneer if you like, shake your empty heads all you wish, but I— *I* know the truth. Why do you think I stayed with him, endured his mockery, his pettiness, his *distaste*? Do you imagine that I enjoyed living in that bleak tower, freezing in winter and roasting in summer, shivering at night while the rats danced overhead, groaning and straining in that putrid jakes, my guts bound immovably by the mortar of his trollop's gruel, do you think I enjoyed all that? By comparison, this place where I am now in exile is very heaven.

Well then, you say, if it was so terrible, why did I remain there, why did I not flee, and leave Copernicus, wrapped in his caution and his bitterness, to sink into oblivion? Listen: I have said that I was a greater astronomer than he, *and I am*, but he possessed one precious thing that I lacked—I mean a reputation. O, he was cautious, yes, and he genuinely feared and loathed the world, but he was cunning also, and knew that curiosity is a rash which men will scratch and scratch until it drives them frantic for the cure. For years now he had eked out, at carefully chosen intervals, small portions of his theory, each one of which—the *Commentariolus*, the *Letter contra Werner*, my *Narratio*—was a grain of salt rubbed into the rash with which he had inflicted his fellow astronomers. And they had scratched, and the rash had developed into a sore that spread, until all Europe was infected, and screaming for the one thing alone that would end the plague,

205

which was *De revolutionibus orbium mundi*, by Doctor Nicolas Copernicus, of Torun on the Vistula. And he would give them their physic; he had decided, he had decided to publish, I knew it, and he knew I knew it, but what he did not know was that, by doing so, by publishing, he would not be crowning his own reputation, but making mine. You do not understand? Only wait, and I shall explain.

*

But first I must recount some few other small matters, such as, to begin with, how in the end he came to give me his consent to publish. However, in order to illuminate that scene, as it were, I wish to record a conversation I had with him which, later, I came to realise was a summation of his attitude to science and the world, the aridity, the barrenness of that attitude. He had been speaking, I remember, of the seven spheres of Hermes Trismegistus through which the soul ascends toward redemption in the eighth sphere of the fixed stars. I grew impatient listening to this rigmarole, and I said something like:

"But your work, *Meister*, is of this world, of the here and now; it speaks to men of what they may know, and not of mysteries that they can only believe in blindly or not at all."

He shook his head impatiently.

"No no no *no*. You imagine that my book is a kind of mirror in which the real world is reflected; but you are mistaken, you must realise that. In order to build such a mirror, I should need to be able to perceive the world whole, in its entirety and in its essence. But our lives are lived in such a tiny, confined space, and in such disorder, that this perception is not possible. There is no contact, none worth mentioning, between the universe and the place in which we live."

I was puzzled and upset; this nihilism was inimical to all I held to be true and useful. I said:

"But if what you say is so, then how is it that we are aware of the existence of the universe, the real world? How, without perception, do we *see*?"

"Ach, Rheticus!" It was the first time he had called me by that name. "You do not understand me! You do not understand yourself. You think that to see is to perceive, but listen, listen: *seeing is not perception!* Why will no one realise that? I lift my head and look at the stars, as did the ancients, and I say: what are those lights? Some call them torches borne by angels, others, pinpricks in the shroud of Heaven; others still, scientists such as ourselves, call them stars and planets that make a manner of machine whose workings we strive to comprehend. But do you not understand that, without perception, all these theories are equal in value. Stars or torches, it is all one, all merely an exalted naming; those lights shine on, indifferent to what we call them. My book is not science—it is a dream. I am not even sure if science is possible." He paused a while to brood, and then went on. "We think only those thoughts that we have the words to express, but we acknowledge that limitation only by our wilfully foolish contention that the words mean more than they say; it is a pretty piece of sleight of hand, that: it sustains our illusions wonderfully, until, that is, the time arrives when the sands have run out, and the truth breaks in upon us. Our lives—" he smiled "—are a little journey through God's guts . . ." His voice had become a whisper, and it was plain to me that he was talking to himself, but then all at once he remembered me, and turned on me fiercely, wagging a finger in my face. "Your Father Luther recognised this truth early on, and had not the courage to face it; he tried to deny it, by his pathetic and futile attempt to shatter the form and thereby come at the content, the essence. His was a defective mind, of course, and could not comprehend the necessity for ritual, and hence he castigated Rome for its so-called blasphemy and idol-worship. He betrayed the people, took away their golden calf but gave them no tablets of the law in its place. Now we are seeing the results of Luther's folly, when the peasantry is in revolt all over Europe. You wonder why I will not publish? The people will laugh at my book, or that mangled version of it which filters down to them from the universities. The people always mistake at first the frightening for the comic thing. But very soon they will come to see what it is that I have done, I mean what they will imagine I have done, diminished Earth, made of it merely another planet among planets; they will begin to despise the world, and something will die, and out of that death will come *death*. You do not know what I am talking about, do you, Rheticus? You are a fool, like the rest . . . like myself."

*

I remember the evening very well: sun on the Baltic, and small boats out on the Frisches Haff, and a great silence everywhere. I had just finished copying the manuscript, and had but put down the last few words when the Canon, perhaps hearing some thunderclap of finality shaking the air of the tower, came down from the observatory and hovered in my doorway, sniffing at me enquiringly. I said nothing, and only glanced at him vacantly. The evening silence was a pool of peace in which my spirits hung suspended, like a flask of air floating upon waters, and wearily, wearily, I drifted off into a waking swoon, intending only to stay a moment, to bathe for a moment my tired heart, but it was so peaceful there on that brimming bright meniscus, so still, that I could not rouse myself from this welcome kind of little death. The Canon was standing at my shoulder. The sky outside was blue and light, enormous. When he spoke, the words seemed to come, slowly, from a long way off. He said:

*"If at the foundation of all there lay only a wildly seething power which, writhing with obscure passions, produced everything that is great and everything that is insignificant, if a bottomless void never satiated lay hidden beneath all, what then would life be but despair?"*

I said:

*"I hold it true that pure thought can grasp reality, as the ancients dreamed."*

He said:

*"Science aims at constructing a world which shall be symbolic of the world of commonplace experience."*

I said:

*"If you would know the reality of nature, you must destroy the appearance, and the farther you go beyond the appearance, the nearer you will be to the essence."*

He said:

*"It is of the highest significance that the outer world represents something independent of us and absolute with which we are confronted."*

I said:

*"The death of one god is the death of all."*

He said:

*"Vita brevis, sensus ebes, negligentiae torpor et inutiles occupationes, nos paucula scire permittent. Et aliquotiens scita excutit ab animo per temporum lapsum fraudatrix scientiae et inimica memoriae praeceps oblivio."*

Night advanced and darkened the brooding waters of the Baltic, but the air was still bright, and in the bright air, vivid yet serene, Venus shone. Copernicus said:

"When you have once seen the chaos, you must make some thing to set between yourself and that terrible sight; and so you make a mirror, thinking that in it shall be reflected the reality of the world; but then you understand that the mirror reflects only appearances, and that reality is somewhere else, off behind the mirror; and then you remember that behind the mirror there is only the chaos."

Dark dark dark.

I said:

"And yet, Herr Doctor, the truth must be revealed."

"Ah, truth, that word I no longer understand."

"Truth is that which cannot be concealed."

"You have not listened, you have not understood."

"Truth is certain good, that's all I know."

"I am an old man, and you make me weary."

"Give your agreement then, and let me go."

"The mirror is cracking! listen! do you hear it?"

"Yes, I hear, and yet I do not fear it."

The light of day was gone now, and that moment that is like an ending had arrived, when the eyes, accustomed to the sun, cannot yet distinguish the humbler sources of light, and darkness seems total; but still it was not dark enough for him, and he shuffled away from me, away from the window, and crawled into the shadows of the room like some poor black bent wounded thing. He said:

"The shortness of life, the dullness of the senses, the torpor of indifference and useless occupations, allow us to know but little; and in time, oblivion, that defrauder of knowledge and memory's enemy, cheats us of even the little that we knew. I am an old man, and you make me weary. What is it you require of me? The book is nothing, less than nothing. First they shall laugh, and later weep. But you require the book. It is nothing, less than nothing. I am an old man. Take it . . ."

*

That was the last I was to see of him, in this world or, I trust, in any other. I left the tower that very night, carrying with me my books and

209

my belongings and my bitter victory. I did not remark the abruptness of this going, nor did he. It seemed the correct way. The inn to which I fled was a pigsty, but at least the air was cleaner there than in that crypt I had left, and the pigs, for all their piggishness, were alive, and snuffling happily in the good old muck. Yet, though I abandoned the tower without a thought, I found it not so easy to do the same with Frauenburg; that was August, and not until September was in did I at last depart. I spent those few final weeks kicking my heels about the town, drinking alone, too much, and whoring joylessly. Once I returned to the tower, determined to see him again, yet at a loss to know what more there was to be said; and perhaps it was as well that the Schillings planted herself in the doorway and said that the old man would not see me, that he was ill, and anyway had given her strict instructions not to let me in if I should dare to call. Even then I did not go, but waited another week, although I should have been in Wittenberg long before. What was it that held me back? Maybe I realised, however obscurely, that in leaving Prussia I would be leaving behind what I can only call a version of myself; for Frauenburg killed the best in me, my youth and my enthusiasm, my happiness, my faith, yes, faith. From that time on I believed in nothing, neither God nor Man. You ask why? You laugh, you say: poor fool, to be so affected by a sick old man's bitterness and despair; O, you say, you ask, all of you, why, and how, and wherefore, you are all so wise, but you know nothing— nothing! Listen.

\*　　\*　　\*

I wished to go straightway to Petreius, but if I were to keep my post at Wittenberg, I needs must return there without further delay, for the authorities at the university were beginning to mutter threateningly over my unconscionably long absence. And indeed they seemed very glad to have me back, for I had hardly arrived before I was elected Dean of the faculty of mathematics! I might have been excused for thinking that it was my own brilliance that had won this honour, but I was no fool, and I knew very well that it was not me, but my connection with the Great Man of Frauenburg that they were honouring, in their cautious way. It was no matter, anyway, for I was confident that

210

before long the goddess Fama would turn her tender gaze on me. However, the promotion imposed new tasks on me, new responsibilities,
and it would be spring, I now saw, before I could find the freedom to go
to Nuremberg and Petreius; might not the goddess tire before then of
waiting for me? With this thought in mind, I decided to have printed
immediately, there in Wittenberg, a short extract from the manuscript,
which would not reveal the scope of the entire work but only hint at it.
(You see how I had learned from the master?) Thus originated *De late-
ribus et angulis triangulorum.* It caused no little stir in the university,
and even in the town itself, and helped me to squeeze out of the burghers and the clerics, and even out of Melanchton himself, several valu-
able letters of recommendation, which I carried with me to
Nuremberg.

*

I arrived there at the beginning of May, and at once set about the
printing of *De revolutionibus orbium mundi* in its entirety. Petreius's
craftsmen made swift progress. I lodged in the town in the house of a
certain Lutheran merchant, Johann Müller, to whom I had been recommended by Melanchton. He was a bearable fellow, this Müller:
pompous, of course, like all his kind, but not unlearned—he even displayed some interest in the work on which I was engaged. Also, his beds
were soft, and his wife exceeding handsome, though somewhat fat. All
in all, then, I was well content at Nuremberg, and I might even say I
was happy there, had not there been lodged in my black heart the ineradicable pain that was the memory of Prussia. From there not a word
came, of discouragement or otherwise, until Petreius broached the
subject of finance, and I told him it was not my affair, that he should
send to Frauenburg. This he did, and after some weeks a reply came,
not from Koppernigk, but from Bishop Giese, who said that he had
just that day arrived there from Löbau, having been summoned by
Anna Schillings to attend the Canon, who was, so Giese said, sick unto
death. This news moved me not at all: living or dead, Koppernigk was
no longer a part of my plans. True, I spent an anxious week while
Petreius underwent an attack of nerves, brought on by the realisation
that he would have to finance the publication of the book himself, now
that the author was dying, but in the end he went ahead, a decision he
was not to regret, since he fixed the price per copy, of the thousand

211

copies that he printed, at 28 ducats 6 pfennigs, the greedy old bastard.

My plans. How cunning they were, how cold and clever, and, in the end, how easily they were brought thundering down in rubble about my ears. The first signals of impending disaster came when I had been but two months in Nuremberg. Petreius had already set up thirty-four sheets, or about two-thirds of the book, and had begun to invite into the printing house some of the leading citizens of the town, so that they might view the progress of the work, and, being impressed, advertise it abroad. Now, it seemed to me only to be expected that these men of influence should above all wish to meet me, the sponsor of this bold new theory, but, though I spent the most part of my days in the caseroom, where the sheets were proofed for their viewing, I found to my surprise, and vague alarm, that they avoided me like the plague, and some of them even fled when I made to approach them. I spoke to Petreius of it, and he shrugged, and pretended not to understand me, and would not look me in the eye. I tried to dismiss the matter, telling myself that businessmen were always in awe of scholars, fearing their learning et cetera, but it would not do: I knew that something was afoot. Then, one evening, the good Herr Müller, twisting his hands and grimacing, and looking for all the world like a reluctant hangman, came to me and said that if it suited me, and if it was not a great inconvenience, and if I would not take his words amiss, and so on and so forth—and, well, the matter was: would I kindly leave his house? He made some lame excuse for this extraordinary demand, about needing the extra room for an impending visit by some relatives, but I was in a rage by then, and was not listening, and I told him that if it suited him, and if it was not a great inconvenience, he might fuck himself, and, pausing only to inform him that I was grateful for the use of his jade of a wife, whom I had been merrily ploughing during the past weeks, I packed my bags and left, and found myself that night once again lodging at an inn. And there, shortly afterwards, Osiander visited me.

*

Andreas Osiander, theologian and scholar, a leading Lutheran, friend of Melanchton, had for some time (despite his religious affiliations!) been in correspondence with Canon Nicolas—had been, indeed, one of those like myself who had urged him to publish. He was also, I might add, a cold, cautious, humourless grey creature, and it was, no doubt, the cast of his personality which recommended him to the Canon. O yes, they were two of a kind. At first, like a fool, I imagined that he had come to pay his respects to a great astronomer (*me*, that is), and congratulate me on winning consent to publish *De revolutionibus*, but Osiander soon dispelled these frivolous notions. I was ill when he arrived. A fever of the brain, brought on no doubt by the manner of my parting from Müller, had laid me low with a burning head and aching limbs, so that when he was shown into my humble room I fancied at first that he was an hallucination. The shutters were drawn against the harsh spring light. He planted himself at the foot of my bed, his head in the shadows and bands of light through the slats of the shutters striping his puffed-up chest, so that he looked for all the world like a giant wasp. I was frightened of him even before he spoke. He had that unmistakable smell of authority about him. He looked with distaste at my surroundings, and with even deeper distaste at me, and said in his pinched voice (a drone!) that when he had been told that I was lodging here he had hardly credited it, but now, it seemed, he must believe it. Did I not realise that I was, in a manner of speaking, an ambassador of Wittenberg in this city? And did I think it fitting that the name of the very centre of Protestant learning should be associated with this . . . this *place*? I began to explain how I had been thrown out on the street by a man to whom I had been recommended by Melanchton himself, but he was not interested in that, and cut me short by enquiring if I had anything to say in my defence. Defence? My hands began to shake, from fever or fear, I could not tell which. I tried to rise from the bed, but in vain. There was something of the inquisitor about Osiander. He said:

"I have come this day from Wittenberg, whither I was summoned in connection with certain matters of which I think you are aware. Please, Herr von Lauchen, I would ask you: no protestations of injured innocence. That will only cause delay, and I wish, indeed I *intend*, to conclude this unfortunate business as swiftly as possible, to prevent the further spread of scandal. The fact is, that for a long time now, we— and I include in that others whose names I need not mention!—for a long time, I say, we have been watching your behaviour with increasing dismay. We do not expect that a man should be without blemish. However, we do expect, we *demand*, at the very least, discretion. And you, my friend, have been anything but discreet. The manner in which you comported yourself at the university was tolerated. I use the word advisedly: you were tolerated. But, that you should go to Prussia, to Ermland, that very bastion of popery, and there disgrace not only yourself, not only the reputation of your university, but your religion as well, that, *that*, Herr von Lauchen, we could not tolerate. We gave you every chance to mend your ways. When you returned from Frauenburg, we granted you one of the highest honours at our disposal, and created you Dean of your faculty; yet how did you repay us—how? You fled, sir, and abandoned behind you a living and speaking—I might say *chattering*—testimony of your pernicious indulgences! I mean, of course, the boy, whose presence fortunately was brought to our attention by the master he deserted, and we were able to silence him."

"Boy? What boy?" But of course I knew, I knew. Already light had begun to dawn upon me. Osiander sighed heavily. He said:

"Very well, Herr von Lauchen, play the fool, if that is what you wish. You know who I mean—and I know you know. You think to win some manner of reprieve by playing on my discretion; you think that by pressing me to speak openly of these distasteful matters you will embarrass me, and force me to withdraw—is that it? You shall not succeed. The boy's name is Raphaël. He is, or was, a servant in the household of the Bishop of Kulm, Tiedemann Giese, at Löbau, where you stayed for some time, did you not, in the company of Canon Koppernigk? You behaviour there, and your . . . your connection with this boy, was reported to us by the Bishop himself, who, I might add, was charitable enough to defend you (as did Canon Koppernigk himself!), even while you were spreading scandal and corruption throughout his household. But what I want to ask you, for my own benefit, you understand, so that I shall know—what I want to ask you is: why, *why* did you have this boy follow you across the length of Germany?"

"He did not follow me," I said. "He was sent." I saw it all, yes, yes, I saw it all.

"*Sent?*" Osiander bellowed, and his wasp's wings buzzed and boomed in the gloom. "What do you mean, sent? The boy arrived in Wittenberg in rags, with his feet bandaged. His horse had died under him. He said you told him to come to you, that you would put him to schooling, that you would make a gentleman of him. Sent? Can you not spare even a grain of compassion for this unfortunate creature

214

whom you have destroyed, whom you could not face, and fled before he came; and do you think to save yourself by this wild and evil accusation? Sent? Who sent him, pray?"

I turned my face to the wall. "It's no matter. You would not believe me, if I told you. I shall say only this, that I am not a sodomite, that I have been slandered and vilified, that you have been fed a pack of lies."

He began a kind of enraged dance then, and shrieked:

"I will not listen to this! I will not listen! Do you want me to tell you what the child said, do you want to hear, do you? These are his very words, his very words, I cannot forget them, never; he said: *Every morning I brought him his food, and he made me wank him tho' I cried, and begged him to release me.* A child, sir, a child! and you put such words into his mouth, and made him do such things, and God knows what else besides. May God forgive you. Now, enough of this, enough; I have said more than I intended, more than I should. If we were in Rome no doubt you would have been poisoned by now, and spirited away, but here in Germany we are more civilised than that. There is a post at Leipzig University, the chair of mathematics. It has been arranged that you will fill it. You will pack your bags today, now, this instant, and be gone. You may—*silence!*—you may not protest, it is too late for that: Melanchton himself has ordered your removal. It was he, I might add, who decided that you should be sent to Leipzig, which is no punishment at all. Had I my way, sir, you would be driven out of Germany. And now, prepare to depart. Whatever work of yours there is unfinished here, I shall take charge of it. I am told you are engaged in the printing of an astronomical work from the pen of Canon Koppernigk? He has asked that I should oversee the final stages of this venture. For the rest, we shall put it about that, for reasons of health, you felt you must abandon the task to my care. Now go."

"The boy," I said, "Raphaël: what has become of him?" I remembered him in the courtyard at Heilsberg, in his cap and cape, mounted on his black horse; just thus must he have looked as he set out from Löbau to come to me at Wittenberg.

"He was sent back to Löbau Castle, of course," said Osiander. "What did you expect?"

Do you know what they do to runaway servants up there in Prussia? They nail them by the ear to a pillory, and give them a knife with which to cut themselves free. I wonder what punishment worse than that did Giese threaten the child with, to force him to follow me and tell those lies, so as to destroy me?

*

I could not at first understand why they, I mean Koppernigk and Giese, had done this to me, and I went off to exile in Leipzig thinking that surely some terrible mistake had been made. Only later, when I saw the preface which Osiander added to the book (which, when he was finished with it, was called *De revolutionibus orbium coelestium*), only then did I see how they had used me, poor shambling clown, to smuggle the work into the heart of Lutheran Germany, to the best Lutheran printer, with the precious Lutheran letters of recommendation in my fist, and how, when all that was done, they had simply got rid of me, to make way for Osiander and the *imprimatur* of his preface, which made the book safe from the hounds of Rome and Wittenberg alike. They did not trust me, you see, except to do the hackwork.

*

Did I in some way, I asked myself then, merit this betrayal? For it seemed to me inconceivable that all my labours should have been rewarded thus without some terrible sin on my part; but I could not, try as I might, find myself guilty of any sin heinous enough to bring down such judgment on my head. Throughout the book, *there is not one mention of my name.* Schönberg is mentioned, and Giese, but not I. This omission affected me strangely. It was as if, somehow, I had not existed at all during those past years. Had this been my crime, I mean some essential lack of presence; had I not been *there* vividly enough? That may be it, for all I know. Frauenburg had been a kind of death, for death is the absence of faith, I hardly know what I am saying, yet I feel I am making sense. Christ! I have waited patiently for this moment when I would have my revenge, and now I am ruining it. Why must I blame myself, search for some sin within myself, all this nonsense, why? No need of that, no need—it was all his doing, his his *his!* Calm, Rheticus.

Here is my revenge. Here it is, at last.

*

The *Book of revolutions* is a pack of lies from start to finish . . . No, that will not do, it is too, too something, I don't know. Besides, it is not true, not entirely, and truth is the only weapon I have left with which to blast his cursed memory.

The *Book of revolutions* is an engine which destroys itself, yes yes, that's better.

The *Book of revolutions* is an engine which destroys itself, which is to say that by the time its creator had completed it, by the time he had, so to speak, hammered home the last bolt, the thing was in bits around him. I admit, it took me some time to recognise this fact, or at least to recognise the full significance of it. How I swore and sweated during those summer nights at Löbau, striving to make sense of a theory wherein each succeeding conclusion or hypothesis seemed to throw doubt on those that had gone before! Where, I asked, where is the beauty and simplicity, the celestial order so confidently promised in the *Commentariolus*, where is the pure, the pristine thing? The book which I held in my hands was a shambles, a crippled, hopeless mishmash. But let me be specific, let me give some examples of where it went so violently wrong. It was, so Koppernigk tells us, a profound dissatisfaction with the theory of the motions of the planets put forward by Ptolemy in the *Almagest* which first sent him in search of some new system, one that would be mathematically correct, would agree with the rules of cosmic physics, and that would, most importantly of all, save the phenomena. O, the phenomena were saved, indeed—but at what cost! For in his calculations, not 34 epicycles were required to account for the entire structure of the universe, as the *Commentariolus* claimed, but 48—which is 8 more at least than Ptolemy had employed! This little trick, however, is nothing, a mere somersault, compared with the one of which I am now about to speak. You imagine that Koppernigk set the Sun at the centre of the universe, don't you? He did not. The centre of the universe according to his theory is not the Sun, *but the centre of Earth's orbit*, which, as the great, the mighty, the all-explaining *Book of revolutions* admits, is situated at a point in space some three times the Sun's diameter distant from the Sun! All the hypotheses, all the calculations, the star tables, charts and diagrams, the entire ragbag of lies and half truths and self-deceptions which is *De revolutionibus orbium mundi* (or *coelestium*, as I suppose I must call it now), was assembled simply in order to prove that at the centre of all there is nothing, that the world turns upon chaos.

*

Are you stirring in your grave, Koppernigk? Are you writhing in cold clay?

*

When at last, one black night at Löbau Castle, the nature of the absurdity which he was propounding was borne in upon me, I laughed until I could laugh no more, and then I wept. Copernicus, the greatest astronomer of his age, so they said, was a fraud whose only desire was to save appearances. I laughed, I say, and then wept, and something died within me. I do not willingly grant him even this much, but grant it I must: that if his book possessed some power, it was the power to destroy. It destroyed my faith, in God and Man—but not in the Devil. Lucifer sits at the centre of that book, smiling a familiar cold grey smile. You were evil, Koppernigk, and you filled the world with despair.

He knew it, of course, knew well how he had failed, and knew that I knew it. That was why he had to destroy me, he and Giese, the Devil's disciple.

If I saw all this, his failure and so forth, even so early as the Löbau period, why then did I continue to press him so doggedly to publish? But you see, I wanted him to make known his theory simply so that I could refute it. O, an ignoble desire, certainly; I admit, I admit it freely, that I planned to make my reputation on the ruins of his. Poor fool that I was. The world cannot abide truth: men remember heliocentricity (they are already talking of the *Copernican revolution!*), but forget the defective theory on which the concept of heliocentricity is founded. It is his name that is remembered and honoured, while I am forgotten, and left to rot here in this dreadful place. What was it he said to me?—*first they will laugh, and then weep, seeing their Earth diminished, spinning upon the void* . . . He knew, he knew. They are weeping now, bowed down under the burden of despair with which he loaded them. I am weeping. I believe in nothing. The mirror is shattered. The chaos

218

Well I'll be damned!

-*Freunde!* What joy! The most extraordinary, the most extraordinary thing has happened: Otho has come! O God, I believe in You, I swear it. Forgive me for ever doubting You! A disciple, at last! He will spread my name throughout the world. Now I can return to that great work, which I planned so long ago: the formulation of a *true* system of the universe, based upon Ptolemaic principles. I shall not mention, I shall not even *mention* that other name. Or perhaps I shall? Perhaps I have been unjust to him? Did he not, in his own poor stumbling way, glimpse the majestic order of the universe which wheels and wheels in mysterious ways, bringing back the past again and again, as the past has been brought back here again today? Copernicus, Canon Nicolas, *domine praeceptor*, I forgive you: yes, even you I forgive. God, I believe: resurrection, redemption, the whole thing, I believe it all. Ah! The page shakes before my eyes. This joy!

\*

Lucius Valentine Otho has this day come to me from Wittenberg, to be my amanuensis, my disciple. He fell to his knees before me. I behaved perfectly, as a great scientist should. I spoke to him kindly, enquiring how things stood at Wittenberg, and of his own work and ambitions. But behind my coolness and reserve, what a tangle of emotions! Of course, this joy I felt could not be contained, and when I had enquired his age, I could not keep myself from grasping him by the shoulders and shaking him until his teeth rattled in his head, for just at that same age did I, so many years ago, come to Copernicus at Frauenburg. The past comes back, transfigured. Shall I also send a Raphaël to destroy Otho?—but come now, Rheticus, come clean. The fact is, there never was a Raphaël. I know, I know, it was dreadful of me to invent all that, but I had to find something, you see, some terrible tangible thing, to represent the great wrongs done me by Copernicus. Not a mention of my name in his book! Not a word! He would have done more for a dog. Well, I have forgiven him, and I have admitted my little joke about Raphaël and so forth. Now a new age dawns. I am no longer the old Rheticus, banished to Cassovia and gnawing his own liver in spite and impotent rage, no: I am an altogether finer thing—I am Doctor Rheticus! I am a believer. Lift your head, then, strange new glorious crea-

219

ture, incandescent angel, and gaze upon the world. It is not diminished! Even in that he failed. The sky is blue, and shall be forever blue, and the earth shall blossom forever in spring, and this planet shall forever be the centre of all we know. I believe it, I think. *Vale.*

# IV

---

*Magnum Miraculum*

The sun at dawn, retrieving from the darkness the few remaining fragments of his life, summoned him back at last into the present. Warily he watched the room arrange itself around him: that return journey was so far, immeasurably far, that without proof he would not believe it was over. Outside, in the sky low in the east, a storm of fire raged amidst clouds, shedding light like a shower of burning arrows upon the great glittering steely arc of the Baltic. None of that was any longer wholly real, was mere melodrama, static and cold. The world had shrunk until his skull contained it entirely, and all without that shrivelled sphere was a changing series of superficial images in a void, utterly lacking in significance save on those rare occasions when a particular picture served to verify the moment, as now the fragments of his cell, picked out by the advancing dawn, were illuminated integers that traced on the surrounding gloom a constellation, a starry formula, expressing precisely, as no words could, all that was left of what he had once been, all that was left of his life. One morning, a morning much like this one, a fire fierce as the sun itself had exploded in his brain; when that dreadful glare faded everything was transfigured. Then had begun his final wanderings. It was into the past that he had travelled, for there was nowhere else to go. He was dying.

*

The sickness had come upon him stealthily. At first it had been no more than a faint dizziness at times, a step missed, a stumbling on the stairs. Then the megrims began, like claps of thunder trapped inside his skull, and for hours he was forced to lie prostrate in his shuttered cell with vinegar poultices pressed to his brow, as cascades of splintered multicoloured glass formed jagged images of agony behind his eyes. Still he persisted in denying what the physician in him knew beyond doubt to be the case, that the end had come. An attack of ague, nothing more, he told himself; I am seventy, it is to be expected. Then that morning, in the first week of April, as he had made to rise from his couch at dawn, his entire right side had pained him suddenly, terribly, as if a bag of shot, or pellets of hot quicksilver, had been emptied from his skull into his heart and pumped out from thence to clatter down the arteries of his arm, through the ribcage, into his leg. Moaning, he laid himself down again tenderly on the couch, with great solicitude, as a mother laying her child into its cradle. A spider in the dim dawnlight swarmed laboriously across the trampoline of its web strung between the ceiling beams. From without came the burgeoning clatter and crack of a horse and rider approaching. Poised on the rack of his pain he waited, calmly, almost in eagerness, for the advent of the black catastrophe. But the horseman did not stop, passed under the window, and then he understood, without surprise, but in something like disappointment, that he was not to be let go before suffering a final jest, and, instead of death, sleep, the ultimate banality, bundled him unceremoniously under its wing and bore him swiftly away.

*

It was sleep, yes, and yet more than that, an impassioned hearkening, a pausing upon a deserted shore at twilight, a last looking backward at the soon to be forsaken land, yes, yes: he was waiting yet. For what? He did not know. Mute and expectant, he peered anxiously into the sombre distance. They were all there, unseen yet palpable, all his discarded dead. A pang of longing pierced his heart. But why were they behind him? why not before? was he not on his way now at last to join that silent throng? And why did he tarry here, on this desolate brink? A brumous yellowy sky full of wreckage sank slowly afar, and the darkness welled up around him. Then he spied the figure approaching, the massive shoulders and great dark burnished face like polished stone, the wide-set eyes, the cruel mad mouth.

Who are you? he cried, striving in vain to lift his hands and fend off the apparition.

I am he whom you seek.

Tell me who you are!

As my own father I am already dead, as my own mother I still live, and grow old. I come to take you on a journey. You have much to learn, and so little time.

What? what would you teach me?

How to die.

Ah . . . Then you are Brother Death?

No. He is not yet. I am the one that goes before. I am, you may say, the god of revels and oblivion. I make men mad. You are in my realm now, for a little while. Come with me. Here begins the descent into Hell. Come.

And so speaking the god turned and started back toward the dark land.

*Come*!

And the dying man looked before him again, to the invisible ineluctable sea, wanting to go on, unable to go on, turning already, even against his will, turning back toward the waiting throng.

*Come* . . .

And as a soldier turns unwillingly away from a heart-rending vision of home and love only to meet full in the face the fatal shot, he turned and at once the great sphere of searing fire burst in his brain, and he awoke.

\*

The pain was in his right side, although he seemed to know that rather than feel it, for that side was paralysed from ear to heel. Tentatively, with eyes averted, not wishing really to know, he sent out a few simple commands to arm and flank and hip, but to no avail, for the channels of communication were broken. It was as if half of him had come detached, and lay beside him now, a felled grey brute, sullen, unmoving and dangerous. Dangerous, yes: he must be wary of provoking this beast, or it would surely lift one mighty padded paw of pain and smash him. Bright April light shone in the window. He could see the Baltic, steel-blue and calm, bearing landward a ship with a black sail. Was it too much to expect that this burdensome clarity, this awareness, might have been taken from him, was it too much to expect at least that much respite? Below, Anna Schillings was stirring, setting in motion the

225

creaky mechanism of another day. Despite the pain, he felt now most acutely a sense of anxiety and scruple, and, weirdly, a devastating embarrassment. He had not known just such a smarting dismay since childhood, when, marked out by some act or other of mischief, a dish broken, a lie told, he had stood cowering, all boltholes barred against him, in the path of the awful unavoidable engine of retribution. To be found out! It was absurd. Anna would come in a moment, with the gruel and the mulled wine, and he would be found out. Cautiously he tested his face to find if it would smile, and then, despite himself, he began quietly to blubber; it was a tiny luxury, and it made him feel better, after all.

By the time she came sighing up the stairs he had stanched his tears, but of course she sensed disaster at once. It was the stink of his shame, the stink of the child who has wet his breeches, of the maimed animal throbbing in a lair of leaves, that betrayed him. Slowly, with her face turned resolutely away, she set down on the floor beside his couch the steaming pewter mug of wine and the bowl of gruel.

"You are not risen yet, Canon?"

"It's nothing, Anna, you must not trouble yourself. I am ill." He found it difficult to speak, the blurred words were a kind of soft stone in his mouth. "Inform the Chapter, please, and ask Canon Giese to come." No no, no, Giese was no longer here, but in Löbau; he must take care, she would think him in a worse way than he was if he continued raving thus. She stood motionless, with her head bowed and hands folded before her, still turned somewhat away, unwilling or unable to look full upon the calamity that had alighted in her life. She had the injured baffled look of one who has been grievously and unaccountably slighted, but above all she appeared puzzled, and entirely at a loss to know how to behave. He could sympathise, he knew the feeling: there is no place for death in the intricate workings of ordinary days. He wished he could think of something to say that would make this new disordered state of affairs seem reasonable.

"I am dying, Anna."

He at once regretted saying it, of course. She began quietly to weep, with a reserve, a sort of circumspection, that touched him far more deeply than the expected wild wailings could have done. She went away, sniffling, and returned presently with water to wash him, and a pot for his relief. Deftly she ministered to him, speaking not a word. He admired her competence, her resilience; an admirable woman, really. Something of the old, almost forgotten fondness stirred in him. "Arna? . ." Still she said nothing. She had learned from him, perhaps, to distrust words, and was content to allow these tangible ministrations to express all that could not be said. Sadly and in some wonder he gazed at her. What did she signify, what did she *mean*? For the first time it struck him as odd that they had never in all the years learned to call each other *thou*.

*

Day by day the sickness waxed and waned, pummelling him, flinging him down into vast darknesses only to haul him up again into agonising light, shaking him until he seemed to hear his bones rattling, binding up his bowels tonight and on the morrow throwing open the floodgates of his orifices, leaving him to lie for hours, nauseated and helpless, in the stench of his own messes. Bright shimmering patterns of pain rippled through him, as if the sickness, like a gloating clothier, were unfurling for a finicking taste a series of progressively more subtle and exquisite rolls of silken torture. Always, unthinkingly, he had assumed that his would be a dry death, a swift clean shrivelling up, but here were fevers that lasted for days, wringing a ceaseless ooze of sweat from his burning flesh, robbing him of that precious clarity of mind that at first had seemed such a burden.

Sometimes, however, he was sufficiently clear in his thinking to be surprised and even fascinated by his own equanimity in the face of death. That moment was now at hand the terror of which had been with him always on his journey hither, present in every landscape, no matter how bright and various the scenes, like an unmoving shadow, and yet now he was not afraid: he felt only vague melancholy and regret, and a certain anxiety lest he should miss this last and surely most distinguished experience the world would afford him. He was convinced that he would be granted an insight, a vision, of profound significance, before the end. Was this why he was calm and unafraid, because this mysterious something toward which he was eagerly advancing hid from his gaze death's true countenance? And was this the explanation for the prolonging of his agony, because it was not the death agony at all, but a manner of purification, a ritual suffering to be endured before his initiation into transcendent knowledge? Although he was gone too far now to expect that he might put to living use whatever lesson he was to learn, the profundity of the experience, he believed, would not be thus diminished. Was redemption still possible, then, even in this extremity?

Searching for an answer to this extraordinary question, his fevered understanding scavenged like a ragpicker among the detritus of his life, rummaging fitfully through the disconnected bits and scraps that were left. He could find no sense of significant meaning anywhere. Sometimes, however, he sank into a calm deep dreaming wherein he wandered at peace through the fields and palaces of memory. The past was still wonderfully intact there. Amid scenes of childhood and youth he marvelled at the wealth of detail that had stayed with him through all the years, stored away like winter fruit. He visited the old house in St Anne's Lane, and walked again in quiet rapture through the streets and alleyways of the town. Here was St John's, the school gate, the boys playing in the dust. A soft golden radiance held sway everywhere, a stylised sunlight. Tenderness and longing pierced him to the core. Had he ever in reality left Torun? Perhaps that was where his real, his essential self had remained, waiting patiently for him to return, as now, and claim his true estate. And here is the linden tree, in full leaf, steadfast and lovely, the very image of summer and silence, of happiness.

But always he returned from these backward journeys weary and dispirited, with no answers. Despair blossomed in him then, a rank hideous flower. Numbed by an overdose of grog, by an unexpectedly successful blending of herbs, or by simple weariness, he withdrew altogether from the realm of life, and lay, a shapeless piece of flesh and sweat and phlegm, in the most primitive, rudimentary state of being, a dull barely-breathing almost-death. Those periods were the worst of all.

At other times the past came to his present, in the form of little creatures, gaudy homunculi who marched into the sickroom and strutted up and down beside his couch, berating him for the injuries he had done them, or perched at his shoulder and chattered, explaining, justifying, denouncing. They were at once comic and sad. Canon Wodka came, and Professor Brudzewski, Novara and the Italians, even Uncle Lucas, pompous as ever, even the King of Poland, tipsy, with his crown awry. At first he knew them to be hallucinations, but then he realised that the matter was deeper than that: they were real enough, as real as anything can be that is not oneself, that is of the outside, for had he not always believed that others are not known but invented, that the world consists solely of oneself while all else is phantom, necessarily? Therefore they had a right to berate him, for who, if not he, was to blame for what they were, poor frail vainglorious creatures, tenants of his mind, whom he had invented, whom he was taking with him into death? They were having their last say, before the end. Girolamo alone of them was silent. He stood back in the shadows some way from the couch, with that inimitable mixture of detachment and fondness, one eyebrow raised in amiable mockery, smiling. Ah yes, Girolamo, you knew me— not so well as did that other, it's true, but you did know me—and I could not bear to be known thus.

*

Where?

He had drifted down into a dreadful dark where all was silent and utterly still. He was frightened. He waited. After a long time, what seemed a long time, he saw at an immense distance a minute something in the darkness, it could not be called light, it was barely more than nothing, the absolute minimum imaginable, and he heard afar, faintly, O, faintly, a tiny shrieking, a grain of sound that was hardly anything in itself, that served only to define the infinite silence surrounding it. And then, it was strange, it was as if time had split somehow in two, as if the *now* and the *not yet* were both occurring at once, for he was conscious of watching something approaching through the dark distance while yet it had arrived, a huge steely shining bird it was, soaring on motionless outstretched great wings, terrible, O, terrible beyond words, and yet magnificent, carrying in its fearsome beak a fragment of blinding fire, and he tried to cry out, to utter the word, but in vain, for down the long arc of its flight the creature wheeled, already upon him even as it came, and branded the burning seal upon his brow.

> *Word!*
> *O word!*
> *Thou word that I lack!*

And then he was once again upon that darkling shore, with the sea at his back and before him the at once mysterious and familiar land. There too was the cruel god, leading him away from the sea to where

229

the others awaited him, the many others, the all. He could see nothing, yet he knew these things, knew also that the land into which he was descending now was at once all the lands he had known in his life, all! all the towns and the cities, the plains and woods, Prussia and Poland and Italy, Torun, Cracow, Padua and Bologna and Ferrara. And the god also, turning upon him full his great glazed stone face, was many in one, was Caspar Sturm, was Novara and Brudzewski, was Girolamo, was more, was his father and his mother, and their mothers and fathers, was the uncountable millions, and was also that other, that ineluctable other. The god spoke:

Here now is that which you sought, that thing which is itself and no other. Do you acknowledge it?

No, no, it was not so! There was only darkness and disorder here, and a great clamour of countless voices crying out in laughter and pain and execration; he would know nothing of this vileness and chaos.

Let me die!

But the god answered him:

Not yet.

Swiftly then he felt himself borne upwards, aching upwards into the world, and here was his cell, and dawnlight on the great arc of the Baltic, and it was Maytime. He was in pain, and his limbs were dead, but for the first time in many weeks his mind was wonderfully clear. This clarity, however, was uncanny, unlike anything experienced before; he did not trust it. All round about him a vast chill stillness reigned, as if he were poised at an immense height, in an infinity of air. Could it be he had been elevated thus only in order that he might witness desolations? For he wanted no more of that, the struggle and the anguish. Was this true despair at last? If so, it was a singularly undistinguished thing.

He slept for a little while, but was woken again by Anna when she came up with the basin and the razor to shave him. Could she not leave him in peace, even for a moment! But then he chided himself for his ingratitude. She had shown him great kindness during the long weeks of his illness. The shaving, the feeding, the wiping and the washing, these were her necessary rituals that held at bay the knowledge that soon now she would be left alone. He watched her as she bustled about the couch, setting up the basin, honing the razor, painting the lather upon his sunken jaws, all the while murmuring softly to herself, a tall, too-heavy, whey-faced woman in dusty black. Lately she had begun to yell at him, this unmoving grey effigy, as she would at a deaf mute, or an infant, not in anger or even impatience, but with a kind of desperate cheerfulness, as if she believed she were summoning him back by this means from the dark brink. Her manner irritated him beyond endurance, especially in the mornings, and he mouthed angry noises, and sometimes even tried to smack at her in impotent rage. Today, however, he was calm, and even managed a lop-sided smile, although she did not seem to recognise it as such, for she only peered at him apprehensively and asked if he were in pain. Poor Anna. He stared at her in wonderment. How she had aged! From the ripe well-made woman who had arrived at his tower twenty years before, she had without his noticing become a tremulous, agitated, faintly silly matron. Had he really had such scant regard for her that he had not even attended the commonplace phenomenon of her aging? She had been his housekeeper, and, on three occasions, more than that, three strange, now wholly unreal encounters into which he had been led by desperation and unbearable self-knowledge and surrender; she had thrice, then, been more, but not much more, certainly not enough to justify Dantiscus's crass relentless hounding. Now, however, he wondered if perhaps those three nights were due a greater significance than he had been willing to grant. Perhaps, for her, they had been enough to keep her with him. For she could have left him. Her children were grown now. Heinrich, her son, had lately come out of the time of his apprenticeship in the cathedral bakery, and Carla was in service in the household of a burgher of the town. They would have supported her, if she had left him. She had chosen to remain. She had endured. Was this what she signified, what she meant? He recalled green days of hers, storms in spring and autumn moods, grievings in wintertime. He should have shown her more regard, then. Now it was too late.

"Anna."

"Yes, Canon?"

"*Du*, Anna."

"Yes, Herr Canon. You know that the Herr Doctor is coming today? You remember, yes? from Nuremberg?"

What was she talking about? What doctor? And then he remembered. So that was why he had been granted this final lucidity! All that, his work, the publishing and so forth, had lost all meaning. He could

231

remember his hopes and fears for the book, but he could no longer feel them. He had failed, yes, but what did it matter? That failure was a small thing compared to the general disaster that was his life.

Andreas Osiander arrived in the afternoon. Anna, flustered by the coming of a person of such consequence, hurried up the stairs to announce him, stammering and wringing her hands in distress. The Canon remembered, too late, that he had intended to send her away during the Nuremberger's visit, for her presence under his keen disapproving nose would surely lead to all that *focaria* nonsense being started up again—not that the Canon cared any longer what Dantiscus or any of them might say or do to him, but he did not want Anna to suffer new humiliations; no, he did not want that. She had hardly announced his name before Osiander swept roughly past her and began at once to speak in his brusque overbearing fashion. Confronted however by the sight of the shrivelled figure on the couch he faltered in his speechifying and turned uncertainly to the woman hovering at the door.

"It is the palsy, Herr Doctor," Anna said, bowing and bobbing, "brought on by a bleeding in the brain, they say."

"O. I understand. Well, that will be all, thank you, mistress, you may go."

The Canon wished her to remain, but she made a soothing sign to him and went off meekly. He strained to hear her heavy step descending the stairs, a sound that suddenly seemed to him to sum up all the comfort that was left in the world, but Osiander had begun to boom at him again, and Anna departed in silence out of his life.

*

"I had not thought to find you brought so low, friend Koppernigk," Osiander said, in a faintly accusing tone, as if he suspected that he had been deliberately misled in the matter of the other's state of health.

"I am dying, Doctor."

"Yes. But it comes to us all in the end, and you must put yourself into God's care. Better this way than to be taken suddenly, in the night, the soul unprepared, eh?"

He was a portly arrogant man, this Lutheran, noisy, pompous and unfeeling, full of his own opinions; the Canon had always in his heart disliked him. He began to pace the floor with stately tread, his puffed-up pigeon's chest an impregnable shield against all opposition, and spoke of Nuremberg, and the printing, and his unstinting efforts on behalf of the Canon's work. Rheticus he called *that wretched creature.* Poor, foolish Rheticus! another victim sacrificed upon the altar of decorum. The Canon sighed; he should have ignored them all, Dantiscus and Giese and Osiander, he should have given his disciple the acknowledgment he deserved. What if he was a sodomite? That was not the worst crime imaginable, no worse, perhaps, than base ingratitude.

Osiander was poking about inside the capacious satchel slung at his side, and now he brought out a handsome leather-bound volume tooled in gold on the spine. The Canon craned for a closer look at it, but Osiander, the dreadful fellow, seemed to have forgotten that he was in the presence of the author, who was still living, despite appearances, and instead of bringing it at once to the couch he took the book into the windowlight, and, dampening a thumb, flipped roughly through the pages with the careless disregard of one for whom all books other than the Bible are fundamentally worthless.

"I have altered the title," he said absently, "as I may have informed you was my intention, substituting the word *coelestium* for *mundi*, as it seemed to me safer to speak of the *heavens*, thereby displaying distance and detachment, rather than of the *world*, an altogether more immediate term."

No, my friend, you did not mention that, as I recall; but it is no matter now.

"Also, of course, I have attached a preface, as we agreed. It was a wise move, I believe. As I have said to you in my various letters, the Aristotelians and theologians will easily be placated if they are told that several hypotheses can be used to explain the same apparent motions, and that the present hypotheses are not proposed because they are in reality true, but because they are the most convenient to calculate the apparent composite motions." He lifted his bland face dreamily to the window, with a smug little smile of admiration at the precision and style of his delivery. Just thus did he pose, the Canon knew, when lecturing his slack-jawed classes at Nuremberg. "For my part," the Lutheran went on, "I have always felt about hypotheses that they are not articles of faith, but bases of computation, so that even if they are false it does not matter, provided that they save the phenomena . . . And in the light of this belief have I composed the preface."

233

"It must not be," the Canon said, his dull gaze turned upward toward the ceiling. Osiander stared at him.

"What?"

"It must not be: I do not wish the book to be published."

"But . . . but it is already published, my dear sir. See, I have a copy here, printed and bound. Petreius has made an edition of one thousand, as you agreed. It is even now being distributed."

"It must not be, I say!"

Osiander, quite baffled, pondered a moment in silence, then came and sat down slowly on a chair beside the couch and peered at the Canon with an uncertain smile. "Are you unwell, my friend?"

The Canon, had he been able, would have laughed.

"I am dying, man!" he cried. "Have I not told you so already? But I am not raving. I want this book suppressed. Go to Petreius, have him recall whatever volumes he has sent out. Do you understand? *It must not be!*"

"Calm yourself, Doctor, please," said Osiander, alarmed by the paralytic's pent-up vehemence, the straining jaw and wild anguished stare. "Do you require assistance? Shall I call the woman?"

"No no no, do nothing." The Canon relaxed somewhat, and the trembling in his limbs subsided. There was a fever coming on, and a pain the like of which he had not known before was crashing and booming in his skull. Terror extended a thin dark tentacle within him. "Forgive me," he mumbled. "Is there water? Let me drink. Thank you, you are most kind. Ah."

Frowning, Osiander set down the water jug. He had a look now of mingled embarrassment and curiosity: he wanted to escape from the presence of this undignified dying, yet also he wished to know the reason for the old man's extraordinary change of mind. "Perhaps," he ventured, "I may return later in the day, when you are less wrought, and discuss then this matter of your book?"

But the Canon was not listening. "Tell me, Osiander," he said, "tell me truly, is it too late to halt publication? For I would halt it."

"Why, Doctor?"

"You have read the book? Then you must know why. It is a failure. I failed in that which I set out to do: to discern truth, the significance of things."

"Truth? I do not understand, Doctor. Your theory is not without

234

flaws, I agree, but—"

"It is not the mechanics of the theory that interest me." He closed his eyes. O burning, burning! "The project itself, the totality . . . Do you understand? A hundred thousand words I used, charts, star tables, formulae, and yet I said nothing . . ."

He could not go on. What did it matter now, anyway? Osiander sighed.

"You should not trouble yourself thus, Doctor," he said. "These are scruples merely, and, if more than that, then you must realise that the manner of success you sought—or now believe that you sought!—is not to be attained. Your work, however flawed, shall be a basis for others to build upon, of this you may be assured. As to your failure to discern the true nature of things, as you put it, I think you will agree that I have accounted for such failing in my preface. Shall you hear what I have written?"

Plainly he was proud of his work, and, a born preacher, was eager to descant it. The Canon panicked: he did not want to hear, no! but he was sinking, and could no longer speak, could only growl and gnash his teeth in a frenzy of refusal. Osiander, however, took these efforts for a sign of pleased anticipation. He laid down the book, and, with the ghastly excruciated smile of one obliged to deal with a cretin, rose and thrust his hands under the Canon's armpits, and hauled him up and propped him carefully against the bank of soiled pillows as if he were setting up a target. Then, commencing his stately pacing once more, he held the book open before him at arm's length and began to read aloud in a booming pulpit voice.

"Since the novelty of the hypotheses of this work—which sets the Earth in motion and puts an immovable Sun at the centre of the universe—has already received great attention, I have no doubt that certain learned men have taken grave offence and think it wrong thus to raise disturbance among liberal disciplines, which were established long ago on a correct basis. If, however, they are willing to weigh the matter scrupulously, they will find that the author of this work has done nothing which merits blame. For it is the task of the astronomer to use painstaking and skilled observation in gathering together the history of celestial movements, and then—since he cannot by any line of reasoning discover the true causes of these movements (you mark that, Doctor?)—to conceive and devise whatever causes and hypo-

235

theses he pleases, such that, by the assumption of these causes, those same movements can be calculated from the principles of geometry for the past and for the future also. The present artist is markedly outstanding in both these respects: for it is not necessary that these hypotheses should be true, or even probable; it is enough if they provide a calculus which is consistent with the observations . . ."

The Canon listened in wonder: was it valid, this denial, this spitting-upon of his life's work? Truth or fiction . . . ritual . . . necessary. He could not concentrate. He was in flames. Andreas Osiander, marching into windowlight and out again, was transformed at each turn into a walking darkness, a cloud of fire, a phantom, and outside too all was strangely changing, and not the sun was light and heat, the world inert, but rather the world was a nimbus of searing fire and the sun no more than a dead frozen globe dangling in the western sky.

". . . For it is sufficiently clear that this art is profoundly ignorant of causes of the apparent movements. And if it constructs and invents causes—and certainly it has invented very many—nevertheless these causes are not advanced in order to convince anyone that they are true but only in order that they may posit a correct basis for calculation. But since one and the same movement may take varying hypotheses from time to time—as eccentricity and an epicycle for the motion of the Sun—the astronomer will accept above all others the one easiest to grasp. The philosopher will perhaps rather seek the semblance of truth. Neither, however, will understand or set down anything certain, unless it has been divinely revealed to him . . ."

The walls of the tower had lost all solidity, were planes of darkness out of which there came now soaring on terrible wings the great steel bird, trailing flames in its wake and bearing in its beak the fiery sphere, no longer alone, but flying before a flock of others of its kind, all aflame, all gleaming and terrible and magnificent, rising out of darkness, shrieking.

"And so far as hypotheses are concerned, let no one expect anything certain from astronomy—since astronomy can offer us nothing certain—lest he mistake for truth ideas conceived for another purpose, and depart from this study a greater fool than when he came to it!"

No! O no. He flung his mute denial into the burning world. You, Andreas, have betrayed me, you . . .

Andreas?

236

The pacing figure drew near, and swooping suddenly down pressed its terrible ruined face close to his.

You!

Yes, brother: I. We meet again.

*

Andreas laughed then, and seated himself on the chair beside the couch, laying the book on his lap under the black wing of his cloak. He was as he had been when the Canon had seen him last, a walking corpse on which the premature maggots were at work.

You are dead, Andreas, I am dreaming you.

Yes, brother, but it is I nevertheless. I am as real as you, now, for in this final place where we meet I am precisely as close to life as you are to death, and it is the same thing. I must thank you for this brief reincarnation.

What are you?

Why, I am Andreas! You have yourself addressed me thus. However, if you must have significance in all things, then we may say that I am the angel of redemption—an unlikely angel, I grant you, with dreadfully damaged wings, yet a redeemer, for all that.

You are death.

Andreas smiled, that familiar anguished smile.

O that too, brother, that too, but that's of secondary importance. But now, enough of this metaphysical quibbling, you know it always bored me. Let us speak instead, calmly, while there is still time, of the things that matter. See, I have your book . . .

Behind the dark seated smiling figure great light throbbed in the arched window, where the steel-blue Baltic's back rose like the back of some vast waterborne brute, ubiquitous and menacing. Above in the darkness under the ceiling the metal birds soared and swooped, flying on invisible struts and wires, filling the sombre air with their fierce clamour. The fever climbed inexorably upward along his veins, a molten tide. He clutched with his fingernails at the chill damp sheets under him, striving to keep hold of the world. He was afraid. This was dying, yes, this was unmistakably the distinguished thing. Minute fragments of the past assailed him: a deserted street in Cracow on a black midwinter night, an idiot child watching him from the doorway of a hovel outside the walls of Padua, a ruined tower somewhere in Poland inhabited

237

by a flock of plumed white doves. These had been death's secret signals. Andreas, with his faint and sardonic, yet not unsympathetic smile, was watching him.

Wait, brother, it is not yet time, not quite yet. Shall we speak of your book, the reasons for your failure? For I will not dispute with you that you did fail. Unable to discern the thing itself, you would settle for nothing less; in your pride you preferred heroic failure to prosaic success.

I will accept none of this! What, anyway, do you know of these matters, you who had nothing but contempt for science, the products of the mind, all that, which I loved?

Come come: you have said that you are dreaming me, therefore you must accept what I say, since, if I am lying, it is your lies, in my mouth. And you have finished with lying, haven't you? Yes. The lies are all done with. That is why I am here, because at last you are prepared to be . . . honest. See, for example: you are no longer embarrassed in my presence. It was always your stormiest emotion, that fastidious, that panic-stricken embarrassment in the face of the disorder and vulgarity of the commonplace, which you despised.

There was movement in the room now, and the pale flickering incongruity of candles lit in daylight. Dim faceless figures approached him, mumbling. A ceremony was being enacted, a ritual at once familiar to him and strange, and then with a shock, like the shock of falling in a dream, he understood that he was being prepared for the last rites.

Do not heed it, brother, Andreas said. All that is a myth, your faith in which you relinquished long ago. There is no comfort there for you.

I want to believe.

But you may not.

Then I am lost.

No, you are not lost, for I have come to redeem you.

Tell me, then. My book . . ? my work . . ?

You thought to discern the thing itself, the eternal truths, the pure forms that lie behind the chaos of the world. You looked into the sky: what did you see?

I saw . . . the planets dancing, and heard them singing in their courses.

O no, no brother. These things you imagined. Let me tell you how it was. You set the sights of the triquetrum upon a light shining in the

238

sky, believing that you thus beheld a fragment of reality, inviolate, unmistakable, enduring, but that was not the case. What you saw was *a light shining in the sky;* whatever it was more than that it was so only by virtue of your faith, your belief in the possibility of apprehending reality.

What nonsense is this? How else may we live, if not in the belief that we can *know?*

It is the manner of knowing that is important. We know the meaning of the singular thing only so long as we content ourselves with knowing it in the midst of other meanings: isolate it, and all meaning drains away. It is not the thing that counts, you see, only the interaction of things; and, of course, the names . . .

You are preaching despair.

Yes? Call it, rather, *redemptive* despair, or, better still, call it acceptance. The world will not bear anything other than acceptance. Look at this chair: there is the wood, the splinters, then the fibres, then the particles into which the fibres may be broken, and then the smaller particles of these particles, and then, eventually, nothing, a confluence of aetherial stresses, a kind of vivid involuntary dreaming in a vacuum. You see? the world simply will not bear it, this impassioned scrutiny.

You would seduce me with this philosophy of happy ignorance, of slavery, abject acceptance of a filthy world? I will have none of it!

You will have none of it . . .

You laugh, but tell me this, in your wisdom: how are we to perceive the truth if we do not attempt to discover it, and to understand our discoveries?

There is no need to search for the truth. We know it already, before ever we think of setting out on our quests.

How do we know it?

Why, simple, brother: we *are* the truth. The world, and ourselves, this is the truth. There is no other, or, if there is, it is of use to us only as an ideal, that brings us a little comfort, a little consolation, now and then.

And this truth that we are, how may we speak it?

It may not be spoken, brother, but perhaps it may be . . . shown.

How? tell me how?

By accepting what there is.

And then?

There is no more; that is all.

O no, Andreas, you will not trick me. If what you say were true, I should have had to sell my soul to a vicious world, to embrace meekly the hideousness, yes—but I would not do it! This much at least I can say, that I did not sell—

—Your soul? Ah, but you did sell it, to the highest bidder. What shall we call it?—science? the quest for truth? transcendent knowledge? Vanity, all vanity, and something more, a kind of cowardice, the cowardice that comes from the refusal to accept that the names are all there is that matter, the cowardice that is true and irredeemable despair. With great courage and great effort you might have succeeded, in the only way it is possible to succeed, by disposing the commonplace, the names, in a beautiful and orderly pattern that would show, by its very beauty and order, the action in our poor world of the otherworldly truths. But you tried to discard the commonplace truths for the transcendent ideals, and so failed.

I do not understand.

But you do. We say only those things that we have the words to express: it is enough.

No!

It is sufficient. We must be content with that much.

The candleflames like burning blades pierced his sight, and the grave voice intoning the final benediction stormed above him.

Too late!—

You thought to transcend the world, but before you could aspire to that loftiness your needs must have contended with . . . well, brother, with what?

Too late!—Death's burning seal was graven upon his brow, and all that he had discarded was gone beyond retrieving. The light, O! and the terrible birds! the great burning arc beyond the window!

With me, brother! I was that which you must contend with.

You, Andreas? What was there in you? You despised and betrayed me, made my life a misery. Wherever I turned you were there, blighting my life, my work.

Just so. I was the one absolutely necessary thing, for I was there always to remind you of what you must transcend. I was the bent bow from which you propelled yourself beyond the filthy world.

I did not hate you!

There had to be a little regard, yes, the regard which the arrow bears for the bow, but never the other, the thing itself, the vivid thing, which is not to be found in any book, nor in the firmament, nor in the absolute forms. You know what I mean, brother. It is that thing, passionate and yet calm, fierce and coming from far away, fabulous and yet ordinary, that thing which is all that matters, which is the great miracle. You glimpsed it briefly in our father, in sister Barbara, in Fracastoro, in Anna Schillings, in all the others, and even, yes, in me, glimpsed it, and turned away, appalled and . . . embarrassed. Call it acceptance, call it love if you wish, but these are poor words, and express nothing of the enormity.

Too late!—For he had sold his soul, and now payment would be exacted in full. The voice of the priest engulfed him.

*"Only after death shall we be united with the All, when the body dissolves into the four base elements of which it is made, and the spiritual man, the soul free and ablaze, ascends through the seven crystal spheres of the firmament, shedding at each stage a part of his mortal nature, until, shorn of all earthly evil, he shall find redemption in the Empyrean and be united there with the world soul that is everywhere and everything and eternal!"*

Andreas slowly shook his head.

No, brother, do not heed that voice out of the past. Redemption is not to be found in the Empyrean.

Too late!—

No, Nicolas, not too late. It is not I who have said all these things today, but you.

He was smiling, and his face was healed, the terrible scars had faded, and he was again as he had once been, and rising now he laid his hand upon his brother's burning brow. The terrible birds sailed in silence into the dark, the harsh light grew soft, and the stone walls of the tower rose up again. The Baltic shone, a bright sea bearing away a ship with a black sail. Andreas brought out the book from beneath his cloak, and placing it on the couch he guided his brother's hand until the slack fingers touched the unquiet pages.

I am the angel of redemption, Nicolas. Will you come with me now?

And so saying he smiled once more, a last time, and lifted up his delicate exquisite face and turned, to the window and the light, as if listening to something immensely far and faint, a music out of earth and air, water and fire, that was everywhere, and everything, and eternal, and Nicolas, straining to catch that melody, heard the voices of evening rising to meet him from without: the herdsman's call, the cries of children at play, the rumbling of the carts returning from market; and there were other voices too, of churchbells gravely tolling the hour, of dogs that barked afar, of the sea, of the earth itself, turning in its course, and of the wind, out of huge blue air, sighing in the leaves of the linden. All called and called to him, and called, calling him away.

D. C.

# Notes

Quotations from writings other than Copernicus's:

p. 189  "It seemed as though a new world . . . possession of the whole community." from Henri Pirenne's *A History of Europe*, translated by Bernard Miall (New York, 1956)

p. 192  "If at the foundation . . . but despair?" from Søren Kierkegaard's *Fear and Trembling*, translated by Walter Lowrie (Princeton, N. J., 1968).

p. 192  "I hold it true . . . the ancients dreamed." from Albert Einstein's Herbert Spencer Lecture, Oxford, 1933 (quoted by Jeremy Bernstein in *Einstein*, London, 1973)

p. 193  "Science aims at . . . of commonplace experience." from Sir Arthur Eddington's *The Nature of the Physical World* (Cambridge, 1923).

p. 193  "It is of the highest . . . we are confronted." from Max Planck (quoted by Bernstein in *Einstein*, p. 156)

p. 193  "The death of one god is the death of all." from Wallace Stevens's "Notes Toward a Supreme Fiction", *Collected Poems* (London, 1955).

## JOHN BANVILLE

was born in Wexford, Ireland, in 1945. His first book, *Long Lankin*, was published in 1970, and was followed by *Nightspawn* a year later. A third novel, *Birchwood*, published in 1973, won the Allied Irish Banks prize in that year, and was also awarded a Macaulay Fellowship by the Irish Arts Council. In 1967 he won the American-Irish Foundation Literary Award, and in 1976 *Doctor Copernicus* was awarded the James Tait Black Memorial Prize for the best work of fiction published in that year. *Kepler*, first published in the U.K. in 1981 and in the U.S. by Godine in 1983, was the winner of the Guardian Prize for Fiction. *The Newton Letter*, a contemporary novel, published in London in 1982 to wide acclaim, will appear under the Godine imprint.